OTHER TITLES BY CATHY YARDLEY

Smartypants Romance

Prose Before Bros, Green Valley Librarian book 3

Fandom Hearts

Level Up
Hooked
One True Pairing
Game of Hearts
What Happens at Con
Ms. Behave
Playing Doctor
Ship of Fools

Stand-Alone Novels

The Surfer Solution
Guilty Pleasures
Jack & Jilted
Baby, It's Cold Outside

LOVE, ~~LIKE,~~ COMMENT, SUBSCRIBE

CATHY YARDLEY

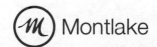

Montlake

Text copyright © 2021 by Cathy Wilson

Published by Montlake, Seattle

www.apub.com

Amazon, the Amazon logo, and Montlake are trademarks of Amazon.com, Inc., or its affiliates.

ISBN-13: 9781542030007
ISBN-10: 1542030005

Cover design and illustration by Philip Pascuzzo

Printed in the United States of America

*To my "crew" of recovering honors students from SDHS,
the inspiration for this . . . the ones who taught me that
it doesn't matter if you're weird, so long as you're together.*

PROLOGUE

Ten years ago . . .

This was it. This was the year.

Lily Wang straightened the hem of her tiered skirt and tried not to fidget. It was the first day of her senior year at Ponto Beach High School, the sky impossibly beautiful as only the skies in Southern Cal beach communities seemed to be. Her skirt was shorter than what she'd normally wear, and her mother would give her hell once she saw it—not because it was too trendy, but because it was too short, and her mom was the only one who was allowed to wear short skirts, arguing that it helped promote the family's clothing boutique.

Lily's stick-straight hair was newly cut in a sleek chin-length bob. Combined with her boho inspired pink blouse, it all looked bleeding-edge stylish, still casual, and sexy (but hopefully not trying-too-hard sexy). She was wearing makeup, a more pronounced smoky eye, something she'd learned from Michelle Phan on YouTube, and her lips were slicked with pink gloss.

If she was ever going to fit in with the popular kids, it would be this year. She'd never be more ready.

Now it was lunchtime. She'd defaulted toward the Bowl, a little grassy hillside by a concrete circle where the school regularly held assemblies. This was where the nerds and geeks hung out and ate lunch—a small collective that ironically called themselves the Nerd Herd, despite the fact that they were almost all honors students, headed toward lucrative careers and bright futures. This was where she'd had lunch for the past three years. Several people she knew had already congregated. Hayden and Asad were trading comic books. Keith and Melanie were talking about setting up a group outing to catch some sci-fi movie that weekend. Vinh and Emily, who had been dating since the beginning of junior year, seemed to be just as in love as ever, heads close together, chuckling and speaking softly.

"Hey, Lily," her friend Tam said, scooting over on the concrete step. She was wearing jeans and a graphic tee with Pikachu on it, along with black suede skate shoes. Her dark hair was overlong, teeming with flyaways. She pushed her glasses up her nose, studying Lily, then smiled broadly. "How was Taiwan? You look tanned. Seems like you were gone most of the summer!"

"Just three weeks," Lily demurred, refusing to sit. "Hung out with cousins, mostly. Went shopping."

"I can see," Tam said, looking over her outfit. "You look nice."

Lily refused to feel uncomfortable, even though this was awkward. Tam was obviously waiting for her to sit down.

"Well, look who decided to show up," a voice drawled.

Lily rolled her eyes. "Tobin."

Tobin Bui, the group's jokester. His glasses were askew, topaz-brown eyes sparkling with mischief as he smirked. "We were starting to think you were going expat," he said. "You missed it. *Epic* pranks. Homemade fireworks. Josh and I even made a parody trailer for *Toy Story* as if it were a slasher film. I put it up on YouTube; I can send you the link."

Lily sighed. Tobin had been recording skits and editing parody trailers since junior high. He'd roped all of them into them at one point or another. She winced as she remembered playing a medieval maiden in something he'd filmed. "Don't you think we're getting a little old for that?"

He looked genuinely surprised. "Josh!" he yelled. "Are we getting too *old*?"

Their friend Josh walked up, his blond hair a mussed mess, his T-shirt scrupulously clean but obviously faded, his pants hems frayed. "Too old for what?" he asked, taking the empty seat next to Tam and nudging her hello. Tam nudged him back absently before taking a bite from half of her sandwich, offering him the other half.

"For fun, I guess," Tobin said sarcastically. "Our little Lily's all grown up and says we're getting too old for videos."

"You are such a . . . *goofball*," Lily said sharply.

"Oh, God. Not a goofball," Tobin said, clutching at his chest with exaggeration. "How will I sleep at night?"

"Does everything have to be a joke to you?"

Tobin's smile was broad and unrepentant. "Pretty much, yeah."

"Ugh." She didn't know why Tobin got under her skin so much. They'd known each other since elementary school and had hung out since junior high, or at least had had the same group of friends that hung out. They were in the same honors classes. She'd even thought he was cute there, for a little bit.

But he drove her *crazy* with his cringeworthy antics. It was like the guy had no sense of shame.

"So, did you bring lunch, Lily," Tam quickly interrupted, before Tobin could respond and the squabbling could continue, "or do you still need to buy it? I can go with you."

This was it. Lily stiffened. "Um . . . I, uh, brought some." She took a deep breath. "But I'm not staying."

"Huh?" This from Tobin.

"I'm eating lunch over there." She nodded in the direction of a fat palm tree in the nearby grassy area, closer to the bleachers and the football field. It was where the popular kids sat: largely football players, cheerleaders. But it wasn't purely "jocks." The two kids who were most likely to become valedictorian and class president sat there, too,

and there were some other kids from the honors classes that somehow managed to secure a place as well. And this year, dammit, she
was determined to eat lunch there. Hang out with them. Spend her
time at crowded keg parties with scandalous stories to follow. Trade
makeup tips with the homecoming court. Date one of the popular
boys—despite having no real dating experience.

She was tired of being seen as nerdy and gauche. Ignored by cute
boys and teased—gently or not so gently—by popular girls. It was
probably the most clichéd thing on earth, the subject of a million teen
movies, wanting to be part of the in crowd. But those movies had never
captured how it *felt*, it seemed, to want to be beautiful and noticed and
valued by people who made those kinds of decisions.

Because, being honest, as much as she loved her friends—they
didn't *choose* her. Most of them had some degree of social awkwardness,
and they simply didn't fit anywhere else. It was solidarity by default.

And somehow, that made her bitter, for all of them.

"You're eating lunch *there?*" Tobin squawked in disbelief.

If anything was going to goose her into action, it'd be Tobin's evident derision. "Yes," Lily said sharply. "I am."

With that, she started moving, heading toward the group under the
palm tree, arranged in small knots of people, laughing and joking. A
few of the boys were doing the half-wrestling, half-shoving thing that
teen boys seemed determined to do, while others jeered and cheered
them on.

Lily targeted Vanessa, someone she knew from Honors English and
Journalism. They'd worked on a few projects together. Vanessa wasn't a
friend per se, but they were *friendly*. Lily had even gone to a pool party
at Vanessa's house sophomore year. So she walked up, as bold as she
could. "Hey, Vanessa!"

Vanessa's dark eyebrows went up. "Um, hey, Lily," she said, obviously puzzled. She brushed her long, flatiron-straight, sun-streaked

brown hair over her shoulder. Then she glanced at the girl sitting next to her, who shrugged slightly.

Lily suppressed a wince. The blonde girl sitting next to Vanessa was Kylee Somers. She was in Honors English, too, and a shoo-in for homecoming queen and probably prom queen and whatever other sort of queen competition was available. She had a friendly smile for everyone, and there were rumors that you shouldn't piss her off. Rumors Lily staunchly believed.

"How . . . was your summer?" Lily asked.

The girls exchanged glances again. "Great," Vanessa said slowly.

"Sucks to be back at school, though," Lily added, when they didn't keep going.

"Nah, I'm glad to be back," Kylee countered, with a genteel shrug that made Lily feel like an idiot. "It's good to see everyone again. I went to Belize for like a month, and I missed Travis *so much!*"

"You're so lucky," Vanessa said with enthusiasm. "I just hung out at Ponto Beach most of the summer. Oh, and we hit Baja . . . went camping for a week."

"I went to Taiwan," Lily offered. Vanessa looked at her sympathetically but didn't acknowledge the statement.

Kylee's boyfriend, Travis, tromped up, settling himself down with a huff. "Hey, Big Wang," he said with a snicker. "How's it hanging?"

Lily felt blood rush immediately to her face. God, she hated that nickname.

An awkward silence fell.

"So . . . did you, um, want something?" Vanessa finally asked, looking directly at Lily.

Lily blanched.

"I . . . I, uh, thought . . ." Her grip on her lunch bag tightened.

I want to sit here and eat my lunch with you all. I want to be a part of your crowd.

"I guess we'll see you later, then?" Kylee prompted.

Before Lily could respond, Vanessa had turned back and was quickly talking with Kylee about Belize as Travis nuzzled Kylee's neck, to her continued murmuring of *stawwwp, Travis!*

Lily had been dismissed.

She felt shame bubbling in her chest. She wasn't more than a few yards away when the trio started whispering, then burst into laughter. Lily wasn't sure that it was even about her. Maybe they were talking about Belize, for all she knew.

But it *felt* like it was about her.

Like they were judging her. Mocking her.

She swallowed hard. She wasn't going to cry. She had worked too hard on this makeup, this look. She was *not* going to give anyone the satisfaction of seeing how they'd affected her.

"That went well," Tobin remarked as Lily went to sit on Tam's other side.

"Fuck off, Tobin," Lily said, opening her lunch bag.

"Dude," Tam snapped at Tobin, then put an arm around Lily. "You okay?"

"I'm fine," Lily said, even though she knew she really wasn't. "It's nothing." She bit into her sandwich. It tasted like paste.

It's not your year.

But one day . . . she was going to show them. She was going to be popular, and recognized, and valued.

And they would be *sorry.*

CHANNEL: *Everlily*

Subscribers: 3.87M
Video views: 179M
Most recent video: "Picking the Sexiest Heel for Your Hemline"

RECENT COMMENTS:

Gina Pagano: Your voice is so smooth! I love these videos!

Hai Mai: I didn't know that about ankle straps no wonder I look like I have cankles UGH

Breathless Belle: I love wedge heels, I would wear them with anything.

Emily Anderson: Great video as always, Lils! ☺

CHAPTER 1

Present Day

"Is this weird?"

Lily looked around the crowded party, frowning at her friend Mikki's question as she took in the scene. "Weird, how? What do you mean?"

Mikki made a face, his flawless, glittery makeup at odds with his sour expression. "We're hanging out at the unholy love child of a prom and a strip club," he pointed out, gesturing to the go-go dancers and the sloppy-drunk people surrounding them, dancing badly and taking selfies. "I could be at an actual club, having a better time."

"If you want to be a beauty influencer," she said, nudging him with an elbow in his ribs so his eye-shadowed eyes widened, "then this is part of the gig."

She wasn't kidding. This was an after-party from the earlier CreatorCon, which they'd dutifully attended despite not having booths or speaking on panels. CreatorCon was one of the smaller conventions for YouTube and TikTok "celebrities," with only eight thousand or so attendees, but because of its location in LA, it still managed to attract some big names. She and Mikki had scored tickets to this after-party, hosted by a camera company or something, after much flirting and begging. It was touted to be "fan-free"—creators only, not even press. There were free drink tickets to the wildly overpriced bar. There were even elaborate props set up, encouraging influencers to take selfies—a huge set of lips, a snow globe set, an amusingly phallic banana-shaped chair. And, of course, the company's logo featured prominently everywhere.

It was grasping, she realized, and crassly commercial, and it didn't matter. This was just a hoop to jump through. She was here on a mission; the surroundings weren't important.

"Don't look at it as a party," she counseled Mikki. "Look at it as a job. This is *work*."

He blew a raspberry. "At least they've got guy dancers as well as girls this time," he grumbled. "I need a drink."

She shook her head. Mikki, a.k.a. Mikki MUA (for Make Up Artist), was a relatively new YouTuber. She'd met him at a party, and they'd both waxed rhapsodic about an obscure brand of Chinese eye cream, and they became fast friends soon after. She now often used Mikki as a date of sorts for these kinds of strategic engagements. "One drink," she said. "Then we're going to track down our target."

"Why do you always talk about these things like you're going behind enemy lines and trying to save the world from Axis forces?" Mikki rolled his eyes.

They got their drinks—a beer for him (which was priced at ten dollars without drink tickets, despite being domestic, something Mikki scowled at) and a cranberry juice for her, her drink of choice since it was easy to pass off as a vodka-cranberry. Generally speaking, she didn't drink on the job. You never knew who was filming at these things, and the internet was both eternal and unforgiving. She'd learned she could convincingly fake being drunk if she felt she had to.

"So," Mikki said, then took a long pull of his beer and scanned the crowd. "Where's this guy we're trying to meet?"

"The guy we're looking for is standing over by the banana chair," she said, before taking a sip of her juice and gearing herself up for . . . well, battle, as it were. "Come on. We're going in."

"Who is he, again?"

"He's one of Chrysalis's entourage," she said.

Mikki's eyes bugged out. "*Chrysalis* is here?"

"No, of course not. They're way too big," Lily said. "But this guy is a friend, supposedly, and always brags about being one of their inner circle and having invites to their parties. We've got this."

They made their way to the man and several of his friends, who were goofing around with the banana-chair prop. She laughed, a bit forced, as he positioned the banana to seem to be his equipment. He looked at her with an interested quirked eyebrow. "Well, hello," he said with a smile.

She just smiled in response. Was his lazy survey of her body icky? Sure. But it was also reflexive, and she tried not to take it personally. "Hi. Aren't you Rickalicious? Fitness trainer, skin-care-regimen guru?"

His chest puffed up with pride, and his smile widened. "Sure am. You looking for a workout?"

She tamped down on impatience. Why were men like this?

"Actually, I was wondering," she said, trying to sound friendly but not necessarily flirtatious. "Do you have any extra tickets to the PEACOCK launch? I know you're a close friend of Chrysalis's."

"I might have a few," he drawled, studying her as his friends continued goofing around on the chair. She was wearing what she considered her signature clothing—rose-gold baby doll dress with kitten heels, purse. "Good girl" chic, and he obviously approved. "Who are you again, darlin'?"

"I have a beauty channel, EverLily," she said. "My name's Lily Wang, and this is Mikki MUA."

His smile was bright, making his words seem even harsher. "Never heard of you."

This was irritating, but again, not surprising. She wasn't sure if he was negging her or just being honest, but either way, she couldn't afford to take offense. "I'm more of a niche brand at this point," she said, overemphasizing the sweetness in her voice. "But I'm at close to five million subscribers and growing."

He seemed to mull this over, eyes narrowing as he stared at her face. "Is it in English, though?"

"Yes, it's in English," she snapped, then stopped herself. "I started the channel when I was still at UCLA," she added when her facade was safely back in place.

"Hmph." He pulled his phone out. "EverLily, you said?"

She knew exactly what he was doing—checking her numbers and profile on Social Blade. She didn't blame him. She waited until he verified her stats: number of subscribers, number of views, followers on Instagram, Twitter, TikTok. Then he looked at her. "Okay, those are decent numbers," he admitted grudgingly, typing something else in and frowning. "I don't recognize your sponsorships, though—they seem pretty small, a lot of them foreign."

"I've got some things in the works," she hedged. He saw through it and frowned.

"What about your own cosmetics?" he pressed. "Any deals?"

She shook her head. "Not quite yet."

He looked unconvinced, judgmental, and she felt a pang of desperation but knew better than to show it.

"I just really want to see the palette," she gushed. "I've been waiting since Chrysalis teased they were launching the new eye shadow collection, back in January. I would just *love* to see it and test the samples on my channel!"

She'd chosen that plea specifically. Rick was a member of Chrysalis's entourage, sure, but he was a fitness YouTuber, not a beauty influencer, and his numbers were a lot lower than Chrysalis's. (He wasn't the only one who could use Social Blade, and there was no way Lily was going to go into something like this blind.) Lily knew he'd have tickets to the party. Chrysalis's assistant had distributed a lot already, to the crème de la crème of LA's influencers, but there was social currency in *inviting* people to the party—showing you had the access to invites, sure, but also inviting the right people. Rick would stand to curry some favor if he brought in someone with good numbers who could spread the word about the launch—a good review on a subscriber-heavy channel could only help. On Lily's side, writing about the launch would bring more viewers to her site who wanted to know more about the palette. Win-win, which Rick would recognize if he had any intelligence at all.

That was not to say that he did. She waited.

"All right," Rick said with just a hint of reluctance in his voice. "Give me your number, and I'll get an invitation sent."

"Two," she corrected, looking at Mikki.

Rick seemed to size Mikki up, then shrugged. "Sure, two, why not," he agreed. "It wouldn't hurt to have some nobodies there, to pad out the crowd."

She could feel the ire coming off Mikki in waves, so she quickly gave Rick her number and then dragged Mikki off.

"The *nerve* of that asshole," Mikki growled. "Just because I don't have a lot of subscribers or anything . . ."

"You know how it is," she said, trying to console him. "It's a numbers game. It's just the way things are with the beauty community. Or any YouTube or social media community, I guess."

"It's fucking high school all over again."

High school.

She couldn't help it. She winced.

And *of course* Mikki had to notice it. "Ooh. That struck a nerve," Mikki said, his impish face looking immediately curious. "So what happened? Tell me all about it."

She shot him a nervous glance. She liked Mikki. He was the closest thing she had to a friend in Los Angeles. But it had been years since she'd really had best friends . . . not since high school, really.

She noticed that Mikki was still waiting impatiently and smoothed on a smile. "It wasn't a big deal," she said. "I spent years as one of those nerdy kids—you know, advanced classes and extracurriculars, journalism and academic team, California Scholarship Federation and National Honor Society. You name it."

"That doesn't surprise me," Mikki said, before taking another sip of beer. "You're sort of insanely organized and, like, super smart."

"Yeah, well, by senior year I was sick of just being seen as one of the 'Nerd Herd'—can you believe we actually *called* ourselves that?—and I wanted to hang out with the popular crowd." She squirmed. "That sounds terrible, doesn't it?"

"I'm not judging."

She looked at him, and it really seemed like he wasn't, so she kept going. "I just . . . they were all so good looking. They always had stories about these parties and glamping trips where they'd get drunk and get wild, and they were having sex, and it was *so* damned exclusive, even though there wasn't anything specific, you know? It wasn't like they were a country club or something. You just . . . you fit in, or you didn't."

Mikki paused for a second. "I'm guessing it didn't go well," he said finally when she didn't automatically continue.

"It went about as well as expected," she said, even as memories swamped her.

Vanessa's judging, puzzled expression. "So . . . did you, um, want something?"

Lily felt her stomach knot, even after all these years.

"Anyway," she said brightly, "we did what we set out to do."

"Was there any doubt?" Mikki said, clinking his beer bottle against her glass. "You, my dear, are an absolute *beast*, and I think there's nothing you can't get if you set your mind to it."

She smiled back at him. Being a YouTuber might seem frivolous, but she knew better than anyone it was a business, one that took hard work and dedication, one you had to take seriously.

No one took success more seriously than she did.

CHANNEL: GOOFYBUI

Subscribers: 9.1M
Video views: 300M
Most recent video: "Killing Potatoes for Fun and Profit"

RECENT COMMENTS:

Xxvibe_kingxX: 2:51 "Listen, tuber, I am not fucking around" LMAOOOOOO

T3Ch Warrior: I find your love-hate relationship with potatoes disturbing.

Skeptic_Sketcher: Die, potato! *gun slide clicks* NOT TODAY!

Hayden the Greaten: Can we combine your potato slaying with Tater Theater next time?

CHAPTER 2

I am amazed that I get to do this for a living.

Tobin Bui grinned. It had taken six months of planning, a lot more money than he'd anticipated, and a shit ton of coordination, but now he—or rather his YouTube alter ego, GoofyBui—was ready to pull off his most epic "goof" yet.

His house was in a decent development in Ponto Beach, and like most of the houses in the area, it had a seven-foot fence surrounding the relatively small backyard. Unlike most of the houses, his home had two things: a tree house, and a fifteen-foot scaffolded platform.

He was in the tree house, next to his friend and cameraman, Hayden. "Everybody ready?" he said into the walkie-talkie he held in his hand. "Over," he added absently.

"Ready!" a chorus of voices crackled back through the tinny-sounding speaker.

"Okay . . . three . . . two . . . one . . . *go!*"

Tobin held his breath, staring at the platform and hitting the remote control. Then, slowly, like a majestic phoenix rising from the ashes, a red form unfurled, curling up toward the sky.

Well, less a phoenix and more a big red *tube.*

With a smiling face.

And . . .

"WOOT!" Tobin yelled, as the tube man's arms started flailing wildly.

He looked past the flailing arms, over the crisscross of fences parceling out his neighborhood, only to see in the distance, a second later, *another* tube man emerging with fiery-red flailing arms. He vaguely heard the cheer of triumph. Then, yet another tube man sprang up, farther on the hilltop. Pretty soon, there were seven tube men, dancing and wiggling along the ridge of the neighborhood.

It was *glorious*.

"How's the footage?" he yelled into the walkie-talkie.

"It is *fucking awesome!*" his friend Asad answered, laughing. "Drone's picking up everything!"

Tobin stuck his head in front of the camera. *"The beacons of Minas Tirith are lit! Gondor calls for aid!"*

"And Ponto Beach will answer!" This came over the walkie-talkie, from his other friend and frequent collaborator Shawn, a.k.a. Skeptic Sketcher.

Tobin felt downright nuclear, happiness radiating from him in what had to be a maniacal grin. Hayden's answering grin was ear to ear. There were seven tube men, covering *miles*, all within eyesight of each other.

It was epic.

Hours later, they reviewed the footage. Asad had controlled the drone while his boyfriend, Freddie, drove through the corresponding roads, getting an aerial view of the domino of tube men. So far, the video looked awesome. After driving around town collecting the tube men to return to the rental place and thanking the people who had donated their time (and their backyards) to help pull off the prank, Tobin celebrated, popping open a few Newcastles with Hayden, Freddie, and Asad.

"That," Asad said, lifting his bottle in a toast, "was legendary."

"Gonna take all night to edit that thing, but I'll post it by the afternoon, latest," Tobin answered.

"Bet this one goes viral," Hayden said sagely. "Seriously. I mean, your playthroughs are fun, and I laugh my ass off at your skits and that stuff where you do movie dialogue with crazy chat filters, but this? Instant classic. LOTR nerds are gonna eat this up."

"I thought I was gonna choke when that first tube man popped up," Asad added.

Tobin took a little mock bow before settling down into his patio chair. Now that the filming was over, he felt the endorphins and adrenaline that had been fueling him all day start to ebb . . . the crash after the high.

Which sucked. Back in the day, when he'd been haphazardly loading videos in between engineering classes in college, he'd been able to ride that giddy sensation for nearly a week. He hadn't really been doing it for the money back then, of course. Now that it was his career—one that he'd quit college to pursue full time—things had changed. Exhaustion seemed to club him as soon as the camera stopped filming, which was going to suck when it came time to edit. He should probably be switching to Red Bull, not drinking a beer.

"What's next?" Hayden asked.

"Next?" Tobin repeated, feeling irritated even though he knew his friend didn't mean anything by it. "I *literally* just finished that 'legendary' video, and I haven't even edited it. Give me a minute to enjoy the afterglow, okay?"

Hayden grinned unrepentantly. "Speaking of afterglow . . ."

Tobin groaned, covering his face.

"Still seeing . . . what was her name? That cutie, with the long hair. Jessica? Angelica?"

"Nah," Tobin said quickly. "That was just casual. We haven't hooked up in a while." He frowned, thinking about it. A couple of months. Actually, more like six months, now that he thought about it.

Huh.

"Seriously? Man, you need to get out more," Hayden said.

"What? I'm social."

Hayden looked at Asad, who grinned by Freddie's side. "Dude. Online gaming with your friends on their Twitch stream doesn't count as social."

"It's important for channel promotion," Tobin protested. "And it's fun."

"Clearing your head is important too," Asad said. "Do you even feel relaxed?"

"Et tu, Asad?" Tobin said, narrowing his eyes.

"Just sayin'. You *have* seemed kind of stressed lately."

"And the answer is . . . sex?" Tobin suggested with a small smile.

"Now, I didn't say *that*," Asad said.

"I might've implied that," Hayden added with a smirk.

"I mean, you're under pressure." Asad's expression was concerned. "Self-care is important."

"Sounds like *all* he's doing is 'self-care,'" Hayden said. Tobin and Asad both ignored him.

"I've been working out. Regularly," Tobin said, knowing he sounded stubborn and defensive, and hating it. "I got that meal-service thing, so I'm eating healthier. I even tried meditating."

That had gone laughably wrong, but he got the feeling he didn't have a particular aptitude for sitting still while spa music played in the background.

Asad looked skeptical. "Well, at least you're trying."

Tobin pulled his phone out of his pocket, glancing at the time. "Okay, I gotta get going on these edits. Thanks again for all the work, and for just being awesome."

"Anytime," Asad said, clapping him on the back as he and Freddie headed out.

"Let me know the next time you want to go out," Hayden said in the doorway. "Oh! That reminds me. You're going, right? To the reunion?"

"Shit." Tobin grimaced. He'd been so wrapped up in this shoot he'd lost track of time a bit. "Is that soon?"

"You forgot, didn't you?" Hayden shook his head. "Doesn't matter— I'll remind you. You really need an assistant, you know."

"Heh. Bad enough that I've got an agent," Tobin joked, then corrected himself. "Two, actually, now."

"How's the coagenting thing going?"

"It is what it is." He'd liked his original agent, Bastian, but Bastian had signed on a slew of new talent, and some of his clients had exploded in popularity. Tobin knew he was still a priority—he'd recently hit nine million subscribers, which wasn't nothing—but he wasn't pushing for big endorsements, and he didn't embody the hustle that a lot of other YouTubers seemed to have in spades. The agency had then suggested Bastian split some of his agenting duties with a new "coagent," Jeffrey.

Tobin got the feeling Jeffrey didn't quite get him. Or YouTube, really. Jeffrey wanted to do TV and movies and streaming services. It wasn't that Tobin had anything against any of those things; he just didn't see where he fit into that picture.

"Seriously. If you want to go hang out, see people IRL, hit me up," Hayden said, reminding Tobin that he was lucky he had the friends that he had. "Couple of the Herd townies are gonna get together anyway— sort of a prereunion thing. Maybe in a few weeks? Game a little, hang out. Let me know if you're in."

"Sure," Tobin said, then shut the door behind him.

Tobin rubbed at the back of his neck, then tossed his bottle in the recycle bin and headed for his office. He still had footage to download and compile, editing to do. He could hire an editor and usually worked with several he trusted, but he wanted to play with this video particularly before he made final cuts, see what worked best. It would probably take all night.

You ought to get out more.

He grimaced.

In the end, it had taken all night, and he'd fallen asleep watching TV on his couch while it was rendering, which was stupid. The thing was comfortable enough to sit on but too short to really accommodate his whole body. Now, he had a crick in his neck as he uploaded the video and retreated to his shower.

He spent the day watching movies and catnapping. After a quick workout and meal, he found himself wandering back to his computer. Tomorrow would be a video prep day. Then, he'd probably record a playthrough of a video game—he wasn't sure which one yet. He had a loose content calendar, but he didn't like being tied down to anything.

Maybe I'll do a farm sim. He hadn't done that before, he thought, scrolling through Steam, looking for new indie releases. Maybe he'd see if there were any new horror games. Those were always popular, although he was getting a little bored with . . .

He'd opened his YouTube account on his second monitor, and he glanced at the views in the corner of his screen. Then he blinked and focused on it again.

Wait.

That wasn't right. Was it?

He called Hayden. "Dude, have you—"

"*Holy shit,*" Hayden said, all but singing with excitement. "You're awake! Are you *seeing* this?"

"This can't be right," Tobin croaked. "Glitch, maybe . . . ?"

"Damn right it's right!" Hayden shouted. "Your viewers went *nuts.* Shared it everywhere! I am seeing this all over social media. Buzzfeed's sharing it, big YouTubers, it's all over Twitter. Hell, I think Peter Jackson's shared it!"

"Are you kidding?" Tobin leaned back in his gaming chair, suddenly feeling light headed. "But this is . . ."

"Congrats, buddy!"

"Thanks," Tobin said and hung up, still staring at the screen.

One. Million. Views.

He ought to be thrilled. He ought to be shouting, dancing (badly—he knew his skill set), screaming out of his windows. Opening champagne. Well, buying champagne, then opening it.

But he didn't feel that. He felt . . . *numb*.

He took a deep breath. Then he kept quietly scrolling through Steam, wondering if maybe Asad had a point about his stress levels.

CHANNEL: *Everlily*

Subscribers: 3.88M
Video views: 190M
Most recent video: "Palette Review: Lip Gloss Couture by PeachyPink"

RECENT COMMENTS:

Breathless Belle: I like pink, but I don't know if it goes with my skin tone . . . ?

Karen Roel: Daisy Blackwell said those lip glosses were SHIT

Annabel Lee: I love that you pick delicate colors! Not everything needs to be metallic!

Decemberist Girl: Please review Wild Cherry's lip gloss next!! *hearteyes*

CHAPTER 3

Lily sat in the lobby of her talent management company, waiting for her quarterly meeting. She was wearing one of her favorite spring outfits—a midi skirt of the palest pink and a matching sleeveless silk blouse with an ivory cardigan. Her kitten heels were ivory, as was her clutch purse. Her accessories were a rosy gold: hoop earrings, a woven bracelet with some chunks of pale jade interspersed. She'd deliberately gone professional but soft with her makeup, brightening her skin. She'd been having some trouble sleeping the past few nights, but thanks to Fenty and some skilled highlighting, nobody here in the office would know that but her.

"Lily?" Her manager, Maria, walked out, shaking her hand and smiling. "It's great to see you. How are you?"

"Fine, thanks." Lily followed Maria into her office. There was a view of downtown Los Angeles in the floor-to-ceiling windows, and the skies were relatively clear. Lily took the proffered seat across from the black lacquer desk as Maria sat behind it. After exchanging some pleasantries, Lily took a deep breath, broaching the subject at hand . . . the reason she'd come in. "For this quarter, I wanted to focus on seeing if I could upgrade my profile a bit. Expand my brand." She was still stinging from Rickalicious's sneering dismissal of her current sponsors and lack of cosmetic partnerships. It was stupid, but she knew that he wouldn't be the only one who made that kind of snap judgment.

"You're not happy with your current sponsors?" Maria asked, taking notes.

"I'm thrilled with my current sponsors," Lily said quickly, not wanting Maria to think her ungrateful. "But I was thinking: Isn't it time we started aiming a little higher?"

"You know I'm always about aiming higher," Maria said with an encouraging smile. "What'd you have in mind?"

"Lots of other beauty vloggers have their own palettes with various cosmetic companies," Lily said. "It feels like if you want to be a popular influencer, that's a key component."

"Did you have any companies in particular in mind?"

"The bigger the better." Lily's reply was swift, so she softened it with a smile. "I don't necessarily mean some huge conglomerate—L'Oréal or Elizabeth Arden is probably out of the question, but a midrange with a good following . . . I'm sure we could find a good fit."

Maria's soft sigh instantly put Lily on her guard, although she schooled her expression not to show it.

"The beauty community is so glutted right now, is the problem," Maria said. "Every day, there's a new influencer on Instagram, YouTube, TikTok. It's a struggle to stay relevant. You know that."

Lily felt her jaw tighten. She forced herself to relax. "There was that big shake-up," she pointed out. "Karmageddon . . ."

"Yes, but that didn't really open up spaces so much as reveal the dark underbelly of the community," Maria protested, steepling her fingers on the desk surface and looking at Lily sympathetically. "A lot of the people who were 'canceled'? You know they could afford to shed a few million viewers and they still have careers. People always forget the drama, which is unfortunate. And worse . . . a lot of people *want* the drama."

Lily nodded. She had not gotten into many—*any*, really—online feuds. She didn't get called out, and there wasn't any drama. She'd thought that was largely a good thing. She couldn't afford to lose sub-scribers or get canceled because of doing something stupid.

Besides, the idea of being called out for terrible behavior, engaging in petty drama? Her family would be furious, and she wouldn't blame them.

"You're doing great as far as avoiding those kinds of pitfalls," Maria continued. "Still, staying neutral can sometimes mean being *too* neutral. Sometimes it's problematic. Just something to consider."

Lily stilled. "What do you mean?" She was proud that her voice sounded calm. "I'm close to five million subscribers on YouTube, three million on TikTok, and I'm still building my Insta, but that's near two million. My numbers have been growing steadily. I don't see that as being a problem."

"The numbers have been plateauing," Maria pointed out. "And again, there are only so many topics you can cover without repeats when you're not reviewing palettes negatively. 'Forty daytime-to-night-time looks'? Or 'five must-haves in your spring wardrobe'? You need to come up with something more compelling. Something people haven't seen before."

Lily bit her lip. She knew what Maria was saying, and her manager wasn't wrong. Still, it made anxiety knot in her stomach.

"I guess you need me to do something more original."

"And hit maybe six million," Maria agreed. "Show that you're grow-ing strong. Have you considered some collaborations?"

"I've done collabs."

Maria smiled gently. "I meant with somewhat more prominent YouTubers," she clarified.

"Well, I've *thought* about it," Lily said. "But it's not that easy. And I don't want to be seen as a social climber, necessarily."

She had a brief flashback to senior year in high school and swal-lowed hard.

"Besides," she added, "that's not going to help me with the 'original content' problem."

"Well, I'm sure you'll think of something," Maria said. "Let's set your goal as building your audience as much as you can, shooting for six million as a baseline. And see if we can't get some of your content to go viral. That's the game changer."

"Most of the beauty community's stuff doesn't go viral unless it's a scandal, an apology for a scandal, or spilled tea about a scandal," Lily protested.

"Not true," Maria said. "There are those cosplay ones that tend to capture a larger audience."

Lily couldn't help but wrinkle her nose. "Well, yeah. But that's a slightly different audience, isn't it?"

"Is it?" Maria countered. "It's a *larger* audience. Geek is chic, sweetie."

Lily's smile was forced. As if she wasn't familiar with geeks. "Touché."

"Speaking of geek—did you see that latest viral video?" Maria said, tapping on her keyboard, then turning her computer screen. "This is brilliant."

Lily watched, unsure of what she was seeing, until one of those inflatable tubes with the waving arms popped up; then another one did. She snickered as she realized what it was from.

Suddenly, Tobin Bui's face was in the screen. *"The beacons of Minas Tirith are lit!"*

It was like a slap. She glanced at the channel name.

GoofyBui. Because of course it was.

She watched the rest of the video, then automatically went to the views counter.

Four million views? Already? What the hell?

"Now that is clever," Maria said, not noticing Lily's frozen dismay. "If you could get that level of views, your subscribers would shoot up."

"I'll see if I can't come up with a few more approaches," Lily said faintly, "and email you some ideas." She got up, reaching to shake Maria's hand.

"I know you'll come up with something," Maria said. "And I'll see who I can reach out to. Brainstorming some future merch wouldn't be a bad idea either. And think of what you'd do with either a cosmetic or fashion line—how you'd make it stand out, besides simply being a Lily Wang original."

Lily nodded and retreated back to her condo in West Los Angeles, just down the street from UCLA. It wasn't super luxurious, but it was a decent neighborhood, and it was close to the freeway. Besides, she'd managed to decorate it in her signature style, on a relatively tight budget—living in LA wasn't cheap.

Lily flopped down on her couch, rubbing at her temples.

I need to get more creative. More clever.

Lily grimaced. She ought to go over to her desk and grab her bullet journal, the one that housed her content calendar for the next three months. Given her conversation with Maria, what she had there was not going to work, which made her both annoyed and dismayed. She would have to redo it . . . possibly the whole thing.

Considering she normally put the content calendar down in permanent ink, this was obviously a big disturbing step. But she couldn't keep doing the same things. If she wanted to become a big-time success—which she did, more than anything—then she'd need to make the changes Maria was suggesting. No matter how daunting that might seem right now.

How the hell am I supposed to go viral? It wasn't like anybody *planned* for those things—they just blew up. It was like a lightning strike.

Lily changed into her scrubbiest yoga pants and a T-shirt she'd had since junior high, one with a cartoon turtle. After washing her face and moisturizing, she sank down in her chair in front of a clean whiteboard, waiting for her leftovers to heat.

Her phone rang, and without even looking, she answered it. There was only one woman who called her regularly rather than just texting her like a normal person. "Hello, Mom."

"Lily," her mother said in Mandarin. "How did the meeting with your manager go?"

Lily smiled with weariness. "All right, I guess?" she answered, also in Mandarin. "I want to expand into bigger sponsorships. I really want to get my own palette or beauty products with a cosmetics company."

Her mother made a contemplative noise. "Your own palette, or maybe clothing line," she mused. "Or accessories? I can source some things for you, if you're interested, from Taiwan."

"Palette first," Lily said firmly. "My makeup tutorials are getting more views than my clothing ones, so I'm probably going to tailor my content more that way."

"Good idea. Have any companies in mind?"

"A few," Lily said. "American. Probably smaller to start; then I'll move up to larger ones as my brand grows."

"What's in your way, then?" her mother asked, her tone prosaic.

"Right now? Subscribers," Lily said, throwing herself on her couch. "Maria says that if I want to get a makeup deal, I'll need at least six million subscribers, and I'm barely at five."

"So get more subscribers."

Lily rolled her eyes, glad her mother wasn't into video chatting. "Sure, Mom. Because it's just that easy to get *a million people* to sign up for my YouTube channel."

Her mother made a dismissive sound. "I didn't say it would be *easy*, did I? I'm just saying you know what to do. Now, you just have to go do it."

Lily grinned, shaking her head. Her mother was like this about everything, whether it was about grades, getting into a good college, or making her career a success. "I'm working on it." She paused. "Maria mentioned that I need to be more creative. And maybe look at collaborating with more popular influencers."

"That's a good idea," her mother said. "Networking is crucial. Remember that venture capitalist, the one from San Jose? Utter asshole. But your father and I laughed at his jokes, went to his Christmas party. I even played *golf*," she said with obvious distaste. "So we got the next round of funding, and the business is growing more than ever!"

"How is Dad?" Lily asked. "How are things in San Francisco?"

"San Francisco is fine, and as for your father . . . you know how he is," her mother said with fond exasperation. "Binging historical dramas on Netflix and Viki, what else? And his doctor told him to cut down his sodium. I'm finding salty snacks hidden all over the house. He thinks he's some kind of . . . what is it called? A sneaky *squirrel*."

Lily laughed just as her microwave dinged. "That's my dinner."

"I'll let you eat," her mother said. "And don't worry about the subscribers. You'll do this the way you do everything, just like with school."

Lily smiled. "Love you, Mom. Hug Dad for me."

"Love you, too, Lily," her mother said before hanging up.

Lily took her dinner out of the microwave, then headed to her computer, putting the plate on her desk. She decided to open her email, poking at the pasta and vegetables with her fork as it fired up. She glanced through emails—a few promotional coupons, newsletters, and the like—and saw an email forwarded from her friend Emily. Emily had been one of her best friends at Ponto Beach, one of the Nerd Herd. Lily still kept in touch with them—loosely—via a Slack channel their friend Asad had set up, but she rarely participated, often forgetting she had access to it. She and Emily usually exchanged texts and GIFs every few weeks or so . . . although, now that she thought about it, it had been longer than a month since their last exchange. She opened the email with a touch of guilt.

The subject read: ARE YOU GOING?

Lily glanced at the forwarded message. Then she reread it.

Ten-year reunion?
Good grief. Had it been *that* long?
Emily had attached a little note: hope you'll be there! Tam's MIA, but the rest of the Herd are going to show up, from the sounds of it. Miss you!

Lily grimaced. It was so weird—she'd just been talking about high school to Mikki; then her mother had mentioned it in passing, and Maria showed her Tobin's video. Now this. It was like the universe was shouting at her: *You may think you're over high school, but it's not over you.*

Well, she had bigger things to worry about than her damned high school reunion, she thought, stabbing a snow pea and crunching on it savagely. Namely, making her channel a success.

CHANNEL: *GOOFYBUI*

Subscribers: 9.8M
Video views: 306M
Most recent video: "Beacons Are LIT"

RECENT COMMENTS:

Peter Jackwad: Fucking. Epic!

Tony Guidice: Saw this on Twitter! Totally subscribed!

Xxvibe_kingxX: How the hell did you pull this off?

Big Dill: Meh. I like your playthroughs better.

CHAPTER 4

Tobin groaned as he saw yet another notification from his agents, Bastian and Jeffrey. The video had gone up on Tuesday night, and now on Friday it had passed the five-million-views mark. It was easily one of his fastest-climbing and most popular videos, and of course his agents were going to want to capitalize on it, even if they hadn't interacted much with him since signing.

It was so weird, the idea that he had even one agent, much less two.

Now, they were requesting a Zoom meeting for that morning. He'd agreed, even though he didn't particularly like meetings, and he *hated* ones on Zoom. With any luck, they'd congratulate him, ask a few questions, and then he could get on with his workout.

It was probably not going to work out that way, especially knowing Jeffrey. Still, a guy could dream.

Bastian was in his late thirties, maybe early forties. He wore suits that made him look stylish and sophisticated, emphasizing his slim figure and darker complexion. The guy looked like a *GQ* model. Which made it all the funnier, considering Tobin knew for a fact that Bastian played the newest *Assassin's Creed* releases like someone was paying him, cursing like a sailor the entire time. They'd met playing *Fortnite*, actually, and then *Among Us*. They even teamed up on Bed Wars on a *Minecraft* server just for laughs. Bastian was a gamer, and he . . . well, he *got* it.

That's why Bastian had signed him in the first place. Since then, Bastian had managed to sign several bigger names: actors, influencers, the works. He was smart, savvy, and driven, but still approachable. His career was skyrocketing.

So to help lighten the load, they'd assigned Tobin . . . Jeffrey.

Jeffrey was in his twenties and eager to make his mark. He wore suits, too, although he didn't rock them like Bastian did. He wore a pair of glasses that just had plain glass in them, fashion rather than prescription. The sides of his hair were trimmed short, with longer locks on the top that started to flop toward his eyes. He wore fashionable clothes and judged people who didn't, based on some comments he'd made about Tobin's nonfilming attire when they'd met in LA. Basically, Jeffrey was a poser, and that drove Tobin bugshit.

Alas, while Tobin was a pretty-good-size fish in the YouTube pond, he wasn't bringing in the endorsements and other media that Bastian's other clients were raking in. Tobin took the addition of Jeffrey in stride and just gritted his teeth, trying to keep his focus on Bastian when he could whenever they had meetings.

He clicked "join," and after a second, Jeffrey's face filled his screen.

"Congrats on the video, buddy!" Jeffrey shouted, leaning forward, his face getting even larger. "Over five million views and growing! Even got picked up and shared by *Good Morning America*—holy shit, am I right?"

"Thanks." Tobin surreptitiously turned down the volume. Jeffrey had some loudness issues, particularly when excited. Of course, considering a lot of Tobin's reactions were yelling, he guessed he couldn't really throw stones. "Where's Bastian?"

"Oh, he's working on a deal with one of his new clients. An actress who started on TikTok, doing microsketch comedy. They're working on a series, little episodes on a new streaming service," Jeffrey said. "It's just going to be you and me today."

Oh, goody. Tobin saw himself in the camera, displaying the slightest wince. Thankfully, Jeffrey didn't seem to notice.

"So . . . what's next?" Jeffrey pushed his glasses up the bridge of his nose. "You've got an audience. We need a follow-up."

Tobin shrugged, glancing at the large whiteboard out of sight of the camera. "Um . . . let's see. I could do a few playthroughs. There are some great games coming out."

Jeffrey frowned.

"And I had some skits planned with Skeptic Sketcher," Tobin said, feeling strangely unsettled at Jeffrey's scrutiny, "but we'll need to coordinate that."

"The skits." Jeffrey immediately latched on to that. "Anything funny? Things that could go viral?"

"It's impossible to tell what'll go viral," Tobin protested. "You have to know that."

"Well, are they really *funny*?" Jeffrey pressed. "Because funny sells. That's the content people want."

Tobin felt his jaw clench. Funny, huh? God knows *he* needed some funny right now, to defuse some of the anger he felt bubbling up at Jeffrey's obtuse suggestions.

He decided to mix things up. Clicking over to his filters, he tapped a few keys.

He then grinned as he saw his own camera's view in the corner. His head was now a large doughnut, complete with pink frosting and sprinkles, his mouth forming the hole. "How about this?" Tobin said innocently. "That's funny, right?"

Jeffrey's smile was as fake as his glasses. "Yeah! That's funny. Maybe something with chat filters?"

Tobin sighed. He'd done a video where he and Skeptic had acted out dramatic scenes from popular movies in Snapchat filters. He'd actually done the president's speech from *Independence Day* while looking like a potato with a mouth. They called it Tater Theater. It had done okay, stats-wise.

But Jeffrey apparently didn't know that.

He shifted the filter to Pingu, the Claymation penguin. "Noot noot!" Tobin hooted, doing his best Pingu impression.

He could see Jeffrey's smile strain. "Yeah, that's funny too. So about your next video . . ."

Tobin knew he was probably being an asshole by this point, but he found it hard to care. He shifted to Disco Avocado. "It took six months to set up the Beacons video," he said as his avocado avatar boogied along to his words. "I'm not going to be able to just pull another big-budget, elaborate video out of my ass by next week, Jeffrey."

"Maybe your next one doesn't have to be quite that long and elaborate," Jeffrey clarified, in a way that clearly said, *I have no idea what the big deal is here.* "But I'm sure you can do something that'll capitalize on all this attention. Just do what you've been doing. Only, you know"—Jeffrey made a vague gesture with his hands—*"more."*

"This is pretty much how I work. A few big set pieces a year, unless I get inspired, or . . . I don't know, I get a collab opportunity that I want to pursue. But otherwise, I've got the usual playthroughs and sketches, and weaponized silliness. That's what Bastian signed me for."

"Our job is to get you to the biggest opportunities possible," Jeffrey pointed out. "There is more to life than YouTube, you know."

Tobin gasped. Then he shifted the filter over to Cosmic Cat, lasers shooting out of his eyes as the jaguar head snarled. "There is *not* more to life than YouTube. How *dare* you."

"That's really distracting," Jeffrey carped, then sighed. "Listen, I get it. It's not the usual media: you're not doing the same old crap. You're fresh, you're different. Hey, I'm young too." He grinned. "Actually, I'm younger than you."

If Tobin were editing this video, he would've added himself looking into another camera, like Jim from *The Office*. If you had to tell people that you were young and therefore hip and that you "got" it . . . *sorry, my dude. I really think you don't.*

"What I'm saying," Jeffrey continued, "is that if you want to be a voice actor, which you totally could do, or . . . hell, if you wanted to be a *real* actor, or a stand-up comedian, or go on *SNL*, or have your own series, or *be in a movie*, then we could make that happen! But *not* if you don't take this seriously!"

Tobin sat silent for a second.

Then, without warning, he changed his avatar again.

"What makes you think I'm not taking this seriously?" the eggplant on the screen asked, jiggling ominously.

"Jesus." Jeffrey grimaced. "Can't you turn that thing off?"

"That's just it: I can't just turn this shit on and off," Tobin said, his somber tone at odds with the ridiculous avatar. "I'm either feeling creative, or I'm not."

And lately, it'd been more *off* than *on*. But he wasn't going to tell fucking Jeffrey that.

"Let me ask this, then," Jeffrey pushed. "Are you interested in succeeding in this business? Because it's like being a shark. If you don't keep swimming forward, you drown. There are *no* barriers to entry, and the next GoofyBui is building his audience right now. So I repeat: Are you going to take this seriously?"

Tobin winced. It was too much like a conversation he'd had with his parents.

When are you going to grow up, Tobin?

He sighed. "What do you need from me, Jeffrey?" he asked. Even the eggplant looked somewhat chastened.

"Bastian wants a meeting," Jeffrey said. "Come have lunch with us next Wednesday, here by the offices. We'll talk strategy."

"I have to drive to LA?" Tobin yelped.

"Yeah, well, apparently Zoom meetings aren't a great idea." Jeffrey gestured to the screen.

Okay. So Tobin had screwed himself on that one. Damn his compulsion to annoy.

Unbidden, he pictured Lily Wang—somebody he hadn't really thought of in years. But when he thought "annoy," she was naturally the first person to come to mind.

"Bastian's going to actually be at this meeting, right?" Tobin said, still leaving the eggplant in place.

"Yes." Jeffrey looked irritated. "Bring some ideas for content. Then we'll talk."

Jeffrey closed the meeting, and the screen went blank. Tobin sighed, then went out to his living room, heading for the treadmill. He needed to run off this bad mood, and he knew from experience that if he didn't exercise, he'd spiral into a downward turn of unproductivity and bad moods.

He hated talking strategy. Maybe it was his ADHD, but when there were too many plans, too many constraints, he quickly lost interest in projects. He'd perfected how he worked in the past twelve years or so he'd started messing around with his videos, back when he was in college watching Markiplier and JackSepticEye and all those other gamers. At least, he'd perfected *how it worked for him.* If Jeffrey thought he was somehow going to make Tobin more efficient, to be creative on demand and viral by design . . . well. The guy had another think coming.

His phone rang. It was Asad. He slowed down the treadmill and answered, only slightly out of breath. "What's up?"

"Dude! We're celebrating your accomplishment over at the Belly Up tonight," Asad said, referring to a popular bar in a beach town farther south from Ponto. "How do you feel about taking an Uber down and getting hammered? First three shots are on me and Freddie."

Ordinarily, Tobin drank in moderation, if at all. But he did want to celebrate, dammit. Here he was, hitting a really big milestone—over five million views!—and it was as "meh" as eating a frozen pizza. That was messed up. Besides, after his talk with Jeffrey, he wouldn't mind "altering his state" a little. The guy put him on edge.

"Fine," Tobin said. "What time?"

"Yaaaassss," Asad cheered. "Nine o'clock! I'm inviting some of the Herd. It'll be epic!"

"No shit? Cool," Tobin said, then hung up after ironing out details. The Nerd Herd, he thought with a grin, starting to run again. Or at least the townies—the ones who'd stayed in Ponto Beach, when so many of their peers had gone off to parts unknown. They'd all been honors students, back in high school, often on "most likely to succeed" lists or the academic team. They hadn't been particularly popular, or socially adroit. That said, they'd had each other, and that had mattered more.

Even now, the townies still had each other, and Tobin was grateful.

He again thought, briefly, about Lily Wang. She'd been one of the Herd once upon a time too. Whether she liked it or not—and she'd made it pretty clear: she *did not like it.*

He grinned. He hadn't thought of her in years.

I wonder what she's up to?

CHANNEL: *Everlily*

Subscribers: 3.89M
Video views: 190M
Most recent video: "Getting Rid of Undereye Darkness"

RECENT COMMENTS:

Emily Anderson: You have no idea how badly I needed this video

Gina Pagano: I like that you went over a wide range of skin tones. More beautytubers need to do that.

Hai Mai: I don't have this problem. Can you use these tricks for covering acne, tho?

Annabel Lee: Well, it's not just "get more sleep" LOL! Because THAT'S not happening!

CHAPTER 5

The Chrysalis launch party was just as crowded, just as opulent, and just as over the top as Lily expected it would be . . . and then some.

She was wearing what she considered her signature "look," albeit geared for a dramatic evening: smoky eye, contouring, a dusky but subtle lip, everything from shimmery pearl-pink highlights to dusty rose lows. But as she looked around, she noticed everyone else seemed to have taken a cue from the new palette. Called PEACOCK, it was filled with shocking teal, electric blue, and glitter-filled gold. The people around her were wearing bright colors, their makeup and clothing as dramatic as Carnival in Rio.

Apparently she'd missed the memo.

She forced herself not to hunch, to hold her head up. She had a look, and she stuck to it. *Confidence,* she scolded herself, as she wove through the crowd.

"Lily!" She saw Mikki, waving to get her attention. They'd arrived separately, and judging by his tipsy smile, she guessed he'd gotten here early. She hadn't wanted to, knowing that it was the mark of an amateur, but Mikki said he liked to "pregame" before the bar got too crowded. Now, he was at a high table, next to another YouTuber she was friends with, Val. She gave them both hugs.

"I didn't know you were going to be here," she said to Val.

"I wasn't going to be," her friend Val said, giving her a tight hug. "But I wanted to see the palette, and it's always good to hear what people are up to. I scored an invite through their publicist." Val, short for Valkyrie on YouTube, was a self-described "big ole lesbian" and a lifestyle YouTuber. She and her girlfriend filmed clothing and makeup content, especially for plus-size women who wanted to be more fashion forward. It was a niche that worked for them. That said, it was just that . . . a niche. Her viewership was respectable, but not stratospheric, just a couple of million subscribers.

"Shot?" Mikki offered, nudging one of the small glasses at her. The liquid inside was just as vibrantly colored as the rest of the party. It looked like the Capitol from *The Hunger Games* in here.

"You know that's not really me," Lily said. "I mean, I did take a Lyft here, but I'm not going to be here long. I'll probably try to get a little more work done tonight."

"Tonight?" Mikki said, rolling his eyes. "It's a Friday night, and you're at one of the biggest parties in LA! Why in the world would you *work*?" He sounded like the college student he was, Lily thought indulgently. Maybe not *her*, when she was in college, but other people.

Tobin Bui came to mind, strangely.

"And this is why your subscriber numbers aren't growing, Mikki," Val murmured, tossing back her own shot. "Making it as an influencer is a dog-eat-dog business. You gotta *work*." Mikki leveled an irritated glare at her in response.

"I'm trying to come up with some new content," Lily interjected, before they could start sniping at each other. "My manager suggested that I need to mix things up a bit more. She also said I should be thinking about more collaborations." She bit her lip.

"I'll collaborate with you," Mikki volunteered instantly. "Although I've got midterms coming up, so it might be a little while."

"Midterms?" Lily blinked. "Isn't it summer?"

"I needed to make up that management class I tanked last semester," he muttered. He was still attending UCLA, pursuing a bachelor's in business economics at his parents' insistence. She'd even helped him with some homework, since she'd breezed through her degree in the same major.

"She doesn't mean us, Mikki." Val smiled, shaking her head. "I think her manager means collaborating with somebody with bigger numbers and less of a niche audience."

"That does make more sense," Mikki agreed.

Lily felt a burst of relief. She didn't want to turn down Mikki—and she'd probably collab with him plenty, schedule permitting—but she really needed more star power than his channel would bring.

"We are at a party with some of the most popular BeautyTubers in LA," Val pointed out. "Get out there. I'm sure you could find a big collab."

Lily nodded. "That's the idea." Her mouth suddenly felt dry, her throat scratchy. Her heart and stomach both fluttered with unpleasant nerves.

"Well, go on, then," Val nudged her. "Look! Chrysalis and Daisy are *right there*. You should totally talk to them!"

Lily choked. "That's ambitious," she said, trying not to let her fear show. "I mean, this is their launch party. Chrysalis has fifteen million subscribers, and Daisy has at least twelve. I was thinking of starting a little smaller. Bigger than me, but not quite so . . ."

She could imagine their derision—their judgment. And she felt her stomach drop even more.

"That's perfect," Mikki said, oblivious to her fear. Probably because she was used to masking it, even with her friends. "You could go over there and say hi and congratulations and stuff. Go on, go on!"

Lily looked over to where Daisy and Chrysalis were laughing, surrounded by friends and fans and hangers-on. It suddenly seemed very daunting.

Unbidden, it reminded her of that dreadful time, senior year, at Ponto Beach High. When the so-called popular girls had neatly and coldly dismissed her. That was what was holding her back, she realized. The idea of being rejected, all over again, was hamstringing her—even now, when it really mattered.

Lily closed her eyes for a second, the remembered shame warring with fury. Sometimes she felt like if she'd just gotten over that hump, if she'd just gotten *closure* from that awful, stupid incident, her life would be so much different. So much *better*.

She needed to get over that high school shit *now*.

With an icy determination, she reached over, grabbed a neon-green shot Mikki had in front of him, and downed it. It tasted like honeydew and lighter fluid, and she winced.

"All right," she said. "I'm going in."

She barely registered Mikki's and Val's hoots of encouragement. She walked up to the small crowd sitting on couches talking to each other.

Chrysalis was tall, around six feet, and looked . . . well, like a stunning, larger-than-life demigod, wrapped in a Technicolor rainbow. They wore short-shorts and go-go boots and a silky-looking blouse, all in the signature PEACOCK palette, complete with peacock-feather details. Their makeup was flawless, but that was to be expected. Their hair, which was famous for how often they changed the color and style, was a long, waist-length wig tonight, an iridescent waterfall of blues and greens and purples.

Daisy, on the other hand, would have fit in with Ernest Hemingway and F. Scott Fitzgerald's circle. She was wearing PEACOCK colors, too, but her outfit was flapper inspired . . . her signature. Her red hair was cut in a bob with pin curls. She even had a beaded headband and a small peacock-feather detail. She looked different from anyone else in the mansion, and she *owned* it.

What was it like, to have that? To feel that? Lily was determined to find out. She edged closer to the group, leaning against a couch arm, trying to figure out how to enter the conversation without making a fool of herself.

"God, everything is so *boring* anymore," Chrysalis complained, holding their empty glass out to a waiter, who promptly exchanged it for a full one. "Everything's been *done*."

The crowd murmured its agreement.

Boring. So boring. No originality.

"I *know*," Chrysalis echoed. "I have to wade through *tons* of crap to try to find things to share with my followers. Same clothes, same makeup, same tutorials. It's ridiculous!"

"It's getting harder and harder to make an impact," Daisy added. "I'm just glad you have this new palette. And I'm trying to brainstorm new ideas for content for my channel and Instagram."

Lily's heart started beating fast. This could be her opportunity. But how to break into the conversation without looking like a total douche? At the very least, she could hear about what kind of content they were trying . . .

"I mean, I'm trying out a makeup line from the princess of . . . Monaco, I think?" Daisy continued. "Or maybe Norway? Do they have a princess?"

"Is that the stuff that's, like, sixty-two thousand dollars for a tube of lipstick?" Chrysalis asked.

"Swear to God, it truly *is*," Daisy agreed, rolling her eyes before grinning with a little cruelty. "Fifteen 'exclusive' colors and an eighteen-carat-gold box? Can't *wait* to tear that apart."

Lily winced. No way could she afford to do that kind of content on a regular basis. Besides, bad-mouth reviews weren't her brand or her style. So that wasn't helpful.

"Say, have you seen that viral video that's going around?" This from Daisy's on-again, off-again boyfriend, Todd. "The one with the wiggly-arm things."

Chrysalis laughed. "Yes! Now, see, *that* was clever. Seeing those things go up like dominos over a couple of miles and dance around. *That* took coordination."

"I didn't get it," Daisy said dismissively. "So there were those dumb inflatables. So they were going up one after the other. What's the big deal?"

"It's a Lord of the Rings reference," Lily said without thinking. "Actually, a *Return of the King* reference."

All conversation on the couches stopped for a second as all of them stared at her for interrupting.

Well, you wanted their attention.

"In the movie . . . I mean, it's a fantasy kingdom—they don't have cell phones or anything—and they need to send a signal from one side of the continent to the other, and there's this dramatic scene where they light a big bonfire, and then you look across the landscape, and more and more beacons are lit. That's what they were doing," she finished. She straightened her back, hoping that she looked more confident than she felt.

Chrysalis tilted their head, studying her. "Huh. I just thought it was impressive because the guy obviously shelled out a good deal of money, and did a bunch of planning, to make it work."

Daisy sniffed. "I never saw those movies."

"Also," Chrysalis added, "that guy? GoofyBui? He's *cute*."

Now Daisy's interest was piqued. "Oh?" she added, causing Todd to scowl. She quickly opened her phone, obviously looking him up immediately.

"That video's gotten a crazy amount of views in a short period of time, got picked up everywhere," someone else chimed in. "He's creative, and funny."

"Hmm," Daisy mused, tapping her chin with blue-polished nails. "He is cute. And those stats aren't bad either. Does anybody here know him? I mean, *know him* know him. Like, enough to text, private number?"

Lily cleared her throat. She couldn't believe that this was how she was cracking into their inner circle, but . . . *now or never.* "I know him."

They went quiet, staring at her again.

She hadn't anticipated that her entrée to BeautyTuber society would be Tobin Bui, but at this point, she needed to use whatever leverage she could.

"Really," Daisy drawled.

"We went to high school together," Lily said. *Where he annoyed the shit out of me.* Still, he'd been one of her friends, beyond the irritation. *Nerd Herd for Life.* Before, it had seemed like a sentence. Now, it looked like a saving grace.

Daisy rolled her eyes again, something of a habit, it seemed. "Oh. So you're, like, Facebook friends or something, right? Like, you haven't talked to him in years? You don't *know* him."

"I still see him when I go back to my old hometown," Lily countered, not admitting that her trips to Ponto Beach were infrequent at best, especially since her parents had moved to the Bay Area. "We hang out in the same circles."

Do not tell these people about the Nerd Herd.

"All right, sweetie." Chrysalis patted the couch cushion next to them. Feeling strange, Lily gingerly sat down next to the towering beauty icon. "If you know GoofyBui . . ."

"I do," Lily reassured them.

"Prove it." Daisy's smirk turned sharp as she flanked Lily, boxing her in. "Let's video call him and say hi."

Lily swallowed.

Video call Tobin?

Shit.

CHAPTER 6

Tobin was pleasantly buzzed, sitting at one of the red couches at the Belly Up Tavern. It had great beer on tap and great musical acts. They'd been listening to a cool band he'd never heard of, a mix of rock and EDM. "Maybe I could do a video on a band," he mused, leaning his head back against the cushions.

"I don't know, Tobin," his friend Josh said, taking a pull from an Arrogant Bastard Ale. "You set the bar pretty high with that Beacons video. Congrats on that, by the way."

Tobin raised his glass with a little nod. "Thanks. Congrats on your new restaurant-thing opening. Or should I say your five restaurants?"

Josh grinned. He was the proud creator and owner of five "ghost kitchens" in San Diego that delivered food via Door Dash and Uber Eats, and he was making *bank*. Josh was usually too busy to hang out with the Nerd Herd crew much anymore, at least those townies that had remained in Ponto, so the fact that he'd made time to hang out with Tobin and the rest of them was a big deal, and Tobin appreciated it.

"All I know is, people expect consistency, even when they want something fresh," Josh said.

Tobin grimaced. "Same but different. I know." He sighed.

Asad plopped down on the couch across from him, his boyfriend, Freddie, sitting next to him and putting his arm around Asad's shoulders. "You still stressed about a follow-up?" Asad asked, looking sympathetic. "Dude. You should be happy, not all stressed out."

"I don't think I've ever seen you stressed," Josh mused.

"Hey! Will you all stop saying *stressed*?" Tobin complained, rubbing at his temple with his fingertips. "I'm . . . *concerned*. Just having a little trouble coming up with a new idea, that's all."

He was concerned that he was starting to have trouble coming up with ideas. His conversation with Jeffrey hadn't helped that process one bit. He'd tried mind mapping, free journaling, doodling.

Nothing. Nada. Zip.

Now, he was trying beer and brainstorming with his buddies. If this didn't work, he was going to look into a vision quest or something. Or maybe one of those physical challenges where you were alone out in the wilderness living on twigs and berries.

He frowned. "Hey. What if I did, like, a hard-core survival thing? You know. Film myself for a week or something in, like, Antarctica or the Yukon or whatever."

Josh's eyes widened. "Um . . . I think you'd die."

"I love you, man," Asad agreed, "but let's just say it: you're indoorsy. Rugged, you ain't."

Tobin frowned. They had a valid point. He wasn't quite so desperate that he was going to risk permanent bodily harm for content.

Not yet, anyway.

"I am stuck," he finally admitted.

Josh leaned forward, looking intent. Tobin knew that look. It was his "thinking face."

"I wish I'd brought my Post-its," Josh grumbled. "Hold on a sec." He got up, heading to the bar.

"Maybe some old-school game playthroughs?" Freddie offered. "Like, *super* old school. Old Activision *Pitfall* or something from ColecoVision, like *Zaxxon*."

"Who the hell has a Coleco?" Tobin said with a little laugh. "That's not a bad idea, though. And I do like the idea of *Pitfall*, but the graphics are so crap, I think it might not translate well. Still, at the end of the day, they're just playthroughs. I don't know if that moves the needle enough?" He frowned. *Maybe do a live-action* Pitfall? *How would that work?* He stored it away in the metaphorical file cabinet in his mind that stocked the seeds for weird ideas. "Anything else?"

"LEGO reenactment of . . . ," Asad began, but Freddie quickly interrupted.

"Nope. *Hard pass.*"

"What? Why?" Asad protested.

"One, filming stop-motion is a pain in the ass," Freddie pointed out, "and two, there are channels that do that already, and do it better. He ought to stay in his lane."

"Weaponized silliness," Asad agreed. "Okay. So, what's silly?"

"That's just it," Tobin moaned. "I have lost touch with my silly. I am currently silly-*less*. This is a disturbing state of affairs."

Josh returned to the table with a small stack of white cocktail napkins and a pen, and the surrounding friends groaned.

"Not your cards," Tobin begged. Josh had developed this obsession with "creative life design," like, six years ago—something their friend and fellow Nerd Herd member Tam turned him on to—and now he seemed to believe every problem could somehow be solved with sticky notes, thoughtful doodles, and a bunch of brainstorming. The guy sketched out *everything*. "That's cruel and unusual."

"My kitchens are making millions because of these cruel and unusual cards, my dude," Josh said mildly. "I used this system to go from being a dishwasher to a restauranteur and businessman. So suck it up, and let's ideate."

They kicked around ideas for a half hour, until Tobin was ready to punch himself in the head. He was relieved when his phone rang. "Sorry, I have to take this," he blurted, fleeing the noisy bar and heading outside to where it was quiet. He didn't care if it was a telemarketer pimping burial plots. He just needed a *break*.

But the caller was even more of a shock, and he stared at it for a second.

Lily Wang wants to video call me?

Curious —and, admittedly, at least half-bagged—he hit the answer button.

Lily's face filled his screen as the sounds of a noisy party surrounded her. She looked . . .

Well. She looked beautiful, like some cherry blossom goddess in a really good anime. Only, you know, Taiwanese. Of course, she always looked beautiful. She probably spent hours carefully constructing her look.

But she always looked good, makeup or not, his beer-soaked brain provided, not necessarily helpfully. He shushed his errant thought.

Not today, Satan.

"Well, well, well," he said instead. "Lily Wang. What's up?"

"I just, uh, wanted to congratulate you," she said, her voice smooth as Parisian hot chocolate. "The viral video. It's a big deal."

And there it was. The reason he was suddenly hearing from Lily.

He knew she was a YouTuber now, too, although beauty YouTubing was hardly his area. He hadn't really kept track of her—they'd lost touch since she moved to LA and her parents moved to the Bay Area, giving her one fewer reason to head back to Ponto.

"Thanks," he said, hating how wooden he sounded. "How are you doing, anyway?"

"Fine," she said. "I'm, um, at a party . . . well, a launch party, and—"

"Is that really you, GoofyBui?" a woman's voice drawled off screen. Suddenly, what looked like a flapper popped in front of Lily's face. "This one here claimed she knew you personally, and, well—"

"We didn't believe her," another voice chimed in, as another heavily made-up face crowded onto the screen. "Shame on us! Is it really you?"

He thought he recognized the second person: Chrysalis, an absolute titan in the beauty community. Influential enough that even he'd heard of them.

"It's, um, really me," Tobin said, feeling odd, although part of that might've been the beers and brainstorming session. "And yes, I know Lily."

"That's so sweet," the flapper said, sounding saccharine. "And you've known each other since high school?"

"Since grade school," he corrected. "Went to the same elementary, middle, and high school. I've known her forever."

Lily, or at least what he could see of her, looked mollified. The other two looked curious.

"She's actually not a bad gamer," he added, feeling a little looser after the beers. "I mean, she's kind of a psychotic rage warrior, and she always killed me, even when I was on her team. But she had some button-mashing skills."

Chrysalis burst out laughing, and Daisy snickered. Lily looked less entertained. "Tobin . . ."

"You know," he said, feeling pretty damned amused himself by this point, "she actually tried to kill me in real life before, now that I think about it. Remember? Sixth-grade camp?"

"You *got kicked out of camp*," Lily said, sounding like she was talking through gritted teeth. He couldn't help it. He grinned broadly. *"For drawing on my face."*

"In my defense, she fell asleep first," he pointed out, watching as Chrysalis and the flapper leaned on each other, chuckling. "And I was pretty proud of my artwork. Drew the Darth Maul pattern in full detail. She didn't wake up once."

"You drew it in *Sharpie!*" Lily snapped. "It didn't come off all week!"

52

Chrysalis actually hooted. "God, I can't tell if it's enmity or fore-play," they said, gently dabbing at their eyelashes. "But you two are hilarious. You've got this whole kiss-me, kill-me vibe. You two ever get together?"

"*Absolutely not*," Lily said, sounding so disgusted that Tobin's ass-hole response triggered like a bear trap.

"Oh, there was that one time," he teased, waiting for Chrysalis and the flapper to lean in, obviously interested. "In ninth grade . . ."

"*Do. Not.*" Lily's tone was the voice of doom. Alas, by this point, he could not give less of a shit.

"Somebody smuggled Goldschläger to a little party we were having—just us geeks, not like a kegger or anything," he clarified, unsure of why he bothered to do so. "Anyway, we wound up somehow playing seven minutes in heaven? And I got Lily in a hall closet, and shot my shot."

Flapper giggled. Chrysalis arched a perfectly drawn eyebrow. "So what happened?"

"I was about to kiss her." He waited for a moment, a dramatic beat. Then he grinned. "Then I puked on her shoes."

"Oh, God, kill me," Lily moaned.

Chrysalis laughed, while the flapper shook her head. "You are *too funny*," the flapper said with a look of interest. "And so cute! EverLily, you ever think about collaborating with *him*?"

"Not really," Lily said, her voice so tight you could bounce a quarter off it.

"Oh, you should!" Chrysalis said, clapping their hands.

"Yeah, Lily," Tobin echoed, knowing his over-the-top cheer would drive Lily bananas. "We should *totally* collaborate!"

"We'll see," she said, even though he could tell she looked ready to shoot fire out of her eyes before driving down to Ponto to murder him.

"I'll call you, sweetie!" he yelled. "We'll totally *hook up*! On this collab, I mean!" He winked.

She growled. Then she hung up on him.

He laughed, harder than he had in months. He did not know what it was about Lily Wang that tempted him to push every single one of her buttons. Maybe it was her uptight attitude and her evident disapproval of his approach to life. Or maybe it was her strange and mistaken belief that she needed the approval of people who, ultimately, didn't matter to who she was. Whatever it was, she managed to wave a red cape in front of the bull that was his subconscious, and before he knew it, he was off and running.

He went back into the bar, still chuckling. "What took you so long?" Josh said, the cards spread out like some kind of drunken-doodle tarot spread. "We think we're really on to something."

"You won't believe who called me," he said, then plowed forward before they could guess. *"Lily Wang."*

"Lily, who hates you?" Asad asked, expression bewildered.

"Last time you two were together, she threatened to give you a vasectomy with a weed whacker," Josh added.

"She was a bit perturbed," Tobin agreed with a grin, feeling the tension he'd been carrying flow out of his shoulders. He probably shouldn't get this kind of hard charge from teasing Lily, but it had been a long time since he'd been able to—she didn't visit as much as she used to. And there was absolutely no stress relief quite like winding Lily up.

"Oh! That time we all tried to go camping, and you pretended you were a bear?" Freddie said.

"You are so lucky she didn't murder you," Asad breathed. "Like, for real. I am surprised she didn't run you over with her car."

"What the hell *is* it between you two, anyway?" Freddie asked. "I've only seen you together a handful of times, and I can't tell if it's, like, 'I tug her hair because I like her' or you're just literally trying to drive her insane."

Asad rolled his eyes. "You should've seen them in high school. It was even worse."

Josh snickered. "Like 'get a room' worse."

"Trust me, we have never gotten together," Tobin said with a grin. "She would probably literally kill me."

But what a way to go.

He frowned at himself. No. He didn't think that.

Did he?

He sighed. "She was just calling to score some points with influencers," he said, and his heart fell a little, the buzz from the beer and the phone call starting to wear off. "She's focused on the job. So I guess I'd better get my own act together, huh?"

With that, he forced himself to focus on the stupid cards, and the stupid brainstorming, and hoped like hell he'd come up with some kind of new idea.

CHAPTER 7

Lily stared at her now blank phone screen. She wanted two things. She wanted the ground to swallow her up. But not before she drove down to Ponto Beach and pummeled one Tobin Bui to a pulp.

"So, that happened," she murmured, looking at Chrysalis and Daisy, who were still snickering. God, they must think she was the biggest geek and loser on the planet.

Chrysalis shook their head. "That man," they said. "Such a *character!*"

"And decent numbers," Daisy added, with an avaricious gleam in her eye. "If I could think of doing anything with him, I would."

"Oh, I can just imagine what you'd do with him," Chrysalis said suggestively, bringing out a fresh round of laughter from the two of them (and a scowl from Todd again). It was like Lily wasn't even there.

Which was not the point. At all.

Lily cleared her throat. "I really love your new palette," she said to Chrysalis, keeping her voice steady and not tentative at all. "I'm looking at developing my own makeup line."

Chrysalis nodded, not really paying attention. Daisy, on the other hand, sniffed, rolling her eyes slightly.

"I don't suppose you have any tips on how to build your brand and your viewership?" Lily continued. "I'd love any insights you might have. Especially around collaborations."

Daisy's laughter was dismissive. "Here's a tip: don't collab with anybody who has less than eight million subscribers." She shot Lily a look that clearly said *don't even ask*.

Lily forced herself not to shrink back at Daisy's sharp words. Chrysalis, at least, had a kind expression.

"Daisy's right on one point," they said. "Working with a YouTuber who has a larger audience can be a great boost."

That's what I'm trying *to do!* Lily wanted to scream, but she kept her face placid, hoping her expression was just mildly inquisitive.

"You could do worse than collaborating with someone like GoofyBui," they added.

"A gaming channel?" Lily asked with doubt. "I just don't see any audience crossover."

"You'd be surprised," Chrysalis replied. "People aren't just one thing, you know."

"But wouldn't that dilute my brand?"

Chrysalis frowned. They hated being defined or pigeonholed, Lily remembered, and quickly backed off.

"Maybe your brand is too narrowly focused," Chrysalis said, a bit more coolly. Then they turned back to Daisy. "Anyway . . . did I hear you were considering a fashion line?"

"Just accessories to start," Daisy said, fanning herself with her hand. "But down the road a bit, I was thinking . . ."

After a few minutes of being pointedly ignored, Lily registered the dismissal. They were obviously done talking with her, and the longer she stayed, the more humiliation seeped into her. It was bad enough that she wasn't important enough to warrant their attention. But to let everyone see her being ignored and then realize that either she was too stupid to recognize that she was being shut down or that she was so desperate she was trying to force a connection that would never happen?

She winced internally. It was high school all over again. Just as she'd feared.

She pasted a small smile on her face, trying to look as blasé and uncaring as possible; then she got off the couch, retreating back to her friends. Mikki's eyes were wide, and Val was grinning.

"Oh my God, how did it go?" Mikki asked breathlessly.

"Are either of them going to collab with you?" Val tacked on. "It seemed like y'all were getting on like a house on fire."

"And what were they doing with your phone? Were you showing them your content?" Mikki pressed.

"It wasn't like that." Lily felt herself deflate. "They were talking about Tobin Bui."

The two looked at her with blank expressions.

"*GoofyBui*," she clarified. "You know. Waving-arm tube-man video?"

"Oh! I saw that," Mikki said. "What about it?"

"I know him." Lily still felt anger seething through her system. "They didn't believe me, so I wound up calling him."

"And?"

"*And he is one of the biggest dinguses alive*," Lily hissed. "Seriously. I could strangle him with my bare hands."

Mikki looked horrified. "What did he say?"

"He just . . . he brought up all these embarrassing stories from when we were kids," she said, the mortification rolling over her all over again. She'd wanted to impress Chrysalis and Daisy. Instead, she'd looked like a geekish, dweebish child. An *idiot*. Certainly no one they'd want to collaborate with—Daisy had made that painfully clear from the jump.

"That doesn't sound so bad," Val said, but her face looked skeptical. "Maybe they just thought the stories were funny, or cute."

"Trust me, they didn't." Lily ground her teeth together. "I'm headed home. I still need to . . ."

Figure out how she was going to boost her subscribers. Find a collaborator who would work with her and actually make a difference.

And come up with some content that was creative and original—and apparently something she wasn't doing presently.

The shot she'd drunk hastily earlier was gurgling in her stomach. She pressed a hand to it.

" . . . I need to go," she finally finished. She hugged them both, then left the mansion before catching a Lyft and heading back to her own loft. When she got there, she got cleaned up, changed, and broke into her emergency chocolate truffles, ones she saved for special, stressful occasions. The prettiness of the box, and the luxurious, luscious flavors of the sweets, soothed the worst of her temper.

Do something different.

She looked at her old content calendar. Maria was right: it had things that had been done a million times before. Creating a minimalist wardrobe palette without being boring? Jeez, the tagline itself *was* boring! Testing different Asian skin-care routines? That was more niche—maybe too niche. For pity's sake—*How to rock earth tones?*

What had she been thinking? It was amazing she had as many subscribers as she had, putting this stuff out!

She grabbed a blank notebook and her favorite colored markers, then started to write a list of possible ideas. It wasn't one of her favorite blank journals—she collected those and hoarded them like a dragon, since they were really too pretty to waste on brainstorming and things she'd cross out or revise—but she needed some place to experiment.

After an hour, she felt like banging her head against a wall. So far, she'd come up with ideas like cartoon makeup, but she knew that some big YouTubers had already done that. She'd considered "makeup when you're shame-walking to work," but frankly, that wasn't her experience. In the past few years, she'd mostly had boyfriends, few and far between though they were. And she always traveled with makeup remover and a travel pack of makeup. The few casual hookups she'd had, she'd refused to stay the night, hating to be seen so disheveled and making do with someone else's toiletries. She hated waking up somewhere she didn't know, and she really hated making small talk with someone who was (hopefully) great at giving orgasms but had nothing more in common with her than that. That awkward "Um, so last night was nice" or "I'll call you" (when neither of them had any intention) was wretched, and at this point, she'd rather do without unless she was really, really stressed.

She sighed, cudgeling her brain to try to come up with something fresh and new.

Club looks: *done it.*

Daytime looks: *yawn.*

Wedding looks: *not her wheelhouse. At all.*

By two in the morning, she had scoured fellow YouTuber accounts and had gone to desperate lengths to try to find *something* that fit her personality, would be considered original and noteworthy, and involved someone who would collaborate with her. All she had to show for it was a headache and a list full of expletives and crossed-out video ideas.

Sandy eyed, she looked at a recommended video. It was Tobin's beacons thing, yet again. She was too tired to be mad. Instead, she decided to click over to his channel. It had been a while since she'd looked at it. She wasn't a gamer by any stretch of the imagination, and his antics tended to remind her of the behavior that made her want to punch him when they were younger.

She found herself falling down a rabbit hole of his old content. He still played plenty of video games, yelling and laughing and basically making a fool of himself. He still did funny little skits and fake movie trailers and song parodies. She didn't play video games all that much anymore, but found herself cracking up at his attempts at winning a simple game that required pogo-jumping up increasingly difficult, increasingly ludicrous terrain. His swearing was colorful and inventive. He also did bigger, stupider things, like the ill-advised filling of a weather balloon with propane and lighting it (complete with huge warning disclaimer and subsequent "this was the stupidest thing I have ever done" epilogue). It reminded her of the Nerd Herd, back in high school, when they'd done things out of the *Anarchist's Cookbook* as a result of their honors chemistry classes.

The more she watched, the more she realized: as much as she hated to admit it, he was incredibly creative. He managed to pack a twist and a shock even into small segments, and she found herself laughing out loud, although she was irritated at the fact.

He really was talented.

She wasn't into cringe humor, and she didn't like the idea of making a fool of yourself to get laughs or get views. But he was more than that. He had a flair.

Maybe it wouldn't be the worst idea in the world to collaborate with him.

She blinked. Was she seriously considering this?

She looked at his stats on Social Blade. His numbers were more than respectable: he had nine million YouTube subscribers, even if her Instagram and TikTok followers dwarfed his, largely because he didn't really produce much content in either of those accounts. He seemed to focus more on YouTube and Twitch. He was slowly but steadily growing, and he'd seen a jump after the Beacons video went viral.

The more she thought about it, the faster her heart beat. Sure, it wasn't an obvious connection. Beauty influencer and gamer? Where was the connection? But the thing was, he *wasn't* just a gamer. He wasn't all playthroughs, all the time. She'd enjoyed his comedy stuff—always had, even when he drove her up a wall. Her audience would probably find him funny too. Beyond that, the guy was unbelievably creative. If anyone could help her come up with an off-the-wall, viral element for her beauty channel, it'd be Tobin. And she'd do whatever she needed to on his channel, which would mean more exposure as well as diversification in her content.

She took a deep breath.

The problem was . . . she'd have to *work with him*. Historically, that was like putting a cobra and a mongoose in a burlap sack. It did not go well.

Although she'd like to think she was the mongoose.

She rubbed her temples. She needed to talk to him about this. Not over the phone—she growled at the memory of their last video call. She wanted this to be face to face. If she could manage to keep her temper, and if he could manage to be serious for more than five minutes, then maybe . . . *maybe*, this would work out well for both of them.

She wasn't holding out a lot of hope, she realized. She'd drive down to Ponto Beach tomorrow, and head to his house, and see if they could help each other without some kind of bloodshed.

CHAPTER 8

Lily didn't usually do things on impulse. But she realized as she drove up the cul-de-sac to Tobin's house that this might not have been the best idea she'd ever come up with.

She'd been second-guessing herself the entire two-hour drive from Los Angeles to Ponto Beach. Driving was usually a good way for her to clear her head—at least, when she was actually *moving*, not just sitting in exhaust-filled stopped traffic and crawling her way across LA—but now her brain seemed like it was on an infinitely running loop.

This is stupid.

No, this will work.

No, this is really stupid.

It'll work. It has to work.

Tobin was many things: annoying, hyperactive, compulsively incapable of taking anything seriously. But the guy was also insanely creative. She could take things seriously for both of them, she thought with a frown, if it meant some of that creativity rubbed off.

She'd stopped at a bakery on the way and was now armed with doughnuts, which she knew he had a weakness for. Weirdly, she'd even remembered what kind he liked: bavarian creams. Taking a deep breath, she pulled her MINI Cooper into his driveway, then grabbed the white paper bakery bag and headed for the door.

His house was like any number of houses in Southern California: cream-colored stucco, red ceramic tile roof. She'd been here once before, when he'd first bought it a few years ago. She'd been visiting her friend Emily, and the Nerd Herd had an impromptu gathering to celebrate Tobin's milestone. She'd remembered feeling some envy, since she was still renting. Still, it was a hell of a lot easier to buy a house in Ponto than it was to buy a condo in LA, and she'd decided to either invest her money back into her business or sock it away in savings—just in case.

She was a big fan of planning and contingencies. She had graduated from UCLA with her major in business economics and a minor in digital humanities, all in four years. She'd actually planned out her college classes—*all four years' worth*—at her parents' kitchen table during her senior year of high school. Her parents had watched, nodding with approval. They were just as meticulous as she was. Nature or nurture, she came by it honestly.

Of course . . . she didn't have a contingency if Tobin said no to this.

She took a deep breath, going up his walkway, then rang the doorbell and waited.

Abruptly, panic gripped her. She probably should've called first. What if he didn't mean it about collaborating with her? He'd had that teasing tone, like he was messing with her. And what if he hadn't even come home the night before? He seemed kind of drunk.

She winced. What if he'd come home but wasn't alone? She didn't want to have a conversation with him while his hookup poured herself coffee in the background.

Gah! Gah! GAH!

She took another deep breath—and strongly considered turning on one kitten heel and driving the hell out of Ponto—when suddenly she heard a voice from the other side of the door.

"Comin'. Just give me a minute," Tobin's scratchy voice said; then the door opened. Lily couldn't help it. She gaped.

He was standing in blue-plaid sleep pants, rubbing at his eye with one hand. He had serious bed head, his dark-walnut hair sticking up at odd angles, and he had stubble on his jaw.

He also wasn't wearing a shirt.

She blinked. Apparently, he'd started exercising in the ten years since high school—fairly seriously. She suppressed a gasp, taking in the definition of his chest, the bulge of his arms, the hint of a six-pack.

Holy shit! Tobin Bui is ripped*!*

"Lily?" He seemed just as surprised as she was, his sleep-droopy eyes widening. "What are you doing here?"

She laughed, but it sounded breathless and raspy and weird. "Um . . . I wanted to talk to you."

He blinked. "Ohhhh-kay?"

She thrust the bakery bag forward like the world's most aggressive gift. "I brought doughnuts," she added. "Your favorite. I think."

"Thanks?" He still looked confused as hell, and she did not blame him. The slow seep of embarrassment was heating her cheeks and making her squirm.

She gritted her teeth. Apparently she was going to need to just dive in and spell it out for him.

"Were you serious about collaborating with me?" she asked without preamble.

He stared at her. Then he ran his hand over his face, slowly. "Tell me you didn't just drive all this way to talk about YouTube."

She scowled.

"But of course you did," he continued before she could answer. "Come on in. If we're going to talk, I desperately need coffee. And ibuprofen. I am hungover as hell."

She followed him. His house was nicer than she remembered— of course, it had been unfurnished at the time. Now, he had a taupe couch and a big coffee table, and of course the requisite "dude-bro" huge-screen television. He also had some framed pictures, surprising her. Pictures of him with his parents, and some older people who she assumed were his grandparents, and maybe aunts and uncles. Then there were pictures of him with the Nerd Herd: Tobin, Josh, and Vinh fooling around at the beach; that time when they all tried camping out in the desert; late night on the Coronado bridge.

There was even a picture of all of them graduating from Ponto High School, the group of them so young, smiling wildly in their caps and gowns, honors cords and Hawaiian leis around their necks. They weren't like the artistic and carefully composed photos she had hanging in her apartment, mostly black-and-white studio shots her parents had meticulously curated and professionally framed, but she had to admit, it felt . . . nice. Homey.

He also had a treadmill, a stationary bike, and a set of free weights, in what would've been the dining room. Which explained how he was now looking like a *Men's Health* cover, she supposed.

He yawned, stretching, and she felt her mouth go a little dry at the play of muscles across his back. It had been a while, she argued with herself, since she'd been with a guy. So that would explain why she was acting so stupidly thirsty.

About *Tobin frickin' Bui*, of all people.

"Coffee?" he asked, as he measured out ground coffee and got his pot started. She shrugged, not trusting herself to speak. They waited in increasingly tense silence as the stuff gurgled and finally brewed. He paused it long enough to get his own cup. Then he dumped in sugar and cream, and turned to her. "So. You want to collab. Badly enough to drive a few hours, all the way down here, to my house, to ask me in person."

She bit her lip. "Yes," she said. "I know it seems crazy. Believe me, I balked when Daisy suggested it, but the more I thought about it . . ."

"Wait a minute, wait a minute," he said, holding up a hand, then taking a sip of coffee. "Who the hell's Daisy?"

"The woman, last night," Lily said, trying to curb her impatience. "Daisy Blackwell. One of the biggest beauty influencers in the world."

"The flapper one?"

"Yes, the flapper one," Lily agreed, suppressing a grin. It was so *great* to hear someone sum Daisy up so offhandedly. She'd been insulated in the beauty YouTuber bubble for so long it never occurred to her that others might not have the same level of fear and awe. "Anyway, she pointed out that it might be a good idea, and Chrysalis agreed. And the more I thought about it, the more I thought we could really help each other."

She took a deep, steadying breath. She'd gotten up early to prepare herself, to show why, exactly, a partnership between EverLily and GoofyBui was a viable and potentially profitable one. Now, she felt her nerves melt away as she snapped into what she considered her "pitch" mentality.

"You have a large base of subscribers and followers," she said. "You've definitely got a bent toward gamers, but some people just watch you because they like your humor and your creativity. I don't think they're just watching exclusively for playthroughs, and I don't think they'll mind you collaborating with a beauty YouTuber."

He kept sipping, his expression betraying nothing. He was still listening, at least, rather than being distracted. He took out a doughnut, taking a large bite.

She took a deep breath. "And I've got a following that might enjoy a crossover," she said. "My content may not be as viral," she said, thinking *gross understatement!* "But it's consistent: my viewers know when to expect videos. I haven't deviated from that schedule in five years." Not even when she had bronchitis, although she'd wound up doing a silent video with text overlays. It had been a bitch.

But she'd gotten it done.

Tobin blinked at that one. "Not once?" he marveled. "In *five years?*"

"And my viewers are really loyal," she said. "That said, I think they'll be open to new content, and I . . . I want to bring some more originality to my videos."

There. She'd admitted it. It felt like showing her jugular to a jaguar, admitting a weakness, and she hated it.

She rushed forward. "What I'd like to propose is a collaboration between GoofyBui and EverLily. Maybe a short video series—half on your channel, half on mine."

"Doing what kind of content?"

She felt her stomach knot a little. He was the creative one. That's why she was here. "I'm sure we can think of something," she hedged. "I wanted to get your buy-in before we developed more concrete ideas."

He made a vague noise. What did it mean? Was he interested? Not interested? Still fricking *hungover* and not paying attention?

"So, what you're saying," he said slowly, after finishing the doughnut in a few bites, "is that you want to use me. You want to boost your numbers, and you want to leverage my channel to get there."

She winced like she'd been slapped. It wasn't like he was *wrong*, per se, but still. "I wouldn't put it like that, but that's how collabs work, Tobin," she said, feeling affronted . . . and vaguely ashamed.

"What are you bringing to the party?" he said. "Because I'm doing fine, and I don't think that a bunch of fashion and beauty viewers are going to be signing on to my channel, frankly."

"You'd be surprised," she snapped. "It's like Chrysalis says: people aren't just one thing. And I really think it would depend on the content we produced."

His brow wrinkled in thought. "There's one other problem," he pointed out. "I'm a dog, Lily."

She blinked. "You're a *what*?" she asked, confused as hell. "What, like a womanizer? Why are you telling me this? Are you planning on hitting on me or something? Because we both know *that's* not going to work!"

His eyes widened. Then he burst out laughing, hard enough that he had to put his coffee cup down. "No, no. Not like that," he said. "Like . . . like a Labrador retriever, I mean."

"I see," she said slowly. Although, honestly, she didn't.

"I'm silly, and happy, and mostly harmless," he explained. "You, on the other hand, are a cat. You're beautiful and finicky, and despite any attempts for a dog to play with you, you would probably hiss before clawing the hell out of me."

"That feels overly simplistic," she protested.

"We don't get along, Lils," he pointed out. "I get you want to grow your channel, but there is a good chance that we would be filming a murder. I'm just not sure it's a good idea."

"You think I can't be professional?" she asked, bristling.

"No," he said with exaggerated patience. "I know you can. Just like I know, odds are good that I *can't*."

Her mouth dropped open.

"I can almost guarantee I will do something stupid," he continued. "I will ruin your takes. I will make inappropriate jokes. I cuss like an overly imaginative sailor. If you thought I was goofy in high school . . . I assure you, it's only gotten worse."

"I've seen your content," she protested. "It's good, Tobin. I think I can work with it."

"Yes," he said, sighing. "But will you be able to work with *me*?"

She wanted to growl. The damned thing was—he was just voicing the same concerns she had. She wasn't sure, not 100 percent. But she *needed* this.

"I know I can," she said with more confidence than she felt.

"I'm really sorry, Lily," he said, and to his credit, he did sound like he was. "But . . . I just don't think it's a good idea."

Just like that, she felt her confidence crumble like a sandcastle. She refused to let it show, instead crossing her arms. "That's fine. It's fine," she repeated, as if repetition would make it somehow better. "You're probably right."

He leaned against the counter, then yelped. "Shit, that's cold," he said, rubbing his lower back and glaring at the granite countertop. Then he looked down, his eyes widening. "Annnnnd I'm not wearing a shirt."

Despite feeling tears pricking at her eyes, she smirked. "I noticed."

"Shit," he repeated, putting down his coffee. "Uh . . . listen, I feel bad that you came all this way for nothing. Let me put on some real clothes and . . . I dunno, take you out to breakfast or brunch or something?" He grinned. "You strike me as the brunch type."

"I really need to record today," she said. No way in *hell* was she going to keep up a brave face, choking down eggs Benedict with the guy who'd shot down her idea and refused to help her career. "But thanks."

She turned to the door and stopped for a second when Tobin gently put his hand on her arm. "I really am sorry," he said.

"Don't be," she said. "I really should've just called."

With that, she walked out the door, going back to the car, and shortly thereafter pulling back out of the driveway.

Well, that was a huge waste. And the worst part?

She had no idea what to do next.

CHANNEL: *GOOFYBUI*

Subscribers: 9.9M
Video views: 310M
Most recent video: "Trying to Come Up with an Idea"

RECENT COMMENTS:

Skeptic_Sketcher: Add in eating whipped cream straight from the can, and that's my process, dude

Hayden the Greaten: I coulda lived my whole life not seeing you yodel in the shower

Emily Anderson: LMAO

Han Solo Cup: This is some funny shit

CHAPTER 9

Tobin hated driving into LA. Unfortunately, it was ground zero for YouTubers—there were probably more YouTubers per capita there than in any city in the country. It was entertainment central as well, and technically only a few hours from Ponto, depending on traffic. Still, if he was going to Los Angeles, he was damned well going to make it worth his while, because he didn't want to make multiple trips if he could help it.

So, even though rigid scheduling was something he rarely submitted to unless it was absolutely necessary, he booked a few different things. He left Ponto super early—like "oh my God, where is the sun?" early—and had a quick breakfast at Tommy's Diner with two of his favorite podcasters, GameOrDie, before recording a show with them at their house. Then he stopped and visited one of his gamer friends, TwitchyBird, and they did a joint livestream of a quick jaunt through a few levels of the latest *Zelda* release, yelling and laughing the whole time. While it was fun, it was kind of exhausting, especially since he'd recorded, edited, and uploaded a video the day before and still felt kind of wiped out. His video wasn't anything special, just a "trying to come up with an idea" skit that he'd kicked around. If he'd been more on the ball, he would've done full animation, but he'd already gone several days with no posts, and while he wasn't as strictly scheduled as Lily apparently was, he knew that at least a marginally consistent release schedule was important. No content meant bored viewers. Bored viewers tended to disappear. He wanted to keep his audience happy. Normally, that meant a sixty-forty mix of game stuff and silly shit—approximately. He probably needed to keep better track of that sort of thing.

He bet Lily had a spreadsheet that mapped that kind of thing out. *Why are you thinking about Lily again?*

He took a few deep breaths, forcing himself to regain focus. After all, he was slated to have lunch with his agents and discuss his future. Or something.

He sighed. Because the livestream had finished early, he was early to lunch, so he was sitting at a bougie restaurant, drinking Dr Pepper and playing *Clash of Clans* on his phone. The place was swank— linen tablecloths, well-dressed waiters, the offer of three different kinds of *water*, for God's sake—which suggested Jeffrey had picked it out for their lunch meeting. It was probably a place to be seen by people in Hollywood, or something. Tobin was wearing a T-shirt that had Baby Yoda (he would never, *ever* call him "Grogu") on it with the word *WANTED* printed under it, a pair of skate shorts, and his old pair of Chucks. He was not exactly dressed to impress.

On the other hand, he didn't really give a shit, so there was that.

"Tobin," Bastian said, greeting him, completely unfazed by his client's casual attire. Tobin stood, and they shook hands, then did the bro hug, one shoulder and a pat. "Good to see you, brother."

"Same," Tobin said with a genuine grin. Bastian might look slick and sleek, but he was good people. Then he held out his hand to Jeffrey, who definitely shot him a judgy look as he took in his outfit. They shook hands quickly; then they all sat down.

"Congrats on the Beacons video," Bastian said with a warm smile. "I know it took a while to pull together, but . . . shit! That thing took off."

"Thanks." It was funny how much more Bastian's approval meant to him.

Cathy Yardley

"We were talking about how important it is to have a follow-up," Jeffrey jumped in. Tobin fought the urge to flip the guy off. *What a tool bag.* "So. What are your concepts? What do you have in mind to capitalize on the traffic? Your subscriber numbers have been growing steadily."

Tobin gritted his teeth, then pulled out the "cards" he'd brainstormed with Josh, Asad, and Freddie. "Keep in mind, these are just spitballing," he warned. "It's only been a few days."

Bastian and Jeffrey looked at him, expectant.

Tobin sighed, then plowed forward. "Water-balloon jai alai. Or maybe water balloons in a T-shirt bazooka."

Bastian frowned. "Didn't they do something like that in *Jackass?* Also—won't they break? And I think that'll hurt like hell."

Jeffrey, on the other hand, chuckled. "If it hurts, that'll be gold. People love that shit. Like treadmill-fail videos."

Tobin grimaced. It was not one of the better ideas, which was why he'd led with it. "Um—this is a bit more elaborate, and it'll take some time, but . . . capture the flag." He paused a beat for emphasis. "In the Mall of America."

Bastian grinned, shaking his head.

"Liability issues," Jeffrey kiboshed immediately, shaking his head. "God, the lawsuit. Let's not go there."

"Also, didn't you do something similar at University Town Center, in San Diego?" Bastian asked, quirking his eyebrow. "I mean, it was popular, and this would be a step up—but it's more of the same, isn't it?"

Tobin had actually liked that idea—enough that he'd done it more than once. In fact, he and the Herd had pulled off something similar in high school, at a mall downtown. And yeah, to Jeffrey's point, the security guards had been none too pleased by their antics. He let out a slow breath. "Live action *Pitfall?*"

Jeffrey gave him the thumbs-up. Bastian, on the other hand, wrinkled his nose. "You've got to think about it: the vines, the pits, the rolling logs . . . the scorpions and snakes, for God's sake. How much money and how much time is it going to take to set this up?"

"I hadn't really worked out the details," Tobin admitted, feeling like he'd been called on in class and hadn't done the homework. But the damned thing was, he'd *tried*. And it was one thing to disappoint that douchebag Jeffrey. Disappointing Bastian felt like . . .

Failure.

Bastian cracked his knuckles, a move at odds with his suave, sophisticated front. It was a gamer thing, one Tobin knew Bastian did before he started playing. "Listen, Tobin, shooting high is all well and good," he said, "but the best thing about the Beacons video wasn't the expense, or the scale—it was the fact that it was so unexpected. People value originality, creativity. You're a smart fucking guy with a twisted sense of humor. Don't think that you have to go bigger. You're smart, and you think differently." Bastian clapped him on the shoulder. "Lean into *that*."

Jeffrey frowned but followed the lead of his senior agent.

Tobin nodded, then drank some of his flavored seltzer water, which tasted like chalky sparkling water that had been in the same room as a watermelon at one point. "I've been feeling a little stuck." He drew out the words, unwilling to admit it.

"That's nothing," Jeffrey said quickly with a barracuda smile. "You'll snap right back to it. You just haven't come up with the right idea."

Before Tobin could, indeed, snap, Bastian held up a hand. "Have you considered doing another collab?" he asked. "Sometimes working with new blood can shake up your creativity."

He thought immediately of Lily, showing up out of the blue on Saturday morning when he was viciously hungover and utterly unprepared, asking to work together. "Funny you should mention," he said wryly. "I have had somebody approach me to collab recently."

Jeffrey groaned. "Another gamer cross-promo, Bas?" he asked the older agent. "We're getting *really* niche here. I don't know that we're going to get any kind of series just based on gaming . . ."

Bastian leveled a cool glare at Jeffrey, and the younger man quieted down. "There are plenty of opportunities for you, just as a gamer," he said to Tobin, but he did also sound a bit hesitant. "We could pitch a series on one of the new streaming networks—some of them are looking for ten-minute episodes. There's enough of a specialized audience—"

"Wait, no. I didn't mean . . . this actually wouldn't be . . ." Tobin chuckled at himself, feeling like an idiot. "She's a beauty YouTuber, actually."

For a second, Bastian and Jeffrey just stared at him. Then they both started cracking up, Jeffrey practically braying like a donkey. "You mean, like, makeup and fashion and shit?" Jeffrey croaked, breathless.

Tobin laughed weakly. "Yeah. Don't worry, I told her no."

"Why in the world did she suggest it?" Bastian said, gesturing to the waiter to take their order.

"She's building her stats, just like I am. She's not quite there yet, but she is determined. Like a pit bull." Or whatever the cat equivalent of a pit bull was, he thought with a grin, thinking of his dog-and-cat analogy. "She may not be the most creative, but she's a content machine. And a beast when it comes to consistency."

Jeffrey was still snickering to himself when Bastian's eyes narrowed. "What's her name?"

"Lily Wang," Tobin supplied, then clarified. "Her channel's name is EverLily."

They ordered lunch from the patient waiter, then Bastian whipped out his phone, quickly typing. His eyes widened.

Jeffrey looked over Bastian's arm at the phone display, then let out a low whistle. "Holy shit. She is *smokin'* hot. I'd hit that."

"Watch it," Tobin snarled. "She's a friend. Like, since grade school."

He could practically see the gears turning in Bastian's head. "What kind of content did you have in mind with her?"

"Huh? I didn't have *any* content in mind with her," Tobin said, startled. "Like I said, I told her no."

"I think you might be missing an opportunity here," Bastian replied, thoughtful. "Jeffrey's right: there's something to be said for going a bit more mainstream. Whether she can act or not, you could probably come up with some funny, fresh material. Think about it: a gamer and a beauty guru? What the hell would they have in common?"

"Other than the fact that we grew up together? Um, *nothing*," Tobin said, feeling bewildered.

"Well, what kind of chemistry do you two have?" Bastian pressed.

Tobin rolled his eyes. "She's spent most of her life wanting to kill me, so there's that."

Bastian's smile was like the Cheshire cat's. "Tension, maybe some dirt from when you were kids . . . hell, she can be straight man to your silliness. And while I wouldn't necessarily word it the way Jeffrey did, a pretty girl is never a bad thing to incorporate into your content. I sense a lot of potential here," he said. "I'm not telling you what to do. I'm just saying, it might be the perfect way to shake things up without spending a ton of prep time and money. You might work up to a bigger set piece on your own, but that could take months. In the meantime . . ." He trailed off, with a *voilà* gesture.

Tobin felt for a moment like he might be crazy. "Me. And Lily." He stared at Bastian, waiting to hear that he'd gotten it wrong, that Bastian was not, in fact, suggesting he work with a childhood frenemy beauty YouTuber who probably had pee breaks blocked out on her planner.

"Just an idea," Bastian said.

Yup. That's exactly what he's saying. Tobin grimaced. Of course, Bastian's suggestion was just that—a suggestion.

Unfortunately, he didn't have a single better idea.

Which meant talking to Lily. *Again.* And seeing what they could do.

CHANNEL: *Everlily*

Subscribers: 3.90M
Video views: 190M
Most recent video: "Palette Review: PEACOCK by Chrysalis"

RECENT COMMENTS:

Annabel Lee: More metallics. Ugh.

Hai Mai: OH MY GOD you are so lucky!!!! I want that palette SO BAD!!!

Breathless Belle: You met Chrysalis? Seriously? What were they like?

Decemberist Girl: Wild Cherry Lip Gloss review PLS!!

CHAPTER 10

Lily usually followed a religious posting schedule: film and edit on Saturdays, Mondays, and Wednesdays; post and promote on Sundays, Tuesdays, and Thursdays. She ran her schedule like a Swiss watch.

But now she sat at her computer, staring at her own face, and felt a deep, dread-filled feeling of wrongness.

"The key to perfect interview makeup," video-her said in a calm voice as she applied foundation, "is not being too dramatic. Well, depending on what job you're going for, I guess. But you want the statement to be about *you*, more than about your makeup."

She grimaced. There was nothing technically wrong with the video. She'd come a long way in her YouTube career, improving her cameras and microphones and lighting equipment. She knew how to flag her good takes. She probably ought to hand off her editing to someone else, really—she was a content creator, not a video or audio editor. But the last two editors she'd hired had disappointed her, either by returning work late or by not performing up to her standards, and she had trouble leaving the quality of her channel in somebody else's hands.

Control freak, she could imagine Tobin saying.

He wouldn't be the first. But she wanted things the way she wanted them, and it had gotten her this far. She wasn't going to apologize for wanting to be the best.

She kept editing, frowning at the thought of Tobin. Ever since her ill-advised little jaunt to Ponto Beach on Saturday, she'd been in a bad mood, which hadn't helped anything. She should have just called, she told herself for the thousandth time. What had she been thinking?

His voice echoed in her head: *I just don't think it's a good idea.*

He was right. It wasn't a good idea. It was crazy, just this side of stupid. He drove her up the wall on good days. Working together? She'd probably go after him with a golf club. No, better that she do this on her own, or find a more appropriate collaborator to work with.

She sighed, trying to focus on her video, organizing the media files she'd be using, editing the audio, smoothing out the levels. Then she added on-screen text and added the royalty-free music she'd found. Normally the spa-like sounds were calming, but today she found them grating. She finally went through the whole thing one last time, like she always did before rendering and exporting it.

"And there you go," video-her said with quiet resolve, as she covered the final face with finishing powder. "Nothing too flashy, nothing too sexy. Utterly professional, and totally appropriate. Just what you want to make your way up the corporate ladder."

She blinked. Then she stopped the video and winced.

Ugh. Seriously.

Interview makeup?

Make your way up the corporate ladder?

What was she, eighty?

It was, literally, *not sexy*. It said so right there in her monologue! If it were any more boring, it could be used as a tranquilizer!

She put her face in her hands. She wanted to cry. She wanted to *scream*.

She looked at her watch. Six o'clock. That meant she'd been filming and editing all day. If she scrapped all of this video and audio, she'd be starting from scratch. She'd need to pull an all-nighter to try to catch up, to stay on schedule. And she had not been late on a video in five years. She wasn't going to let that slide now. Boring or not, she had to post this. Didn't she?

For the past week, she hadn't been able to come up with any new ideas, although she'd been banging her head against the proverbial wall trying. She'd posted on Sunday, the earth-tones post, and she already knew that was boring. Now, she felt like she was sliding into a pit of *meh*, and if she posted this stupid video, there was no way she'd be able to claw her way out of it.

Besides, what else would I post about? If she'd had a better idea, she would have filmed *that*.

That was the biggest problem. The one that was making her want to yank her hair out.

Her phone buzzed, and she grabbed it, eager for the distraction. It was a text. But it wasn't from Mikki or Val, or even Emily . . . who she *still* hadn't texted, now that she thought about it.

It was Tobin.

She considered, briefly, being petty and ignoring it . . . maybe even deleting it without reading it. But she was too curious. She opened it.

TOBIN: U busy?

She grumped privately, then texted back.

LILY: Editing. What do you want?

She hated it when people used text shorthand. Maybe that made her weird or old fashioned, but it just *bugged*. And yeah, her text was sort of rude.

Tough shit, she thought unrepentantly.

TOBIN: I wanted to talk to you about the collab.

She blinked. Well. That was unexpected.

LILY: I thought it was a bad idea?

TOBIN: Probably is. Doesn't mean we shouldn't do it.

He added a bunch of crying-laughing emojis at the tail end.

Now she was really confused. He'd made it clear that he thought their collaborating wasn't going to help. What had changed between Saturday and now?

TOBIN: I'm in town. Let's meet and talk, K?

Her mouth dropped open. Without thinking, she hit call. "Hey, Lily," he said, his voice sounding rueful. "Got a minute?"

"You're in LA?" she asked. "Why?"

"Meeting with my agents," he said. "I talked to them about you, and . . . well, they think that a cross-collaboration might be a good thing for both of us. *If* we hit on the right idea, anyway. I thought maybe we should discuss it in a little more detail." He paused. "I mean, if you're still interested, and if you have the time."

She glanced at her watch again. She couldn't post this damned "interview makeup" video—it was wretched. But if she went and talked to Tobin, it would eat up time she didn't have. Not if she wanted to keep to her schedule. The posting schedule she hadn't deviated from *once*. In *five years*.

She took a deep breath.

"I could spare a little time," she said and felt a brief wave of disorientation hit her.

You can always post on Friday.

"That's great!" he said, oblivious to her brief existential crisis. "How about we have some dinner, talk it over?"

"Fine. I'll text you my address," she said. There was no sense in both of them fighting for parking spots or paying for valet.

"Great." He sounded enthusiastic. Like a puppy, she realized, then remembered his "I'm a dog, you're a cat" analogy. "See you in, like, half an hour, okay?"

"Okay." She hung up. Then she looked at her clothes. She hadn't asked where they were going, she realized. She looked down at what she was wearing. It was casual, just a pair of sweats and the tank top she usually did makeup videos in, a plain ivory that didn't detract from the cosmetics. She frowned.

She wasn't dressing to impress Tobin, per se. It wasn't like it was a date. It was a business dinner. She just needed to look professional. Then she grimaced, remembering her "interview makeup" fiasco.

Maybe . . . maybe she could be a little sexy. Not because she was going to seduce Tobin or anything weird like that. It was just like war paint: it could only help her confidence.

And Tobin wouldn't know what hit him, she thought, smiling for the first time in hours. She just had to get ready, that's all. Then they'd get down to business.

Actual business, she chastised herself, before rushing to the shower. If she had only half an hour to get ready, she was going to be in a hurry.

CHAPTER 11

Tobin was dragging ass by the time he found Lily's condo. In a combination of his ADHD time blindness, his underestimation of LA traffic, and the stupid-long drive-through line at In-N-Out, he was almost an hour late, and cranky as hell. As he parked in a ridiculously small visitor parking space at her building, he realized he just wanted to talk to Lily about how they might work together, maybe sketch a couple of ideas out, and come to an agreement on working together. Then he wanted to drive the hell home and get some sleep.

If they could come to an agreement, he thought with a scowl. Despite Bastian's obvious enthusiasm for their partnership, he still wasn't sold on this being a good idea.

What the hell do a gamer and a beauty influencer have in common, anyway?

He'd grabbed burgers, fries, and shakes. He was pretty sure she still ate burgers. He probably should've asked. *Oh well. Too late now.*

He took the elevator up to nearly the top level, then found her door, knocking awkwardly since his hands were full. The door opened.

"Hey, Lils, sorry I'm . . ."

He stopped abruptly as he took her in.

She was wearing a black skirt that was all skinny fitting, a pair of black high heels, and a sleeveless white top that had one of those swoopy-material necks. Cowl neck? Was that a thing? Her hair was up in a bun, with little sexy wisps of curls coming out. As always, her makeup was like something out of a movie: her lips were painted a deep red that somehow looked darker in the center, like a rosebud, and her eyes looked unbelievably huge.

She looked like somebody who negotiated soul contracts, he realized. And abruptly understood why a person might actually sign those things if someone like her was offering the pen.

She smiled at him, her eyebrow quirking up. "You're sorry you're . . . ?"

"Late," he finished, then realized . . . "Oh, shit. You thought we were going *out* to dinner, didn't you?"

And here he was, wearing scrubby clothes and holding a sack full of fast food. Strangely, though he hadn't been embarrassed at all at the fancy lunch place where he'd met his agents, he now stood in Lily's condo entryway, utterly mortified.

"I'm guessing we're not, then?" she said, and her cheeks pinkened.

"No! I mean . . ." He looked at the food he was holding. "I can just . . ."

"No, this is fine. Actually, it's probably better if we talk here. We can hear each other, for one thing," she said, kicking off her shoes and picking them up. "Also, I've got all my stuff, and it'll be easier to write things down."

He nodded, then toed off his own shoes out of habit, putting them under the bench by the door. Just like he always had at her family's house when they were kids.

"C'mon," she said. "Let me put these in my closet; then I'll give you the grand tour."

He let out a low whistle. Her place was *nice*. It probably cost twice what his place did, and his was a single-family house. Granted, Ponto Beach wasn't exactly Los Angeles, but it was still kind of beach adjacent. All her appliances were gleaming stainless steel. She had a long oak table in the dining area. He set the food down, then continued exploring. She had a set of black sofas in the living room, some framed paintings, some plants out on the balcony that he could see through sliding glass doors. In the corner of the loft, she'd obviously set up an office: a large desk, with several boards, all posted with neatly written notes, pictures, and surprisingly artistic doodles. "Is this where you record?" he called out.

"No," she said, from the doorway of the room she'd disappeared into. "I record here, in my bedroom. Want to see my setup?"

His body tightened, and he blinked. "Um . . . sure?"

Gingerly, he peeked in. Sure enough, there was Lily Wang's bedroom. She had a queen-size bed, he'd guess, looking like something out of an interior design catalog . . . a deep-gray quilt with shiny silver pillows, tons of them. Matching nightstands on either side with sleek stainless lamps, and a black lacquer dresser. It all looked sophisticated, even sexy—much like Lily herself.

Which was honestly the last thing he needed to think about Lily, *in her bedroom*, for God's sake.

He forced himself to focus. The walls, on the other hand, were the dark industrial gray of noise-canceling egg crate. He was well acquainted with the stuff, since he used plenty himself. She had a nice camera, he noted with professional interest. "You've got good equipment," he said, his voice slightly husky. Which was ridiculous.

"The acoustics suck in the main room," she said with a shrug as she closed her closet door. "Although the light's better out there, so I still do some filming there—shows off the makeup better. I do fashion stuff out there, too, and I take almost all my Instagram pictures on the balcony."

He nodded, feeling himself getting back into the groove as they left the bedroom and headed back to the food. At least he wasn't grumpy anymore. "You sure you're okay with burgers?" he asked. "I'm sorry, I should've asked."

"Sure. I haven't had In-N-Out in forever," she said, shaking her head. "Although my trainer is probably going to scream at me when she finds out."

"You've got a trainer, huh? I shouldn't be surprised," he said. "Your body is insane."

The two of them blinked.

"I mean that in the most respectful, my-goodness-you-look-healthy way possible," he added immediately. "How about I shove a burger in my mouth before I say anything else horribly inappropriate?"

"No, no," she said, but the pink was still up on her cheeks. She sent him a look under her long eyelashes—which was not an expression he understood until he stood there and *watched her do it*. "Thanks? I mean, I just try to stay healthy. You know my Dad has, um, heart issues. Also, I find that exercise helps my energy levels, and let's face it, posting three videos a week? Can be kind of tiring."

"Exactly," he said as they sat down at the kitchen table. "My doctor said that exercise helped with my ADHD . . . increases my concentration for the stuff I'd otherwise want to ignore and keeps my attitude positive. Also helps me stay motivated." He handed her a burger, then held up the shakes, asking, "Chocolate or vanilla?"

"Vanilla," she said, and he grinned.

"Does not surprise me." He handed over the shake, smiling as she frowned.

"Why?" She took a sip—or rather tried to take a sip . . . the thing was *thick*—and then glared at him. "You think I'm boring? Vanilla?"

"No," he said, taking his own attempted sip of his shake. Then he gestured to her. "Chocolate doesn't go with your outfit."

She pulled back in surprise, then shook her head. "You are so weird."

"That does bring up a point," he said, digging into his burger. "I *am* weird. My content is weird. If we're gonna work together, you're going to have to be okay with that."

She wrinkled her nose, studying her burger. "Did you get this animal style?"

He grinned. "Is there another way to eat it?"

She sighed. "Hold on a second." Then she got up, disappearing back into the bedroom and shutting the door. When she emerged, she was wearing a pair of cut-off denim shorts frayed around the hem and a T-shirt that had the name of some promotional party on it. "Sorry," she said, when he looked at her curiously. "I was all geared up for a business meeting, but no way was I going to get a bunch of onions and burger sauce on a silk blouse."

"Smart move," he agreed. It was a little jarring to see her in full makeup with the casual clothes—but that said, she still looked good.

Real talk, though. Did the woman ever not look good?

He cleared his throat after taking another large bite. "But this brings up another point," he said. "My content, my work style, is messy. And there's the little problem of us driving each other nuts."

"You drive *me* nuts," she said, taking a much more delicate bite of her burger and rolling her eyes. "Deliberately. Gleefully. Without remorse. I don't drive *you* nuts."

"Oh, you don't?" He tilted his head at her. "What about that time we had to work on that paper on *The Grapes of Wrath* junior year, and you went to war with me over copyedits until I wanted to pitch you out a window?"

"I was being *thorough*," she countered, her dark-brown eyes flaring wide. "If it were up to you, you wouldn't even hit spell-check."

"You argued with me for half an hour," he pointed out. "*Over a semicolon versus a colon.* You made me look it up in the *Chicago Manual of Style* AND the MLA, after frickin' Strunk and White! It was a high school essay! Who does that?"

"Things just need to be done the right way," she said, and he could hear the edge of stubbornness in her voice. They ate in silence for a minute. He finished his burger, then turned to dunk his fries in his shake. *Mmm.* She rolled her eyes again, noticing his actions.

"There is no style guide for what we do," he said, hoping that she understood how serious he was being. "Which is why I initially thought this was a bad idea."

"What changed your mind?"

"My agents," he admitted. "They think it could help me go mainstream a bit more. Also, my channel needs a little shaking up."

Also, they think you're smokin' hot, and that would only help.

He grimaced. No. Not gonna bring that up. Nope.

"My channel definitely needs shaking up," she said, her tone rueful. "And you're right: I've been a little too . . . rigid. I need to figure out how to be more creative. I'm hoping you can help me with that."

He swallowed the fry he'd been chewing. "How do you want this to work?"

"I'm thinking six videos . . ."

"Six?" he yelped. She ignored him.

"Three on my channel, three on yours," she continued. "Plenty of cross promo between us. The stuff on my channel could be more like my brand, I guess, only with your twist on it? And the stuff on your channel . . . I don't know. Whatever you want to put on your channel, I guess."

Tobin frowned. "If it's on my channel," he warned, "then it's going to be my content. My house, my rules. Are you seriously okay with that?"

He saw a cloud of concern pass over her features, before she nodded with resolve.

"I can do that."

"And maybe we ought to do one video, and see how it goes," he added, feeling nerves knot in his stomach.

"I'm sure it'll be fine," she said. "But okay. One video to start. Your channel, just to show you I can be okay with all of this and not kill you. Deal?"

"I've got a bad feeling about this," he muttered, and she grinned.

"We'll be fine, Han. You'll see. What kind of content did you have in mind?"

He should've figured she'd get the *Star Wars* reference, and he reluctantly grinned back. Rule freak or not, beauty guru or not, she was still a Nerd Herd member.

"I didn't have much on the slate," he admitted. "Just some game playthroughs. I didn't even have any silly sketches written up for the month."

Because I've been totally creatively blocked.

"I don't really game anymore," she admitted. "Don't have the time, and I tend to get a little obsessive when I do play. Maybe I could do something, a playthrough, with you?"

He started to protest that it wouldn't necessarily be that exciting— his viewers liked to see him matched against equally dominant players, or else doing crazy stuff or hacks in game. Watching a noob play, pretty girl or not, was probably not going to be all that interesting . . . and it probably wasn't going to look good, from a feminist optics standpoint, for a pretty girl to look like a novice at video gaming. He had too many women gamer friends who would kill him for inadvertently pushing such a damaging stereotype. If there was a way around . . .

He jolted, struck by an idea like a bolt of lightning.

"I know just the game we can play," he murmured, then grinned. "Can you come down to my place? Friday or Saturday? We'll film then."

"Friday," she said, nodding. "Saturday I'll be filming and editing my own stuff. What were you planning on doing?"

"It's a surprise, if I can pull it off," he said.

And that was the question: Could he pull it off? Because it would either be hysterically funny . . . or she really, truly would murder him.

Either way, he thought with a grin, it would be epic.

CHAPTER 12

Lily drove down to Ponto Beach Friday morning. She'd told Tobin she'd be there early—she didn't want to hit too much traffic, either the mess in Los Angeles or the tail end of San Diego's nightmare, so she left at five and got there by seven, seeing the sunrise on the way. She half expected him to still be asleep. She didn't muck around with doughnuts this time. She did pray he had coffee ready to go, though.

When she got there, she saw the lights were on, the soft glow edging around the living room curtains. She went up the walkway and knocked.

There was a pause—*ha, I'll bet he was asleep!*—and then she heard the dead bolt unlatch. Then he opened the door. She started to talk, then stopped abruptly as she took in what he looked like.

He was wearing basketball shorts and a T-shirt that was pulled tight across his chest. His hair was damp with sweat. In some ways, it was less suggestive than when he'd greeted her sleepy and bare chested. In other ways, it was hotter, although she wasn't quite sure *why*.

She sighed at herself. This was ridiculous. She made a mental note to ask Mikki if he knew any cute boys she could play with. She didn't even need to keep them. She just needed to take the edge off, and a hookup was probably the best solution, even if it wasn't something she practiced regularly. Honestly, she hadn't had a hookup in at least . . . what, a year?

"Sorry," he apologized, sounding sheepish. "I didn't know how long we'd take filming, and I try to fit in cardio in the mornings, and I thought I could sneak in a workout before . . . anyway. Um. You're right on time."

"Always," she agreed faintly, kicking off her canvas espadrilles by the untidy rows of shoes to the side of the front door.

"I lost a little time, got a little sidetracked getting ready, so I got off to a late start. Anyway! Let me just take a quick shower and get changed, and then we can get going. Okay?"

"Mmm," she said, nodding like a bobblehead.

He really did look good.

She frowned. "Okay if I use the bathroom?" she asked.

"Sure!" he called, as he disappeared down the hallway. Then he popped his head out of what she assumed was his bedroom. "Oh! And if you could just turn the coffee on? It's all ready to go."

She went about her business—a must after the long drive—and then got the coffee started, sighing with happiness at the scent. By the time he emerged from the bedroom, the pot was full. He rubbed a towel over his head, his face alert and bright.

He's got good skin, she noted clinically. He filmed well, something she'd picked up on when she was going through his content. She'd now gone through more of his past content. She wasn't into all the video games he played, and he yelled kind of a lot. Not in an angry way, but in a silly, staged kind of way. But apparently it worked for his audience, so who was she to complain?

When they both had coffee, she followed him to his office—"where the magic happens," he said with a grin and a wink—and settled into the second gaming chair he had set up. Like her bedroom, it had noise-absorbing material on the walls. It was a bigger room, though, complete with a small couch by the window and a bunch of bookshelves. He had a swanky computer setup, too, a weird neon affair that she knew was supposed to be one of the best gaming computers in the world. And his lighting setup was different from hers, since it was more important for him to film his screen than, say, capture his face and the application of makeup.

She felt a little frisson of nerves bubble through her, surprising her. This was important for her career, granted, and it was something she had no experience with. Still . . . it was *Tobin*. She'd known him since second grade, when her parents had moved from Taiwan to Ponto Beach. For God's sake, they'd been around each other in one capacity or another for . . .

She did the math. *Twenty-one years.* Holy crap.

"So," he said, leaning back in his own chair with a smile, "we're going to be playing a dating game, okay? Like *The Sims*." He paused. "I'm assuming you're familiar with *The Sims*."

"Yes, I know *The Sims*," she said, rolling her eyes. "I played that for hours when I was in college. For a while, anyway."

"Oh?" He fired up his computer. "Why'd you stop?"

"I realized I was spending hours working, cooking, going to the bathroom, and studying," she said. "I was basically doing what I did in real life . . . in a game."

"Yeah, I burned out on it too," he admitted. "Did a few play-throughs, but it wasn't really my bag. Still, some fans like it."

"But this is a *dating* game?" she asked, puzzled. "I haven't played one of those."

His grin was like quicksilver, bright and fast. "Then this'll be *fun*," he said, his eyes shining. "The goal is to find the guy you want, snag his attention, build the attraction, then close the deal."

She startled, glaring at him. "This isn't a sex game, is it?" Because *eww*.

"What? No," he said, giving her an "Are you crazy?" look. "I might cuss a lot, but by and large I keep it more on the ridiculous side of the spectrum. I'll play some violent games, on occasion, so there's some gore. But I don't feature, like, *porn*."

"Well, I didn't know," she grumbled. "So we're going to play this game, and I need to get a boyfriend."

Story of my life.

She frowned. Not that she needed a boyfriend, she quickly chastised herself. Who had time to maintain one of those, anyway? She couldn't keep a plant alive.

"You'll pick out clothes and put on makeup," he continued. "It's a game I found, released out of Korea, with English translation."

"Sounds up my alley," she said. "How does it work? How long will it take?"

He looked at the ceiling, like he was doing mental math. "Well, I think the full game play, depending on the choices you make, takes about six hours."

"Six hours?" she yelped. "We're going to be filming for *six hours*? Do we have to do the whole thing?"

"We're not going to *air* the whole thing, obviously," he said. "But . . . yeah. You're going to be playing for a few hours. Then I'll edit it down to something workable, somewhere between twenty and thirty minutes, maybe."

"Oh my God," she said, staring at him. "My beauty videos take a while, but . . . *six hours*?"

"We can even split this into two different videos, if it works," he said. "But we can at least get the first two hours or so, I'd say, and that'll be a good start."

"Only two hours, huh?" She bit her lip, thinking. "Okay. Why don't you turn it on, I'll do a bit of practice, and then we'll go."

"Practice?" He blinked at her, then shook his head, laughing. "Hell no."

"What?" She bristled. "But . . . but I always do at least one practice run when I do my videos."

"Sure. When you're doing *your* videos," he said. "These are *reaction* videos, Lils. Viewers want to see the unvarnished, unpracticed responses

94

to whatever you're playing. They want to feel what you're experiencing, as you're experiencing it."

"I'm sure I can recreate it," she said, feeling nervous.

"You mean you're sure you can *fake* it?" Tobin blew a raspberry. "Yeah, *no*."

She crossed her arms.

"I told you this was gonna be messy," he pointed out in a low voice. "Trust me, when it's your turn to do a video—if you even still want to—then you can practice and plan and overthink it to your little anal-compulsive heart's content, okay? But you came to me first, and if we're doing my content, it's like I said: my house, my rules."

She scowled at him. She wanted to complain. But this was her deal, wasn't it? This was what she wanted. She set her jaw, nodding. "All right," she conceded. "Let me just freshen up my makeup, and we can start filming."

He nodded absently, already getting his camera in place and adjusting lighting. She sighed, touched up her eyeliner and lipstick. Then he got them started.

"Hey-oh! It's GoofyBui," he said, in that bouncy, hyperhappy way of his. "Today I've got a special collab. Everybody, please say hi to EverLily, one of the hottest beauty YouTubers around." He paused, and she swore he blushed. He turned to her. "Is it okay to call you that? I meant, like, popular. I can always edit that out."

"It's fine," she said, feeling her own cheeks heat. "Let's keep rolling."

"Okay. Well, gang, today we're going to be testing a sim that I've heard a lot about. It's called *Mr. Perfect*, and it's by a little indie game company—details and link in the description, okay? Oh, and there will also be a link to Lily's channel. We've been friends since forever, but I thought I'd introduce her to the wild and wonderful world of gaming. You ready, Lily?"

"Ready as I'm going to be," she said, trying to match his energy. She was usually much more placid, and she felt weird, but she wasn't going to let it stop her.

With that, he started the game. It was cute, and surprisingly realistic. It started with her choosing her avatar, kind of like making a character on *The Sims*. She tried not to take too long creating it, which she made match herself as much as possible. Then Tobin guided her through using the controller, moving her character, interacting through the world. She chose the "first person" mode, moving through the college campus where her Mr. Perfect was presumably waiting. She got to interact with her friends, choose different dialogue options to "flirt" with different characters, and even go shopping for things for her avatar. It was more fun than she thought it would be.

"Okay, now you're going to meet your candidates for perfect boyfriend," he said.

The choices were varied, all members of a fraternity. She eventually picked a guy who was cute, Asian, and sort of sporty. A bit like Tobin, she realized. And felt herself blush at the realization.

"Thirsty?" Tobin asked.

She turned back to him, as if he'd read her thoughts. "Excuse *you*," she said.

He burst out laughing. "I've got water here," he said, handing her a water bottle. "It's got ice and some lemon slices. Sometimes when you're talking a lot . . ."

"Oh! Right. Right." She took one of the containers, removed the lid, and chugged some down. He was right: her voice was tight from talking so much. She wasn't used to doing it for this long and consistent a time frame. "Thanks."

"No problem. Okay, you've hit an achievement," he pointed out. "Hottie McSexyPants has asked you to the fraternity's Halloween party! What are you going to wear?"

More choices. She finally settled on "sexy baseball player," which was the least provocative of the outfits. It even had a little hat and bat. She smiled.

"All right. To the party!" Tobin said, rubbing his hands together. "Time to charm the pants off of McSexyPants!"

She rolled her eyes. This wasn't quite what she was expecting, but it wasn't too bad. She wasn't sure if it was going to be all that exciting for viewers to watch. She was almost positive it wasn't going to go viral, something that made her wonder about how viable this partnership was going to be.

Just keep going. It was too soon to make a judgment. And she was all about working hard until you made it.

"Oh, here we go. Look! He thinks you look beautiful, and he wants to take your relationship to the next level," Tobin said, and she looked over to find his eyebrows wiggling. "He wants to *invite you up to his room.* Says he's going to get things ready, and for you to meet him up there. You gonna go?"

She groaned. "You promise this isn't, like, porny . . ."

"No, no," he reassured her. "Nothing like that. You'll probably just make out or something. Serious kissing. No biggie."

"Okay." Using the controller, she navigated through partygoers and various scary Halloween decorations, through the convincingly spooky "haunted house," until she got to McSexyPants's room.

"All right, this is it," Tobin said. God, he was good at this. He could take something as simple as a dating game and make it sound riveting.

Why can't I do that?

She was pondering this as she opened the door . . . then stared blankly at something that made no sense.

Her "perfect boyfriend," Hottie McSexyPants, was lying on the bed in the center of the room, wearing only a pair of shorts.

Also, he was decapitated and disemboweled. His legs and arms were no longer attached to his body.

"What the absolute fuck?" she yelped, as she processed what she was looking at.

Without warning, something—some creepy, shaky-motion creature— jumped out of the closet, holding a scythe, wearing a sadistic smile. She froze, genuinely terrified.

"Oh *shit*!" Tobin yelled, snapping her into action. "Run, Lily! Run run *RUN*!"

Letting out a squeak, she quickly moved as best she could, helping her character flee with the controller, bumping into walls, bursting out of the room. There was now carnage everywhere, the partygoers getting murdered left and right. She ran into the haunted section again, but the lights were now flickering, making the whole thing hard to see. Her heart was beating in her chest like a jackhammer and she felt like she had more adrenaline than blood in her veins.

"Look ou . . ."

A face popped up, covering the entire screen. More skull than face, with floating eyes. It laughed, its razor-toothed mouth going wide.

She couldn't stop herself. She shrieked.

CHAPTER 13

I am going to hell.

Tobin grinned. He was probably going for other things, too, let's face it. But waiting to jump scare Lily, under the pretense of a dating sim that was actually a horror game, definitely earned him a first-class ticket on the downward escalator to Scorchville.

"Run, Lily!" he shouted. Her eyes wheeled like a panicked horse, and she started button mashing so hard that he wondered if he'd have to buy a new controller. "Hit him! Hit him with the bat!" he tried to instruct, then realized she had no idea how to do that.

It made it that much funnier, to be honest.

Then the main horror antagonist—ironically called Mr. Perfect, the titular character—filled up his large computer screen, and she screamed and dropped the controller, throwing her hands in front of her face.

He couldn't help himself by this point. He let out a shout of laughter, both at her reaction and at the sheer delight that the plan he'd devised for this video had actually *worked*. She couldn't have reacted more beautifully if he'd designed her in a computer.

He saw the exact moment her fear shifted into something else.

Rage.

She was no longer paying attention to the screen, which was probably just as well. Mr. Perfect slaughtered her in a splatter of blood, and a text box stating "YOU DIED" showed up in white text on red, taking up the center of the screen, over a chorus of bloodcurdling moans of torture.

"What the *fuck*, Tobin?" she shouted, which was a big clue: she only swore when she was truly pissed off, or scared, or both.

He was still laughing. In fact, he was laughing *harder*.

He really should have known better.

She got up out of the chair and started smacking him on the shoulders with her delicate open palms. "What! Did! You! Do!"

He let out a little yelp and tried to evade, doing a rolling dive out of his chair, still laughing. She followed him, yelling obscenities.

Honestly, it was just like old times.

"You *jerk*!" Her voice was loud enough that his neighbors would probably hear it if they weren't at work. "You . . . you *asshole!* You knew that was going to happen, didn't you?"

His smirk must've been answer enough. He held his hands up defensively, grinning like a fiend.

She surprised him by *tackling* him. A full-on tackle, right onto the small couch behind his gaming setup. He was so literally blindsided by it he fell onto the short sofa with an *oof*. She was straddling him—not in a sexy way, but more in a way that would've made it hard to breathe if she didn't weigh next to nothing. She grabbed a nearby decorative pillow that had "for fox's sake" cross-stitched on it with a little illustrated fox (a gift from one of his viewers), and she started systematically whacking him right in the face.

"Son! Of! A! Bitch!" she yelled, pounding him to punctuate each furious word. *"Son! Of! A! Bitch!"*

He couldn't breathe, the result of her bearing down on him, the pillow periodically covering his mouth, and his hysterical laughter. Tears rolled from his eyes. "Mercy! Mercy!" he gasped, as best he could.

She got up off him, creating a moment of relief.

Then she took the pillow and absolutely *belted* him, teeing off like she was Tiger Woods.

Okay, that actually hurt. He rubbed his jaw, disgruntled. But he was still amused, his chuckles slowly dying down.

She spun on her heel and stalked out of the room, slamming the door behind her.

He stopped the video, then opened the door, following her. "Lily! That was *gold*," he crowed, heading for the kitchen, where he sensed she'd retreated. "The traffic is going to . . ."

He stopped abruptly as he took in her face. She was crying, her makeup smeared, her full rosebud mouth pursed in a suppressed sob.

"Whoa! Hey, hey, hey," he said, rushing to her and rubbing her shoulders, trying to pull her into a hug. "It's just a game! Nothing to be scared of."

She shoved him away. "This isn't because I'm scared, you idiot," she replied, but it lacked snap because of the soft, teary hiccup that emerged. "This is . . . that was . . . Tobin, that was not okay."

Guilt welled up. "Let me explain . . ."

"I *assaulted* you."

He blinked. Not where he thought this was going. "That was nothing," he said, brushing it off, but her dark eyes remained intense.

"I shouldn't have hit you. It's *really* not okay."

He sighed. "Lils, you've been 'assaulting' me since we were in grade school," he pointed out. "I've gotten hurt worse in jujitsu classes. You have all the arm strength of overcooked spaghetti, and the worst you've ever managed to do to me is kick me in the nuts once in the pool when we were twelve, and I almost drowned."

"Oh, God, I forgot about that," she said, rubbing at her face and making her makeup smear even more.

"In your defense," he added, "I was being a dick at the time, I think." He couldn't actually remember what he'd done, but odds were good. Besides, he wanted to take that stricken look off her face.

"You were a dick just now too," she countered, and he smiled, hoping she was rallying. "But back then, we were just kids. We're

101

twenty-eight now, for God's sake, Tobin." She glared at him. "This is stupid, and immature, and wrong."

He felt his gut clench. "This," he said, his tone serious, "is my job."

When are you going to get a real *job, Tobin?*

He brushed the unwelcome thought aside. He'd heard the comment enough from his parents in person; his subconscious didn't need to play the rerun on a loop. "I get paid well for being *stupid, immature,* and *wrong.* And you came to me, knowing the kind of content I do," he said, a sharpness of his own creeping into his voice. "You want to back out now?"

She let out a long huff of breath. "I . . . I don't know. I just don't like being made fun of on camera. It feels cruel."

He winced. If he posted what he'd just done on the Am I the Asshole board, he wasn't quite sure what kind of sentence he'd get . . . but he had a bad feeling he'd probably get a thousand "Asshole" votes.

"Tell you what," he said. "Let's add me giving you an apology on camera afterward. We can explain that you smacking me was just play fighting, something we've done since we were kids. And I promise . . . I'll never jump scare you again. At least not without you having some advance notice. Okay?"

She looked at him with dark, serious eyes, her eyelashes still damp with tears. Slowly, uncertainly, she nodded. "Okay, I guess."

"Good. Trust me, though. The video? Will be epic."

"I'll bet," she muttered. "I'm getting mocked, I screamed like a frightened six-year-old, and I look like a complete idiot."

"You looked adorable."

She blinked at him. He realized that probably came out a bit more earnest than he'd intended.

"More importantly, you looked *authentic,*" he pointed out. "Do you know why reaction videos are so popular? Because people want to recreate the feeling of experiencing something for the first time. You were totally, utterly *real*, and people are going to eat that shit up with a spoon."

She still looked uncertain. He took her hand.

"Go on. Fix your makeup, and we'll do the ending, okay?"

He waited in his recording room while she got herself together. When she came back, she looked like nothing had ever happened: her makeup was perfect, her expression almost zen. Maybe a little more subdued.

He turned to the camera. "So *that* happened," he said. "It has been pointed out to me that fooling someone into playing a horror game when they *think* they're playing a dating sim is a bit of a dick move."

"Kinda," she agreed.

"And I feel a little bad about laughing," he said, then smiled. "Although you have to admit, it *was* also a little funny."

"I bet a bunch of AITA posters would disagree," she muttered, echoing his earlier thought. He sobered, clearing his throat.

"Right. So I am formally apologizing to EverLily here, for putting her in this situation and yelling at her and scaring her."

"And I am apologizing to Tobin," she said, sounding gracious as a queen, "for . . . um . . ."

"Beating the shit out of me," he finished, and her eyes flashed at him. "In her defense, though, it was really just play fighting, mostly. Totally consensual."

"His safe word is *Captain Crunchyroll*," she added, deadpan, surprising a laugh out of him.

"Besides, it's something we've done since—how long have we known each other?"

"Twenty-one years," she said, and he gaped.

"No kidding? That long?" He shot a grin at the camera. "And yet, in all that time, she still hasn't killed me."

"Yet." She grinned herself, nudging him with her shoulder, which surprised him enough to make him pause. She sounded *playful*.

"So, right, bottom line: no YouTubers were harmed in the making of this video—and, gang, don't do this to your friends." He paused. "Enemies are fine, though."

They wrapped up the video with a little more patter, and he shut off the camera. "Okay. I'll edit all of this and probably post it tomorrow. Or maybe Monday? I don't want to step on your Sunday traffic."

"If you can get it edited, tomorrow's fine."

"When do you want to film the next video?" Normally he'd be all wrung out after a day of filming, but he found himself eager to schedule the next. Because it had been *fun*. And not in a vaguely stressed way, like the Beacons video had been. It had just been hanging out, having a good time, for the most part. Kind of like when he'd done goofing-around videos back with the Nerd Herd.

It was nice. He wouldn't mind doing that again.

She cleared her throat. "About that."

He stiffened. "I thought we were cool?"

"We are." She sounded prim. "But . . . maybe we should see how well the video does, before we commit to the whole series."

He frowned. It was logical. It made sense. And it was probably good that he kept the fact that she was doing these collabs to get a boost in stats, rather than any particular personal fondness she had for him, front and center.

"How long do you want to wait?" he countered, glad that his own voice sounded calm and rational.

"Well, I can't imagine that it will go as viral as your wavy-arm thing," she said. "But . . . if you post on Saturday, we could check back on Monday and decide from there, maybe? See what the numbers look like?"

He nodded. Then he looked at the clock. They'd played all morning and through lunch. "Wanna grab something to eat?"

Her stomach growled, but she shook her head. "I should head back," she said. "I'll grab something on the way."

"Suit yourself." He felt unsettled for some reason. "So . . . we'll talk on Monday?"

"Talk on Monday." She headed for the door.

He felt his jaw clench, and he sighed. "Lils?"

She glanced up from where she was putting shoes on. "Yes?"

"I really am sorry."

She looked at him, hesitant, as if checking to see if he was making fun of her again. Something in his face must've convinced her, because she shrugged.

"Talk to you Monday, Tobin," she said, then let herself out.

CHANNEL: *Everlily*

Subscribers: 3.88M
Video views: 179M
Most recent video: "Makeup for Interviews"

RECENT COMMENTS:

Adriana Rodriguez: I love that you list the products you use, as well as the techniques. And that you suggest stuff for other skin tones than yours. Great channel!

Hai Mai: I'm 16 I don't go on interviews but still love you, Lily!

Naomi Whittier: Does it matter what job you're going after? Like, corporate versus retail? Or I.T. versus marketing or something?

Diana Princess: You have the best smile! And your voice—have you considered doing those ASMR videos, with the whispering and soothing voices and stuff? You'd be so good.

CHAPTER 14

Lily didn't usually work out on Sundays. She usually took it as a lazy day off—well, as lazy as she got. She promoted whatever video she'd posted, went over content stuff for the week, looked at other YouTubers' content, logged her stats, and tracked her progress on social media. Nothing as intensive as actually filming and editing. If she was lucky, she indulged in a nice brunch or something with a friend like Val and her wife. But ever since she'd recorded with Tobin, she'd felt . . . antsy. Like a battery that had been overcharged and was consequently overheating.

As a result, she'd asked Mikki if he wanted to hit the gym, which was one of his favorite things. Which is how she found herself at a gym in Westwood Village, near Mikki's apartment and UCLA, walking steadily on a treadmill while looking out over Wilshire Boulevard.

"The hotties are checking you out today," Mikki noted, increasing the incline on his neighboring treadmill. "I mean, they're sort of frat boy, but if you like that sort . . ."

"We could've gone to that gym in WeHo," she pointed out.

"True, but that would've been for me. I figured we'd go somewhere there were prospects for *you*." He smiled at her. "You said you wanted a hookup, did you not?"

She shushed him hastily. "Why not just announce it over the loudspeaker?"

"I'm sorry," he said, rolling his eyes. "I didn't know you were trying to be all discreet about it. Is there an interview process too?"

"I just told you that I was feeling a little, um, *wound up*," she tried to say delicately. "And that finding someone to help me *unwind* was welcome."

"Wow. Way to be subtle." He snickered. "Sweetie, you can say that you just want to hit it. No shame."

"I'm not ashamed! It's just . . . there's a difference between being open to meeting someone for a casual, erm, *you know*," she said, feeling her cheeks heat in a way that had nothing to do with the speed of her treadmill, "and posting a free-for-all Craigslist ad saying open for business, anyone welcome."

"You're picky, which I can appreciate," Mikki said with a sniff. "Sometimes a little too picky, though, especially considering we're talking, like, a one-night stand." He paused. "Which is what we're talking about, right? Do you still have your Bumble profile?"

"You know how I feel about apps," she said, suppressing a groan. "Why do men feel like their dick pic is some kind of positive advertisement? Seriously."

"If you're looking for sex," Mikki pointed out, "isn't it, though? I am serious. I have no idea what straight women are looking for, and I am okay with that."

She shot a glance at him, increasing her speed. He matched it easily. "I mean, you don't like a bunch of janky pictures of randos' junk sent to you, do you?"

Mikki laughed. "I do get a bunch of janky pictures of randos' junk, so I get what you're saying, but I also get the occasional nice—and solicited—specimen, so I can see how some men would get confused."

She sighed. "It's just so demoralizing. I think that's why I've just ignored it for . . ." She did some mental math. It turned out to be harder than she thought. "A while. A long while."

"When *was* your last boyfriend?" Mikki asked, frowning and apparently doing his own math. "It was that Insta model, yeah? What was his name?"

"Rafael," she said, wincing. He was beautiful and ambitious, and for a while, that had been enough. They hadn't exactly had long conversations when they'd been together, and she'd spent so much time working that what they had was perfect—he didn't demand anything, he understood her pursuits, and he had his own stuff going on. Of course, she hadn't realized that he was seeing three other women for the same purpose until she'd seen pictures of his "girlfriend" and himself in a compromising position accidentally posted on his public Instagram account. She'd known they were casual, but that had just stung.

"Rafael, right. Good lord, was that two years ago?" Mikki's eyes widened. "You've been living like a nun for *two years*?"

"No, I haven't," she snapped. "There was that one guy, from the launch party for Jacqueline's Fierce palette. And . . . um . . . that other guy. From Tinder."

Which, incidentally, was why she no longer used Tinder.

"So you've only had *bad* sex for two years?" Mikki amended, appalled.

She sighed. "I really need to rethink having these conversations with you in public places."

"Sweetie, I don't know that hooking you up with guys is in my wheelhouse," Mikki said, frowning. "I'm not necessarily *that* gay best friend, you know?"

"You push me outside my comfort zone and get me to do stuff I need to do, even when I'm whining or dragging my feet," she said with a smile that Mikki returned. "I focus more on the 'best friend' bit of the equation."

They were companionably quiet for a moment as Mikki mulled over her dilemma. Then he looked past her and frowned. "I am not just saying this," he said in a low voice, "but a *lot* of guys seem to be checking you out. Or possibly me. But I'm thinking you."

She started to glance over to where he was looking, in the free weights area. Sure enough, a number of guys were staring at them intently. Several seemed to be whispering to each other, excited.

She felt a shiver of discomfort. This didn't seem like leering, which on the one hand was good, but on the other hand—what the hell were they looking at?

She looked down at her black shorts. Had her period started, and she didn't know it? She tried to look at herself as innocuously as possible. No, she seemed fine.

"Ten dollars says one of those frat boys comes up and asks you out," Mikki teased. "They seem really, really interested."

"Or I've got camel-toe that's internet worthy," Lily shot back, causing Mikki to burst out laughing.

"Take the compliment, sweetie," Mikki said. "You wanna do some of the machines? I'm pretty warmed up now, and it's leg day."

"Every day is leg day," Lily crooned, off key, and he chuckled again. "But sure. I didn't really have anything planned for today, but that should be fine."

She slowed down, then stopped her treadmill, getting off gingerly. She grabbed her towel, covering her face and wiping off the sweat.

When she took the towel away, there was a man's face, just inches from hers. "BOO!" he shouted.

She yelped, then swung out on reflex, slapping him across the face with her sweaty towel.

A raucous burst of laughter emerged from a small crowd of guys who were now waiting around her treadmill. The guy she'd inadvertently slapped with her towel scowled.

"The *fuck*?" Mikki snarled, stepping in front of her and glaring. He might not be all that ripped, but he definitely had muscle definition, and his expression was one of pure anger. "What are you doing?"

"She's the chick from the video, isn't she?" the slapped guy protested.

"What? What video?" Lily asked, feeling confused. "What are you talking about?"

"GoofyBui," one of the others offered, at least looking somewhat chastened. "The, um, jump-scare video?"

Her mouth dropped open. "You've seen that?"

"Hell, yeah. It was *hilarious*," the slapped guy said, snickering. "You were all 'eeeeek!' and freaking out, and then all pissed off, chasing him around . . ."

"Son! Of! A! Bitch!" the other three guys chimed in, laughing some more.

Lily looked over to see Mikki staring at her, his eyebrows around his hairline.

"He shouldn't have scared you, though," the embarrassed dude bro said, by way of apology. "Sorry. He's a dick."

"You don't have to apologize for Tobin," she said before realizing he was talking about his friend, not the video. "Um . . . yeah. Okay."

She got the feeling that she was going to get asked out, by one or all of these men, and she was *really* not feeling it. "C'mon, Mikki," she said, heat flushing her face. They retreated to the weight machines.

"What the hell was *that*?" Mikki hissed.

"Tobin posted the video," she said. "Obviously."

"Was it that bad?"

She groaned, covering her face. "I don't *know*. I was too nervous to watch, honestly."

"You haven't seen it?" Mikki grumbled, then fired up his phone.

"Oh, God, don't . . ."

Mikki watched, fast-forwarding, until she heard her own voice. *"What the absolute fuck?"* Then the sound of shrieking, and yelling, and her . . . well, chasing and tackling Tobin.

She wanted to die. She wanted to just disappear from the earth.

She heard Mikki laugh. "Good for you—you should've kicked his ass," he said. "But really, it's not that bad."

"Not that *bad*?" She wanted to tear her hair out. "Are you *kidding* me? I just got approached because I was acting like a total weenie, then a total *psycho*, and people are finding that hilarious! I am totally humiliated!"

"I thought it was funny too," Mikki said. "Not in a mean way. You know I wouldn't want anyone to embarrass you, and I'm not into cringey humor . . ."

"Dammit. I am going to kill him," she promised. "I should have known better. I just wanted those damned numbers so badly . . . I am going to *kill* him."

Mikki studied her for a long moment, tilting his head. "Lily," he asked slowly, "is there a reason you wanted to go trawling for a man? Right this second, I mean? Because you've been going without for months, even years. What triggered you?"

She reared back. "What does *that* have to do with anything?" Couldn't he see how upset she was?

"Because," Mikki drawled, "this Goofy guy? I think . . . do you *like* him?"

She gaped at him. "I . . . of course . . . *no!*" she spluttered.

He grinned. "Suuuuure."

"I am going to kill him," she said. "And I am going to kill *you*, if you keep this up."

"For someone who runs one of the most chill, positive beauty channels I've ever seen, you sure are murderous," Mikki said with a smirk. She let out a low groan of frustration. "All I'm saying is, you two have chemistry."

"We have history," she corrected, then scrambled to explain herself. "*Not that kind of history!* We've known each other since we were kids, and I've actively hated him for a good portion of that time. It's not like that."

"Whatever helps you sleep at night," Mikki said, dismissing the subject, and she felt so much frustration she thought it would crush her. "Anyway . . . what're you going to do now?"

"Well, obviously I'm not going to continue doing a series with him!"

He blinked. "Are you kidding? Have you seen the numbers?"

She felt her stomach turn into a ball of ice. She grabbed his phone. Nine hundred thousand views . . . and climbing.

"Oh, shit," she said. She had to talk to Tobin. *Now.*

CHANNEL: GOOFYBUI

Subscribers: 10M
Video views: 311M
Most recent video: "Mr. Perfect, Meet EverLily"

RECENT COMMENTS:

Peter Jackwad: What the hell?

Skeptic_Sketcher: Please let me meet her.

Han Solo Cup: LMAOOOOOOOOOOOOO

CHAPTER 15

Tobin sat at his parents' kitchen table, eating a turkey sandwich with homegrown tomatoes and lettuce and sharp cheddar cheese, wondering if there was a discreet way to drown himself in his own cup of tea.

It wasn't like he didn't know how these things worked. He had lunch with his parents once a month, whether he wanted to or not. Most of the time, it was "not," even though he loved them dearly.

"So I told him, in perfect German, that they were either going to get the shipment to me on time or 'this bitch' was going to put him through the wringer," his mother, Abigail, said with a small, delighted smile. "Can you imagine? He thought I didn't speak a word! Well, *he* was in for a surprise."

Tobin grinned. His mother was deceptive. She was what you'd call an English-rose type: all porcelain pale, with those weird rosy cheeks, like you'd see on painted collectibles. Her hair was still gold blonde, cut in a short, no-nonsense style. She looked amazing for fifty-three. "You are a terror."

"Only if you deserve it," his father said with a fond smile. "I should've turned you loose on that idiot that kept insisting on changes to the designs. I kept trying to point out that the laws of physics wouldn't actually allow for a room with no load-bearing walls the way he wanted, and even if I did set up the room the way he wanted, the internal structure would nearly double or triple the cost." His father rolled his eyes. "Why do they insist on this stupidity?"

Tobin made noncommittal noises of agreement as he glanced at the clock. They'd been eating—and his parents had been sharing stories of their various workplaces—for over an hour. He was almost home free. If he could just . . .

His mother cleared away lunch plates and brought out a selection of cookies. Then she pinned him with a shrewd gaze as he reached for one. "How are your little videos going, then?"

His heart sank. *Damn it. I was so close!*

"They're doing fine," he said in as neutral a voice as possible. "You know. Working hard, making content."

His father's lips pulled taut as he studied his son. "Working hard," he said with a slight scoff. "Playing video games and recording it."

Tobin fought the urge to bristle. They loved him; he knew that. But they didn't *get* it. The shouting match they'd had when he dropped out of school had been the worst fight he'd ever had with them—they hadn't spoken for months afterward. Now, they were back to a truce, but it didn't stop them from needling him, once a month, about his life choices.

"A recent video I did was very successful," he said, feeling himself fall into the trap, but talking anyway. Hell, he was *jumping* into the trap at this point. "It racked up several million views, and it's still climbing. They showed it on *Good Morning America*." There. You couldn't get more mainstream than that.

"Oh?" His mother sounded unimpressed, sipping her tea. "What was it of?"

"It was . . ." He abruptly realized there was no way he could describe it without it sounding frivolous, and somewhat stupid. *And that's why it's called a trap, moron.* "A parody of the beacons of Minas Tirith. From *Lord of the Rings*," he clarified.

His father looked at his mother, who shrugged. "And you're getting paid for this?"

"Ad revenue," Tobin said tightly. "More views, more subscribers . . . more money." *Which I have explained to you approximately one million times.*

"Hmm." His father nodded. "What are you doing next, then?"

God, would people stop asking him that? He felt his turkey sandwich sit like a ball of concrete in his stomach, and he nudged away the cookie his mother had offered. "I'm doing a collaborative video series, with another YouTuber," he said. "Lily Wang, actually. Do you remember her?"

"Oh! I do remember her," his mother said, smiling. "Beautiful girl. Always so fashionable. Not to speak badly of you and your friends, but I swear, sometimes I wondered if you all got dressed in the dark."

She grimaced, nodding at his T-shirt, on which was printed, *"YOU'VE READ MY T-SHIRT. That's enough social interaction for one day."*

"Of course," she said, shaking her head, "that hasn't changed noticeably. Why don't you wear those shirts I bought you for Christmas? You're twenty-eight, dear. Surely you can dress like a grown-up at this point."

He suppressed a sigh.

"What videos are you doing with Lily?" his father asked, puzzled. "I barely remember her, but she never seemed the silly type. Does she like video games?"

"She's a beauty YouTuber, but we're doing some crossovers," Tobin tried to explain. Then it occurred to him: this might be a way to finally show that being a YouTuber could be a valid occupation. "She's making a living from it, like I am. We're actually pretty close in numbers of subscribers and followers—that's why we're doing the collab. So we can help build our viewerships, and generate some viral buzz . . ."

"Where did she go to college?"

Dammit. "UCLA," he said.

"And she got her degree, didn't she?" His mother's expression was innocent, deceptively so. "What in?"

"I don't know," he admitted. "Something business related, I think. Or maybe communications?" He'd genuinely never asked. He'd always been more of a hard science guy himself.

"But she got her bachelor's."

"Yes, Mom, she got her degree," Tobin admitted, feeling sullen.

"See, that's smart. She has something to fall back on," his mother said, taking another sip of tea and glancing at his father.

Fuck. My. Life. Tobin fought against the urge to yank his hair by the roots.

"There's nothing that says you couldn't take courses part time at UCSD." His father picked up the thread. "A light course load, and you could still do your little videos. It would take more time to get the degree, but you'd *have* it."

Tobin gritted his teeth. "My *little videos* are a full-time job," he said. "Between the filming itself, the editing, the processing and posting, promoting, and administrative stuff, it's actually more than forty hours a week."

"Maybe you need to streamline, focus a bit more?" his mother offered, and while he loved her, he wanted to tear out his hair and scream at her. "I mean, why would it take hours to film those? Most of them are twenty minutes or so, I thought?"

He felt a headache starting to pound. "It's complicated."

"It's just . . . it's an interesting hobby, but is it really viable in the long run?" his father said with a note of concern.

Tobin grimaced. "We've had this talk, Dad," he warned.

"I know, but . . . well, we're just concerned."

Tobin looked over to see his mother nodding in agreement. "No one's saying that you haven't been successful . . ."

"Yeah, I'd hope not," Tobin snapped before he could stop himself. "Seeing how I bought my own house with my income."

His father's face darkened like a storm cloud. His mother shook her head, almost imperceptibly. "But it's like winning the lottery, isn't it? It was a wonderful windfall, and it's been an exciting ride. But is it sustainable? What happens if the ad revenue drops, or you aren't popular anymore?"

"There are a million YouTubers entering the market, aren't there?" his father added.

"There are a million electrical engineers, too, Dad," Tobin said, feeling hopelessness hitting his chest like a baseball bat. "Getting a degree doesn't protect me from anything."

"You're more likely to get a job with a degree than having a résumé that says, 'I played video games and made silly jokes for money,'" his father shot back.

Before Tobin could defend himself, his phone rang. He frowned. He rarely got calls. He glanced at the display.

LILY WANG.

He hit ignore. "I've got a solid base of viewers," he protested. "And my agents say that I can translate this into something bigger."

"Something bigger?" His mother sounded suspicious. While most YouTubers would give their left nut to have an agent, his parents viewed them as somewhere between enablers and heroin dealers, encouraging his pipe dream of a career. "Like what?"

"Having my own streaming series or something. Doing live shows—a lot of YouTubers do things like that."

"Live shows?" Now his father sounded bewildered. "Are you telling me that people would pay money to sit somewhere and just . . . watch you yell at your computer while you're shooting at things?"

Way to oversimplify! Tobin growled, "It's more like . . ."

His phone rang again. He glanced at it.

LILY WANG.

He sighed. "I'm sorry—would you excuse me a minute?" With that, he walked from the kitchen to the living room, in front of one of the windows. "Lily? Are you okay?"

"No, I am *not* okay."

His heart stopped for a second. "What's wrong?"

"The *video*, Tobin." She sounded ready to spit nails.

God, he did not need this. "I posted it yesterday," he said. "You're just now having an issue with it?"

"Yeah, well, I hadn't gotten *accosted in a gym because of it* yesterday, had I?"

"*What?*" he barked out. "Are you all right? What the hell happened?"

"A guy thought it'd be hilarious to jump scare me when I got off the treadmill," she said. "And now, it seems like everybody's thinking it's *hilarious* that I'm such a goddamned *weenie*, Tobin!"

"So, you're not hurt." God. His heart finally started beating double-time in his chest, and the tightness of his breath relented. "He didn't hurt you."

She paused, and he swore her tone softened reluctantly. "No, he didn't hurt me. Scared me," she amended. "And I, um, may've slapped him with my workout towel."

Tobin couldn't help it. He let out a burst of laughter.

"It was *reflex*, okay?" she said, which made him laugh harder. "And it just makes things worse! Do you have any idea what this is going to do to my reputation? This is a disaster!"

"No, it's not," he promised. "Listen, I'm at my parents'. Let me get home, and we'll video chat, okay? I will show you that it's okay."

"I highly doubt that."

"Trust me, Lils." With that, he hung up. Then he took a deep breath, heading back to the kitchen table. "I'm sorry. Gotta go. Work, um, emergency."

"Everything all right?" his mother asked, sounding concerned.

"Yeah," he reassured her, giving her a hug. "Or at least it will be."

His father gave him a hug. "Just think about what we said, will you?"

Tobin nodded, unable to trust himself to speak. It was the same conversation they always had. Every time they had it, he knew that they worried about him. They loved him.

They just didn't trust him to make the right decisions for himself. And dammit, that hurt.

CHAPTER 16

Lily had spent an hour pacing. She'd put up her own video—a positive one on a new set of nail colors that YouTuber Rainbowslicker had developed and that she'd totally loved—and was proud of the results. Still, she knew Maria would tell her that it wasn't original enough. That was why she'd gone to Tobin in the first place. She was trying new, exciting things . . . or so she thought.

Now, she couldn't help but feel like she'd made a horrible, stupid mistake.

The idea of doing collabs with Tobin had been a mistake born of desperation, and now it was biting her in the ass. She was too nervous to even look at her stats, which was unheard of for her. She just needed to pull the plug before things got any worse. No more videos . . . she was done.

Her phone signaled her that he was video calling, and she answered. "Hey, Tobin," she said in a rush. "Listen, I don't want to keep you. I just wanted to say that, um, I've thought about it, and I don't think doing any more videos together is a good idea."

"Okay, Lily, just calm down. It's not a big deal."

Unfortunately, he chose the two worst words on the planet if he actually expected her to calm down. She'd had a much worse temper when she was younger, and the words *calm down*—especially when wielded by a man—tended to engender the opposite reaction. "Really?

Calm down. Just like that." She rolled her eyes, knowing he could see it, and she let her voice drip with sarcasm. "What a brilliant idea! I can't believe I didn't think of it. Just calm down! Man, you should write a frickin' book!"

He sighed. "Let me try this again," he said, his voice cautious. "What, exactly, is upsetting you?"

"Besides looking like a total wimp on your channel?" she said, her voice continuing to pitch higher and louder. "Good grief! Look at the comments on your video, Tobin. This was a stupid idea. You made me look like a complete fool, and now it feels like hundreds of thousands of people are laughing at me!"

She felt her eyes sting with tears, and she knuckled them away, embarrassed to be showing even this much emotion in front of Tobin. Now, instead of irritation and frustration, his expression shifted to something even worse: pity, and what she had to interpret as conde-scension. And like *hell* did she need Tobin Bui looking down on her, even if he had done her a favor by collaborating with her. He could take his pity, and his millions of viewers, and shove them directly up his ass.

He sighed. "What kind of comments?"

She blinked. "Did you really not see?"

"I've been at my parents' house, Lils," he reminded her. "And I don't check the comments religiously. Usually too busy brainstorming the next idea or doing social media or cross promo on other platforms."

His matter-of-fact tone stopped her short. It was a surprise. "Well," she said, "there are the comments laughing at me, saying it was hysterical."

"It *was* hysterical," he pointed out.

"And mean spirited."

"It was a surprise, a prank. That's how they work," Tobin said with almost exaggerated patience. "And I already promised I won't do it again. So why not keep doing videos? Just a few. I feel like we're on to something here."

She blinked. He did? "Why in the world would you think that?"

She could tell that he was looking at another monitor—he must have had Skype on the one he'd called her from and YouTube on the other. "Okay, I am genuinely sorry about these," he said.

"Which ones?" she asked. She'd opened up the video about five minutes after she got home from the gym—she'd opted not to have mimosa brunch with Mikki because she was too freaked out—and then five minutes after she opened the video, she quickly closed it. Now, she opened her own computer, calling up the video and starting to scroll.

She saw some of the comments she'd originally viewed, ones that said that it was epic, and hysterical, and LMAO. Now that she had a little distance, she could see why Tobin thought she was overreacting. Not that she'd admit he was right quite yet, but she felt herself calm. At least, until the next batch of comments.

SHOW ME YOUR TITS.

WHO'S THE HOT NOOB?

WHAT IS THIS BITCH DOING ON THIS CHANNEL?

Her heart sank. "Now I definitely don't think we should do any more collabs," she said firmly, her stomach roiling.

"I'll delete those comments." Tobin's voice was harsh, rough with anger. "That's bullshit, and my viewers should know better. If they don't, they can fuck off and watch somebody else."

She didn't know why she felt startled. Tobin could be annoying—hell, he was usually annoying. But he also wasn't generally sexist, and he was . . . well, goofy. To her knowledge, he'd never cussed at her, nor had he ever referred to women in misogynistic terms. The fact that he'd stand up for her and refuse to allow his viewership to treat her poorly, to slap back at misogynistic speech and risk his own viewership . . .

It was a tiny bit hot.

She took a deep breath. "I don't . . ."

"Now, here are some good comments too," he pointed out, and she scrolled to try to see what he was viewing. "Look. See? WonderYonder75401's comment."

She glanced down, then snickered.

Goofy scaring a beauty noob by fooling her into playing a horror game that she thinks is a dating sim: funny.

Watching said beauty noob beat the ever-loving shit out of him with a pillow: hysterical.

She grinned. Well, at least that had gone over well.

"And look below that," Tobin said, his grin widening. "We're getting shipped."

"What?" She rolled her trackball, scrolling down in the comments.

SO CUTE! I TOTALLY SHIP THEM!

THE BANTER. I CAN'T EVEN WITH THESE TWO.

OKAY, WHO THINKS THEY'RE HOOKING UP? BECAUSE THEIR CHEMISTRY IS RIDICULOUS.

And, finally: JESUS, GET A ROOM.

She cleared her throat. "That's . . . interesting."

"That's viewership," he pointed out. "Not all my viewers are douchebros. Gamers attract guys, girls, nonbinary people . . . I've got a wide spectrum of followers. A lot of them are here for the funny stuff, and I think we provided that."

"The thing is," she said, "I . . . damn it. I'm supposed to be more original. I'm trying to move outside of the usual beauty-product reviews and tutorials. But I don't know if your stuff will work for me. People watch my channel to find out how to look . . . you know. Perfect. And my video with you just made me look like an idiot."

"Nobody's asking you to turn EverLily into GoofyBui," he said, and she couldn't believe it, but his deep voice was comforting, supportive. She blinked in surprise. He wasn't wearing his ever-present smirk, either. He seemed thoughtful, earnest.

She was a little freaked out by it, to be honest.

125

"Just think about what you do best, what you like—and then think about what you could do with me," he said, then winked. "I promise I'll be a willing subject. You were a good sport—it's the least I can do."

She smiled back, feeling oddly shy. Which was stupid. She had known this guy for literally most of her life, and been his frenemy for at least three-quarters of that time. Why would she be shy?

GET A ROOM.

She sighed. "Okay. I'll, erm, come up with something."

"That's what I like to hear."

"Can you come up on Tuesday?"

He blinked. "Come up? To LA?"

Now it was her turn to smirk. "Yeah," she pointed out. "Remember? Your videos in your setup, at your house . . . my videos at mine. And yeah, we'll probably practice."

He groaned, covering his face. "Lils, you're *killing* me."

"Cry me a river," she shot back, then laughed. "I will come up with something sufficiently torturous."

"Like drag?" he said. "Because I have to warn you: I've done that, for my channel. I looked amazing." He paused. "If somewhat stocky. And I tripped on my heels. Actually, that might not be a bad idea at all."

She sighed. She'd toyed with the idea, but of course he'd done it. Was there any idea that he hadn't done?

"It'll be a surprise," she said. "See you on Tuesday."

She hung up, then looked around her apartment. It was now Sunday evening. What the hell was she going to do with a half-crazed gamer who did sketch comedy? How was she supposed to be original in the face of *that*? Especially while being true to her own brand and her own skill set?

It took hours. She brainstormed, looked at videos. In sheer desperation, she started flipping through TV channels while simultaneously searching Reddit. She needed some kind of inspiration. This was what Tobin was supposed to be helping her with. Instead, she felt challenged . . . and like she was falling short.

She looked up to find *Queer Eye* on. She watched with half her attention. She enjoyed the show, loved the heart and emotion of it, but she had too much on her plate to really give it the focus it needed.

Then, suddenly, it hit her like a lightning bolt.

She knew *exactly* what she'd do with Tobin. And it was going to work.

CHAPTER 17

Tobin got a little lost.

He was lucky he'd left early, but he still smacked into LA traffic. God, he hated LA. Still, he knew it was where most of the successful YouTubers lived—that was probably why Lily had moved here. She was nothing if not a planner, and she did what she needed to, to succeed. She'd been like that since he'd known her in high school. She had studied for the SATs like she'd been planning the Normandy invasion, and she'd attacked the APs like they personally insulted her. He'd never seen anyone as prepared as she had been.

He'd winged it, knowing that a three in an AP course was basically as good as a five, if you were just looking at getting out of electives. She had *hated* that "half-assed" approach, he remembered with a smile.

Maybe she was right. Maybe their collaborating *was* a bad idea.

He pulled into a warehouse parking lot. He'd never been in this part of LA. The area was super industrial, and the building itself looked like a gray concrete factory, although he wasn't sure what the factory was for. It was probably a good artistic backdrop for fashion stuff, he mused. He thought he'd seen a previous video where Lily had wandered through someplace straight out of a Soviet bloc, all rusted metal and exposed brick and concrete blocks, while she was wearing something gauzy and floral and feminine. She worked the hell out of it, he seemed to remember.

Not that he'd been paying too much attention to that, he thought with a huff, double-checking the address and then getting out of his car. It was just that he was trying to see more of her content, figure out what the Venn diagram intersect between what she did and what he did was. The problem was, she was right: their partnership might be a little too much of a stretch. She was just *so* rigid, so controlled. He worked hard, but there was a lot of guesswork and a lot of flexibility in his videos. He was jazz. She was a military march . . . the kind where the band would get shot if they got a note wrong.

He walked up to the door, looking around. The place only had a few cars. It was weird, considering it was the middle of the week.

On the other hand, he thought, *there's a chance she's taking me somewhere empty to kill me without witnesses.* She had been pretty pissed about the jump scare, and he knew that she tended to hold a grudge about that sort of thing, especially if she felt like people were making fun of her afterward. She wasn't like their friend Vinh, one of the Nerd Herd, who was ridiculously old-school vengeful. That guy made Clint Eastwood look like Barney the Dinosaur. Vinh would wait a couple of months to a couple of years, then utterly destroy anything you cared about. Tobin remembered hearing about Vinh's adventures at NYU, when some classmate had stolen one of his class projects, turned it in as his own, and tried to frame Vinh as a plagiarist. After researching the guy and his family for six months, Vinh had not only gotten the kid kicked out of school; he'd gotten his father arrested for insider trading with an anonymous tip and a buttload of evidence. Ultimately Vinh was a good guy, but if you crossed someone he cared about, the guy was scary.

Tobin shook his head. No, Lily could be pissy, and occasionally spiteful, but she wasn't going to punish him for being late and scattered. At least, he hoped she wouldn't.

Tobin buzzed the intercom. "Who is it?" a scratchy female voice said.

"Hey, Lils. It's me, Tobin."

"You're late."

"Just a little," he protested. "I got lost. Stupid GPS."

"No problem. I'll send someone down to get you, okay? Just wait there."

Where was he going to go? And who was "someone"? He'd done shoots with whole crews before—Shawn, Hayden, Asad, and whatever other merry band he could rope into helping him—but from what he could tell, Lily tended to work alone. He didn't even know who her friends were anymore. *Did* she have a lot of friends in LA? Had she replaced the Herd?

It occurred to him that despite his penchant for doing things off the cuff, he might have asked a few more questions before he got here.

He waited, rocking back and forth from the balls of his feet to his heels. She hadn't prepared him for this, although she'd told him that she knew exactly what they'd be doing. He glanced around. This place was the type of place where he could see a bunch of street runners parkouring. Maybe he should try a video where he attempted parkour. *Mental note: see if Skeptic's up for it.* Although he doubted it. If Tobin was indoorsy, Shawn was downright subterranean.

The door opened, and he found himself confronted with a woman, taller than he was, with an undercut dyed bright purple, a baby doll dress, and a pair of platform combat boots that he was frankly amazed she could walk in. "You must be the goofy one," she said, sizing him up.

"Yup. That'd be me," he admitted. What the heck was going on here? "And you are . . . ?"

"The designer." She turned, walking down the hallway. He glanced around, then followed. He'd assumed that was what he was supposed to do.

"Designer, huh? You're going to be working on the shoot with us?"

The woman grunted. He wondered if Lily had told her what had happened with the previous video. If Lily wanted him dead . . . well, odds were good she could handle it herself, honestly. But he imagined this woman might be handy at disposing of a body.

She took him into a large workroom. There were bolts of fabric, and large tables, and workstations with sewing machines. He looked around with curiosity. It was cool.

"Tobin." Lily sounded smug, and she walked over to him, cocking a hip and crossing her arms. "Perfect. You ready to get started?"

"Ready to get started with what?"

"You said my video, my rules," she warned him. "And you said you'd go along with anything I came up with. Are we still good with that?"

He abruptly regretted that particular agreement. What did she have in mind? It was a workshop . . . obviously of a clothing designer. It couldn't be that bad, really. He had already admitted that he'd been dressed in drag, and that was actually kind of fun. He wondered if he could steer her toward cosplay too. That might be a good combination of what they both liked, he realized.

"Tobin?"

He realized that his brain had gone off on a tangent. "Um, yeah. Of course. No problem."

She nodded. "Then I have some people I want you to meet." She gestured to a kind of buff Latino guy, who emerged from a small side room. "This is Santangelo, and you've already met Ion."

He turned to the tall woman. The name kind of fit her, actually. He greeted them both. "Great! What are we going to be doing?"

She ignored his query, turning instead to Santangelo. "So, what do you think?"

Santangelo walked around him. "Dude, when was the last time you got a haircut?" he said, shaking his head. "It's healthy, though. Use any product?"

"Not really." Tobin realized he was feeling uncomfortably like a horse or car being auctioned, and ignored the impulse to cover his chest with his crossed arms. "Unless I'm cosplaying. I mean, I once put an entire bottle of hair gel in my hair to make it stick up like Goku from *Dragonball Z*."

"Well, it's shiny and has a lot of body, but you gotta do something with . . . all that," Santangelo said, brushing past his anime reference and gesturing vaguely around his head. "And colors . . . how do you feel about changing it?"

"I dyed my hair purple once," Tobin replied, then nodded his head at Ion. "Kind of like her color, but a little brighter."

"No, I mean . . . ," Santangelo said, then stopped, looking at Lily. "Well, we don't want to be here all day, I guess."

"It'll be fine," Lily assured Santangelo. Tobin wondered when she might assure *him*, seeing as he was the one who was possibly dying his hair or shaving his head or something. "Ion, what do you think?"

Now it was Ion's turn to circle him. "I'm going to need to adjust a few things," she said. "Nothing off the rack's going to be quite right— he's shorter than I was expecting, and he's got a broader chest—but some quick tailoring ought to be enough. I'll think about what I have that would work."

Tobin didn't want to show his impatience, but he was feeling it. "Um, what are we doing?"

Lily smirked. "Why, Tobin? Feeling nervous?"

He chuckled, or at least he tried to. It sounded a little wooden to him. "I am hardly nervous. Did you see the video I did with Skeptic where I waxed my entire body except for my head? And that other time, when I went tandem skydiving?" He scoffed. "Trust me. This is going to be a snap."

"It really will be," she said, and he swore she sounded like she was trying to soothe him. The idea seemed ludicrous. It also made him feel even guiltier—he hadn't tried to reassure her when it had been his turn to do a video. If anything, it made him more of a dick.

"So, you're going to make me dress in drag, then? Like we discussed?" he said. "That should be fun."

"It probably would be," she agreed. "But as you've said, you've done that already. Also, I think too many channels go for drag in a mean-spirited way. I don't want that to happen."

"Neither would I," he agreed immediately. But he was completely at a loss. "So . . . what are we doing?"

She grinned. "We're going to give you a makeover, of course," she said with a placid smile.

"A . . . makeover?" He glanced down at his clothes. "Um. Okay."

He wasn't expecting that. He wasn't sure why he wasn't expecting that. It actually made perfect sense, considering her usual content. Still . . .

"Isn't that a little . . ." He cleared his throat, unsure of how to say it, then just plunged forward. "I don't know, boring?"

He expected her to be offended and felt bad the moment the words were out of his mouth. Instead, her brown eyes glinted with humor.

"Trust me," she said, in a way that absolutely meant he probably shouldn't. "When I'm done, this is not going to be your typical makeover video. You are gonna be *hawt*."

He couldn't stop himself from barking out a laugh. "I sincerely doubt that."

"So do I," Ion muttered, causing Santangelo to laugh. Tobin winced at the conviction in Ion's voice.

"My video, my rules, right?" Lily said, and there was no missing the smugness of her voice.

He grumbled his agreement.

"Perfect," she said, smiling. Then she pointed to the little room. He started walking over.

"Oh . . . and, Tobin?"

"Yeah?" he asked over his shoulder.

"Strip."

CHAPTER 18

It occurred to Lily, a little late probably, that she might've picked an easier video than trying to make her dorky high school nemesis "hawt." Because right now, he was shivering in a pair of boxers and a hairdresser's cape, and talking nonstop to Santangelo, who looked like he was going to strangle his client.

Still, difficult or not, she was committed. Tobin had been right: their cross collab had been an unbelievable boost to her numbers. The bump she'd gotten from her first collab with Tobin had been impressive enough that Maria had texted her: Keep up the good work! with a bunch of smiling emojis. She knew that Maria kept casual tabs on her numbers but generally didn't reach out unless there was a deal in the works or they were brainstorming strategy. To have Maria contact her out of the blue meant she was definitely headed in the right direction.

From here on out, she was all gas, no brakes.

"You've got a lot of hair," Santangelo said, cutting across Tobin's running commentary. "And do you ever shut up?"

"Yes," Tobin said. "And no. Lots of hair. Like, literally every hairdresser or barber I've ever gone to has commented on it. And I don't really shut up. I even talk in my sleep. Or so I've been told." He frowned. "I should record that. That'd be a good video. What do you think, Lils?"

She shook her head. "I think you should let Santangelo cut your hair," she said, then turned to Ion. Ion rolled her eyes, then pulled out her phone. In a flash, Lily's phone buzzed softly in her pocket. She pulled it out to read Ion's text.

ION: He's annoying, isn't he?

Lily grinned. Welcome to my world, she answered.

ION: remind me why you're doing this again?

LILY: he's got nine million subscribers and I gained over a hundred thousand just from one video with him. In a day.

Ion's eyebrows jumped up. "No shit?" she mouthed silently, cognizant of the microphone.

Lily nodded. Which was why she was continuing the video. She had felt humiliated . . . but the numbers didn't lie. Tobin had been right, galling as that fact was. A little embarrassment, taking a risk, moved the needle.

She was willing to do a lot to move that needle.

She may have aimed a touch too high to claim that she was going to make Tobin "hawt." He was cute—there was no denying that. There were people all along the gender spectrum who called out his looks (and his "do-ability") in the comments on his channel, at various points. But she wanted to make him undeniably smokin'. She wanted to be able to take him to a party full of influencers in LA and have them drool uncontrollably. She knew that was probably petty, but she didn't feel too bad about that. Petty worked. Spite motivated her in more things than she cared to admit.

"Hey, Lily?" Santangelo said, interrupting her thoughts. "What are we thinking about the beard? Right now, he's looking eight-o'clock shadow, and it's only, like, noon."

"Hey," Tobin said, sounding a little hurt.

She walked in, knowing she was on camera. She studied Tobin's face, holding his chin. He crossed his eyes. She ignored it. "Keep the shadow," she said with more confidence than she felt, then surprised herself by rubbing her palm against his jaw. He had a good jaw, she realized with a start. "It looks good. Sorta Oscar Isaac-ish, you know? Sexy."

"Sexy?" Tobin squeaked. Then he cleared his throat, pitching his voice lower. "I mean . . . yeah. *Sexy.*"

"Okay. But I'm shaping this bitch," Santangelo muttered, producing his clippers and getting to work. "When we're done here, you're gonna get the brush and the product I told you, yeah?"

"Yes, sir," Tobin said, his eyes wide. He seemed to be mocking a little, but he also seemed a little cowed. Lily grinned at him in the mirror, and he grinned back, until Santangelo told him to knock it off "so I can work."

"All right, I've got three looks here," Ion said. "Classic, rugged, and . . . well. The third's a combo, based on this guy's whole ethos."

"That sounds good."

"What does any of that mean?" Tobin asked.

"Classic's a suit; rugged's, like, jeans and a tee," Ion said.

"That doesn't sound very makeover-y," Tobin noted, sounding more curious than anything. "I mean . . . I don't generally wear suits, so I guess that'll be different. But I live in comfy clothes."

"Yeah, that much is obvious," Lily teased, as Santangelo brushed off his neck and shoulders, getting rid of all the small hairs and sweeping up the clippings.

"We can't all be fashion models, Lils," Tobin shot back. "You color coordinated your nail polish to your purse to your damned *phone case*. And you had, like, fifteen phone cases!"

"As opposed to you," she said with a smirk, "who actually wore two different shoes and never noticed until I pointed it out."

"Thankfully, I've got a career where, for the most part, I don't even have to wear pants if I don't want to," Tobin joked. "I deliberately didn't want a job that required me dressing like a grown-up. Now, I feel like I'm going to prom. Or what I imagine prom felt like, anyway."

Lily blinked, then tilted her head as the memory came over her. "That's right. You didn't go."

"Hey, I gamed for twenty-four hours straight over at Vinh's house with Josh and Asad," he said with a grin that felt slightly off. "That was way better than wearing some gross rented tux and listening to bad pop music in a hotel ballroom."

She was going to say something cutting about gaming versus fashion, but something in his eyes made a truth suddenly hit her. She'd always assumed that he didn't want to go to prom, like the other guys. But now, something in his tone made her wonder. Had he simply been too self-conscious? Too nervous to ask someone and go?

"Who would you have asked?" she blurted out.

He blinked. "I wouldn't have asked anyone. I *didn't* ask anyone. Because I didn't go to prom."

"Yeah, but if you had decided to go . . . if it weren't some big political or 'I'm too cool' statement," she pushed. "Who would you have asked?"

He frowned. Then he grinned. "Isn't it obvious?" He winked. "I would've asked you. If only to piss you off."

She shook her head. Santangelo, on the other hand, glanced at them both curiously. "You went to high school together? You knew each other?"

"Yup," Tobin said with a grin. "She's hated me for years."

"We have a complicated relationship," she said and sighed when Tobin hooted. "Okay, Goofy. Time for you to get dressed. Not that I'm not digging the boxers."

"If I'd realized I was going to be in my undies on camera, I would've worn something more festive," he said easily. "I've got a pair with T. rexes wielding laser guns. And a sort of strategic unicorn one, but that probably would be distracting."

Santangelo chuckled. "Your boy's a mess," he said. "But a funny one. Once you get used to him."

"He has his moments," she said, tugging Tobin to Ion. "All right. Let's get him set up."

Ion pulled him behind a set of dressing screens. Ion wasn't particularly well known, but she was incredibly talented, and she did very solid menswear. Lily had known her for several years, after meeting at a fashion influencer party where they'd both been deathly bored, and Lily was glad to be able to show Ion off on the channel. It hadn't occurred to her before, since so much of what EverLily did was more stereotypically feminine. She pulled out her phone, making a note: *more masculine-themed content, maybe?*

"You got that camera ready?" Ion said.

Lily checked. "Yup, let's go. Ready for the big reveal."

"Are you sure?" Tobin said from behind the screen, and she heard his deep voice rumble, "I feel like an idiot."

"Revenge is mine," Lily said, and found herself grinning when he laughed in response. "Come on, get out here and strut that stuff. I want to see you work it."

"All right. But if you get blown over by my sheer overpowering sexiness, it's on you," he warned, then chuckled again. And with that, he emerged from behind the screen.

Lily was glad that the camera was on a tripod, because if it had been in her hands, she would've for sure dropped it onto the concrete floor. Her jaw dropped slightly, and her eyes widened, like it would help her take in more of what she was seeing.

He was wearing a black suit that might as well have been tailored to his fit figure, broad across the shoulders but nipping into his waist. His shirt was blinding white, and his tie was a bright bloodred. His hair was perfectly groomed. Combined with the shadow, he looked like a hit man. A sexy, dangerous, sharp-as-a-razor hit man. He looked at her with surprising hesitance and a little, shy half smile. "I look stupid, don't I?" he asked.

She swallowed, trying desperately to get some moisture in her mouth. "Try giving me a sexy look," she said instead. Her voice, to its credit, sounded demanding.

He quirked an eyebrow, then did an exaggerated duck face. "Blue Steel!" he said, cracking himself up.

"Dude, *no*," Santangelo said, shaking his head. "You cannot pick up women like that, man."

"Good lord. Is *that* what I'm doing?" Tobin asked, sounding bewildered.

Santangelo stood next to him. "You need to be confident. You look rich, dangerous. Only thing missing is the confidence."

"I have literally no idea how to do that," Tobin said with a frustrated laugh.

"All right, let me think." Santangelo tapped his own bearded chin with his fingertips. "You ever play, like, a tournament or something? Ever trash-talk?"

"Ye-ees," Tobin drew out.

"Imagine some young punk-ass bitch just told you that they're better than you," he said. "Like, some sixteen-year-old. Or some frat boy that has maybe played, like, a month. And he's talking shit."

Tobin scowled. "I . . . okay."

"Now, imagine you're about to go into a game with him," Santangelo prompted, backing away so it was just Tobin in the shot. "Like you're about to destroy his ass. Like he's a dead man, and he don't even know it yet."

Tobin's smile was . . .

Oh. My. God.

Lily felt her entire body go hot as Tobin unleashed a feral smile, his whiskey-brown eyes absolutely molten. He even let out a low little chuckle that she seemed to feel in every nerve ending.

"Holy shit," Ion murmured behind her.

"I know, right?" Lily whispered in response.

Tobin blinked, and the spell was broken. "That it? I just have to be in gaming-beast mode?"

"You wear that suit, go to a bar, and do that," Santangelo said, nodding in approval, "and you are going to be so crowded by thirsty women, you're going to need one of those rescue lines to get you out."

Lily cleared her throat, realizing she was losing her grip on the video. "All right! That was awesome. Let's go on to the next outfit."

She thought that would help. She had a kink for guys in suits. So what if Tobin looked good in one? He still talked, and that tended to be the main problem. Besides, he wasn't going to keep giving her "the look" either. She just needed him to go back to comfy clothes, and he wouldn't be appealing anymore. It was the suit, not the man.

Except he did it again. He was now dressed in a pair of distressed jeans that Ion had somehow miraculously made look like he'd owned them for ages, soft as a cloud, worn in just the right places.

Did his ass look like that normally? She wanted to ask, but she was afraid of what the question might reveal about her. She simply kept filming, laughing when he goofed around.

"I like this leather jacket," he said, examining it, twisting around. That twisting movement made the slate-blue T-shirt he was wearing pull across his chest. But at least it was relaxed. She didn't know what she'd do if it were tighter.

"All right, last look," Ion announced, and Lily felt a burst of relief. She'd definitely gotten in over her head on this one. "I call this 'if a geek went jock,' and I think it'll work perfectly. Because . . . you know, he's a geek. And a jock."

"Excuse *you*," Tobin said, his eyebrows jumping up. "I am hardly a jock."

"With a body like that? Are you kidding me?" Ion said, calling him on his bullshit.

"I take care of myself," he said with overblown wounded pride. Lily snickered.

"Well, get in there, Mr. I Take Care of Myself," Ion said, gesturing to the changing area.

"All right, all right."

Lily heard rustling, then a snort of disbelief. "Where's the rest of this?"

"Just put it on!" Ion called, then turned to Lily. "This isn't what I normally do, but I was playing with some concepts. This should be fun."

He stepped out. He was wearing his own high-top sneakers, a pair of black basketball shorts that were obviously silky, with an almost mirror sheen. It somehow showcased his muscular legs.

She didn't even know she liked legs that way.

"I am wearing a crop top," he said, gesturing to his abs. "I look like a Hulk Hogan video. But, you know, Asian."

"You look great, six-pack," Ion said, rolling her eyes. "Relax."

"You try relaxing when you look like an eighties Jane Fonda exercise video," he muttered. "Does a headband come with this? Or do I order that separately?"

"Don't make me come over there and thump you," Ion warned, and Tobin grumbled but shut up. "There is a hoodie in there you can pull over, if you absolutely must. I made it custom for a slightly larger client, but it should fit you. Actually, that probably works better—he was taller, but his chest wasn't as broad, so it should even out. If it doesn't, I can find something else."

Tobin crowed, retreating back to the dressing area. Then Lily heard him making what sounded like yummy noises.

"Oh my God, this is the softest thing I have ever felt, *ever*," Tobin said. He came back out wearing the pullover hoodie, looking ecstatic. "And it's got a wizard's kinda hood, not one of those stupid little puny hoods! And deep pockets! Oh my God, did you line this thing with kittens? This is so frickin' *soft*!"

Ion grinned.

"You gotta give me your buy links," he enthused, bouncing around with the hood up. "And you realize I am buying this and keeping it, right? I am wearing it out of this shop. I may never take it off. I want to *live* in it. This is like a cloud. With a hood. This is *perfect*."

Ion turned to Lily, an amused little grin on her face. "He's like a puppy, isn't he?"

I'm a dog . . . like a Labrador retriever.

Lily smiled back. "You know, he really is." She turned back to Tobin. "All right. Up to this point, I would say we were successful. We have achieved hawt."

"We did? We have?" he said, stopping his bouncing.

"Which means next video is your turn."

He grinned. And despite the fact that he was in just a pair of athletic shorts and a hoodie, grinning like a fool, she still felt the tiniest tug . . . like she had when he'd done the sexy "I will destroy you" look in the suit.

Hmm. That would be something to consider.

"You coming to my place on Friday?"

She swallowed.

"Of course," she said.

It was just business, after all. She could handle a man like Tobin Bui.

CHAPTER 19

Tobin meant to be ready by the time Lily got there. He really did.

He'd been thinking of possible videos for them to shoot since the last time he'd been up in LA and she'd made him "hawt," quote, unquote. He hadn't felt particularly hot, truth be told. If anything, he'd felt self-conscious as hell, which pushed all his anxiety-driven humor and an almost intolerable amount of talking. Normally he was able to channel that nervous energy into his videos. Some had joked that he sounded like a hamster on crack in a lot of his videos, and admittedly, with a lot of game playthroughs especially, he tended to rattle off a lot. But it wasn't a big deal.

Also, he tended to not film videos in his underwear. He imagined that was Lily's revenge, and he couldn't really fault her for that, per se.

He sighed. Lily was going to be here any minute. He'd told her specifically to come on Friday, because it seemed to fit her sense of schedule: film in Ponto, at his place, on Fridays, up in LA at her place (or wherever she deemed appropriate, like Ion's workshop) on Tuesdays. So that worked.

He just didn't have a damned idea.

He jolted when she rang the doorbell. At least he was fully clothed, he thought with a rueful grin. He let her in. "Sorry for the late start," he said. He'd told her not to show up too early, making up something about an appointment, when the only appointment he'd had was trying to somehow cudgel creativity out of his tired brain.

"You're all right?" she asked, with casual curiosity.

"Yeah, yeah, I'm fine." Completely uninspired and without a video idea, but fine. "Um. Right. Are you hungry? Do you want to eat something? I've got some food, or we could go out and grab lunch."

She frowned at him. "It's a long drive, Tobin," she pointed out. "Probably better if we just jump right into the video, don't you think?"

"Um, yes . . . ," he hedged. "About that."

Her eyes widened. "What's wrong? What happened?"

"I, uh, may not have an idea quite ready yet."

She goggled. "Are you kidding me? We need to post a video tomorrow!"

"Technically," he said, "my viewers aren't, like, religiously following my posting schedule. I try not to go more than four days without posting, but I also mix things up."

"Well, I am supposed to have a video up on Sunday," she said, her voice firm, "and my viewers are kind of rigid about it. I've only missed a video posting once in the past five years, remember?" She paused. "And that was because of you too."

"I told you that filming with me was going to be more of an unstructured experience," he carped back at her, feeling both guilty and attacked. "And in my defense, I knew we'd need to film, and I figured I would have an idea by now. I tend to come up with things best under pressure. Either that, or just before I go to sleep."

"Well, that's not very helpful, is it?" Lily snapped. "So what are we going to do now?"

He gestured to his office. "Now, we brainstorm."

She sighed, then walked in, settling herself in on the small couch with the "fox" pillow, hugging it to her. "I am interested in seeing how you brainstorm," she admitted.

"Well, I don't go all design crazy like Josh," he said, remembering the brainstorming session that had spontaneously burst out at the Belly Up. "He'll have you color-coding Post-its and index cards and doing doodles, and he has, like, a whole system. I just mind-map a little, or write words that help me think of things."

She nodded. "I do that too. Like springs, florals, new makeup palettes, designers and MUAs I want to promote."

He wiped down his whiteboard before pulling out a dry-erase marker. "The trick is coming up with stuff that will fit both of us," he said. "The intersection between our two audiences. Personally, I think that funny works."

"You're the funny one," she pointed out. "Not me. So I don't know what I can contribute there."

"I think you're funnier than you give yourself credit for," he said and was surprised to see a shy half smile emerge. "Besides that, though, you're a great straight character to my goofy over-the-top one. You need the balance for the jokes to land."

"You don't usually work with a partner, though."

He shrugged. "I still understand the theory. And I think that, other than the dick factor of scaring you, our initial video worked wonders."

"Our last video did pretty well too," she said.

"I know. I got a bunch of new subscribers," he said. His agents were pretty happy with the collab, too, telling him to keep it up. "A lot of them said that I was 'hawt, if somewhat annoying.'"

"You could put that on your tombstone," she said with a grin. "Hawt, if somewhat annoying."

"I should have T-shirts made," he added and was rewarded with a laugh. "I'll add it to my merch."

"Speaking of . . . thanks for plugging Ion's clothes," she said. "Ion said that she's sold out of those hoodies, and she's scrambling to make up new orders. She's also sold out of a lot of her other stock."

He was glad. He liked supporting smaller, lesser-known businesses of all types, and Ion was pretty cool.

"All right, let's hash out ideas," she said, the getting-down-to-business look in her eye gleaming. He was well acquainted with this expression. "All right. Um . . . dance challenges? They're all over TikTok. Maybe we can do something from that?"

"The fact that they're all over TikTok doesn't help us," he said. "We need to come up with something that's more original."

Her eyes gleamed. "This isn't because you suck at dancing?"

"No," he said, taking the question seriously. "Because my sucking at dancing would actually work even better. It's funnier." He sighed, thinking it over, then wrote DANCE CHALLENGE on the whiteboard. "We'll hold this in reserve for right now, in case we can't come up with anything better. Let's think—and I hate to say this, because it's so clichéd—outside the box."

She frowned. "What do you normally do?"

"Video game playthroughs, like I said. Except you don't play games all that much, and besides, I do Twitch streams all the time, and I have other collabs that might work better for that." He grinned. "You should watch my livestream of the last *Minecraft* bed-wars tournament I was in. That was fun."

"I will," she promised, and he got the feeling she wasn't just saying it to placate him. Of course, she probably saw it as homework. "What else?"

"Um . . ." He pulled out a notebook where he'd jotted down his ideas and past videos. "I've done physical challenges, to a certain extent. The tandem skydive was particularly popular, but I don't know if that's what we want."

She looked green. "That's a no from me," she said, swallowing hard.

"Those kinds of challenges take a hell of a lot more prep than we can do in one day, honestly," he said. "We'll put a pin in that one too. Um, so other than physical challenges, I've done a few cooking things, but those never are as popular. I think I need to rethink how those get done or have a more unique approach than just 'GoofyBui makes char siu bao' or whatever." He paused, rubbing his stomach. *Mmmm. Char siu bao.*

"Hmmm. Maybe something difficult, like a wedding cake? Or, um, like something from a Bake-Off?"

"Maybe," he said, still feeling a little skeptical of the idea. It just didn't *feel* right, and his content needed to if it was going to succeed. He'd been doing this long enough to know that.

"What about your weaponized silliness?" she asked.

He grinned at the sound of the phrase coming out of her mouth, especially when she said it earnestly. "Those are usually skits that I come up with. Those can take a while to percolate. The Beacons video took months to plan out. The Tater Theater ones were quicker, because we already had the speech in place, and it was just the chat filter. Still, those didn't perform as well as I would've liked." He groaned.

It went like that through the afternoon, and he could tell Lily was getting frustrated. Hell, he was getting frustrated with himself. Why couldn't he come up with an idea? Damn it, he'd done this a million times. Why was he stuck *now*?

After they'd grabbed some tacos and burritos from a nearby hole-in-the-wall (the *best* hole-in-the-wall, as far as he was concerned), she was rubbing her face. "That's it. We go with the dance challenge," she pronounced. "We're running out of time."

He grimaced. "You know . . . hold on a second."

He whipped out his phone, calling Asad. "'Lo?" Asad answered.

"What are you doing tonight?"

"What'd you have in mind?"

Tobin looked over at Lily. "You know how Hayden wanted to get people together before the reunion? When is that, anyway?"

"It's in about two weeks," Asad answered. "And you know I'm always down to get the townies together, anytime. Game night, you think?"

"I'll bring Harbinger." Tobin had one of the largest board game collections known to man—he sometimes reviewed them, so he was offered a lot of free ones. "And I'll also bring Lily."

"You're still collaborating, huh?" He could hear the grin in Asad's voice. "How's *that* going?"

"Well, she hasn't killed me yet. So far, so good," he said. "Around six?"

"Sounds good. See you then."

As soon as he hung up, Lily looked at him, angry. "Where am I going?"

"Asad's. We're having a party," he said. "And I'm going to get inspired there. I promise."

She crossed her arms. "We could have an okay video without it," she said. "The dance challenge."

"Yeah, but don't you want the best video possible?" he countered. "The idea is to use these collabs to build our audience. We need stuff that's going to be shareable, viral. Different."

"Do you really, one hundred percent promise me you'll get a video idea out of this?" Her eyes bored into his soul, it seemed. She was not here to play. She was seriously pissed.

He nodded. "We won't stay too late, and if I don't get inspired, then we'll just do the dance challenge, and then I'll edit it myself, okay? It'll be up by Saturday, right on schedule."

She waited a long minute, then rubbed at her temples.

"Fine."

He nodded. "It'll be fun, you'll see," he said.

Now, he just had to come up with an idea. He was getting pretty damned tired of being in this position. But hopefully being with his old friends, and even Lily, would help jump-start his creativity. And if he was lucky, even though Lily had lost touch with a lot of the Nerd Herd since moving to LA, hanging out with their old high school crew might spark a few new ideas for her as well.

CHANNEL: *Everlily*

Subscribers: 4.5M
Video views: 200M
Most recent video: "Makeover! From Goofy to HAWT"

RECENT COMMENTS:

Breathless Belle: Holy crap, that guy really is hawt! And that voice! *fans self*

Hai Mai: I watch his gaming channel all the time. You are so lucky! If I had a boyfriend I'd want him to be like GoofyBui!

Amanda Parker: You should do more male makeovers on your channel!

Emily Anderson: Hey, you didn't kill him! Good job! 😉

CHAPTER 20

Lily hadn't been to Asad and his boyfriend's house before—they hadn't bought it when she was last among the Herd—and she felt a little self-conscious as Tobin's truck pulled up to it. It was nicer than Tobin's, if perhaps a bit smaller—charming, really, with all-native water-resistant landscaping that looked beautiful. Asad had always been into aesthetics, so it didn't surprise her that the place looked like it could be showcased on a magazine cover. She followed Tobin, brandishing the bottle of wine that Asad's boyfriend, Freddie, apparently favored, while Tobin toted the six-pack of beer that would be for Asad.

"Have you met Freddie before?" Tobin asked as they headed up the driveway and toward the front door.

"Big guy? Flame-red hair, bushy beard?"

"That's the one. He looks like a ginger lumberjack," Tobin said with a chuckle.

"I think I met him once, about . . . what, three years ago?" she mused. "At Melanie's wedding."

She frowned. Now that she thought about it, that might have been the last time she was in Ponto, not including this crazy collaboration. She used to visit a lot more, when her parents still lived here. She'd crash at their house and touch base with Emily, or Tam if she was in town—although Tam hadn't been back for even longer than Lily had been. Lily thought about when the Herd had initially graduated from

Ponto Beach High. Those first few years, they'd still stayed in contact. Still had their parties and get-togethers whenever there were school breaks or summer vacations. But as they started pursuing careers and moving forward, things had . . . shifted. Emily had dropped out of college and was wrestling with family problems; Tam had fallen off the map entirely. Her twin brother, Vinh, was some kind of big corporate muckety-muck, although his job itself seemed vague. Even Josh, who had never left Ponto, was rarely seen because he was busy becoming a big restaurant mogul. She could point to all that and justify her own reasons for staying away, but in reality, she'd actually missed the group. She'd just been too fixated to notice.

Thanks to her collab with Tobin, she noticed now.

"He's a great guy," Tobin enthused, and she realized he was still talking about Freddie. "You'd think he'd be this big tough linebacker, but he's just super gentle and mellow. He's like a big sheepdog to Asad's Scottish terrier."

She snickered. That was probably a really apt description, since Asad tended to be hyper.

Tobin rang the bell, then surprised Lily by just opening the door without waiting. "Hey, all!" he called. "The party has now started!"

A chorus of laughs and jeers met this announcement, and Tobin made a dramatic bow.

"That's a bold assertion," Asad said wryly, taking the beer.

"I meant Lily here, not myself, of course," Tobin said with a wink. Lily felt momentarily self-conscious . . . which was stupid. She was friends with all these people. She'd known them for years. But with her new epiphany, plus the residue of guilt, she felt weirdly out of place— something she'd never felt with the Herd before. They were just *there*, always welcoming, never judgmental.

Why haven't I kept in touch better? She'd fix that mistake, she thought, determined. In fact, she'd add it to her planner. *In pen.*

She thrust the wine bottle at Freddie, who smiled. "You shouldn't have," he rumbled.

She smiled back, feeling awkward as hell.

"Why don't you go in, have a seat?" he said. "We've got some nibbles and things. Do you want anything to drink? We've got a full bar, but we've also got a selection of local beers and wine. I can open this to breathe, if you like."

"Gin and tonic?" she asked hesitantly.

"Ooh! Ooh!" Asad gave her a hug. "We have this amazing artisanal gin; it will blow your mind. Let me go grab that for you."

She hugged back before he disappeared in the kitchen. She'd always liked Asad. He had Tobin's energy without the deliberate annoyance.

Tobin was joking with their friend Hayden in the dining room, where an incredible spread was laid out. She'd been expecting crackers and cheese and maybe, maybe, one of those crudité platters in the partitioned plastic trays that you could grab at the grocery store, if someone was feeling particularly grown-up or healthy. But this? "Holy hell," she murmured.

"Now, those are deviled eggs with speck," Freddie said, "and those are gougères with this amazing gruyere we found. And, of course, asparagus wrapped in bacon."

"Because bacon," Asad said with a grin, handing her a squat square glass with a sprig of mint. "Freddie's a caterer."

"You're amazing," she said, and meant it. "I can't even tell you how many influencer parties I've been to in LA that haven't had anything half as nice."

Freddie looked quietly pleased. "I used to work up in LA," he said, shaking his head. "Soul sucking."

"Now he caters for all the rich folk around San Diego County," Asad said, and affection and pride were positively beaming out of his expression.

"I like it better down here," Freddie agreed. "It's not as . . . crazy, you know?"

Lily nodded before she realized she was doing it.

"So you're back in Ponto, working with Tobin on a collab series?" Asad asked, taking a sip of his beer.

"Yes," she said, glancing over at Tobin—who was apparently now wrestling with Hayden on the living room floor as people looked on and laughed. "It's been . . . interesting."

"I warned him that you'd probably kill him," Asad said cheerfully, and Lily laughed. "And in that first video, I really thought you would."

"He deserved it," Freddie said, and Lily felt an immediate warmth at his support. She didn't know him that well, but he seemed nice and obviously protective. "Asad, I would kill you if you did that to me!"

"No, you wouldn't." Asad kissed his cheek, then shook his head. "But I still wouldn't test it, because that was just evil."

"It got a lot of views and shares, and we both got subscribers from it," Lily said with a little shrug. She noticed that Asad looked at her, head tilted with curiosity.

"Well, that's the point, isn't it?" he said, but there was something—not exactly judgy. Just . . . not quite agreeing? "Still, if Tobin suddenly disappears, you have to know you're the first person we're going to look at."

"I'm amazed he's made it this long," another voice piped in, and Lily was surprised by a quick hug around her waist from behind. "Lily! I was hoping I'd see you here!"

She turned to see her friend Emily. She looked different—which wasn't surprising, since the last time she'd seen her was also at the wedding. Emily's burnished-gold hair was pulled back in a low ponytail, and she wasn't wearing any makeup. Her gray eyes looked tired. Actually, her whole expression looked tired. But she also looked happy to see Lily, and that made Lily feel both happy and ashamed. When was the last time she'd really talked to Emily, face to face, not just texts or quickie emails? Or any of her high school friends, for that matter?

"Emily! How are you?" she asked.

Emily shrugged, and the expression definitely turned pained. "Eh. Same shit, different day," she said, her voice so flat that it hurt to hear. "But I'm better now. I wasn't sure if I'd see you until the reunion, if then!"

Lily was about to answer, but she heard a low crash, and Asad cursed, "Dammit, Tobin! And Hayden! What are you, twelve?"

Freddie and Asad both rushed to find out what was going on.

"I see that you're doing really well," Emily said, drinking what looked like a white russian. Maybe a B52. It was funny—nobody Lily knew ordered those drinks. Maybe it wasn't an influencer thing? Not hip and trendy enough? "With the YouTube thing, I mean," Emily clarified. "And Tobin."

"I enjoy it," Lily said. "And I've been working hard at it."

"My brother tried to have a YouTube channel," Emily said, her voice just a touch bitter. A hank of hair escaped from the ponytail, falling around her face, and she absently pushed it out of her eyes. It was all Lily could do not to fix her hair . . . maybe a cute fishtail braid, or something a little more elaborate. But Emily was always no fuss. "Needless to say, it didn't work. But not before he bought a lot of equipment."

Lily grimaced. Emily's big brother, Greg, was a problem—always had been. He was three years older, so they'd only been in high school with him the one year, and Lily hadn't seen his shenanigans firsthand, but she'd heard Emily's horror stories often enough. Various run-ins with the law. Mild gambling. Lots of get-rich-quick schemes. He'd tried to pull a scam of some sort with a few friends, and it had cost the family thousands—money that her single mother simply did not have. It had cost Emily her college education as she'd dropped out to help her mother keep the house. So Emily had gone from Stanford to Ponto

Community College, and to her credit, she didn't seem to resent living back at home with her family.

At least not much.

"You have always worn the coolest clothes," Emily said, and there was no hint of envy or cattiness. There was just warmth and support. "I wasn't surprised at all that you made your channel a success."

"Haven't quite made it yet," Lily demurred, but she gave Emily a hug. "I've missed you, and I've been a crap friend."

"You've been busy," Emily said with a sad smile and a little headshake.

"You know what? You should totally come up and visit me in LA," she said, even as she realized she lived in an expensive one-bedroom with an uncomfortable couch. Well, they could always share a bed.

Emily's smile was sad. "Um . . . I have kind of an unpredictable work schedule," she said regretfully.

"Remind me again . . . what are you doing now?"

"I work customer service," she said. "For a cell phone company."

"Oh my God, that sounds like hell," Lily said, then winced. "I'm sorry! I didn't mean it like that! I just meant that . . . customer service, especially for cell phones, probably means a lot of people yelling at you all day."

"That's okay, I knew what you meant. And yeah, it *is* hell," Emily said with a laugh, and for a second, it was just like it was back in high school, when she and Emily were on the same wavelength, complaining about some shared annoyance, laughing at a common joke. Lily couldn't help but smile, even as she felt a pang. "But hey, it's a living. C'mon—Juanita and Melanie are here, and obviously Hayden, and I think Keith might be by later."

There were so many people she hadn't connected with in so long. She spent the next hour pleasantly hanging out, even with the ever-joking Tobin. They ate food and reminisced, as well as discussing movies coming out, or changes to Ponto Beach. They played a game of Cards

Against Humanity, and Lily wrecked her makeup by laughing so hard she cried.

"So you never answered my email. Are you going to the reunion?" Emily asked.

Lily felt her cheeks heat with embarrassment. "I'm so sorry—I meant to get back to you, but I've just been slammed with . . ." She stopped herself from continuing the excuse. "When is it, again? I will absolutely be there."

"It's in two weeks," Emily said. "I'm so glad you can make it! It should be hilarious. And it'll be nice to see some of the people who moved, you know? Like Tam, if she manages to show up. I haven't seen her in ages." She frowned. "Her asshole boyfriend wouldn't let her go to Melanie's wedding, can you believe?"

"*Let* her?" Lily barked, eyes wide.

"Well, she came up with some excuse, but you could tell he was pressuring her," Emily said, eyes rolling. "God, I hate that guy."

"Speaking of Tam," Lily said, glancing around. "Where's Josh, anyway?"

Emily laughed. "I know, whenever I think Tam, I think Josh too," Emily admitted. "He's still relatively local—has a big house in Ponto, over by the bluffs—but he's so busy with his businesses we hardly ever see him."

Lily bit her lip. "And what about . . ."

"Vinh?" Emily, who was normally so warm and expansive, grew pinched and irritated. "I don't talk to him anymore. Last I heard, he and Tam were both living in New York City—different places, obviously, since Tam lives with the jerk-wad boyfriend. I'm sure Vinh has some cushy, expensive apartment in Manhattan or something."

Lily almost shivered at Emily's frigid tone. She'd known that their breakup was bad. But it had been nine years ago. The fact that Emily was still this icy about it meant it had been even worse than she'd thought.

"Well, I think I can come down for the reunion," Lily said quickly, changing the subject. Then she frowned. "I wonder if the popular girls are going to be there. You know—like Vanessa and Kylee. Although I don't even know if they stayed in town?"

"Oh, they're in town," their friend Juanita said, shaking her head. "I own a coffee shop over on Main and Third, Uncommon Grounds. I see them in there all the time."

"How long have you been open?"

"Four years this December," Juanita said, beaming. "You should stop by. The coffee's phenomenal, if I say so myself."

"She's right," Emily agreed. "I would load it up in an IV if I could. Sometimes it's all that gets me through the day."

Lily smiled. "That sounds amazing. I'll have to stop by next time I'm in town. Hey! Maybe we can have coffee together?" she asked Emily and Juanita. "Or maybe breakfast, even?"

"We can definitely do breakfast. I've got quiche, pastries, you name it," Juanita assured her. "Maybe not on Freddie's level—*unless he'd start making me some damned food*," she called out, which was met with a burst of laughter. Obviously, it was a conversation they'd been having for a while.

"Juanita, sweetie, you know I can't keep up with your demand," Freddie called back, which caused even more chuckles.

"Him and every other man," Juanita grumbled, then winked. "Well, let's definitely make a plan. Emily? You in?"

Emily nodded, lifting her glass in salute. "If I'm not working, I'm in."

They talked a little longer, but Lily couldn't help the niggling thought. "So, you still see Kylee and Vanessa. Have they changed?" Lily asked, hoping she just sounded curious. "Or, you know, have they . . . I don't know? Let themselves go?"

"Well, it's not like they're interacting with me much, other than to ask me for almond milk or stevia or something," Juanita said with a wry smile. "But they're all married to successful dudes, and they don't seem to work, because like I said, they're in there a lot."

Huh. Lily felt a twinge of . . . anger? Not exactly. Irritation. And that tiny flame of desire for vengeance that she'd thought she'd long outgrown.

She thought about the PEACOCK launch party.

Had she really outgrown anything, though?

"I bet if you show up to the reunion, point out that you're this super-successful beauty YouTuber, they would be totally green," Emily said with an evil little chuckle. She'd been so pissed on Lily's behalf after Lily's disastrous attempt to eat with the popular kids, it helped Lily feel less bad about potentially abandoning the Herd in her quest for popularity.

"C'mon. It's been ten years," Lily said, but she couldn't help it—there was an appeal to the idea. She switched subjects, but her mind kept toying with the image, as if she couldn't leave it alone. Like a tongue rubbing the vacancy of a missing tooth.

After a few hours, it was getting close to one in the morning, to her shock. She'd had two of Asad's excellent G and Ts, and now she was sleepy and happy . . .

And no closer to getting a video done with Tobin.

Dammit. This wasn't what was supposed to happen. At all.

CHAPTER 21

"How are you doing over there?" Tobin asked tentatively, glancing over at Lily in the passenger seat as they headed back to his place. He hadn't meant to stay at Asad and Freddie's for quite so long. Obviously, had he been on his own, he would've hung out for as long as the party went on—he'd been over there until four in the morning before, playing *Call of Duty* or even Cards Against Humanity. Hell, he'd crashed over on their couch or their floor before, when the games had gone late. But he'd told Lily that they wouldn't stay too long . . . that they were going to work on the video. That he'd find some kind of inspiration or motivation once he shook out the cobwebs and hung out with friends.

Ordinarily, that would be the case. He'd started to feel the subtle claws of desperation digging in, though, as the night grew later and he still didn't have a single damned idea. He didn't want to open it up for discussion, like he had with Josh and Asad back at the Belly Up. That had only made him more frustrated. But now he was creatively empty and starting to feel anxious that he might be completely out of luck. Only this time it was worse—because Lily was counting on him.

He found himself really not wanting to disappoint her.

"I'm fine," she said with a drowsy smile in her voice. "It was fun. I should hang out with friends more."

His eyebrows went up at this. "Do you not have friends in LA?"

"Oh, I do! I do," she quickly clarified, and he realized she was a tiny bit tipsy. "But . . . um, they're other YouTubers. And they're lovely, wonderful people, don't get me wrong. But . . . you know. We don't just hang out and have fun. We're usually talking stats or talking shop, or . . . I don't know. Talking about other influencers. That kind of thing."

He nodded. That world could get really insular, really fast. "I like hanging out with Shawn—Skeptic Sketcher—but I like hanging out with my other friends too. And I know it probably seems weird, all us townies still hanging out ten years later. But I've liked staying in touch."

"I should have stayed in touch more," Lily said, a little mournfully. Then she perked up. "I'm gonna go to the reunion in two weeks, though! I told Emily I would. I missed Emily."

"She missed you too," Tobin said as they pulled into his driveway. "Um . . . I hate to say this, but I don't think you should be driving."

She let out a deep sigh. "I agree," she said. "Honestly, I wasn't planning on going back to LA this late anyway, especially if we haven't, you know, filmed anything."

Guilt hit him like a slap. "I'm really sorry about that," he said. "I know I told you . . ."

She waved a hand at him, stumbling ever so slightly on the way to his front door. "Whatever. We'll just start early tomorrow, huh?"

He felt relief at the reprieve. "Sure thing. I'll set an alarm."

She blinked heavily at him. "Guess I ought to get a Lyft, find a hotel."

The relief fled, and guilt hit him twice as hard. "I'm not . . . you don't have to get a hotel. Christ's sake, it's, like, one thirty in the morning," he said. "I've got a spare room—you can crash there, and we'll get going early tomorrow. Okay?"

She nodded. "Sure," she said, the slightest slide of slurring in her voice; then she grinned at him. "I can't believe I'm sleeping at your house."

"You and me both," he said.

"You got something I can sleep in?" she said. "Since I wasn't planning on staying somewhere tonight, I didn't bring anything."

He blinked. "I . . . um. Sure." He went to his bedroom and rummaged in the drawers until he pulled out a pair of shorts and a T-shirt. He handed them over to her and pointed her to the bathroom, the location of which she knew perfectly well. "You can, um, shower if you want?"

She shrugged. "Sleepy," she announced, then went into the bathroom and shut the door.

He quickly went to the spare bedroom. He hadn't been in there in a while. That fact became abundantly clear when he opened the door, turned on the light . . . and then winced. He'd been doing videos for some time, with a surprising number of props. One included about a thousand rubber ducks in various sizes—which he'd stored here, in big plastic bins, meaning to eventually repurpose in another video. He also had a surprising array of plush animals and hand puppets, some sent by fans, some that he'd gotten for various skits. There was a large Hula-Hoop and a five-foot-tall stuffed teddy bear. There was even part of a skateboard ramp. He tried clearing the way to the room's bed, a futon that was currently upright in a couch position. The mattress was harder than he remembered, and the whole thing was covered in dust and a disturbing amount of LEGO.

Getting new sheets and clearing all this off was going to take a while, he realized, aghast.

"I'm supposed to sleep in here?" Lily's voice came from the doorway, filled with amusement.

"I'd kinda forgotten about all this crap," he admitted, then turned and just about swallowed his tongue. "You're . . . um. Not wearing the shorts?" he squeaked.

She shrugged. "They were these huge basketball shorts, and they kept falling off my waist," she said matter-of-factly. "The shirt's long anyway."

Lily Wang had perfect legs, he realized. Like, stunning, curvy, long-limbed legs. Her figure was slight, but pixieish and graceful. She had her hair pulled back, her face damp and clean.

"You know," he mused, "I don't think I've seen you without makeup since junior year at Ponto High."

She shot him an exaggerated frown. "Be very careful what you say next," she said. "Because if you say that you think I look better with the makeup, I'm going to be annoyed. And if you act like all girls look better without makeup, I'm going to probably be pissed too."

He chuckled. She was so funny—especially when she was being honest and put her filter away. He'd known that, even back in school. It was probably why he was such an ass all the time, pricking at her to get a response. "Honestly, I think you look good either way."

She narrowed her eyes, as if waiting for the punch line. He let it lie.

"Um . . . this is going to take me a few minutes," he said. "I have to find the sheets, and, um, put these LEGOs somewhere," he said, holding his breath as she walked up next to him, poking at the futon.

"This thing is hard as a rock, Tobin!"

He clenched his jaw. *Too. Many. Jokes.*

But there was no way in hell he was going to make a "hard as a rock" joke to Lily, who was currently tipsy and only wearing a T-shirt and underwear. That just felt creepy. Instead, he said, "I'm sorry. I mean, it's a futon—there's only so much we can do there. But, um . . . maybe one of the couches? You're short."

Her eyes flared. "You have *love seats*, Tobin. I'm not tall, but I'm also not a toddler. I can't sleep on those!"

He grimaced. He ought to take her to a hotel. He was the one who . . .

She turned, walking past him. "I'm sleeping with you," she announced, then looked over her shoulder. "Coming?"

He gaped. "I'm . . . excuse me?"

She rolled her eyes, then headed to his bedroom. He followed her, too stunned to even be a smartass. She opened his door. He was glad that he didn't have laundry all over the place—he used his hamper religiously and kept things relatively tidy otherwise—but his bed was still unmade. "See? You've got a nice king-size bed," she pointed out, "and I am exhausted. Besides, I have standards. I think we can safely share a bed without anything weird happening."

His eyes widened. "Uh . . . okay?"

She nodded with satisfaction. "Great. Good night." With that, she climbed into his bed, hunkered down into one of his pillows . . . and fell asleep.

He blinked again. What the hell had just happened?

He went to the master bathroom, getting ready for bed. He pulled on pajama pants—which was weird, since he didn't usually wear pajamas, but again—no way in hell was he sharing a bed with Lily and just wearing his usual boxers. He turned off the lights and climbed into bed.

He could smell her perfume. He could hear her soft, even breathing.

Just like that, his body went harder than his damned spare bedroom futon.

Warning! Warning! Danger, Tobin Bui!

He was *not* going to share a bed with Lily while he was sporting . . . *this.* No way in hell. The last thing he needed was for her to feel weird or threatened or . . . ugh. Just *no.*

He quickly went through his mind, trying to find some way to fix the situation. He went through his usual thoughts: that weird stinky Scandinavian fish, oversteamed broccoli, coffee grounds gone moldy. But unfortunately, his body just wasn't getting with the program. He turned away from her, all but yelling at his own body. *Knock it off, stupid!*

Horror. He thought about the goriest, grossest movies and games he could think of. Razor-blade-and-eyeball stuff. It started to work, which he took consolation in, upping the ante. He thought about the stuff that had scared him as a kid. Bloody Mary. Ghost stories. That stupid Ouija . . .

He blinked, then sat straight up. "Lily!"

"*Hngh*?" she mumbled, her head mostly in the pillow.

"Get up. Get up!"

"Wha?" She sat up, groggy.

"I got it!"

"Got what?" she mumbled.

"An idea for the video," he said as pure electricity jolted through him. "Let's go!"

CHAPTER 22

Lily rubbed at her eyes, trying desperately to figure out what Tobin was going on about.

"Scary sleepover games," he said. "We just have to do a few of those. And film them. It'll be hysterical!"

"What are you talking about?" She reached for the mug of coffee he handed her, taking a fortifying sip. The gin and tonics she'd been drinking earlier had mostly worn off, but she was very sleepy at this point, and Tobin was not helping by being confusing and dragging her out of bed.

His bed.

She frowned. That really wasn't that big a deal. Not that she spent a lot of time sharing beds with people, but . . . she liked the way Tobin smelled. It was hard to describe, probably just some combination of his soap and him. He smelled . . . warm. A little like chai, actually. And sort of . . . she frowned.

Fuzzy?

No, that wasn't a smell. But being surrounded by his scent in the bed had been like sniffing a hug, somehow. It made her feel warm and sort of sigh-y.

Tobin snapped his fingers in front of her. "I promise it won't take that long. I don't think," he tempered. "You sure you're okay? I have, um, five-hour energy drinks around here somewhere."

She shook her head quickly. "Absolutely not. I tried one once, and the stupid niacin flush was ridiculous . . . you know, where your face turns red, because of all the B vitamins? I looked like a cherry tomato." She thought about it for a second. "Oh, and also, my heart started beating erratically. That's probably not good."

"No energy drinks for you, then," Tobin said, looking appalled. "So. Let's see." He guided her toward his whiteboard. "I'm thinking Bloody Mary, Ouija board, and . . . um, something else."

"Well, that sounds comprehensive," she joked. She wasn't as tense as she'd usually be when working, probably because she was so out of it. She needed a full eight hours of sleep to be optimal, and the later it got, the loopier she got. It's why she avoided all-nighters whenever possible. "What do you need me to do? You're not going to jump scare me again, are you?"

"No. Although, ideally, this ought to be kind of creepy," Tobin said, shrugging. "We'll just have to see how it pans out. But it should be fun. Most videos cover what the games are and why you shouldn't do them—as in, 'the devil might get you!' or 'you'll get pulled into an alternate dimension!'—but they don't show people actually *trying* them."

Lily shook her head. "Isn't this how most horror movies start?" she asked. "Like, they're messing around with unseen, unholy forces—because they wanted to be famous, or make a movie, or because they're bored?"

"Well, if I get sucked into hell, I have no one to blame but myself," Tobin said, setting up some lights and a camera in his living room. "I'm thinking Ouija board, over here. Oh! And candles."

She watched as he rummaged around, getting a small selection. He adjusted the lights, muttering to himself as he got the camera together. She sat down on the floor by the coffee table, looking at the Ouija board. "Why do you even have one of these?"

"Huh? Oh. I host game night a lot," he said. "I think I had a plan that we'd give it a try at some point, but we never even opened the box. So hey, this'll be the game's virgin run. No other people vibes on it."

Lily studied him with a smirk. "Tobin Bui, are you superstitious?"

He laughed, shaking his head. "No. Well. Maybe a little. But not really."

"Don't you play horror games all the time?" she pressed. "I remember you liked watching horror movies in high school."

"Eh. Sometimes I like feeling, you know, freaked out. Don't you?"

She leaned her head back on the love seat cushion behind her. "Not really," she said. "Besides, I'm usually too busy to be scared."

He sat down across from her, and she felt his knees brush against hers as he sat cross-legged and tucked himself closer to the surface. "Okay. So . . . shoot. Maybe I should look at the instructions?"

"How hard can it be?" she asked. God, she was sleepy. "I mean, does Hasbro include, like, a book of spells or something? Because I bet they just have a warning disclaimer that says don't conjure Satan and don't swallow small game parts."

He grimaced at her. "I feel like you're not taking this seriously."

"I'm just saying—exactly how specific do you think they get?" she asked with what she thought was inarguable logic. "They also make, like, Candy Land, and you don't see a cookbook in there."

He rolled his eyes at her, too intent on what he was doing to even deign to reply.

"Wait, wait. We need an intro." He looked at the camera, doing his signature smile. "Hey-oh, it's GoofyBui, and we're continuing the crossover series with EverLily. Today, we're going to be testing spooky sleepover games—OoooOOooohhh!"

She couldn't help it. She started cracking up at his lame ghost rendition, and he rolled his eyes at her. She fell over to the floor, then straightened herself out.

"Um. So, yes," Tobin said, shaking his head at her. "We're going to start with a classic: the Ouija board. Unfortunately, it's been years since

I've been around a Ouija board, and I haven't read the instructions, but as EverLily here says, how hard can it be, right?" He looked at the camera. "So if we get possessed by demons, you'll know it's because Lily told me to wing it, and you probably shouldn't improvise when it comes to, you know, dealing with the supernatural."

"Oh, shush," she said around a giggle. "There's no such thing as ghosts, anyway."

"And *now* we're headed into horror-movie territory," he pointed out. "All you have to add is 'how bad could it get' or something, and we're right in a slasher."

She smiled. Then she put her fingertips on the pointy, tear-drop-shaped plastic disc that was supposed to point to the letters. "This look right?"

"Perfect," he said, putting his own fingers opposite hers, the tips brushing together, much like their legs were. It was surprisingly intimate. She frowned.

"All right. Um . . . I think we're supposed to call someone?" he grumbled. "Damn it. I really need to read those instructions."

"Oh, Ouija board spirit . . . or possibly spirits?" she interrupted, closing her eyes and adopting a séance-styled intense expression. "Come and answer our questions." She paused, then added, "Thanks?"

Tobin laughed. "Well, sure. How could a ghost resist that?" he said, shaking his head. "I guess we ask . . . well, how are we going to know someone's there?"

"Um, we wait until the pointy thing starts moving?" Lily responded. "I don't know. This isn't my area."

"The pointy thing is called a planchette, I think," Tobin corrected, and Lily didn't even think—she just stuck her tongue out at him, causing him to start laughing again. "Anyway, okay. We'll say, 'Are you there? Move the planchette if you're there.' And then we'll see what happens." He looked around. "Um, hello? Anybody there?"

"Mooooooove the pointy thingy if you're there," Lily intoned, in her best séance-mistress voice.

The plastic wiggled, ever so slightly, and her eyebrows went up.

"Did you move it?" Tobin asked.

She glared at him. "If you're trying to scare me again," she said, "I will throttle you."

He shook his head. "No, I promise, I'm not going to jump scare you tonight," he said. He frowned down at the planchette. "So . . . I mean, it was a millimeter, but it did move. Kinda."

She shrugged. Honestly, either of them could have nudged it. Or there'd been a mild earthquake. "Anyway. What do you want to ask?"

"I don't know, but I know what we can't ask it," Tobin said. "No asking the name of the spirit, or you can get possessed or haunted or something equally unpleasant. And no asking how you die, because . . . ugh, why would you want to know that?"

"You *are* superstitious!" She crowed it, lifting her finger long enough to point at him. "Ha!"

"I think we need to keep our fingers on the planchette the whole time," he scolded lightly, and she could not help it. He'd messed with her? She would mess with him. Just a little.

"Maybe we can ask when we're going to get married, or who our soul mates are," she suggested.

He gave her a skeptical roll of his eyes. "Sure. And then you can braid my hair and we can write down our crushes' names with hearts around them in our notebooks."

"Hey, some guys would like that sort of thing. And it might be cool to find out if anyone could even stand your stupid butt for that long," she shot back with a grin.

"Fine! Fine. Ouija Board Spirit . . . do I have a soul mate?"

She nudged the plastic piece, gently, subtly, until it hit YES.

"Are you moving it?" Tobin looked a little wild eyed.

"No!" she lied. "And hey—you have a soul mate! That's surprising."

"Shut it, you," he said, but he was grinning. "Um . . . what's her name?" he asked the open air.

She let the plastic sit idle for a minute, and it scooted a little—he was probably tugging a little, too, she realized. And she wondered what he might want. It never occurred to her that he might be interested in someone. Actually, before she'd offered to spend the night in his bed, it never occurred to her that he might be seeing someone.

The thought was more disconcerting than she would've realized.

She smoothed out her expression, then kept her eyes almost entirely closed—just open enough to see what was going on with the board. She nudged the planchette toward letters, slowly, with little jerky motions.

"S . . . T . . . U . . ." Tobin followed along. "Shit! I should be writing this down. Except I'm not supposed to stop touching the planchette. What if it's a whole . . . P . . . I . . ."

Then he stopped, scowling at her.

"D," he finished. "So, you're saying my soul mate is stupid?"

"I imagine that's a surname," Lily said, trying for innocent, then bursting into laughter as he shook his head.

"Okay. So that didn't work so well. How about Bloody Mary?"

She grinned back, still feeling giggly. She had definitely reached the dazed-and-silly stage of sleep deprivation, and it showed. "Why not. What do we do there?"

"We bring the candles in the bathroom," he said. "And then we'll see from there."

"Sure," she said with a shrug and followed him in.

CHAPTER 23

It shouldn't be this damned difficult, but here they were, Tobin thought with a scowl. They'd finished the Ouija board segment and shut the camera down, and now he was setting up for the next section, the Bloody Mary thing. Then they'd break down and set up the camera over again with the third game. It was a pain, certainly more so than his usual game playthroughs. Still, it was easier than the beacons shoot, and the editing shouldn't take that long. He hoped.

Lily was sitting on the closed toilet, watching him with sleepy, heavy-lidded eyes as he struggled, yet again, with the light balance.

"What are you trying to do?" she asked around a yawn.

"Well, Bloody Mary is usually played somewhere dark, with a mirror—hence the bathroom," he explained, as he futzed with the aperture on the camera and adjusted the frames per second again. "The dark is what makes it creepy. But the damned light sensor's not working if I have the light too low. There's no point in doing this if we can't, you know, actually see it on the video." He grimaced. "And I don't want a mic in the shot, either. Gah!"

She snickered. "I've never done anything in the dark," she said.

He smirked at her. "Oh, really?"

"Perv," she said, but there was something amused in her voice, and he shot her a grin. "I mean, with makeup or clothes, you want to show them to their best advantage, which means showing them in plenty of light, especially natural light if you can get it, but regulated artificial light otherwise. That's crucial."

"Huh. But most people don't have those kinds of ideal conditions, do they?" he asked, as he lit a few more candles and then looked at the video feed. Too slow, damn it . . . it was kicking up all kinds of visual noise, making the background look pixelated and messy. Totally amateur. He sped up the frames-per-second rate a little, trying to eliminate that, and the scene went darker. He growled softly in the back of his throat, tugging at his hair.

He was frustrated. He'd thought this was a brilliant idea as he was falling asleep, and if he hadn't promised Lily that he was going to keep to her video schedule, he would've put this idea in a "marinate" file—give himself a few days to a few weeks, or longer, to figure out whether the idea would work at all, and then the mechanics and setup. He didn't do full shot-by-shot setups or anything—he did a lot of simple stuff like playthroughs and whatnot—but for skits and silly stuff, it needed more thought.

There was a good chance this wasn't going to work, he thought with irritation. Which would mean that they were wasting their time. The Ouija board bit was kind of funny, but sort of limped along. He needed to figure out a way to punch things up if he was going to post this tomorrow. Otherwise, it would just be some lame video of him and Lily, and that wasn't going to help either of them. If anything, it would just make people question what the hell he was doing, collaborating with someone so opposite to his brand.

He finally got the lighting, the mic, and the camera the way he wanted them. He tugged Lily in front of the mirror. She looked, then yelped.

"I'm not wearing makeup, Tobin!"

"I know?" He hadn't realized she wasn't aware, especially since they'd shot the Ouija board stuff where she had a bare face . . . man, she must be really tired. "Please tell me you're not going to put a bunch on. It's almost three in the morning."

She grumbled. "Just . . . give me a minute." She shuffled out, turning on the light and causing him to squawk as his eyes adjusted to the sudden brightness.

"Damn it!"

"Oh, hush. Just give me a minute," she said, pulling out a few things. She rubbed something into her face, then slicked on some eyeliner, and something on her cheeks, then something that made her lips just the slightest bit darker. When she turned to him, it looked like she wasn't wearing makeup at all. Instead, her features seemed somehow more pronounced.

"That's a neat trick," he said, reluctantly impressed.

"It's what I do," she said with a shrug, tucking the little accoutrements back into her voluminous bag and then tossing it into the corner. She shut the light off, and for a second, he felt nearly blind, the candlelight so dim he could barely make out Lily's form. He reached forward, his hands brushing against her back, her hip.

"Hey, watch it!"

Oops. Her butt, he realized, and yanked his hand away as if he'd been burned. "Whoa, sorry, sorry! That was an accident, I swear."

"Sure it was."

"No, I mean it," he said vehemently. "I would *never*."

She seemed to be staring at him—at least, that was the impression her silhouette gave. Then she let out a little huff of agreement, just a puff of breath. "Actually, I believe that," she said. "You've always been touchy feely, granted, but you're not a horndog about it, and you don't just . . . you know, grope people. And you're just as likely to tackle or hug a guy as you are a girl."

He frowned, mulling it over. "I guess I am," he said. "Never really thought about it before."

"You're pretty confident in it," she said. "I always thought your parents must be too. You know. Physically affectionate."

He let out a sharp bark of laughter. "Oh, hell no. My dad's Vietnamese, and my mom's British. I think we'd mail each other Christmas cards when we were living under the same roof." He shook his head. "We are many things, but 'touchy feely' is not one of them."

"Really?" He could see her features better now—his pupils had finally settled, and he was able to read more details in the low light. She looked curious, her eyebrows drawing together delicately. "My family's not that physically demonstrative, either, I guess, although they're warm and supportive. Why are you so different, then? You seem to hug, noogie, or tackle everyone."

It made his stomach clench a little. "Trust me, if I had the answer to that, we'd all be happier. All I know is, I'm totally different from my parents."

And it was something they'd noted, seemingly all his life. He swallowed.

"Okay. Let's give this a try."

"Right. What do I need to do?"

He tugged her in front of the mirror. "You need to look into your own eyes—like, really intensely—and then say 'Bloody Mary' at least three times, but more if necessary."

"Oh-kay," she said, rolling her eyes. "And that does . . . what?"

"Um." He frowned, trying to remember what he'd quickly googled. "You're supposed to see her face, I think? And in extreme cases, she's supposed to come out of the mirror."

Her eyes went wide. "Okay. That'll be eventful."

"Here, I'll do it, too, with you," he volunteered, standing next to her. He wasn't terribly tall—about five foot ten—but Lily was only five foot three. He realized that their heads weren't going to line up. "Maybe, um, kneel?"

She blinked at him. "Excuse me?"

He knelt first, then tugged at her shirt—his shirt, he remembered. "I want our heads to be closer to the same height in the shot," he said.

"Oh. Right." She knelt next to him. "That didn't help much."

"Dang it." He really, really needed to think through logistics on this. "Um . . . chairs, maybe?" He went and grabbed two folding chairs from the kitchen, setting them up quickly. She sat next to him, and he checked the shot one last time. "Um. Okay. Let's give this a try."

He stared at his own face, then nudged her. "On the count of three, okay? One, two, three . . ."

"Bloody Mary," she said, and he chimed in along with her. "Bloody Mary. Bloody Mary!"

They paused.

"Um . . ."

"Keep going?" he prompted.

They went on like that for a good minute. Then he shook his head. "Okay. So that's a big fat goose egg."

She laughed. "Yeah, I had my doubts about that one."

"I don't even know if that's going to be good enough to post," he groused, turning the light back on and then blowing out the candles. "Damn it!"

"Hey, are you okay?" she said. "I never see you this frazzled."

He grimaced. "I'm not frazzled," he said. "It's just . . . I told you I'd stick to a shooting schedule, and I'm trying to keep up my end of the bargain, but sometimes it works and sometimes it doesn't, you know? I mean, haven't you ever had an idea just not pan out, or need a day or two to . . . I dunno, recharge? Get your head on straight?"

She blinked at him. "No."

"Oh. Just me, then." He was a little harsher than he needed to be, shutting down the camera and putting things away. "Great."

He froze when he felt her tiny hand on his shoulder, making him pause. "It's okay," she said. "I think it's probably better than you realize, if anything, so don't worry about it, okay?"

He tried to feel heartened, but it just felt like he'd been tired for too long. He sighed.

"Did you have anything else you wanted to try?" she said.

He realized that she was standing there in just a long T-shirt and the tiniest whisper of makeup. And she looked both amazing and encouraging. And he felt warmth for her, which was surprising in and of itself.

"Um," he said, trying to get his mind clear. "There's a game called, uh, sinking into the floor that we could try."

"What's that?" she asked, curious.

"It's kinda stupid," he admitted.

"Can't be worse than Bloody Mary," she pointed out, and he rolled his eyes.

"Yes, thank you for that reminder. Anyway, it's sort of the opposite of 'light as a feather, stiff as a board' . . ."

"Oh! I remember that!" she said, her laugh like a bell. It made him grin—it was a sound of sheer delight. "I swear, we got Melanie up to about a foot off the ground one night, over at Emily's house."

"Honestly, you probably didn't," he pointed out. "But yeah, we don't have enough people to do that. This is more like a mindfuck." He glanced around, then set up the camera in the living room again, where his carpeting was the thickest. "Okay. So. This is 'sinking into the floor,' and it'll be our final spooky sleepover game," he said for the benefit of the camera. "Lily, can you come here?"

She stepped up to him, and he got down on the floor. She followed his lead, but he stopped her before she could stretch out. "Nope. I'm going to be the corpse that gets dragged to hell in this scenario. You're the, um, torturer?"

She grinned at that. "Oh, I'm in."

"Figured you'd like that," he muttered. He spread himself out on the floor, on his stomach. "Okay. So, the trick here is to lift me up by my shoulders and hold me for a while, okay? Then you're going to let go, and it's going to feel like I'm going through the floor, all the way down, like the damned. In theory, anyway."

"Huh." She knelt in front of him, and he saw the smooth skin of her thighs. Which seemed, again, vaguely inappropriate, so he looked away. "Sounds like a yoga pose," she noted.

"Don't stretch me too much. I'm not Gumby," he warned, as she started to lift him.

"Ugh, you're heavy," she replied, tugging at him. It wasn't comfortable, he'd say that.

"A little higher," he said. "I think I need to feel the stretch?"

"Have you never heard of leg day?" she groused, and he laughed as her fingers dug into his shoulders. She crouched a little, trying to get a better grip, get some leverage. For a second, they were face to face. He found himself holding his breath. She was flushed, and grinning—until for a second, she wasn't.

He hadn't felt a damn thing when he'd been staring in the mirror saying Bloody Mary. But now? He felt his stomach knot, his heart pound. Just from looking into Lily's deep, dark-brown eyes.

"Lily," he breathed.

She smiled.

Then she dropped him.

His face hit the carpet with a thump. He was lucky he'd turned a little at the last second, or he might've broken his nose. "Ugh," he mumbled.

"So," she asked, tilting her head and putting it close to his ear. "Feel like you're going to hell?"

"Pretty damned close," he admitted. "And that ought to wrap it up for us. Thanks."

She laughed, then gave him a hand up. "C'mon. Let's go to bed."

He grumbled, shutting everything off. She washed off her reapplied makeup. Then they both tumbled onto his king-size mattress. "Three o'damned clock in the morning," he muttered, jostling for bedding as she curled next to him. "Hey! Blanket hog much?"

"Shut up, Tobin," she said, then paused. "Hey, remember what we were talking about earlier? About you being, you know, touchy feely?"

He blinked in the darkness. "What about it?"

"Does that mean you're one of those snuggling-type boyfriends?" she asked, around a yawn. "I've never had one of those, and they always sound nice."

He thought about it. "I never got why guys wouldn't be into snuggling," he admitted. "It's been a minute since I've had a girlfriend, but when I do, I like it when they spend the night. They're all soft and warm and feel great and smell better."

"You're a hair sniffer, aren't you?" He could hear the smirk in her voice and burst out laughing.

"Yup, that's me," he teased back. "Just sucking in that air like a pervy Roomba. Now get some sleep, or I'll snuggle *you*."

"Heh." Then, to his shock, she wriggled until she was flush against him, then dragged his arm over her like a blanket. "Don't threaten me with a good time."

He froze momentarily, especially when she wiggled *again* to settle herself firmly in the little spoon position.

Fuck it. He curled around her . . . and yeah, he found himself inhaling her scent, the one that reminded him of jasmine and cinnamon and something indefinably sexy. He pressed a kiss on the back of her head.

"G'night," she murmured, sleep heavy in her voice.

He held her tighter. "Good night, Lils."

CHANNEL: GOOFYBUI

Subscribers: 10.1M
Video views: 327M
Most recent video: "Creepy Sleepover Games"

RECENT COMMENTS:

T3Ch Warrior: Dude, does she live there now or what?

Hai Mai: Hi, GoofyBui! I came over from EverLily's channel! I love this video! You two should totally keep collabing!

Hayden the Greaten: Did I tell you about the time we lifted Melanie like 2' doing "Light as a Feather, Stiff as a Board?"

Skeptic_Sketcher: Next segment: raising demons! Special Halloween edition!

Hayden the Greaten: I'd watch that.

CHAPTER 24

A few days later, Tobin was still thinking about big spoons, jasmine perfume, and Lily's smile. At some point in their collaboration, things had shifted, and he found himself zoning out and thinking about Lily. Remembering little things—like the way she'd smacked him around with the pillow, or their shared smiles at Asad's house, or the way she'd stared at him for just a second when he'd stepped out in that suit, with a look that was just as heated as it was shocked. He hadn't really registered it at the time, but now it was like catching Easter eggs from films he'd watched a dozen times that were only just starting to make sense.

He wasn't sure what it all meant, but he was pretty sure it was a bad idea.

Tobin left for LA around nine thirty in the morning. He'd still catch some of the morning traffic—that couldn't be helped—but by the time he reached LA proper, the worst of it would've dissipated. The only other alternative was to leave at five in the morning, and he was too much of a night owl to go that route.

Also, he didn't want to seem too eager. Especially since when he woke up *after* their last video, Lily was gone, leaving a brief note saying "see you soon."

This was going to be his second EverLily video. He wasn't sure what she had in mind, but it couldn't go worse than the stupid spooky games video. He'd managed to edit the clips so they were funny, at least, culminating in his face-plant, which actually was pretty damned humorous. She was also adorable, giggly, and obviously overtired, so her filter was disengaged. The commenters seemed to zero in on that, anyway. Of course, other commenters focused on "what is she doing *in your house* in the middle of the night?" but he had largely brushed them off. There was a contingent of commenters who were full-blown shippers at this point, and they were conjuring up scenarios where he and Lily were in a relationship. Said they were cute. There were some haters, but for the most part, there was just an unbridled, almost obsessive curiosity.

He could only imagine what their response would be if they knew Lily had spent the night snuggling with him—before vanishing the next morning. *With a note, of all things.*

Okay. It bugged him. He wasn't sure why, but it did.

He wondered if Lily faced as many shipping comments on her own channel. He knew that he'd gotten a gratifying number of new subscribers after that makeover video, as well as some comments that made him blush uncomfortably. He had people post that they'd thought he was attractive before, and he largely brushed it off, but the fact that they were actively commenting on how he'd looked in the suit, or with the leather jacket, had been eye opening. Whereas previously he'd gotten "you're so cute" comments, he was now getting "oh my God, I want you to break me in half" sorts of things . . . and while he supposed on some level it was flattering, it also made him weirdly uncomfortable.

Of course, on his channel, there were people who were saying similar things about Lily, except in reverse—"oh my God, I want to break *her* in half." He deleted those comments. Those didn't just make him uncomfortable. Those *pissed him off.* She was beautiful, no question, but that kind of thing was objectifying and vaguely threatening, and he wasn't fucking having it. Not on his channel.

He also tried desperately to convince himself that there wasn't any possessiveness or jealousy whatsoever. Because, you know, he had no right to feel those things, and it was getting weird enough with Lily as it was.

He'd made it past Camp Pendleton, headed for the 405 toward LA, when his phone rang. He groaned when his phone announced that it was his parents, which he should have known, because honestly . . . who called anymore, when texting was available? He weighed the pros and cons of just ignoring the call. It was his father. Finally, he sighed and accepted the call. He might get away with it, but the guilt trip that would come later simply wasn't worth it. "What's up, Dad?"

"We need you to pick up Aunt Helen from the airport on Thursday," his father announced. "She's coming in for a visit from Manchester—it's a long flight, she'll be exhausted, and she's not renting a car or anything. I will text you her flight information, all right?"

Tobin blinked. "But . . . why do *I* need to pick up Aunt Helen?"

"Because your mother and I are working," his father said, as if surprised that he needed to explain it at all.

"But I'm working too," Tobin pointed out.

"Yes," his father said slowly, "but . . . your schedule is obviously flexible. You have time."

Tobin gritted his teeth. "I really need to work," he said, keeping his tone civil. Or at least trying to. "I'll send a driver to get Aunt Helen, okay?"

His father scoffed. "Why would you waste that kind of money? No. You'll go pick her up."

Tobin tried to avoid arguments with his parents; he really did. His mother would've gone the passive-aggressive route by now, saying "fine" and then freezing him out. His father was more like a bull, plunging forward and insisting as if there would be no argument. Which, frankly, was what caused the arguments in the first place. "Dad, I really need to work," he said with a sharpness that surprised even him.

"Oh? Is there some kind of YouTube emergency that you desperately need to attend to?" his father asked sarcastically. "You have plenty of time to film your little videos. It's just a trip to the airport, for God's sake, Tobin. For family."

"It's an hour to the San Diego airport from Ponto Beach, and then another hour back, plus wait time. Not to mention possible traffic," Tobin added, through gritted teeth. "Just tell her I'm sending a driver, all right?"

His father sighed. "Why do you always fight?"

Tobin choked at that bit of unfairness. "You yourself told me how important a work ethic is!"

"That's when you have a real job!"

Tobin felt it like a slap. "I'm driving right now," Tobin said. "I have to go."

"So you'll pick up Aunt . . ."

Tobin hung up before he could say anything else rash. He knew he'd hear about it later, but damn it, he'd *deal* with it later.

On the plus side, he wasn't thinking about Lily anymore. He was too pissed off.

A little while later, he'd almost calmed down as he passed the 5-405 split, listening to his "chill out" playlist, when his phone rang again. He groaned, hoping it wasn't his father. But it wasn't. It was Jeffrey—which was just as bad, maybe worse, now that he thought about it. He was in no mood for Jeffrey's shit right now, so he ignored it. Then ignored it again when the guy called back. On the fourth call, Tobin's head hurt, and he was gripping the steering wheel like he'd like to grip Jeffrey's neck. "WHAT, JEFFREY?" he snarled.

"Dude, do you never pick up your phone?" Jeffrey sounded high strung, like a Chihuahua on speed. "I've got big news!"

Despite himself, Tobin felt a prick of curiosity. "What?" he repeated, albeit less harshly.

"There's a new animated series that wants you to do a recurring character!" Jeffrey sounded ready to pee himself. Maybe he *was* a Chihuahua. "It's going to get plenty of promotion! It'll be awesome!"

"What's the character?" Tobin asked, a little excited despite himself. He didn't do a lot of voice acting—mostly jokey dubs for other YouTubers, or stuff like Tater Theater—but he could see himself having some fun if the character was right.

"It'd be an old Chinese character, like a ninja master, I think," Jeffrey said. "Except he's sort of crotchety and over the top and funny, like the dad on *Kim's Convenience*."

Tobin paused. "You know, ninjas are Japanese."

"So?"

"And the dad on *Kim's Convenience* is Korean," Tobin continued. "And I'm not Chinese, Japanese, *or* Korean. You know that, right?"

Jeffrey huffed impatiently. "It's a cartoon character. And you'd still be Asian, and a diverse hire. Take the win."

Tobin frowned, irritated. "Just curious—who's showrunning it? Who's producing?"

"Well, look at you, taking an interest," Jeffrey said with approval. "Um, the showrunner's the two guys who did that zombie Civil War miniseries on Showtime. That did really well—those guys are really hot right now."

Tobin winced. "Those white guys?" he blurted out. He'd seen plenty about that on social media.

Jeffrey paused. "Problem?" he asked.

"Just . . . I remember the buzz on that. I remember seeing one episode of that show," Tobin pointed out. "It was supposed to be funny, like *Ash vs. the Evil Dead*, but it had a lot of white-savior bullshit and its depictions of Black people . . ."

"You can't honestly tell me you buy into the politically correct stuff," Jeffrey said. "You're a YouTuber. You know lots of lines get crossed. It's just comedy."

Tobin bit his tongue.

Jeffrey sighed. "Well, we'll put a pin in that for now. And I'm sure we can get your concerns addressed in a way that works for everyone," he said, in a super-placating tone that made Tobin want to break things. "There's something else too. You've been invited to join a YouTuber tour—the Twisted Humanoids tour. We're talking major cities—Atlanta, New York, Boston, Chicago, Seattle, San Francisco, Austin, New Orleans. It's a good payday, and amazing exposure, and it could open some great doors. As well as give you other possibles to collab with. Win-win-win!"

"When would it happen?" Tobin asked.

"End of August. Three-week tour."

Tobin felt a little bump of excitement, but he was already crispy around the edges. The thought of going and being "on," in a live show, in front of hundreds of people . . . and then traveling, on top of all that?

"It sounds interesting," he said with honesty, "but would you be okay with my audience numbers taking a little hit? Because taking three weeks off filming and posting would probably cause me to lose some people, and my new subscribers would definitely suffer."

"What?" Jeffrey squawked. "Of course you'd keep posting! Are you kidding?"

Tobin swallowed. "So . . . you'd expect me to keep filming . . . while doing an animated series *and* going on a three-week tour?"

"It's called time management," Jeffrey said, and he sounded so fucking patronizing, Tobin wanted to punch him instead of just breaking things. "And what do you think the other YouTubers on the tour are doing? They'll either have a stockpile of videos set up, or they'll be filming while on tour—usually stuff about the cities they're in. Hell, some of them film in their damned hotel rooms."

Tobin growled quietly.

Jeffrey sighed. "Listen, Tobin. I know we have our difference, but this isn't just me being an asshole. These are the facts of our business. Do you know how rare it is to make a living doing what you do?"

"Yes," Tobin admitted.

"If you want to keep making a living at it, if you want to be the best, then that means making sacrifices and working your ass off. Okay?"

"I know." Tobin sighed. "Let me think about it, all right?"

"You can't take too long on this . . ."

"I need to take some time," Tobin said, more sharply.

"Fine, fine. Call me soon, though, or I swear I will call you back repeatedly until you pick up."

Tobin made a mental note to block Jeffrey's number, then sighed. Guy would probably use all kinds of other people's phones to get through. Jeffrey might be an asshole, but he was a persistent one. "Fine. I will call you back."

With that, he hung up . . . and slammed on his brakes, as the traffic all around him turned into a parking lot.

"What the hell?" Tobin yelped. He turned to the AM station that had traffic alerts.

"An eighteen-wheeler full of chickens has jackknifed on the 405," the alert said in cheerful tones. "Take alternate routes."

He groaned. He was already too far on the 405 to back up. He pounded his steering wheel. Then he called Lily. She didn't answer—like most normal people—so he left her a voice mail.

Then he told his phone to pull up his in-case-of-emergency angry playlist and seethed as the bass shook the windows of his truck. It was going to be a long fucking day.

CHAPTER 25

The later it got, the more irritated Lily grew. She'd hoped Tobin would show up closer to lunchtime, but now it was heading toward late afternoon. He'd left her a voice mail around eleven, saying that he was going to be late because of something—the cell reception had cut out, so it had sounded garbled. If he'd looked at traffic, she thought, maybe they wouldn't be in this mess.

It wasn't that she was impatient to see him, she told herself. She just liked being on time.

Also, she wanted to do one run-through, a practice run. It had taken her a ridiculous amount of time trying to come up with an idea for what they were going to film. After the last session, her viewers seemed really impressed—and, honestly, they were getting just as invested in "shipping" her with Tobin as people on his channel were. They'd said that he was cute, and they were impressed by his makeover.

They'd also started asking how long the two of them had been going out. She planned on addressing the fact that they were *not* a couple in this video, she thought with a nod.

Of course, she'd woken up in his arms, in his bed, just a few days ago.

She closed her eyes as the memory swamped her, her heart rate picking up slightly. It wasn't that they'd slept together, obviously. She had slept *with* him, but not *with* with him. They hadn't had sex. It had just been a long time since she'd slept next to anyone. Even dating Rafael, they hadn't spent the night together all that often. She usually slept with a body pillow, something that she'd snuggle up to, gripping tight, even throwing a leg over.

Maybe, just maybe, it had been a bad idea to test Tobin's "snuggle" proclivities. But he'd been game. It probably shouldn't be shocking that she had turned at some point in the night and clamped onto Tobin in her sleep, her arms wrapping around him like an octopus. And that her traitorous leg had hitched itself over his hip, and she'd buried her face against his shoulder.

Her cheeks burned just thinking about it.

Thankfully, he'd slept like the dead as she got up, changed out of his clothes, slipped into her own clothes, and fled like a university morning-after shame walk. It was ridiculous. She'd left a very brief but polite note, and they'd texted logistics since. He hadn't brought up their sleeping arrangement once. Considering Tobin had no filter, she had to believe that it hadn't affected him at all. With any luck, he never woke up enough to notice her grabby hands and uncharacteristic physicality. Because that would be fodder for way too many jokes and confusion, and frankly, she could not bear it.

That irritation, more with herself than with him, only fed her frustration at his late arrival. She was planning on doing his makeup. It wasn't the most original thing, but she didn't do makeup for men often, and since the menswear video had some good response, she thought that she'd show three different looks: a simple tutorial for guys who were just trying to contour a little or cover blemishes and skin flaws; a more advanced tutorial for guys who were looking for a dramatic change; and finally a full-blown colorful palette, for men who were looking for the full range of what makeup could do, including false eyelashes and bright eye shadows. Nothing muted. Tobin was no doubt going to continue screwing around, making jokes, but she would work around that. And she hated to admit it, but his face would work well with makeup. She'd told him to shave so she would have a blank canvas to work with . . . a bit of a pity, because he really was sexy when he had that shadow of a beard. She wondered what he looked like with an actual full beard.

What are you doing?

She shook her head, chastising herself. She hadn't spent this much time with Tobin, one on one, in . . . well, ever. And it was doing weird things to her head.

Attracted to Tobin. What the hell was the world coming to?

She heard her intercom buzz, and she told Tobin to come up. She opened the door for him, then crossed her arms, tapping her foot a little. "Well, look who decided to show up," she drawled as he walked in.

He toed off his shoes and glared at her, which was a surprise. She was expecting him to be his usual goofy self—maybe sheepishly apologetic. "This wasn't my fault," he said, his voice like a flat slap. "Trust me—spending five hours on the 405 isn't exactly my idea of a good time. Stupid fucking chickens."

"Chickens?" she echoed, then shook her head. "Well, whatever. It just means that this video is going to take even longer. Looking at another late night, I think."

"Goody."

It was weird. She'd never realized how relentlessly cheerful he was . . . until he wasn't. He looked stressed, and irritated, and angry. "Do you not want to do this?" she found herself saying defensively.

"You came to me, remember?" he snapped. "You wanted the video series. You're getting subscribers and increases in your numbers. Does it even matter what I want?" He looked around. "All right, where am I going? How do you want to do this?"

"No," she said. "This is not going to do. This is not how I work."

He turned to her, his expression unreadable.

"Are you telling me I just drove five hours in standstill traffic and now you're just . . ." He made a garbled, choked noise. "Sure, fine, why not? The way today's run? What the hell. It's not like I actually have *work of my own* to do. Why would I? It's not like I actually *do* anything, other than make an asshole of myself on camera, just for the LOLs! Which apparently is so easy, *anyone* can do it, right?"

He sat down on the bench by her front door. She heard him muttering something about the airport, and she blinked. He seemed to be having a little bit of a breakdown. "Tobin . . ."

"Shit, I should be working on my racist stereotypical Asian voice and seeing how I can stockpile playthroughs before going on fucking tour," he muttered to himself, trying to pull his sneakers back on and then untangling the knots in the laces. "I mean, it doesn't really matter that I'm having trouble coming up with video ideas. Just keep pushing through! That's how this works. That's the only way to stay on top, right?"

She blinked. She had never, ever seen him so upset. She sat down next to him on the small bench by her doorway. *"Tobin!"*

He glared at her. *"What?"*

She took a deep breath. Then she leaned forward, slowly. He just stared at her.

She waited for him to pull away or snap at her.

He didn't.

So she kissed him.

She didn't know what possessed her. It was a quick brush of her lips over his, barely enough to taste. Enough to make her heart trip-hammer in her chest, though. Then she pulled back. "Sorry," she said quickly. "I just . . . you wouldn't listen, and you seem to be in a really bad mood, and . . ."

He stared at her like he'd never seen her before, his dark-amber eyes wide.

She sighed, sitting on the bench next to him. "When I said that's not how I work, I didn't mean for you to go home. I mean, you're obviously having a bad day, and that's going to translate to the video. You know that. So it's best that we not just dive into filming. Why don't you . . ."

She bit her lip, thinking. "I don't know. Are you hungry? I have some protein bowls in the fridge, or some cheese and crackers, or we could order some delivery? Or maybe, um, a quick drink? I have . . . um, water. And some pomegranate juice. And I have vodka in the freezer—Stoli Razberi, sorry, but it'll get the job done. Oh! I might have some tequila floating around somewhere."

He kept staring.

"Or we could, uh, go . . . for a walk?" She never went for walks. But right now, he looked like she had hit him with a wrench, which was marginally better than him being pissed as hell, but still not a huge improvement. "Blink twice if you can hear me," she finally said, joking weakly.

He was silent for another long second.

Then he leaned over and kissed her back.

Only in his case, it wasn't a brief kiss for shock purposes. He moved in slowly, giving her plenty of time to pull away or say no. Which, honestly, she probably should have done. She wasn't sure what made her freeze, watching him come closer, until his features blurred and she closed her eyes and felt his lips moving against hers, first slowly, then with increasing pressure. His hand cupped her face, holding her steady.

Then his tongue brushed against her lower lip, and she kind of gasped, and then . . .

Oh, holy hell, *then*.

They went from leaning next to each other to wrapped up in each other. He moved, buried his hands in the hair at the back of her head, holding her close to him. Her hands clutched at his shoulders, pulling him closer to her like she wanted to pull him inside her. Their tongues danced along each other, their mouths moving ravenously, almost desperately.

She wasn't quite sure when she shifted her weight—when he tugged her, so they weren't sitting side by side on the bench, but she was suddenly straddling him. His hands moved to her back, supporting her, and now her hands were in his hair as their heads tilted back and forth and the kiss turned feral. She could barely recognize the sounds she was making. And her hips tilting forward . . .

Just as suddenly as they'd started, they broke apart, staring at each other this time in silent disbelief.

"Um." She felt out of breath, like she'd just spent an hour on the treadmill, and she quickly clambered off him. "Oh."

Should I apologize? Say that it won't happen again?

Drag him to the bedroom?

She bit her lip. She had lost. Her damned. Mind.

He swallowed visibly, his eyes looking wild. His lips looked a little puffy. It actually looked sexy as hell.

Not again. She cleared her throat.

"A shower." His words came out raspy, with this deep timbre that just *did* things to her.

Her eyes widened. "Pardon?" she squeaked.

He smirked, but it was tight, almost pained. "I . . . um, could really use a shower. It's the best way for me to get rid of a bad mood. I brought a couple changes of clothes just in case. Once I'm out, then we can get started filming. Sound good?"

"Sounds good," she agreed, feeling a little weak.

He winked at her. "Oh, and I was thinking of something. A twist on your video."

"Oh?" Her voice sounded reedy to her own ears, and she still felt the aftereffects of shock.

"Yeah. When you're doing makeup on me, I thought I could do makeup on you at the same time."

She startled. She'd never let anyone else do her makeup—and she had *lots* of makeup artist friends who would be more than qualified. "That'll be confusing," she hedged. "Visually, I mean. How would that even work?"

"I think it'll be funny as hell," he countered, his voice mild and bemused. "We can practice it. But I think that it'll be less static, give me something to do, and show us both involved rather than just you doing something to me, or a variation on the makeover video." He waited a beat, then said quietly, "I like to be an active participant in things."

She meant to say something cutting, but her throat had gone dry. And that kiss. Oh, holy hell, that kiss.

"We can practice it," she said with as much dignity as she could scrape together.

He stroked her cheek. "Just give me a minute," he said, then headed for her bathroom.

She watched him walk away, duffel bag in hand. She noticed belatedly that he was wearing a T-shirt and shorts. As usual, he looked . . . she sighed.

God. He looked *good*.

She was not going to survive this, she realized. She had to get some distance between them. Because she had just made out with Tobin Bui, desperately wanted to go even further, and the world officially made no sense anymore.

CHAPTER 26

Lily had set up in the living room, rather than her claustrophobic bedroom. The natural light combined with her other lights would be better for what she had in mind, and it'd give her more room to work on his face—and, apparently, for him to work on hers, if that's what he really wanted. She thought about it like the makeover: do the makeup tutorial with the camera focused on his face, and then let him see the reveal in the mirror after she was done. She imagined that he'd do the same to her. She'd originally had three looks in mind—she wasn't sure what he had in mind. Maybe she'd just let him do one?

She sighed. He was so impulsive, so used to doing things on the fly. She wasn't sure how he managed that. Still, she remembered his outburst from when he walked in. He was upset about someone not taking his work seriously. His agents? His family?

Her?

Guilt stabbed at her. She nibbled at her lower lip. He drove her crazy, but he'd never really been mean spirited. And while she'd raged at him in the past, she'd never done anything that deliberately hurt him. Other than perhaps kicking him in the balls in the pool that one time—she hadn't actually meant to connect, but he'd moved forward at the last moment.

And now, with her new *awareness* of him—she found herself not wanting to hurt him at all, in any way.

She took a deep breath. She had to focus on the video. It was her career, and she'd come too far to lose focus now. He'd add the humor, she'd do the looks, and . . . well. That'd be that.

"Thanks," Tobin said as he emerged from the bathroom. His hair was still damp, sticking up a little, since he'd obviously towel-dried it. He was wearing his shorts again but no shirt, and his feet were bare. "This okay? I, um, was wearing the T-shirt that is safe to get makeup stuff on, but after those hours in the car . . ." He grimaced. "Kinda sweaty and uncomfortable."

"Oh. Um . . . let's throw that in the washer while we're rehearsing," she said. "I've got a load of wash to do anyway. That way, by the time we've got the video practiced, it'll be off and the mic won't pick it up."

He produced a bundle of wadded-up clothes, and she threw them in with her clothes, getting her small stacked washer going. Then she turned to find him studying her setup curiously.

"So we're filming out here?" he asked. "Not too much echo?"

We're not going to talk about the kissing, then. That was probably a good idea, actually. God knew, it was running through her head on a constant loop, and she wasn't sure what would happen if they faced what had happened head on. At best, her hands would shake like crazy while she tried to apply makeup. At worst—well, she wasn't quite sure what the worst thing that could happen would be.

Either he'd want to do more, or he'd want to pretend it never happened. She wasn't sure which possibility disturbed her more.

"We'll have to test it," she finally answered. "The lights and mics and stuff. That's part of what the rehearsal's for."

"That makes sense." He looked amused. "I don't know that I've ever met any YouTuber that does a full rehearsal before filming, though. They usually just go through, fix things as they go, then smooth it all out in editing. Why not do that?"

She gestured for him to sit down on a chair that she'd dragged over to the little breakfast table she normally had out on her balcony.

She then fluttered around, getting out the assortment of makeup she'd planned to use for the shoot. "I know it might feel like overkill," she said. "My friend Mikki makes fun of me all the time for being so finicky about it. But I just like to have a sense of where I'm going and what I'm doing. I hate flailing around, and I really, *really* hate trying to edit a video that seems like it's entirely comprised of rambling. I'd rather just plan, and practice, so I have good footage I can work with, right from the start."

"My entire life feels like rambling," Tobin remarked with a smirk. "But I don't mind it. A lot of times, that's how I stumble on creative stuff. Also, I hate redoing the same things over and over. It makes me fidget. I get bored and kind of stressed . . . like all the energy's been sucked out of whatever idea I came up with."

She wanted to bristle. Ordinarily, she would. But after seeing his little freak-out in her foyer, she instead tilted her head. "So you have ADHD?" she found herself asking.

He blinked. "You are, like, the queen of non sequiturs, you know?"

"Sorry." She felt a blush heating her cheeks, and she set up the camera, turning it on and checking the light levels. He was looking at her curiously and possibly with a little embarrassment.

"Why do you ask?"

"Because when you say stuff like that, I kind of . . . uh, take it personally," she said. "Like anybody who does what I do is boring and stuck up and . . . I don't know. Lifeless."

"What? No!" He looked appalled. "Hell no. I just know what works for *me*, Lils. You need to work with what's best for you. Besides, we've got very different audiences . . ."

"Which seem to have some overlap," she pointed out with a little smile.

"Yeah, that's been fun. But I think that it's not bad. You're giving me structure and new ideas. I'd like to think I'm injecting a little spontaneity into your stuff and maybe helping you loosen up a little. That doesn't mean you're . . . what? Boring, or stuck up, or lifeless."

Lily shrugged. "I know we're really different."

"You've been one of my friends for years," he said. "I know you always had problems with being part of the Nerd Herd. I don't know why, but it bothered you."

She blinked at him. "You really don't know why?"

He shook his head, studying her.

"Because people thought we were geeks," she said. Did he really not get it?

"Age of the geek, baby," he said with a quicksilver grin. "Not a bad thing."

"Trust me, they weren't thinking it in a meta, 'hey I watch Marvel movies' kind of way," she said, and she couldn't help it . . . her tone turned scathing. "They were thinking that we weren't good enough."

"You were in all honors and AP classes, you had over a 4.0 GPA, you were in National Honor Society and California Scholarship Federation, and you got into UCLA," he said, enunciating every syllable. "How the hell is that not good enough?"

"Yeah, well, it got me into UCLA, but it didn't get me to parties," she shot back. "It didn't make me good enough to be friends with them, did it? Certainly not good enough to date anybody! I was an outcast. We all were outcasts!"

He looked at her, and it wasn't pity. It was . . . disappointment.

"We had each other," he said, almost under his breath. "That was what I never understood. Why did you give a shit what they thought, when you had us?"

She sighed. This was not a good way to start their video. The last thing she wanted was to drag up the past. But here they were. "They were gorgeous," she said. "Popular. They . . . I don't know. They had everything I wanted, or anybody *could* want. They were the definition of success."

"If they didn't want to hang out with you, why would you want to be around them?" he pressed. "Again: you had us."

"Yeah, but we just sort of . . . you know."

"No," he said, his voice dangerously low. "I really don't."

"We didn't hang out because we liked each other, necessarily," she said. "We were friends because nobody else wanted to be friends with us."

His eyes widened, his jaw dropping a little. She immediately felt like shit.

"Okay, that's too harsh," she said. "I just . . . I don't know. Emily and Tam were definitely my best friends, and I know they cared about me. But at the same time, I do wonder what would've happened if the popular kids decided they wanted to welcome them. Would they have turned their backs on us?"

"Would you have?" Tobin asked quietly.

Lily grimaced. "No! No. Of course not."

"You sure about that?"

She frowned. "I wouldn't. I think I could've managed both. In fact, I think I could've shown them how amazing a lot of us were."

Tobin still looked suspicious, and annoyed.

"Now, I'd like to prove to them that I don't need them," she said.

"Is that why you're into beauty YouTubing?" he asked. "Because you've got something to prove?"

She winced. Was it?

"I like makeup. I like doing what I do," she said, even though there was an ugly undercurrent that she didn't want to investigate. "And speaking of . . . let's get to this, shall we?"

He nodded. "All right," he said. "But I'm not letting you off that easily."

She sighed. Of course he wouldn't.

***

They'd done a test run of filming putting makeup on him. It was less of a full rehearsal than he was expecting, thankfully. She tested the light and the angles of how it'd be filmed, and she showed him what she was planning on doing: putting makeup on him, with him facing the camera and not being able to see what she was doing in the mirror, then the reveal would be him looking at the effects afterward. They decided to do two versions for him, two for her. Not that he had a lot of experience with any of this, but he knew he could make it lively and funny, if he could just get out of his head.

This was what he didn't like about doing videos . . . the not being sure. And he was still mulling over what she'd said about the Herd. Which, he supposed, was right there in the name—and he'd be lying if he said that felt like he completely fit in either. His joking behavior was often mistaken for an almost preternatural confidence, but really, it was just impulsivity run amok, as well as some overcompensating coping mechanisms. He did things that were kind of crazy, and laughed with others even when part of him felt anxious or embarrassed by what was going on. It took a toll. He was better now, he thought. He knew his audience, he knew his friends, he knew what he was doing, mostly. He was doing what he enjoyed, for people who appreciated it.

Lily, he realized, was doing it to show a bunch of girls who would genuinely never give a shit that she was past it . . . and ultimately only proving that really, she kinda wasn't.

"Hi there," Lily said with that super-chill, super-smooth, almost meditative voice that she only used in videos. "EverLily here, with another collaboration with Tobin Bui, a.k.a. GoofyBui. Hi, Tobin!"

"Hi," he said, smiling at what he felt was her silliness. He waved at the camera.

"Last time I collaborated with Tobin, we gave him a makeover, which a lot of you seemed to appreciate," she said, and he wiggled his eyebrows. She rolled her eyes at him, but in a subdued way, not in a "you're pissing me off" way. Well, it was early on in the video—he'd wait for that and maybe not court it for a change. "So today, we're going to try doing two looks for guys who might be interested in trying out makeup. We're not talking drag, by the way—that's something different. This is just an appreciation of men who might want to try cosmetics but aren't sure how."

"And I," Tobin added, trying to match her serious yet tranquilizing tone, "am going to try my hand at being a makeup artist and doing Lily's makeup."

She looked a little nervous at this, but she kept her zen smile in place. "So, first, we're going to try some simple contouring, and a tiny bit of eyeliner. Tobin's got these great light-brown eyes, kind of unusual, and a little bit of eyeliner will really make them pop."

He was startled. "I have great eyes?"

"The color's great," she said, and he still grinned. She cleared her throat. "You washed up, right?"

"Yup. I used that fancy face wash and all that you told me to."

"It just helps to have a blank canvas. And a skin-care regime is important," she said, more to the camera than to him. She then pumped some lotion-type stuff into her palm and rubbed her fingertips over his face. He closed his eyes, which forced him to focus on the feel of her hands on his skin. She wasn't rough: it was more like a little massage for his face, and it was really relaxing. He sighed a little, leaning into her touch.

"Can I open my eyes?"

"If you want," she said. She had a few little bottles of concealer stuff. She looked like a cross between a painter and a mad scientist as she took his arm and blended a light color and a dark color. "Most people don't have the exact shade of foundation to match their skin, although with brands like Fenty and other BIPOC-owned cosmetics companies finally making a broad spectrum of flesh tones, and major makeup brands jumping on the bandwagon, it's getting easier," she said. "Also, you want to find something that warms your skin, and you want to think about what it's going to look like in the lighting you're going to be in. If you're stuck in gross fluorescent lighting, it's going to look gross no matter what you do. And if you apply stuff in crappy bathroom lighting and then go outside, it's going to look different."

"How do you learn all this stuff?"

"Lots of trial and error," she admitted. She mixed stuff on the back of his hand before she was satisfied, then took this weird egg-shaped sponge thing and sopped it up. "Lots of YouTube videos, too, of course. But really, it's all a matter of just diving in there and trying it."

He chuckled when she started rubbing his face with the egg thing. "Hey! That tickles!"

"Stay still," she said, grabbing his chin and forcing his head to stay in one place. He shut his eyes and felt her move the sponge over his skin. He could smell her perfume again. He took a deep breath. There, underneath the perfume or soap or whatever, was her smell—a mix of girl and something spicy. He found himself wishing that he could lean forward farther, bury his face in the crook of her neck where it met her shoulder, and just inhale that scent.

Pervy Roomba, he mocked himself.

Which was probably stupid, especially considering they still hadn't addressed the whole "we just kissed" thing. And not just kissed. Practically gotten busy on a low bench by the front door.

He cleared his throat and forced himself to think of something else so he didn't start springing wood. That would be both awkward and only delay the video more, and frankly, it was going to be longer than he'd meant for it to be.

"All right. For contouring, you want to use a slightly darker foundation, and apply it in these places, depending on what you're trying to accomplish," she said, instructing in that gentle voice. He liked the sound of it, but he couldn't help but think that he liked what he considered her normal voice better. When she wasn't trying so hard, wasn't putting up the front. Even when she was pissed at him, he realized, and smiled.

"Don't smile," she chastised, and his eyebrows went up.

"What? Why not?"

"Your dimples," she said. "Messes up my ability to get even coverage."

He winked at her, and was surprised to see her cheeks go pink. "All right. Bossy."

She stuck out her tongue at him and made it that much harder for him to keep a straight face. He didn't like the eyeliner bit—sharp objects by his eyeballs freaked him out—but otherwise it really wasn't that big a deal.

"Okay, look in the mirror," she said, turning him, and he did as instructed. To his surprise . . .

"Wow," he said, turning his head this way and that, looking at the results. "I have a jawline! I mean, I had a jawline, but this is like . . . I mean, I could carve a wooden bowl with this sucker. And cheekbones! Look out, Tom Hiddleston!"

She shook her head, laughing.

"Not sure about the liner," he admitted. "Just because I hate having pointy things by my eye."

"You could use a brush," she said. "And it's probably more dramatic than you particularly would want to go with—it's a little emo. For you, I mean. Not for other people."

He quirked an eyebrow at her. "Oh, you think? You know me that well?"

"I do know you that well," she said with a smug smile, and he grinned back at her.

"Okay, your turn," he said, rubbing his hands together maniacally. She looked . . . concerned.

When they'd been rehearsing, she showed him the sheer volume of makeup she had. Some of it was obviously expensive, things she'd purchased because she really liked it. Other stuff was things she'd either received to test or received at parties or promotions. He'd deliberately picked things that were different from her usual subdued, classic, sophisticated palette. He also picked things he figured she wouldn't mind losing if he used them up. "All right, all set."

He knew exactly fuck all when it came to makeup, but he had helped some people with cosplay before, both for videos and just for conventions they'd attended. "So, Lily. This may take a while. Why don't you tell me why you got into makeup?" he said, just to provide some patter. He took a brush and grabbed a tray of pressed eye shadow powders. "I always imagined it had to do with your family."

She blinked. "I, um, don't usually talk about my family."

He wasn't sure if that was a warning or not, so he plowed forward. They could always edit it out afterward. "I think it's important to keep some parts of my life private too," he said, coaxing her a little, "but I've found that my audience likes to learn about me a little more. It makes it more personal, gives us more of a connection."

Lily bit her lip, something he found distracting and attractive. Damn, her lips were full.

A fact he was now well acquainted with.

She took a deep breath. "Well, my family owns an import-export business," she said carefully. "And my mother owned a dress store and a beauty salon, really high end, connected with a spa, back when they lived in Ponto Beach. I think I learned about makeup and clothes from my time at the stores."

He continued to pile on the makeup. Then he took another brush and mixed some lip gloss with the eye shadow he'd just used.

"Uh, that's not lipstick," she pointed out.

"It's close enough. Will you let me work?"

She grumbled but quieted. Then he painted her lips. He left her cheeks alone except for some contouring. Then he turned her. "Ta-da!"

She blinked. "What the heck am I?" she said, the chill slipping out of her voice as she stared at herself in bafflement.

"Goth Lolita," he said. "You didn't have black lipstick, so I improvised."

She basically had charcoal and black eye shadow, from her lashes to her eyebrows, and he'd tried to draw those batwing things, sort of like Neil Gaiman's Death from the *Sandman* comics. She looked harsh. And hot, he admitted.

She blinked. "It's not that bad," she said. "All right. Now we wash this off, and we'll try the next round. Okay?"

He nodded. They continued in that vein. She painted him like a rainbow, using what she called the PEACOCK palette, apparently something she was reviewing. "It's . . . really . . . bright," he said. "Yikes. I mean, I am sure there are a lot of people that can really rock this look, but I look like something out of *Splatoon*."

"I am a better makeup artist than that," she said haughtily, but a smile flickered at the corners of her lips.

"And the fake eyelashes . . . good grief. How do you wear them all the time?"

"You get used to them."

"Feels like I've got ten pounds sitting on my eyelids." Actually, now that he'd said that, he felt totally sleepy.

"Do you want to skip doing me?" she said, and he couldn't help it . . . he snickered like a twelve-year-old, even as his body went a tiny bit tighter.

"Nope. Still doing you," he said with just enough emphasis that her eyes went wide and she smacked his shoulder lightly. He got the makeup for her ready, covering her face with white, then painting those full lips red. "This is going to be fun."

"What about you?" she asked, looking up when he told her to so he could do the liner. "How did you get into YouTube?"

He shrugged. "I just really liked watching gamers, and I kept falling into rabbit holes when I was supposed to be studying," he said. "I mean, I knew it'd be a long shot, and that it would mean a lot of hard work. But I just loved it. I love the videos. I love my audience. It's a hell of a lot of fun."

"Yeah, I think so too," she said quietly.

They kept talking, until he was finally done. And then he turned her, showing off his handiwork.

She blinked. "And this is . . . ?"

"Pennywise! The clown? From *It*?"

She still looked baffled.

"Oh my God. Okay, I am totally making you watch that at some point," he said, shaking his head. "How do you not know *It*? It's one of the scariest movies in years!"

"I don't watch horror."

"We'll see about that," he said, rolling his eyes. They looked at each other, flanked in the mirror. He looked like a tropical bird; she looked like a serial-killing alien clown.

"Well . . . that'll do for today," she said, after doing a sign-off. They looked at the clock. "It's seven," she said.

He sighed. They went and washed off the makeup again, and his skin felt weird after all the washing and then makeup and then washing. He felt tired, and hungry, and emotionally exhausted like he usually felt after a video, whether it had gone well or not. Most people thought it was just goofing around in front of a camera, but being "on" required more energy than it seemed. "I guess I'll get going."

She tapped on her phone. "Looks like there's another accident on the 405," she said. "Maybe . . . maybe it'd be better to wait."

He looked at her, surprised. Then not, because of course she was going to look at traffic and weather. She was organized that way, prepared. "I guess I could . . ."

"Want to grab something to eat?" she said. "Or have something delivered?"

He tilted his head, kicking around something smartass to say. Then he just smiled.

"I'd like that."

CHAPTER 27

Tobin decided to take Lily to a nice restaurant. He still felt bad after the whole In-N-Out debacle, and besides . . . he wanted to spend more time with her, without work in the way.

He tried not to focus on *why* he wanted that.

They went to a little French bistro that had opened up in Westwood, a charming place with small marble-topped café tables and exposed brick walls, painted white cabinets, and displays of rustic cookware interspersed with plants. The menu was in French, or at least the titles were, and the actual food was delicious. He got a Thai chicken sandwich with something intriguingly called a "Thai caramel drizzle" as well as papaya slaw and a lemongrass aioli, and even indulged in a side of truffle fries. Lily went with the roasted salmon with arugula, pickled shallots, and remoulade but indulged in a cup of pumpkin bisque beforehand, as well as stealing several of his fries.

"I need to edit, obviously, but I think today went well," Lily said. "Only two more to go—one of mine, one of yours."

That caused a pang. "I think it's been a good idea," Tobin said.

"It's been fun," she remarked, swiping another one of his fries. "Honestly, filming with you has gone so much more smoothly than I would've thought."

He couldn't help laughing. "I wasn't expecting it either, necessarily, but your shock is just this side of impolite."

She reddened, then rolled her eyes. "Ha ha. I wouldn't be surprised if the Herd in town had money on whether or not I'd murder you before the series was over. Like, some kind of box system where people bet on which episode of the series would finally push me over the edge."

"Nonsense," he said, waited a beat, then grinned. "It wasn't just the townies. Hayden set it up on the Slack channel for everybody to vote."

"Damn it!" Lily laughed, shaking her head. "And don't tell me: they also had another running bet of whether or not the two of us would . . . you know."

"You know . . . what?" he repeated.

She huffed out a little embarrassed chuckle. "Hook up."

He felt the tips of his ears heat and took a bite of his sandwich to buy himself some time. "Um . . ."

"Oh, God, they *did*," she breathed, eyes going wide.

"Apparently that particular bet has been going on for years," he said, feeling sheepish. "Way before the Slack channel. I don't know if that helps or not."

"I don't know either," she admitted.

"On the plus side," he added, "we've outlasted most of the bids. So that's something?"

"It's just so weird. We have *never* . . . you know." She was blushing now, too, but grinning. "I've never understood the draw of the whole enemies-to-lovers dynamic, anyway."

"*Enemies* might be a trifle strong," he said. "I'd like to think that we're friends. By this point, at least."

She looked contemplative, nodding as she flaked away salmon and nibbled it delicately. "Friends," she agreed, with a tiny lopsided smile. "That's also weird."

"Well, at the very least, we're good collaborators," he pointed out.

"That we are," she agreed, but the shock was still evident.

"There's that surprise again," he said with a grin of his own, nudging her with one foot.

"I don't know. Beauty influencer and game geek. It's not intuitive."

"We're not that different, though," he said, and he wasn't quite sure why he was making his case; at least, he wasn't sure why he was putting it so strongly. "We were friends back in the day—even if you felt that it was by default."

"I never should have said that. It was shitty," she said, looking morose.

"No. I mean, you can't help how you feel about things," he quickly added.

"I was just so angry at being . . . discounted, you know? For these weird reasons. I knew I could fit in if they'd just have given me a chance."

"So because we didn't make you work for it, it didn't count as much," he said. He wanted to ask it as a question, but figured it'd be better to just make it a statement, as gentle and nonjudgmental as possible.

"I guess." She pushed the arugula around on the plate. Then she brightened. "So . . . next video at your place?"

He winced. If anything was designed to bring down his mood, it'd be that. "Um . . . yes?"

She looked at him with sympathy. "So. You wanna talk to me about the whole freak-out?" she said quietly. "You're having trouble coming up with content?"

"Not exactly *trouble*, per se," he temporized. "I think I'm just tired. I've been doing this for a few years at this point without a break. I mean, I'm not trying to say that I'm special. I know what it takes to make it as far as we have in the community, and I know it's about putting up more and more original content. It's just . . . I don't know. I feel a little worn out." He grinned humorlessly, toasting her with his glass of fresh-squeezed lavender lemonade. "Of course, who the hell am I to complain, right?"

That came out more bitter than he'd intended it to.

"You can't help how you feel about things," she reminded him, parroting his words back to him with a small smile. "And I'm not going to judge you. I get it. It takes more than people realize, to do what we do."

That. There it was, exactly. "I mean, I talk shop with Shawn and some other YouTubers," he said slowly. "But I don't want them to feel like I'm complaining. And they usually just want to fix the problem. Even Josh, who is like a brother to me, just wants to brainstorm a solution and ride to the rescue. But sometimes the answer seems to just be, you know, sitting with it. Does that make sense?"

She sighed, pushing her plate away, but finishing the fries. "I don't know. I've never been what I'd consider particularly creative," she said.

"You've come up with years' worth of content," Tobin challenged. "Like *clockwork*."

"But that's just the thing," she said. "They've been challenges from other people, or whatever. Testing new palettes. Coming up with looks. But nothing truly original or groundbreaking. Nothing to help me stand out in the crowd . . . and it's a big crowd at this point."

"But you've been a success."

She shrugged, smiling a little. "I'm a hard worker," she said, and there was an edge of determination in her voice. "I wasn't the smartest in school, either, but I sure as hell studied and put in the work, more than anybody I knew. That was what mattered."

He nodded. He did know. She regularly studied on the bus, over weekends, even during the trips to and from Academic Team. And yes, it was geeky as hell that they were on the Academic Team together.

Note to self: Maybe do a trivia-night thing? Or a grown-up academic bowl?

He sighed. No. That would probably not work.

"I think that you're a good content creator," he said, because she looked sad and because he believed it. "I mean, I'm no expert on beauty, obviously. But I think that you're positive, you're never mean spirited,

210

and you're just calming. I would watch the shit out of your videos, just to chill out."

She smiled, and it was warm and appreciative. "Thanks," she said. "And I'd watch your videos just to feel better. You're silly, but you're also never nasty or condescending. I hate that, I really do. But it always seems to get ahead."

He nodded. He hated that as well.

They wound up shutting the restaurant down, and he paid for dinner over Lily's objections, leaving a generous tip. He felt tense and wasn't looking forward to the drive back. He also wasn't looking forward to brainstorming another video for the two of them. He felt . . . empty. Like a jug of milk that had a hole in it and just left a mess and no satisfaction whatever.

Or something. He was even too tired to metaphor.

"So you're going to edit tomorrow and post the next day? Or end of day tomorrow?" he asked as they went back to her place. He accompanied her up to get his clothes out of the dryer.

She nodded. "I'll edit tonight. Even if we didn't plan that much, we didn't ramble, and it should be really straightforward. I think it should go pretty well—we've got some good material." She went to the dryer and patted the clothes. "Still a little damp. You okay to wait another half hour, maybe?"

He groaned before he could stop himself. "Sorry, I'm just wiped out," he admitted. "I mean . . . it's not a big deal. Maybe you can just bring me the clothes when we see each other again?"

"All right. And that should be . . . Thursday? Friday?"

He nodded, frowning. He didn't have his calendar on him, but that seemed to be what they'd agreed upon.

God, how was he going to come up with something by Thursday?

He startled a little when Lily put a hand on his shoulder. "Um . . . this is a little weird, but . . . are you okay?"

"Tired," he said. It was becoming his go-to phrase. "Just kind of tired."

"I don't think you should be driving if you're this tired," she said, and she genuinely looked worried.

He took a deep breath and was about to protest but then realized that he was full of shit and chuffed out a breath. "Yeah. I probably shouldn't, actually," he agreed. "I think I haven't been sleeping well lately—just under the gun. A full night's sleep will probably do the trick, y'know?"

"I do that, too, sometimes," she admitted. "I'll go on a spree where I'm working, like, eighteen-hour days, even though I suck when I don't have enough sleep, and then after a few months, I just need to take a day and sleep for twelve hours and then spend the rest of the time watching the fluffiest rom-coms I can find."

He laughed. "I would not take you for the rom-com type," he admitted. "I don't suppose you know of any hotels around here, do you?"

She frowned. "I never use any," she said, and he started to google it . . . only to stop short when she cleared her throat. "You could stay here, if you wanted."

He blinked, his finger frozen on the cell phone screen. "Here?" he croaked.

"I mean, we've shared a bed, and it hasn't been that big a deal," she said. "Also, it brings up my next point. How about we film the next video for my channel instead? That'll give you a bit more time to brainstorm something new."

Relief crashed into him like a wave. "Really? You mean it?"

She smiled brightly, nodding. "Sure. No problem. Why not?"

He hugged her. "You," he said, smooching her cheek, "are awesome. Thank you."

She looked away, a blush painting her cheekbones. "Um. Don't mention it."

Of course, the last time they'd shared a bed was *before* their epic make-out session with their hands all over each other and their mouths devouring each other and . . .

He stopped that train of thought immediately. He didn't know what Lily was expecting, if she was expecting anything. They hadn't discussed what had happened. Maybe she wanted to pretend it never happened. Maybe this was just friendly concern and convenience. Her couches were these artsy, flat things that had about as much padding as a wetsuit, more design than utility. Still, he could always crash on one. Or the *floor*, if need be.

He wondered abruptly if he was making a big mistake. But looking at Lily, he knew he was going to go for it anyway, and damn the consequences.

CHAPTER 28

Lily was nervous. This seemed so stupid. When she'd made the offer, it was with a few things in mind: the fact that their last video idea had come in the middle of the night, sort of turnabout for him offering her a place to stay when she was in Ponto Beach. Who knew, maybe he'd come up with an idea for a video in the middle of the night again. And even if he didn't, she was saving him money on a hotel . . . even if he did have to share a bed.

Sure. That kiss had nothing to do with your offer.

She frowned, getting herself a glass of water. The thing was, he had plenty of money for a hotel, and there were plenty of places for him to stay in Los Angeles. Nice places. He hadn't been drinking, like she had been. He'd hung out with her and kept her company as she'd edited the video more quickly than any she'd ever done, and she'd posted it before she could overthink it. It wasn't even that late at night, now that she glanced at the clock.

So why *had* she offered for him to, essentially, sleep with her?

You're going to need to talk about that kiss, dammit.

Her cheeks burned. "I'm, um, going to take a shower," she said, rubbing her arm and shifting her weight from one leg to another. "Then I guess I'll, um, turn in?"

"I'm gonna watch a little TV first, if that's okay?" he said. He looked a little wild himself.

You have to talk about it!

She took a shower, taking a bit longer than usual, her body feeling almost oversensitive in the spray. This was, potentially, a colossally bad idea. She was working with him, for God's sake.

Wait. What, exactly, did she want here?

Was she trying to seduce him?

She bit her lip. She'd told Mikki that she was looking for a hookup. Was that what this was? Her long-ignored hormones just pushing their way forward and demanding satisfaction?

She pulled on a pair of sleep shorts and a camisole before wrapping her shoulder-length hair in a towel and quickly patting most of it dry. She sighed, then forced herself back out to the living room.

Tobin wasn't wearing a shirt. He was still wearing his shorts, his feet bare. He was on her uncomfortable but stylish couch, watching some sort of sitcom on the big-screen TV. She forced herself to yawn dramatically, stretching her arms over her head. Unfortunately, this made her camisole ride up slightly, and she quickly dropped her posture, covering her stomach.

"I think I'm going to go to sleep now," she said, but her voice was hesitant.

Is that really what she wanted? His eyes were still fixed on her stomach, that flash of skin, and she felt a corresponding flash of heat.

What the hell was she doing?

She had a plan for everything—what she wanted in life, and how to get it. Why didn't she have a plan now?

"I'm kind of tired myself," he admitted, and her heart started beating wildly. "Guess I'll come to bed too."

He followed her into her bedroom. She felt her breathing quicken and tried desperately to calm herself down. "Do you have a preference for which side you sleep on?" he asked.

She quickly shook her head, and he took the side closest to the door. It felt kind of protective, which seemed ridiculous, but still sent a shivery flutter through her stomach. She climbed in gingerly on the other side of him.

"So. You big spoon this time, or little spoon?"

She knew he was joking, but instead of laughing, her heart sped up a bit. She started to roll over to turn out the light, hoping the darkness would at least hide her confusion, when she heard him sigh. She froze when she felt his hand on her shoulder.

"Lily," he said. "Are we really going to ignore what happened? Because I can if you really want to, but it seems like, all things considered, we might want to talk about the fact that we were all over each other, before we go ahead and share a bed."

She spun to look at him. There was a mix of emotions in his expression: amusement, patience. And hunger. So much that she started to lean forward despite herself.

"Um, we can do more than talk too," he rasped, his eyes widening. "If that's what you want. I'm certainly not gonna say no."

He was putting the ball in her court. She could feel the heat coming off him, and her body wanted to curl against that heat *so* badly she thought she'd go mad with it. She swallowed hard. It would be easy to just have sex with him. They both wanted it; that much was clear.

But what would that mean? She wasn't going to sneak out and leave a note, for God's sake. This was her apartment. And they still had more videos to do.

Besides . . .

What if she didn't want it to just be a hookup?

The thought stunned her momentarily. Bad enough she was attracted to Tobin, but at least it was understandable. He was hot, with his dark eyes and that sexy smile and that *goddamned rumbly voice*, ugh. And if his kisses were any indication, sex with the man was going to be devastating.

But he was kind. He was loyal to his friends. He was understanding and a great listener. He was supportive. He snuggled like he medaled in it at the Olympics. She enjoyed spending time with him and joking over texts with him.

So what if she wanted more than just sex?

"You're thinking too hard," Tobin teased, tucking a lock of hair away from her eyes and behind her ear, then gently stroking along her neck until she shivered. "If you really don't want to talk about it, that's fine. If you don't want to do anything, that's fine. Hell, if you want me to sleep on one of those torture devices you call a couch, I'll be happy to. We don't have to do a damned thing, Lils, I promise. I just . . ." He let out a low, strained laugh. "I really like you. I mean, I've always liked you; we've been friends—one way or another—forever. But . . ."

"But this is different," she whispered. "Isn't it?"

He took a deep breath, then nodded. "It is for me," he said quietly.

"Me too." She pressed a hand to her stomach. "This is so weird."

"I know, right?" He laughed, self-deprecating.

"I want to have sex with you," she blurted out, and his laughter stopped like a needle yanked off a record. "You have *no* idea."

"Oh, trust me, I've got an inkling," he croaked.

"But . . . I don't want to screw things up?" she said, frustrated with herself. "I don't want to just have it, and then have it not . . . matter? I don't want it to be something we fell into accidentally, or felt regrets about afterward. Not just because of the videos but because I don't want to lose you again."

He looked surprised at her comment.

"I'm starting to see just how much I lost when I lost touch with the Nerd Herd," she said, feeling sheepish. "And I never saw you. Not the real you. I don't want to go back to radio silence."

"You won't," he said, stroking her cheek. "I promise."

"So . . . maybe we could . . . take things slow?" she mused.

His hand dropped, and she felt its loss. Then he looked at the two of them in bed and burst out laughing. "Um . . ."

"I didn't plan this, okay? I just blurted stuff out, and said, 'Let's share a bed,' and here we are," she grumbled. "This is why I try to think things through!" She buried her face in her hands.

"Hey, hey, hey." He tugged her hands down, then leaned forward and kissed her—a soft little kiss that was over before she could really enjoy it. "We can go as slow as you like."

"Really?"

He quirked an eyebrow at her. She had no idea how outrageously sexy an eyebrow could be.

"Remember that whole seven-minutes-in-heaven fiasco?"

She smiled, shaking her head. "Maybe not the time to remind me that you puked on my shoes, Tobin."

"I paid Josh twenty dollars to rig that game for me."

She gaped at him. "Are you serious?"

"*And* I took that Goldschläger shot to give myself liquid courage to do what I'd wanted to do for a while," he said. "Afterward, I convinced myself that I wasn't into you, or that it wouldn't have mattered if we had kissed, because nothing else would've happened. But yeah, Lily. I've wanted you for well over a decade." His lopsided smile made her stomach swoop. "I'm playing a long game here, so take your time."

She swallowed against the sudden dryness in her throat. Then she turned off the light, and turned back to him.

"I don't like to rush into sex," she said in the darkness, before reaching for him under the covers. Her hands brushed against his chest, and she heard him issue a low groan as she moved toward him, swimming over the sheets until she was flush against his body. "Not when it matters."

"And this matters?" His breath was hot against her ear, and she could feel his heart racing under her palm.

"Yes," she murmured against his lips. "It matters a lot."

"Damn right it does," he agreed and then stopped talking entirely as his mouth plundered hers.

She couldn't remember being kissed like this before . . . like it was the most engrossing act in the world. Most of the guys she'd been with—and that was not a terribly long list—were all right. A few were sloppy or clumsy, but their enthusiasm made up for their shortcomings. This was like a master class in kissing. His mouth was agile and expressive and *oh my God*. They were on their sides, writhing against each other with increasing frustration. He wasn't going for the obvious, her boobs or her ass. Instead, his fingertips were dragging along her back, smoothing under her sleep shirt and pressing her against him. She mimicked the action by winding her arms around his neck, holding him tight as her tongue tangled with his. He sucked on her lower lip, and she let out a little cry of pleasure, melting against him.

Her thighs were pressed together against the dampness that was quickly growing. She could feel his hardness straining against his shorts, poking against her hip. She moved to cradle it against herself, and they both gasped.

"Okay, that's not fair," he said, his voice shaking.

"You know," she said, her breathing ragged. "Slowness? Totally overrated."

In the low light filtering through her bedroom window, she could see his eyes gleam, and he looked ready to pounce. Then, to her shock, he actually threw himself flat on his back, making the blankets tent with his erection. He seemed to be gritting his teeth.

"It matters," he said. "*You* matter."

She bit her lip. He was right. That had been her boundary, and she knew that if she gave in to her hormones now, she'd probably regret it later. He knew it too. And he was making sure that he respected that boundary.

It made her fall for him, just that little bit more.

I am in trouble here.

CHANNEL: *Everlily*

Subscribers: 5.2M
Video views: 263M
Most recent video: "Makeup for Guys (and by Guys) Featuring GoofyBui"

RECENT COMMENTS:

Hai Mai: I can't believe you haven't seen It! It's really good.

Amanda Parker: This is the content I want. Guy make-overs, guys in makeup.

T3Ch Warrior: I would never wear makeup, but Goofy, you got skills. She looks just like Pennywise.

Breathless Belle: KISS KISS FALL IN LOVE

CHAPTER 29

The next morning, despite getting only a few hours of sleep, Tobin woke up feeling like he'd shotgunned five energy drinks. That might have something to do with the beautiful woman he'd woken up with. And the fact that he kinda had blue balls, but so be it.

She matters.

He didn't know what it meant . . . yet. As in, would they be in a relationship? And if so, how would that work? Long distance? Regular commuting? Somebody moving? And how would they handle their channels? Their collaboration had been a huge success, professionally speaking, but he knew how protective Lily was about her brand. It might be daunting for her to suddenly go from EverLily to "The Lily & Tobin Show" in the eyes of some viewers. They'd need to talk logistics, boundaries, compromises.

That said, he knew in his gut that it would be worth it.

So he'd gotten up, taken a cold shower, and was now wearing clean clothes and eating a bowl of oatmeal with blueberries at Lily's kitchen table. She walked out wearing a pink T-shirt with a hedgehog holding a buttercup on it, and a pair of cotton shorts. Her hair was loose around her shoulders. She bit her lip, sending him a lopsided, shy smile that made his body tighten almost painfully.

Without speaking, he reached out for her, and she went to his side, blushing slightly. "Good morning," she said, before leaning down and kissing him.

He knew he shouldn't get too worked up or press too much, but the kiss went a few minutes beyond "good morning" and almost into "let's head back to bed." He stopped himself before it went too far, leaving her with eyes hazy with pleasure.

"So. Video today," he said, sounding like he'd swallowed a frog. He coughed. "I really appreciate your patience, by the way, with how long it's been taking me to come up with ideas. Hopefully it won't throw the viewers off too much when there's two videos back to back on your channel, instead of alternating like we'd planned."

"I was thinking about that," she said slowly. "I mean . . . it's not really original, per se, but I thought of a video that might fit better on your channel than it would on mine."

"You did?" He hadn't expected that. "What'd you have in mind? Not the TikTok dance challenges," he added with a wink to take any sting out of his judgment. "Although at this point, I guess I ought to be more open minded."

"This is pretty basic," she said, tugging at the bottom of her shirt. She looked hesitant, and he just wanted to encourage her. "Remember how, when you were doing my makeup, I told you I don't like to watch horror movies?"

He nodded, studying her. Her cheeks pinkened.

"Well . . . I was thinking we could do a reaction video." Her voice all but stumbled. She was obviously afraid of being considered stupid, of the idea being bad, and he felt terrible. He wanted to hug her but knew that physical proximity at this point was probably not a great answer. "GoofyBui and EverLily react to a horror movie. That way, I'd still be a weenie on camera, and probably I'll yell and hide my face, and you'll do all those funny comments that you do. And it wouldn't take six hours, like a video game, but it'd still have the same vibe."

He blinked. "That's actually really on brand. Or what we kind of have as a brand currently," he said with a huge smile. "That's brilliant. I don't know why I didn't think of that."

She smiled, relief coming off her in waves. "Because you're the one that comes up with the brilliant ideas?" she teased.

He rolled his eyes, his mind already whirring with possibilities. "We'll probably want to film it down at my place. The setup's better—my cameras, the chairs, the monitor," he explained.

"Then we'll need to drive to your place," she said, nodding. "I guess we can wait until, what, Thursday or Friday? The usual?"

He suddenly didn't want to be apart from her, which was crazy because they hadn't spent that much time together until this past month. But after last night, he just . . . he wanted to see her. "Unless you're going to be filming your own stuff," he heard himself say, "I'd love to knock this out, you know? Just get it done."

She frowned, and he realized he'd worded it poorly. "Just 'knock it out,' huh?" she echoed.

He sighed. "As in, I'd love to have you come down with me, to Ponto Beach, today. So we can shoot the video."

There. He'd all but put out a welcome mat. He wanted to see what they could be. And hell, yes, he wanted to have sex with her. Preferably for a few weeks, until he got the hang of exactly what it took to make her shiver and yell and go absolutely insane.

Then he'd probably spend a few more months just perfecting it. But only when she was ready for it, and only if it meant they were leveling up to something more.

She smiled slowly. "I could go to Ponto today, sure."

"Why don't you pack some clothes?" he said. "And I'll drive."

She blinked at him. "You will?"

"No sense in us taking two vehicles when I'm just going to come back up here to film your last video," he said, hoping he seemed reasonable.

"That's true." She smiled, sounding breathless. She sounded the way he felt.

He drove them down, and they talked companionably all during the two-and-a-half-hour drive, about everything. They decided which movie to watch. They talked about how happy Asad was. They talked about the upcoming reunion. Finally, they were at his house.

They'd decided on *Midsommar*, which was on a lot of horror top-ten lists and which he knew was also kind of artsy. He thought she'd respond better to that than to an outright slasher gore fest. They might work up to that.

Would you want to work with her again?

He frowned. Actually, doing videos with Lily had turned out to be more fun and more productive than he'd felt in a long time. He still loved doing what he did, but he'd been wrung out for so long that he wasn't sure what he was going to do moving forward—hence being blocked. Still, if it was a choice between having Lily in a relationship and having Lily on camera, he'd choose the relationship. It sounded like she was on board too. He also wondered, absently, how slow she meant when she said "taking things slow."

Stay focused, dude.

"You all set up?" she asked, completely unaware of the turn his thoughts had taken.

"Huh? Oh, yeah." He cued up the movie, scooching his chair closer to hers as the movie started. "Hey-oh, it's GoofyBui with another video with my good friend EverLily. As it turns out, she's not a fan of horror movies, which we probably could've guessed from the Mr. Perfect horror game video."

"Ha ha," she said, rolling her eyes, but smiling at him with fondness.

"So today, we're going to attempt watching *Midsommar*. Hopefully she does not kick the shit out of me again," he said.

"You gotta dream," she murmured.

He got the movie started, and he was not disappointed. She was interested, and she made surprisingly funny comments of her own, not just playing straight to his goofiness. She also shrieked convincingly. The movie was more atmospheric and creepy than gory, and there weren't a lot of jump scares, but there were some graphic moments. She yelped and buried her head on his shoulder, in his chest, and he laughed . . . and held her tighter.

"Tell me when I can look," she mumbled against his super-soft sweatshirt, and he stroked her hair.

"You got it."

They debated over what an absolute asshole the boyfriend was and commiserated over various deaths. She laughed at the surprising humor. And as the movie went on, Tobin couldn't help feeling more and more enamored of her. He could envision them watching movies on his love seat, not for filming, but just spending time together, enjoying each other.

Finally, the video ended. "He got just what he deserved," Lily said with a toss of her hair.

"Remind me not to piss you off," he said with a laugh. "All right, we've got one more video in this series. Stay tuned on Lily's channel to see what happens!" Then he ended the video. "Okay. That'll just take some editing."

"The thing is, now I don't know what our last video is going to be," Lily said. "I mean, we've done basically two makeover-style videos with you. I want to do something different. Something original. But I'm not sure what."

"We'll think of something," he reassured her. He missed holding her. They'd basically ended the video snuggling each other on the love seat as they watched. He liked it.

"Okay." She bit her lip, looking at him shyly. "When did you want to go back to my place?"

He took a deep breath. "Remember how I suggested you pack a bag?"

She nodded, still staring at him.

"I thought maybe you could stay a day or two," he said. "You know. Hang out."

"Hang out, huh?" She surprised him with a tackle. He laughed until she moved to cover him like a blanket.

"And, um, brainstorm," he stuttered, as she straddled him.

"Hmmm." She rested her chin on top of her clasped hands, peering up at him from his chest. He sat up so he could get a better look at her. "I have an idea."

"Oh?" It came out as a squeak. A manly squeak, he thought.

Her smile was slow and hot. "I know I said slow," she murmured. "But I didn't mean *stop entirely*."

He knew that his answering smile had to be just as hot. "How about you go as fast as you want," Tobin said, "and I'll just make sure we don't jump the rails entirely."

Please God. It had been difficult enough not crossing the line the night before. At this rate, he wasn't sure he had enough willpower. But like he'd told her, she mattered. Until she was sure, he'd damned well stick to her original boundary.

She made a happy little humming sound and then plastered herself against him like wet cloth, her hot, hungry mouth kissing the daylights out of him. He could *definitely* get used to this, was his last coherent thought before his body took over. He kissed her back just as ravenously, his hands roaming over her body, pulling her tight against him. He barely registered her tugging at his shirt until they broke apart, panting, and she pulled the offending article of clothing over his head and tossed it on the floor. He could see her nipples sticking out against her thin T-shirt fabric. Without thinking, he leaned forward, dampening one with his tongue. She gasped, arching her back and pressing deeper into his mouth, so naturally, he sucked harder.

"*Tobin,*" she breathed.

She was moving restlessly against him, and he was hard as titanium at this point. He could feel the damp heat of her through her thin cotton and his silky nylon basketball shorts. He moved his hips to meet hers, stroking her along his hard length as she gasped and strained. He found himself notched right where she needed him, and she picked up speed, molding herself to him, her hips moving frantically.

"Baby," he said as her fingers dug into his shoulders, moving with a quickly devolving rhythm against his arms. He was lifting himself off the couch, trying to get closer to her, and her thighs clenched against his sides as she rolled her body. She was breathing in gasping gulps. He kissed hard along her neck, cupping her ass as she bore down on him.

"*Ahh!*" She cried out and started shivering. He could feel the rush of wetness through her shorts, and her hips swiveled in a way that practically made his eyes cross.

Before he could stop himself, his body jerked, pleasure flooding out of him, into his basketball shorts.

They stayed like that for a long moment, just looking at each other and breathing heavily.

"So that happened," he finally said unevenly.

Her eyes widened, and then she started laughing. He joined her, until they were both laughing hysterically, wiping at their eyes.

"Come on, get up," he said. "I have to change shorts. I haven't come in my pants since I was . . . God, I don't even remember."

"Worth it," she said smugly. Then she surveyed him from under those long damned eyelashes of hers. "So . . . I'm guessing the guest bedroom's still a mess, huh?"

He smirked. "Yeah."

"Guess I'm sharing a bed with you again, then," she said.

Suddenly, bedtime couldn't come soon enough.

CHANNEL: GOOFYBUI

Subscribers: 10.9M
Video views: 389M
Most recent video: "Midsommar Madness: Reaction Video (w/ EverLily)"

RECENT COMMENTS:

Xxvibe_kingxX: 20:12 EverLily saying "this guy is a dick and I hope he dies painfully." LOL!

T3Ch Warrior: Again—is this chick paying rent? Is she going to start Twitchstreaming with you, too?

Skeptic_Sketcher: Do It next! *stops, thinks about how that sounds.* DO IT!!

Han Solo Cup: Does she play first person shooters? Call of Duty, man!

CHAPTER 30

Lily spent the next few days at Tobin's place. In Tobin's bed, if she was being scrupulously honest. They still hadn't progressed past dry humping, like they were teenagers, but it had gotten more intense with each passing day.

She knew that "taking it slow" probably had fallen by the wayside, and she wasn't quite sure what was holding her back.

You just want to be sure.

During the day, they hung out. She filmed a makeup video on his setup, basically showing how to do makeup when you're not at your own place and you only have a few days' worth of clothes, and styled a "boyfriend" look out of his clothes. The resulting heat in his gaze made her actually shiver, which was ridiculous, but this was apparently her life now.

It wasn't all sexual tension and clothed orgasms, though. They watched movies. Ate meals. Joked around. They'd spent some time apart, too—she'd gone out to lunch with Emily when he needed to do some kind of Twitch livestream, playing a video game. She'd spent time at Juanita's coffee shop, which really did have phenomenal coffee. She'd even gone with him to spend time with the Nerd Herd again, buying a new bikini and hanging out in Hayden's pool while Tobin splashed around . . . and, again, shot her some seriously heated looks.

Just being sure, she reminded herself. She knew she cared about him, that she liked him.

But did that mean they were ready for a relationship? There was a lot they'd need to decide, and she wanted to plan.

But how did you do that with a guy who seemed to just go with the flow? Could a relationship between the two of them work like that? They were going to head up to LA the next day, to get back to her place and film the final video in the series. She could see them cross-collaborating more in the future. She was close to the six-million-subscriber mark, and she knew she had Tobin's help to thank for it. Their banter and interplay just somehow worked. She felt looser and funnier when she was on camera with him. He made things easier, and she felt more comfortable. She kind of wished they could still film together when the series was over.

Would he be open to that? She didn't see why he wouldn't be. It could only help both their careers, she thought. Who wouldn't want that?

Her phone buzzed with a new text. She glanced at it, seeing it was Mikki. She opened it. It was a YouTube link, along with a note saying **You need to watch this** as well as a time stamp to look out for. Puzzled, she opened it.

It opened to a channel she didn't check out often, called Dirt Tea. It was a gossip channel, one that usually focused on the drama that seemed to perennially pop up around the beauty community. You couldn't have huge and often controversial personalities and not expect just a bit of drama.

She clicked to the section of the video that Mikki had mentioned, and the narrator's voice cut in over a picture of her own face. Lily gaped.

What the hell?

"Lily Wang, also known as EverLily, has been around the beauty community for about eight years, only coming to prominence recently," the narrator said. "Very recently, she started teaming up with the popular gamer Tobin Bui, a.k.a. GoofyBui."

The video's background shifted, showing her chasing him around and then whacking him with a pillow.

"They claim to have been friends for years, although this is unconfirmed," the narrator said with a note of suspicion in her voice. "And their early enmity seems to have shifted from manufactured tension of one kind to tension of a completely different kind."

Lily felt her stomach knot.

"Hey, Lils, what's . . . ," Tobin said, walking into the living room where she was sitting. She held up a hand, unable to look at him. She could sense him looking over her shoulder.

"According to a fellow beauty YouTuber, despite attending the same high school, Lily doesn't really know Tobin and hasn't been in contact with him for years. She's just sleeping with him, and using him, in order to boost her own numbers. And according to anyone tracking her subscribers on Social Blade, it appears to be working."

Lily let out a squeak of protest. "What the *hell*?" She glanced over her shoulder at Tobin, feeling completely at a loss, and saw him looking similarly gobsmacked. "I'm . . . what?"

"While Lily has not been particularly high profile, her reputation has been one of cultured, above-the-fray niceness," the narrator continued implacably. "She hasn't gotten into feuds with other YouTubers, and her content, while not necessarily original, has created a devoted following. How well will they take the news that she might be selling out . . . and sleeping around to get what she wants?"

"Are you kidding me?" Lily shrieked. "I can't believe . . . who the . . . what *is* this shit?"

She looked over at Tobin. She wanted to punch someone. She wanted to puke. She wasn't sure *what* to do.

Tobin, on the other hand, was grinning. "Aw, you tramp."

She was in no mood for mocking. "You like the idea that I'm just having sex with you to build my business?" she said, her voice icy.

He held up his hands. "I'm laughing," he corrected, looking in her eyes and ensuring that she understood his intent, "because that is so the opposite of who you are it's ludicrous. Whoever gave that sound bite, anonymously, is not only full of shit; they don't know you at all."

She harrumphed. "Yeah, well, that's not going to help me. You know how much viewership these gossip channels get. Look at Karmageddon 2.0. It was a nightmare. Channels bled subscribers and got demonetized and everything!"

Tobin walked around, then sat next to her on his love seat. The small sofa meant that he was pressed up against her side, and he put an arm around her shoulders, comforting her with a side squeeze. "You're not going to lose subscribers," he reassured her. "You're going to be fine, okay? I promise."

"What in the world makes you think that?" she countered, feeling panic hovering around the edges of her consciousness. "How can you be so confident?"

"Because there are always going to be shit stirrers," he said. "And you have literally done nothing wrong."

Her brain was in hyperdrive, and she got up, pacing. "We could post photos from our yearbook," she said. "Or . . . ooh! The Nerd Herd photos. Stuff that shows we used to hang out! They'll know I'm not just using you!"

"We could do that," he said. "Probably want to ask the Herd if that's okay, all things considered, though."

She felt a slash of shame that she'd been so intent on clearing her name that she hadn't thought of that first. "Of course—I wouldn't want to use their photos if they're not okay with it," she said quickly. "But you know what I mean. Show them that I didn't sleep with you to get you to help me, or boost my subscribers!"

He chuckled, and she glared at him.

"Sorry. It's just ironic, since we haven't slept together."

"Yet," she corrected absently. "But by tonight, that won't even be true, so it doesn't matter. I'm just worried that . . . eep!"

She was silenced when he got to his feet and swept her into a long, deep kiss.

"Tonight?" he finally asked, resting his forehead against hers.

"Did I say that?" She could barely keep a thought in her head.

"Lily, it doesn't matter. That gossip channel doesn't know a damned thing. People will believe what they want. And if it's any comfort," he added, "you're obviously doing well. You're threatening *someone*, if they decided to pull this crap on you."

She sighed, biting the tip of her thumb. It was the only thing that prevented her from chewing her nails, a bad habit she hadn't indulged in for years. "I guess you're right."

"Do you have any idea who it might be?"

She frowned. There was really only one YouTuber who had crossed her path lately who had a reputation for trying to salt her competitors with gossip. One who had specifically wanted to work with Tobin.

"Daisy Blackwell," she said, feeling despondent. "If she has it in for me, then lots of people are going to think I'm using you. She'll keep going unless we can prove otherwise."

Tobin kissed her temple. "Don't worry. We'll . . ." Suddenly, she felt him stiffen . . . not in the fun way, though. More like he was startled. "I got it. I *got it!* I have the perfect idea for our last video!"

She blinked. That . . . was a curveball. "You do?"

"Yes. It's not completely original—Superwoman did something similar—but I'll bet we can pull it off and give a giant FU to Dirt Tea and Daisy, and whoever else wants to start shit with you," he said, sounding excited. Like, Christmas-morning excited. "Good thing that new bikini you bought for Hayden's pool party is strapless."

"My bathing suit?" she repeated. "Tobin . . . what do you have in mind?"

"Just wait for it," he said, his eyes gleaming. "This is gonna be epic."

CHAPTER 31

"Thanks for helping us with this, Hayden," Tobin said, after sketching out the rough idea of what they'd be filming for Lily's video.

"No problem," Hayden said. He was used to manning the camera, especially after going to film school, and Tobin was grateful for his help. The stuff he'd be doing with Lily needed more camera work than he could comfortably handle by himself, and they were going to be doing a skit here . . . telling a story.

"All right, so we're starting with the couch, yeah?"

"Yeah." He got on the love seat with Lily. She had dressed relatively casual, her makeup understated, her hair in a high ponytail . . . like she was just hanging out at home. Although, in this case, it was his home. He was wearing a pair of track pants and a T-shirt, one that she'd stared at. She seemed to like it. He clambered onto the love seat next to her. "Okay. Like we rehearsed, okay?"

She giggled, a little nervously. They started the camera.

"Thanks so much for the video series, Lils," he said, his voice pitched just a little louder than usual, just a little more over the top. He put an arm around her shoulders. "I had a lot of fun."

"I don't know what I'm going to do now that we're just doing our own stuff," she said, and rested her head against his shoulder. "Although I will say one thing: it'll be good for people to stop assuming we're dating."

"I know, right?" He stroked her shoulder. "It's the weirdest thing. Why the hell would anyone think we're together?"

"I know, right?" she said, then snuggled a little harder against his chest. He stroked her hair, forcing his body not to react to the proximity. That was the gag: that they were acting lovey dovey while saying things that were perfectly mild. "I mean, it's not like we did anything really intimate."

"I made you play a dating sim that turned into a murder spree, and jump scared the hell out of you," he said with a laugh and was gratified when she nudged him in the rib cage with one sharp elbow. "Ouch!"

"You're lucky I'm nicer than you," she said with a sniff. "I made you hot."

"Some might argue I was hot to begin with," he protested.

She looked him up and down, and it was like being bathed in heat. "You might be right," she said begrudgingly, but her pupils were blown, and she bit her lip.

God damn. He swallowed hard. "We did silly stuff too," he said. "Doing each other's makeup. And the horror movie."

She nodded. "Really just stuff friends would do."

They kept up some banter. Then they shifted, going to a lawn chair in the backyard. She'd changed into her bathing suit and was lying on her stomach. He applied sunscreen to her back, then rubbed her shoulders, segueing into a massage. Hayden snickered at the sheer lasciviousness of Tobin's behavior.

"I mean, don't all friends apply sunscreen onto their half-naked friends?" he asked.

"Of course," she agreed, smiling, her eyes glinting beneath her sunglasses. "Your turn."

She slathered him in lotion, and he had to admit: he could hardly remember his lines and could barely improv because she was really, really damned distracting. He took a deep gulping breath. "How about some lunch?"

The next scene was in his kitchen. They took turns feeding each other chocolate-covered strawberries. He decided to up the ante a little, "accidentally" getting some whipped cream on her collar bone . . . then wiping it off with his thumb.

Then she shocked *him* by putting his thumb in her mouth and sucking.

"Don't tease," he admonished softly, thinking he was definitely going to pay her back for that tonight. When the shot was done, Hayden was looking at him with a huge shit-eating grin. "What?" Tobin said, irritated with the scratchy quality of his voice.

"If I didn't know you two, I would swear you two are already having sex," Hayden said, his eyes curious. "Hell. I'm not a hundred percent convinced you aren't."

"Trust me, we're not." Close to it, but not sex itself.

But tonight . . .

"Not that there'd be anything wrong if we did," Lily added with a grin, winking at Tobin.

"Hey, no judgment." Hayden's amusement was obvious.

"It's a little bit of fan service, and part of it is to rub it in the face of whatever jackass decided to target Lily," Tobin said. He wondered if they'd do a video "coming out" as a couple when they finally defined their relationship.

He then wondered when they were going to define their relationship.

One thing at a time. He ushered Lily into the master bath, where the tub was filling up with bubbles. She still wore her bathing suit, and he wore his trunks. Since the bikini was strapless, and the bubbles were high, it looked like the two of them were naked together in the tub, her back to his front, his knees around hers. He wrapped his arms around her.

"This okay?" he said, then swallowed against the lump in his throat and tried his best to not . . . well, poke at her. *Think awful, nonsexy, softness-inducing thoughts.* It wasn't that kind of video, dammit. "Not too hot or too cold or anything?"

"Nope." If anything, she sounded like she was purring. Glad she was having a good time, he thought.

Hayden got the camera going, suppressing a few guffaws. "This is so convincing," he said.

"It's really ridiculous that people think we're in a relationship," Tobin said, brushing a kiss against the rim of her ear and then cursing himself when she shivered against him—against a particularly sensitive part of him, to be honest. "I mean, what in the world would give them that idea?"

"And even if we were in a relationship," she said, leaning against him, then twisting a little to face him, "what difference would it make, right? Lots of couples collab."

"It's not using someone if that someone is completely, utterly, and totally . . . *willing to go all the way for you.*"

She smiled, and it was like being handed the sun. "Besides, we work so *hard* together."

Something was hard, that was for damned sure. He was losing the thread, so he forced himself to focus. "Um. Yes."

She wiggled. Probably accidentally. But he felt it in the brush against the front of his swim shorts.

His body literally sprang to life He refused to look at Hayden, who thankfully seemed oblivious to what was happening beneath the bubbles.

"That's good," Hayden said. "Looks great. I'm gonna get set up in the bedroom for the last shot, okay?" Without another word, completely unconcerned, he walked out and shut the door.

Lily looked at him beneath damp lashes, her eyes dark and inviting.

"Don't look at me like that," he rasped. "We've got one final scene—then the video'll be over."

She laughed wickedly. "This is surprisingly fun. Teasing you, I mean," she clarified, climbing out of the tub. He opened the drain. "If I had known you'd been interested in high school, maybe I would've teased you differently then, rather than trying to kill you all the time."

"You are *so* going to get it tonight."

"Maybe sooner than that." She stepped into the shower, rinsing the bubbles off. Then, to his shock, she stripped out of the bathing suit.

He couldn't help it. He stared. They'd always stayed clothed up to this point—he knew her by touch, but only with a layer between them.

She was gorgeous.

She glanced at him. "You'll want to get out of those swim trunks," she said as she wrapped up in a towel. "Don't want to get your bed wet."

He almost swallowed his tongue. He tugged off his trunks, unable to ignore her appreciative smile as she took him in.

"Come on, you two," Hayden said on the other side of the door. "I'm meeting Juanita and some of the crew later. Let's gooooo!"

Tobin loved Hayden like a brother, but in that instance, he wanted to yeet him into the sun.

"Let's go," Lily said, her smile slow and seductive. "Don't want to make Hayden late."

"Aren't you putting on anything?"

"Nope." She gestured to the towel. "This should be good enough. And it'll make it . . . realistic."

"Um . . . wait just a sec."

He turned his shower to freezing cold, then jumped in and immediately yelped.

"You okay?" Hayden asked through the door, concerned.

"Just . . . yeah, I'm fine," Tobin said through gritted teeth. Once his erection was gone, he wrapped up in the towel. Lily burst out in peals of laughter.

"Okay. Let's shoot that last scene."

CHAPTER 32

Lily felt excitement skitter across every nerve ending she had, but at the same time, she felt more confident than she'd ever been in her life. And more desirable. Which was weird, since she was currently strutting wearing nothing but a towel in front of Hayden, making her way toward Tobin's bed.

"Hayden, don't look," Tobin barked out, wrapped in his own towel. His hair was tousled and his eyes were wild.

Hayden laughed. "Then how am I supposed to film, stupid?"

Tobin scowled. "I mean . . . ah, shit, you know what I mean."

"Don't worry," Lily reassured him, clambering under the covers before releasing her towel and putting it on the floor. She laughed when Tobin smacked a staring Hayden in the back of the head.

"Holy shit," Hayden said. "I mean . . . so y'all are *really* gonna be nekkid under there?"

"Apparently," Tobin muttered. Lily noticed that he was walking a little funny, and that he essentially dived for the bed. He had a hard-on, she just knew it.

That made her feel confident too. And turned on. She felt her smile turn positively feral. She watched as Tobin dropped his towel off the side of the bed and snuggled in, and caught a glimpse of his hardness. *Oh, yes.* She cleared her throat. "So, let's wrap this up, shall we?"

Hayden snickered again. "This is gonna be so awesome."

"Shut up." Tobin was blushing. But at the same time, his eyes were voracious, looking over every inch of her that was revealed—which, admittedly, wasn't much, just her naked shoulders, collarbone. The hollow of her clavicle. She shifted, the covers lifting slightly, then burst into a broad grin when his eyes popped and his pupils blew wide. She saw his Adam's apple bob as he swallowed hard. "So . . . um. Where were we?"

Lily arched her back a little, like she was stretching.

"Jesus," he breathed, his voice so low the mic probably couldn't pick it up. "You are. *So.* Not. Fair."

She laughed. "Well, Tobin, I guess that wraps up our video series. I'm sure we can do more in the future, but maybe not if everyone keeps making these ridiculous assumptions that we're together."

"Maybe," he croaked, then cleared his throat. "Shit. I mean, *maybe*," he repeated, more clearly.

She laughed. "All right, then. Good night," she pretended.

"Good night," he responded—then, just like they'd planned, he canted forward, pressing a kiss against her lips. It was just supposed to be a quick kiss; then they'd fade to black, like the lights had gone out.

The problem was, it felt *really* good. She purred, parting her lips slightly. Within seconds, she heard a low, rumbling groan—and his tongue teased her lips before tangling with her tongue.

Things went a little haywire from there, and she lost all perspective. She wasn't even sure how long it was before the sound of Hayden clearing his throat theatrically pierced her consciousness.

"I *said*, I'm going to go now," Hayden yelled, sounding utterly amused. "Which, by the way, I've been saying for a few minutes now."

She blinked, and blushed all over, hiding her face in Tobin's chest. She could almost hear the rapid beating of his heart, felt the heat coming off him like a bonfire. "Bye, Hayden, and thanks." He looked over suspiciously. "The camera's turned off, right?"

Hayden laughed. "I'll leave it in your office, just so you're sure," he said. "And I'll leave on that note. Oh, and I'll lock the door behind me?"

"Great, whatever," Tobin said, but it was clear he'd already moved on. Hayden kept laughing, but true to his word, he disappeared with the camera, shutting the door behind him. She heard the noises of Hayden puttering in the office, then heard the sounds of him shutting the front door with a slam and more laughter.

It wasn't until they heard the roar of his engine—some souped-up penis-mobile, Tobin often joked—that Tobin turned back to her.

"You sure you want to do this?" he asked.

She couldn't form words. She just looked at him, her eyes wide. His gaze was positively molten. She looped her arms around his neck, tugging him closer, then pressed her naked body against his. It was a shock. There was no other word for it. Feeling his hardness pressed against her bare belly seemed to set her entirely ablaze. She couldn't remember wanting anybody the way she wanted him at this moment. They were kissing, their mouths fused together. She barely registered that she was making low gasps and mewling sounds in the back of her throat as her fingertips scrabbled for purchase against his heavily muscled shoulders, the ripples of his back.

Good *God*, he was absolutely gorgeous. How had she not known? He maneuvered himself so he was on top of her. She blinked at the suddenness, startled that he was in such a rush. But he wasn't going for the main event, as it were. Instead, he moved that heated mouth of his from her lips, to her jawline, to the little hollow behind her ear. She shivered, stroking her legs against his. He groaned loudly, and she felt his cock jerk slightly. He moved slowly and thoroughly, kissing down the column of her neck, licking at the delicate hollow at the base of her throat. Then he took one nipple into his mouth, sucking gently. She was particular about this. She'd been with guys, like Rafael, who fancied themselves the best lovers in the world. She hated it when, without enough prep, they dove in and messed around with her boobs, either pinching, or sucking too hard, or, worst of all, biting. It jarred her out of the mood.

But Tobin seemed to know her body the way he knew computers. His fingertips danced over her skin, and he smiled at her, making her feel beautiful, as he toyed with her breasts until she was hot and flustered and slowly going out of her mind. Then he reached gently between her thighs as he pressed hot kisses down her stomach, nuzzling her belly button with his nose.

It took her a second to figure out where he was headed, mostly because . . . well, again, in her experience, oral wasn't something guys were into, especially not the first time. "Oh, you don't have to . . ."

"I'd love to, though," he said. God, his voice ought to be illegal. She felt herself go wet just from the deep bass of it, rumbling over her skin. "So unless you hate it, can I?"

She couldn't trust herself to talk, so she nodded. He smiled, took a deep breath . . . then dived in, as it were. He parted her folds, and she squirmed, partly embarrassed (because she always felt that way), but also partly because she was more turned on than she could ever remember being. Who the hell would've thought Tobin Bui would be this damned good at sex? She knew that he was better than anyone at driving her crazy; she just didn't realize that this was part of his repertoire.

They could've been doing this for *years*, she realized.

"Hey, too much thinking," he said, and his hot breath fanning over her exposed flesh made her quiver, made her moan lightly. He leaned down, and suddenly, instead of his breath, it was his tongue, hot and eager, curving around her clit, exploring every crevice. She gasped, then moaned even louder. His tongue seemed to take it as encouragement, moving more insistently. Delving into her. His blunt fingertip pressed in, gently but determined.

"Oh my God, oh my God, oh my God," she found herself chanting, as pressure began to build inside her. Without warning, an orgasm slammed through her, and she dug her fingers into the sheets, her hips shaking. He held her tight, his tongue relentlessly drawing every last drop of pleasure from her.

She was lying there, disoriented, when he lifted his head. "Do you want more than this?" he asked, between licks. "'Cause I can get you off like this again, if you want. In fact, it'd be my pleasure. I don't want you to think we have to do anything more than this."

"Are you bucking for sainthood?" she marveled, and was rewarded by his laugh.

"I don't think this is the last time we'll do anything, Lils," he said with such quiet assurance that she felt more than just lust. She wasn't sure what else she was feeling, and she didn't want to examine it too closely right then . . . but he was right. There was going to be more than just this afternoon.

Still . . .

"I want more," she said, tugging at his hair. He yelped slightly, then laughed, and she laughed too. This was . . . fun. This was unreal. He reached into a side table, pulling out a condom. She got her first really good look at him. He had a thick cock, not too long, with a deep-purplish head. She was panting, out of breath like she'd just run a marathon. He covered her with his body, notching himself at the juncture of her thighs.

"I'm sorry this is so fast," he said, like he hadn't just spent twenty minutes pleasuring her. She was still drenched from her orgasm, so despite his girth, he easily slid into her, letting out a long, low moan of pleasure. "Holy shit, Lils, you feel amazing."

She wrapped her legs around his waist, pulling him in even deeper, and he shouted, his hips jerking forward. She sighed. "You feel amazing too," she rasped. He withdrew, almost all the way, and she let out a squeak of protest. He grinned, then rocked forward, filling her deliciously. He held her hips, picking up a steady rhythm that made her want to lose her mind.

After a while, she couldn't believe it, but the pressure started building again . . . that wonderful, almost desperate sensation where she was close to the edge and just needed him to nudge her over. She lifted her hips with every forward thrust he pressed into her, gripping his fore-arms, which were bulging with effort.

"Gonna come," she breathed. "Oh, God, Tobin . . ."

His tempo picked up speed and grew uneven. She could tell from the drawn expression on his face, the clenched eyes, that he was close. She squeezed her internal muscles, and his eyes flew open.

"*Lily*," he said, like he was being tortured, and his hips slammed forward.

It was just what she needed. The orgasm flung her out of her mind, and her vision whited out for a second. She cried out and arched her back, meeting him thrust for thrust, then collapsed against the bed. His hips stuttered, and she could feel his cock jerk inside her. He collapsed on her, breathing heavily against her neck.

She held him, her fingertips slicking over his sweat-dampened skin.

"That was . . ." She let the sentence peter out. There weren't really words for what that was.

He propped himself up on his arms, then grinned. "It sure was."

CHAPTER 33

It was two days later, and Lily was still there.

After their last momentous shot for the video, and the even more momentous sex they'd enjoyed, they had proceeded to have pizza, laughing and talking, before going back to bed and enjoying round two. It was all still dreamlike.

The next day, he'd told Lily he'd help her edit her video. She agreed, and they'd spent the morning clipping, putting in transitions, adjusting audio and lighting levels, and adding some funny subtitles and tags. It was finally finished, and it was just as he'd hoped: epic. They'd posted it immediately.

Then they'd gone back to bed after a quick sojourn on the love seat. And they'd christened his gaming chair—another first.

He hadn't had this much sex in a forty-eight-hour period in his entire life, and he'd certainly never been with anyone as sheerly stunning, enthusiastic, and just fun as Lily Wang.

The best part was, he knew her. He'd had girlfriends before, although none had really worked out for longer than a few months, largely because of his workaholic tendencies—which never seemed like workaholic tendencies to them. They always thought he was being immature, that he was just "playing games" rather than creating content, that he was just "fiddling around" with his computer. Lily, on the other hand, simply *got* it.

And, even better, she showed no signs of leaving—and he liked that more than he wanted to say.

They still hadn't put a clear definition on what they were, and it seemed too precious, too precarious, for him to push. He was half-afraid if he asked her about it she'd . . . He sighed, unsure. Chase him around and beat him with a pillow? Try to kill him again?

Or . . . maybe she'd be open to something more? And if she was . . . what was he offering her, exactly? Because he liked the idea of spending more time with her. In fact, if anyone could make him balance work and the rest of his life, it might be Lily.

There was also the little matter of her living two-plus hours away. He suppressed a groan. He didn't want to live in LA, but he'd be damned if he asked her to move away from what was important to her. So where did that leave him?

She walked up to him, kissing him gently. "You're doing that thing again."

"What thing?" He tugged her onto his lap, pressing some kisses of his own against her lips.

She smiled against his mouth, then pulled back to rub a fingertip between his eyebrows. "The thinky frown. You're doing that."

"Thinky frown?" He grinned at her. "I didn't know I had that."

"You do it when you're brooding over something." She tugged him up. "Maybe you should work out. It'll help you feel better."

He pulled her closer, wrapping his arms around her and nipping at her neck, gratified by her little gasp and then purr of approval. "If you're looking for some joint exercise . . ."

"Mmmm. I can definitely see that in our future," she said, and he couldn't help it. He held her tighter at the zing that went through him when she said "our future." Which probably made him the sappiest, but he frankly didn't care at this point.

His phone buzzed, and he groaned when he saw the display. Bastian and Jeffrey, asking for a Zoom meeting. He ignored them.

"Aren't those your agents?" Lily said, when he turned the phone over so the next text didn't show. "It might be important."

"I doubt it."

"Come on," she teased, biting at his earlobe and causing him to shiver. A manly shiver, he internally amended. "Work first, play later. Okay?"

He sighed, then kissed her again. "It'll just be a few minutes." He'd make sure of it, even if he had to hang up on them.

She winked at him over her shoulder before flouncing away in a pair of denim short shorts and one of his button-up shirts. His mouth went dry and his body went hard, and he shook his head to clear it. The woman was amazing.

It made it that much harder to stay focused on the call, but he dutifully switched on the meeting. Thankfully, Bastian was there as well as Jeffrey. "Congratulations!"

"For what?" Tobin asked. "You mean for finishing the video series?"

"And going viral!" Jeffrey crowed. He looked like he was ready to throw his hands up and start dancing. "Have you seen the stats? The views? And your subscribers went up even more!"

"I did notice that." He wasn't religious when it came to checking his stats, unlike some other YouTubers—Lily came to mind, actually—but he did keep track.

"Tell me you're going to continue working with her." Jeffrey pressed forward as Bastian looked amused, rubbing a hand over his chin. "She's like gold, and you two together are viral dynamite."

"I haven't seen you this fired up in a while," Bastian added, a little more quietly but no less enthused. "I think she's good for you, dude."

"I'll just *bet* she is," Jeffrey added with a leer. "Her in the tub? And you two in bed? Holy shit, you're a lucky guy. Wish I was at *that* shoot!"

"Jeff?" Tobin interrupted, before the man could continue mouthing off.

"Um, Jeffrey," he corrected, looking puzzled.

"Make another comment about Lily, and I will beat the shit out of you."

Jeffrey goggled. Bastian, on the other hand, lifted his hands in a calming motion. "Whoa. Sorry. That was inappropriate, Jeffrey."

Jeffrey at least looked chastened, if a bit sulky.

"While I think the collabs you two have are very promising, it isn't what we wanted to talk about," Bastian continued. "We've got some deals on the table that we wanted to discuss."

"I'm not doing the ninja thing," Tobin said bluntly.

"No, I didn't think you would, and honestly, I wouldn't have advised it anyway," Bastian said, shooting another glare at Jeffrey. "Which is why I found another vehicle for you. Sketch comedy, animated—you'd be the voice of a variety of characters. Have you heard of the Grayscale Brothers?"

Tobin tilted his head. "Actually, yes," he admitted. "I like their work. They're funnier than hell."

"Well, they're going to have a thing on Adult Swim. They're looking for voice talent, especially diverse voice talent, and they like your work too. Is that something you'd be interested in?"

"What kind of commitment are they looking for?" Tobin asked.

Jeffrey shot Bastian an "Is he kidding me?" look, and Bastian shook his head almost imperceptibly. "They'd want you as a series regular, I think," he replied.

Tobin clenched his jaw. That would mean a weekly commitment at least. Part of him felt excited about it. It could be a fun project—right in his wheelhouse. And it was always exciting and interesting to collab with people whose work he admired. But that creeping exhaustion was also hitting him.

"And there's the live tour," Jeffrey added, his tone still a little sour. "We're going to need a yes or no on that soon. They can't just hold your spot open, you know."

Tobin grimaced. He did know that.

"Hell, maybe your girlfriend might be a better match," Jeffrey said with a scowl. "She might not be funny like you, but she's got a great—"

"Tobin . . . oh! I'm so sorry, I didn't realize you were on a video call," Lily said, walking in with a catlike smile.

Which was bullshit. The door had been open a little. He had no doubt that she'd been listening to what he was saying with his agents—including Jeffrey's earlier gross comments—and was bursting in to basically give him shit. Which worked, since Jeffrey was now turning a tomatoish reddish-purple.

"Um, Lily," Jeffrey said, clearing his throat. "I, uh, didn't know you were at Tobin's."

"I'm sorry, we've never met. You must be one of Tobin's agents." She sounded placid, maybe just a shade derisive. Tobin fucking *loved* it.

"Jeffrey," he muttered.

"And I'm Bastian," Bastian said with his characteristic smoothness. "We've just been discussing how great your collaborations with Tobin have been."

"Why, thank you! I'd like to think I bring a certain something to the project," she said, looking down shyly before smiling with mischief. "And apparently Jeffrey agrees!"

Jeffrey choked.

Bastian muffled a smile, then let out a little cough. "Be that as it may. While your collabs didn't necessarily make sense on paper, I always thought there might be a quirky twist that would produce results. I'd say you've both boosted each other's profiles and hit on something that a lot of people are connecting with. That has opened up a lot of doors for Tobin here."

"Has it?"

"I'm advising that you two keep doing videos together," Bastian said, and Tobin scowled at him. "But, of course, that's up to the two of you. I just see the numbers, and forecasting what you've been able to do . . . well. You understand this business. It's a matter of leveraging attention and striking when the iron's hot."

"I totally understand," Lily said, her beautiful face serious and attentive. "And I haven't discounted any future collaborations with Tobin yet, certainly."

"Maybe *he* has," Jeffrey muttered.

Lily looked at Tobin, then back at the screen.

"Well, you'll have time to think about it," Bastian soothed. "If Tobin goes on this live tour in a few weeks, he'll be gone for over a month."

"But on the plus side, the recording studio for Grayscale is in LA," Jeffrey tacked on. "So he'll be in your neck of the woods more."

Lily's eyes widened. "Wow," she said, studying Tobin for a second. "I had no idea you had so much going on."

"I'm still mulling things over."

"Don't worry," Lily said to his agents, with a flirty grin. "I'm sure we'll figure out something. But for now, I need to get this man fed. Unless you needed to discuss anything else?"

"Nope." Bastian looked cheerful, even if Jeffrey looked disgruntled. "Great meeting you, Lily."

"And you, Bastian, Jeffrey," she said, sounding like a perfect hostess. Tobin muttered a goodbye, then clicked off the meeting. He groaned, lolling his head back. Lily threw her arms around him, squealing a little.

"What?" he said. "You almost deafened me!"

"That's so exciting!" she said. "I mean, that Jeffrey guy seems like kind of an asshole, but a voice-acting gig? And a tour? Between that and your stats, you are kicking ass!"

He smiled. It was nice. Granted, he had support from his friends, the Nerd Herd, and guys like Shawn. But Lily was different, and her appreciation made him feel warm and just comforted. "Thanks."

"Maybe we could keep doing videos," she pointed out. "It's not a bad idea, you know. He's not wrong—viewers are fickle. Now probably isn't the time to get complacent."

"I still need to think about it," he said.

"Well, don't think too long," she said briskly, getting up and tugging his hands. "Work out. Then we'll grab lunch. Then we'll talk about it some more, maybe?" She winked at him.

He nodded, not feeling quite as happy as he had a minute ago.

CHANNEL: *Everlily*

Subscribers: 6M
Video views: 302M
Most recent video: "Why Do People Think We're Together?"

RECENT COMMENTS:

Hai Mai: OH MY GOD IT'S HAPPENING IT'S HAPPENING THANK YOU JESUS

Breathless Belle: YAAAAASSSSSSS

Annabel Lee: You two are so cute!

Decemberist Girl: So are you really a couple????
Watches epic ship set sail You're really together?
You can't tease us this way!

CHAPTER 34

"Oh my God, thank you," a woman said, surveying herself in the mirror. "I had no idea I could look like this!"

Lily smiled at Mikki. Mikki had approached her with the idea of doing a collab and helping out a small beauty boutique owned by a friend of his. They took samples of various foundations, shadows, blushes, and lipsticks, and the two of them offered free ten-minute makeovers for people willing to be in the video. They'd done about twenty makeovers over the course of the day, and she could already tell the before/after shots were going to be amazing.

"It's our pleasure," Lily said as Mikki gave the woman a hug and then presented her with a small, pretty paper bag that held the samples they'd used. The woman waved as she left, and Chloe, the owner of the boutique, ushered the last of the customers out of the store and locked the door, then leaned against it and let out a long exhalation.

"Oh my God," Chloe said. "That was amazing! You two worked wonders!"

"The products are wonderful, Chloe," Mikki said with a wink and a smile. "Thanks for letting us use your store and your samples."

"You're doing me a favor," Chloe countered. "You're promoting my store, and my products. And you did so many people's makeup!"

Lily surreptitiously stretched a little. She *had* done a lot today. She'd almost avoided it, considering how much time she was spending down in Ponto, but she'd planned this video with Mikki at least six months ago, and they'd been friends too long for her to abandon it.

The fact that she'd even considered it showed just how much she'd changed since doing . . . whatever it was she was doing with Tobin.

"All right, now you have to tell me *everything*. That last video, where you were all but making out with him?" Mikki fanned himself with a hand. "Oh my God! I was so disappointed you didn't actually kiss. I swear, that would probably get a billion views. You've got people invested in that ship."

She cleared her throat. They'd edited out the kissing that had been caught on camera, instead recording an alternate ending—still seeming naked in bed, but this time Tobin shutting off the light and the whole scene fading to black. The commenters had gone absolutely bananas, and as predicted, the video had gone viral.

"Wanna grab something to eat?" Mikki said. "I'm starving."

Chloe had to bow out, needing to get back to her husband and kids, so Lily and Mikki headed to a little Thai restaurant. She ordered a spicy green curry, and Mikki ordered pad thai. "So, what's your next video?" Lily asked, taking a sip of her iced tea.

"Finishing up my classes," he said. "Then, maybe take a nice long vacation before fall semester starts up again."

Lily frowned. "Are you going to be filming on vacation, then?" That could be good, she realized. There were plenty of YouTubers who filmed on location, and it worked out well. "Maybe testing the makeup from other places? Or . . . ooh! Street fashion report?"

He tilted his head, taking a long draw of his diet soda. "Oh my God. I forgot you didn't know."

Lily blinked. "Didn't know what?"

"I'm shutting down my channel," he said. "You've been down in that little beach town, doing all your stuff with Tobin, so I just . . . I didn't want to tell you over text, you know?"

"But why?" Lily wailed. "You're doing so well!"

Mikki rolled his eyes as the food was put in front of them. "I do all right," he says. "But I haven't even gotten to a million subscribers, on YouTube or TikTok, or even Instagram. And let's face it: you need at least a million to do anything as an influencer."

She bit her lip, moving her curry around with her chopsticks. "You could get there, though," she argued. "It just takes some time, and work, and collabs."

"We both know it doesn't 'just' take that," Mikki said wryly. "You've been doing this for, what, eight years?"

"I wasn't really serious about it the first two," she said . . . well, lied, really.

"But your 'not really serious' is most people's 'utterly obsessed,'" Mikki said with a grin. "You realize that, don't you?"

Lily fell silent. He might have a point.

"The thing is, if you're not willing to be completely dedicated to this, you know that you can't make it in this business," Mikki said. "You need to be utterly obsessed. You need to devote your life to this craziness, and hopefully, you're enjoying it," he pointed out. "I love it, but I'm not obsessed with it. I still want to get my degree. And God damn it, I kind of want a boyfriend."

She suddenly found herself having a hard time swallowing her curry, and it had nothing to do with the four-fire rating. "You could have a boyfriend and maintain a YouTube channel," she said, almost tentatively. "At the same time, I mean."

He studied her, then leaned forward, his eyes wide. "Do *you* have a boyfriend and a YouTube channel, by any chance?" he teased.

She shushed him, glancing around, but really, nobody gave a damn what they were talking about. "I don't know," she said in a low voice. "I think so? Maybe?"

He did a little butt-wiggling dance in his chair, then froze. "Wait. We're talking about Tobin, right? Because I'm a huge shipper, too, and if I find out that was all fake and you're dating someone else, I am going to be really disappointed."

She suppressed the urge to shush him again. "Maybe," she muttered instead. "I . . . think so? Or maybe not. Maybe it's just sex."

"YOU HAD SEX?"

Now she *really* shushed him. "For God's sake!"

"I totally called this," Mikki said, his grin ridiculously smug. "I knew you were into him! So you had sex, huh? Was it after that last video? Because *oh my God*, that thing was ridiculously hot. You two have more chemistry than a meth lab."

"That is a strange analogy," she said, rubbing her temples. "And . . . yes." She paused. "And possibly a few more times that night."

Mikki's eyes went wide.

"And the following few days," she said.

"You lucky bitch," Mikki said. "I am envious, really. He's a surprising hottie."

"Oh, God," Lily said, rubbing her hands over her face.

"So what's the problem?" Mikki said, digging into his pad thai noodles with his chopsticks. "And please tell me you're not self-sabotaging already. I know that you're the type who loves snatching defeat from the jaws of romantic victory, but for God's sake, you *just* slept with the guy. What's wrong?"

"I do not self-sabotage," she tried to protest, but Mikki's lopsided grin and skeptical expression pinned her in place. "Well, not deliberately. And not that I was aware of?"

He scoffed, but nodded magnanimously. "I'll allow it." He still pinned her with that stare, though. "So, now that you're aware of it, what are you doing about it?"

"I just . . . my work has been my life," she said. "You might think I was self-sabotaging, but frankly, none of my relationships have ever been as important as the work, you know?"

"I know," Mikki said. "That's why you're so good at what you do, and why your channel's a success. But what's different now?"

She frowned. "Tobin is different from anybody I've ever been involved with. He needs more attention, I think."

"What, he's needy?"

"No!" She quickly shook her head. "I don't know. He spends lots of time with his friends, and he just does things spontaneously—doesn't keep a regular filming schedule, mostly does things on a whim. He has lunch with his parents every month even though he doesn't really seem to enjoy it. He loves being in Ponto Beach and hates LA. It's not like he's successful with his channel because he's a machine or has this big strategy. I swear, it's like he's successful *despite* himself, you know?"

Mikki tilted his head to the side. "Still not seeing the problem."

"The problem is, we're very different!" she spluttered, pointing her chopsticks at Mikki. "I plan my content, I rehearse, I schedule stuff months in advance. I go to influencer parties every week. I've got big plans that involve me living here. If I don't, I'll fall behind. What if he doesn't want to have something long distance? Or what if he thinks that I'm an obsessive-compulsive control freak?"

"Is he just meeting you?"

She glared at Mikki, who smiled apologetically.

"You're looking at this very glass half-empty," Mikki said. "Look at it this way: you two could be a total YouTube power couple. You're already doing gangbusters with your cross collabs. I think he does something good for you, and I think you're good for him. You say he's disorganized and doesn't want to go after opportunities? Help him grab them. Show him how to be consistent and successful. Hell, you could launch him into the stratosphere."

She sighed, eating a prawn. "I suppose," she said.

"At least talk to him about it," he said. "Better talking to him than me, anyway."

She wanted to change the subject, immediately. "You going to the party tonight?"

He smirked. "Which one?"

She smirked back. "Daisy's birthday party."

"You know she's the one who dished behind your back to Dirt Tea."

"I kind of suspected," Lily said.

Mikki's smile was sharp as a razor. "Ten bucks says that she acts like your best friend and suggests a collab when you're there."

"I had Chloe make me a special palette—all green," Lily said, and Mikki burst out laughing. "I'm really, *really* looking forward to giving it to her."

"You are amazing," he said. "That's why you're going to be the biggest beauty influencer on the planet."

She nodded. Still, she felt disquieted. Tobin wouldn't care about this kind of stuff, she thought . . . not the way she did. And she wasn't sure how he'd feel about everything else. But Mikki was right about one thing.

She'd just have to convince him. And when she wanted something, she figured out a plan, put in the work . . . and *got* it.

CHAPTER 35

The reunion was tomorrow. Tobin knew he'd have lunch with his parents, and then he'd see Lily there and hopefully convince her to spend the night again. They still hadn't discussed their relationship explicitly—but he had plans. They were going to talk about it . . . just as soon as he put up another video.

The problem was, in the week since they'd posted the "why do people think we're together" video, he hadn't posted anything. He hadn't even planned anything. People were commenting on social media—not a lot, just some chatter about how he'd slowed down or needed "rest" because Lily had "tired him out." Some speculated that he was ramping up for something amazing, the next Beacons video or something. And he was still getting texts and emails from Bastian and Jeffrey, nudging about what he was going to do about the voice-over work and the live tour. And what he was planning next.

He looked at the whiteboard. He had lots of scribbles, more than actual words. It didn't help that some of the "actual words" were INTERESTING SHIT. SOMETHING FUNNY. SOMETHING GAME RELATED?

He was so, so very boned.

I don't know what the fuck to film!

He rubbed his hands over his face and headed for his treadmill, where he set it for a lowish speed and started to walk. He'd already had a creative dry spell, or at least he was starting to feel that way, since Beacons. Working with Lily had helped because she'd made things fresh and fun. But continuing to do videos, especially in light of his recent talk with Bastian and Jeffrey, seemed unpalatable.

He'd thought a lot about why he hadn't wanted to have sex with her while they were working on the video series. It might seem weird, or stupid, or old fashioned. Or basically unnecessary. As she pointed out, plenty of YouTube couples no doubt had sex and did collabs—it wasn't a big deal. But the more he thought about it, the more he was nervous.

He was starting to hate what he was doing. Just admitting that privately was painful. He hadn't realized how much, until he realized that he didn't want that to taint his relationship with Lily. And he wasn't kidding himself: he wanted a full-blown relationship with Lily. This wasn't just sex, not for him. He was in love with her. It might seem sudden, but he'd cared about her for years, been attracted to her for as long as he'd been attracted to girls in the first place. He knew that she was a tough woman but also that she was caring (the way she stood up for her friend Mikki was a great case in point), and she was funnier than she gave herself credit for. She thought all she had was brute determination, but that wasn't true. She was creative, and intelligent, and sweet.

Yup. He definitely loved her. More than he loved his channel.

But without the channel, what the hell was he?

He grimaced, hitting the speed and pushing until he was jogging, nudging the incline up.

He could always go back to college, he thought, even though his stomach knotted at the prospect. The problem was, he had never enjoyed college. He wanted what he had. He'd once loved doing his channel. It was hard work, but it was *fun* work. He loved coming up with silly skits and fun posts. He still enjoyed gaming with friends. He just was tired from being "on" all the time.

So . . . how could he get back to that? Because he was determined to get back. He didn't believe that life was just getting a job you hated and working really hard at it so you could earn enough money to have periodic fun. That was bullshit.

He started running, almost flat-out sprinting. Hoping against hope that he could somehow outrun his problem. But after a few minutes, he felt his vision start to close in on him. Anxious, startled, he grabbed at the guardrails, hurriedly hitting emergency stop. The thing slowed down. He found himself stumbling out his back sliding door and collapsing breathlessly onto his lawn chair, taking in great gulps of air as his heart beat like a war drum.

This wasn't good, he realized. This was very not good.

The last time he'd had something like this was when he was in his second year at college . . . right before he'd decided to drop out. His parents had flipped the hell out, which hadn't made things any easier, but he'd taken some money he'd socked away for a new camera, and he'd taken a trip. He'd never been to Europe, so he'd set off on his own. After hitting hostels and couch surfing with some of his YouTuber friends, he'd seen France, Italy, and England. It was fun, and it gave him just a sense of relief. It was the creative break he needed.

After that three-week trip, he'd come back reinvigorated—and he'd leaped headfirst into the wild world of full-time YouTubing.

Maybe that's what he needed now. He was pushing too hard, to the point where things weren't fun anymore. Where they were torturous. He just needed a reset.

He found himself picking up his phone and dialing Bastian's private number. He rarely used it, thought of it as an "in case of emergency, break glass" thing. But he didn't want this to go through the office—especially not if it might get shunted off to Jeffrey.

"Hey, Tobin," Bastian said, his deep voice filled with concern. "You okay?"

"Because I'm calling the Batphone, you mean?" Tobin said and laughed—a creaky, off sound. "I need to talk to you, just you."

Bastian paused. "Okay. What's up?"

Tobin took in a deep breath, his fist gripping the phone tightly. Then he let the breath out. It felt like standing on one of those high platform diving boards . . . and there was nothing to do but jump.

"Bastian," Tobin said slowly. "I can't do this."

Bastian was silent for a second. "Define *this*."

"I can't do the live tour," Tobin said. "I can't do the voice-over work—at least, not right now. I am crispy. I am totally fried. If I were more burned out, I'd be a charcoal briquette."

"Hmm." He could almost hear the gears in Bastian's mind turning.

"I'm sorry," Tobin said, feeling miserable. He genuinely liked Bastian and hated disappointing people. Jesus, his entire relationship with his parents seemed to encapsulate this.

"No, no. If you're burning out, then you need to take care of yourself," Bastian said.

"I mean, if you need to drop me as a client, I understand . . ."

Bastian's laugh startled him. "Come on, man. We've known each other for too long. I'm not going to do you like that." Bastian let his corporate mask slip, and he sounded more like the gamer Tobin knew. "But tell me straight. What are you planning to do next? Are you abandoning your channel altogether? Shifting into something else? Getting a nine-to-five, for God's sake? Or . . . I dunno, heading off to an ashram or something? Gonna go all *Eat Pray Love* on me?"

"Nothing like that," Tobin said. "I'm not a hundred percent sure about anything. But I know I don't want to go back to college, and I seriously doubt I'd want to get a corporate job. Hell, I don't even know what I'm qualified to do, besides make an ass out of myself online."

"Don't do that," Bastian said. "Don't put yourself down. You're burned out; it happens. Maybe you just need a break, like you said."

"Am I slitting my throat, though? Business-wise?" Tobin asked in a small voice. He hated feeling like this.

Bastian sighed. "I'm not gonna lie. The barrier to YouTube, TikTok, social media . . . it's nonexistent, and new content flows in every day.

Depending on how long you decide to pause, you're going to lose subscribers. That's just the truth of it. The longer you're away, the more your numbers are going to bleed. And if you say no to the opportunities, you may not get new ones. That's just me being honest."

Tobin felt his skin go cold. "I figured."

"Then again," Bastian added, "you're smart, and you're creative. You come up with original content . . . that's why you're successful. So if you need a break to get your mojo back, it might be the best thing for you."

Tobin felt like he was being torn in two. "What do you think?"

"I think I work for you," Bastian said gently. "I can't tell you what to do here. I'll just go along with whatever you decide."

Tobin closed his eyes. Bastian was right, and he appreciated it. That was why he'd chosen to go with Bastian in the first place: because he wouldn't push Tobin to do something that wasn't best for him, just for the money. "I need to think about this."

"Let me know what you decide," Bastian said and hung up.

Tobin looked at the phone. He was more confused than ever . . . but he knew that he couldn't keep going the way he was. Something had to give.

After a few hours and a lot of deliberation, he turned on his camera setup. He didn't have a script or a plan. He didn't need one.

"Hey-oh, it's GoofyBui," he said. "Short video today. I just wanted to let you all be the first to know . . ."

He took a deep breath.

" . . . I'm going to be taking a break."

CHAPTER 36

Lily walked into the party feeling nervous as she stepped back into Daisy Blackwell's house. Not surprisingly, considering the hostess, the bash was Roaring Twenties themed . . . despite the fact that this was not a launch, just a simple birthday party. Of course, nothing Daisy did was simple . . . or without an eye toward business. She probably had everything comped from sponsors who wanted their products "seen" in various Instagram photos from the partygoers. Daisy knew the system, and she worked it.

The house was crowded. There were waiters in tuxes wandering around with champagne, and there was a DJ, also in a tux, playing what sounded like twenties-inspired EDM. Whatever else Lily could say about Daisy—and there was plenty—the woman was an absolute fiend about her brand. It's why she had all those followers, across a multitude of platforms, and had such hefty brands slavering to work with her. She might be a bitch, but she was a bitch with *hustle*.

Lily put her present on the gift table, grinning to herself. She felt . . . tense. Happy. She wished Mikki was there. She was still thrown by Mikki's insistence that he was going to give up his channel, at least for the time being. She'd nudged him but then left him alone when she realized how strongly he felt about it. He didn't think he had what it took, which she knew wasn't true.

No. It wasn't that he didn't *have* what it took. It was that he didn't *want* to do what it took. She frowned. That was very different.

She felt her phone buzz against her hip bone. She loved the dress she was wearing, specifically because it had pockets that were deep enough to accommodate a phone. She was wearing a brass flower head-dress and a fringe-trimmed dress in a delicate peachy gold. She saw that it was Maria, her manager. She pushed through the crowd, aiming for the balcony. People were smoking or vaping in small clusters, and she could smell a mixture of clove and weed. She suppressed a little cough and headed for the far corner. "Hello?"

"I know it's a bit late, but I figured you'd want this news as soon as possible," Maria said, sounding excited, then paused. "Where are you, anyway?"

"Daisy Blackwell's birthday party," she said. "Putting in face time—you know how it is."

"I swear, you're one of the most persistent and hardest-working influencers and BeautyTubers I know," Maria said, and her appreciation made Lily practically wriggle with happiness, like a puppy. "Which makes this all the sweeter, really."

"You've got news?" Lily prompted.

"Don't worry, I'm not going to torture you," Maria said. "I heard back from GlamSlam. They want to do a special collection, with your name on it."

Lily's breath caught. "Really?"

"Everyone's going with highly dramatic, you know? Heavy metallics, 'fierce' looks. You've got something else," Maria said. "After how well your collabs with GoofyBui went, I was thinking maybe anime inspired. Even geek chic. I think you can come up with an eye shadow palette to start; then we'll segue from there into a larger set of offerings: blushes, bronzers, foundation and contouring makeup, lipsticks. Maybe brushes and such down the line. Hell, cleansers and toners, if you want."

Lily felt her heart beating with excitement. This was it. This was everything she wanted.

She couldn't wait to tell Tobin.

She blinked for a second, realizing that he was the first person she wanted to tell.

"We just need to keep your numbers up," Maria continued, "and we'll see how initial sales go for the collection."

Lily swallowed. "I hit six million," she said. "After the last Tobin video."

"I know. That's how we got the deal through," Maria said with just a hint of amused indulgence. "But that's what they're paying for."

Lily's happiness dipped a little. "How do they feel about the cross collab?"

"Keep it up, as far as they're concerned," Maria said. "Which is what I'd advise, by the way. You'll only keep getting subscribers if you work with GoofyBui. Besides, I think he's good for you."

"What do you mean?"

Maria paused. "I think that he brings out a fun side of you, one that people haven't really gotten to see on your channel," Maria mused. "You're more *you*, somehow. More . . . approachable? Or authentic? And, obviously, more original."

Inexplicably, Lily felt her heart sink.

So her success . . . was all due to Tobin?

"Would they give a special collection to anyone who hit that mark?" Lily pressed.

"No, of course not," Maria said, and Lily felt better—for all of a second. "I mean, there are psychopaths out there that have big numbers, absolute toxic drama magnets. Of course, there are other brands that go for that sort of thing, and GlamSlam has certainly backed some questionable influencers in the past, but I do think you're offering them something special here. I wouldn't just say that."

Lily couldn't help it. She didn't feel convinced. She bit her lip.

"Hey, this is a time for celebrating! You've got a full night before you turn into a stress ball," Maria joked. "And before you dive headfirst back into work."

"No pressure," Lily said. "And yeah, you know me well."

"If you're at Daisy's birthday, then she's probably got some fantastic champagne," Maria said. "Go have some, maybe dance a little. I don't suppose Tobin is there with you?"

"No!" Lily realized she'd yelled it when the people on the balcony who were in their own knots of conversation looked over at her curiously. "I mean . . . no. Why do you ask?"

"I might be shipping you two, myself," Maria said, and Lily could hear the smile in her voice. "So . . . nothing there? It's all faked for the camera?"

Lily felt her cheeks heat. "Um. No comment at this time." At least not until they cleared up what their relationship was, and if they were public. She *really* needed to stop dragging her feet on that. She always went straight for what she wanted. Why was she stalling?

But what if it doesn't work?

And there it was. Her biggest fear. That a relationship with Tobin was the one thing that *wouldn't* work, no matter how hard she tried.

Maria burst into laughter. "Well, if you *are* in a relationship, or whatever, you absolutely should keep doing videos. You two together are magic."

Lily swallowed. "I think so too," she admitted.

"All right. I'll call you next week with the details of the deal, all right? In the meantime—celebrate! Congratulations!"

Lily thanked her, then hung up. She wandered back in. She felt dazed at the news. She ought to feel happier.

Why didn't she feel happier?

It's a step, she told herself. A big deal. She knew that she always did this. She never celebrated her successes—she just shifted gears and looked for the next big thing. It was never good enough to hit a milestone. She needed to keep moving toward the horizon.

She suddenly wished, desperately, that Tobin was there. He would celebrate, she realized. Hell, he did a victory dance when he beat his friends at *Among Us*. He knew how to enjoy life, to live in the present. She loved that about him.

She wondered, absently, if she loved him. Period. Point blank.

The idea was kind of terrifying, but also exciting.

"Oh, Lily! It is Lily, right? I didn't know you were going to be here!"

She turned to see Daisy smiling, that small calculating smile. She was waving to people as she wove through the crowd. They did the air-kiss thing, which Lily always felt self-conscious about, then Daisy's eyes brightened like a predatory bird.

"I heard that you've been going viral. Can't believe I gave you the idea to collab with darling Tobin!"

Daisy said it just loudly enough that people around them could hear—and Lily realized that was the point, that this was theater. She knew that Lily was doing well, and she wanted to both dig into it a bit and claim some credit.

"We should *totally* do something together," Daisy tacked on. *Just like Mikki thought she would.*

"Certainly," Lily said, pitching her voice a little louder too. "Maybe when I get to eight million? Because I remember you telling me that there's no way you'd collab with anyone with a smaller following than that."

Daisy's face reddened slightly, as people murmured among themselves. "Well, of course I'd make an exception for you, sweetie," Daisy said through her teeth. "Who knows? Maybe we can get a makeup brand interested in doing a little something with you. I mean, it's a bit of a long shot—you do work with such *muted* tones—but hey, anything's possible, right?"

Lily felt a bubble of pettiness expand in her throat. "As it happens, I'm already signing with someone to bring out a special collection," she said, trying to sound apologetic while really gloating.

Daisy looked like she'd been goosed. "Oh? Do tell. I want to know everything."

"Can't until the contract's signed—you know how it is," Lily said. "But I'd love it if you could help spread the word when the collection drops. You've been so helpful!"

She nodded, ready to leave on a high note, and started to turn her back on Daisy. But to her surprise, Daisy stepped in front of her, smiling broadly and leaning closer to Lily's ear. "You know, of course, that you'd be fucking nothing if you hadn't gotten traffic from that stupid gamer," she hissed, even though her face looked almost affectionate. "Once you stop working with him, your numbers will tank, and then good luck with those sponsorships and deals. You don't have what it takes to succeed in this game."

Lily felt like she'd been slapped. She studied Daisy's face as Daisy patted her upper arms, like she'd just told her a secret. "I am *so* happy for you," Daisy said for the people around them and then had the audacity to hug her. "Talk soon!"

Lily watched as she walked away. Mind games, she thought . . . but still felt her stomach clench. Now she didn't want to call Tobin. She was too confused, and too upset. Too angry.

I will show you exactly how well I can succeed at this game.

She'd wait to talk to Tobin until the reunion tomorrow.

CHAPTER 37

"Well, this is unexpected," Tobin's mother said as she put sandwiches in front of him and his father. "We didn't plan to see you for another week or so."

"What, I can only have lunch with you once a month?" Tobin tried to joke, even as he squirmed uncomfortably in his chair.

"No. But that certainly seems to be all you have time for," his father said dryly.

Tobin squelched a sigh. "I do actually have a reason for stopping by," he said. He nudged the sandwich—a ham and brie with wilted spinach. One of his favorites, actually. He took a big bite.

"Don't keep us in suspense," his mother said as she sat down with her own plate and a glass of water. "What's going on?"

Tobin kept chewing, trying to think of how best to approach it.

"I think we already know what it's about," his father said, and Tobin stared at him, startled.

"You do?"

"I can't say that I approve," his father said. "That last video. Good grief. What does Lily's family think?"

Tobin choked.

"Are you all right?" Once his mother was assured that he wasn't dying of asphyxiation, she also tutted. "I can't imagine the Wangs are happy with their daughter climbing into bed with you—on tape, Tobin! Honestly. What is wrong with you?"

Tobin spluttered. "That's the joke, Mom," he protested. "Lily and I had been making these videos, and everyone insisted that we were together romantically. So we decided to make a parody, just a big joke video. It was a joke."

"She was *naked*," his father said. "First in a tub with you, then in bed!"

"She was wearing a bathing suit," Tobin said, conveniently leaving out that when they were in bed, she really wasn't. He felt his body heat, just for a second, as he remembered that moment.

Thankfully, being at his parents' house tended to crush any possible feelings of desire into dust. "You know people are going to judge her more harshly because of this," his mother pointed out, ignoring his bathing suit comment. "You'll seem like a big stud, but she's going to look like—and forgive me—but she'll seem like a slut."

He forced himself not to roll his eyes. "All part of the gag, Mom. Besides, she already has to run the gauntlet of people who judge what she does and call her a slut, and worse."

"Worse?" His mother sounded appalled. "And she wants to be a part of this business? *Why?*"

"Because . . ." He stopped himself. "We're going far afield."

"Just a big joke," his father muttered. "Does that mean you're not seeing her?"

Tobin grimaced. "We're dating," he said, which he was pretty certain was the case.

His mother at least looked pleased. "She's lovely," she said. "So polite! Although I have to say I'm a bit surprised. You two usually seemed to be at each other's throats."

"Sexual tension," Tobin drawled, and his father scowled.

"More respect, please," his father said, then bit into his sandwich. "I suppose she's going to be at that reunion of yours tonight."

Tobin was looking forward to it with every fiber of his being. They'd been apart for a few days now, although they'd texted each other the whole time. She said she had big news for him tonight, and he texted the same—although his was asking her to officially be his girlfriend—and go with him to Australia and New Zealand for his "rejuvenating" adventure. He smiled, thinking of it.

"Well, you must be in love, with a smile like that," his mother teased. "She's good for you."

He nodded. "I think so."

"So that was it? You wanted to let us know you're dating Lily Wang?" his father clarified.

Now or never. Tobin put his sandwich down, wiped his hands, then surveyed his parents. "I'm going to be taking a break," he said.

They looked at him with obvious confusion. "A break from what? Lily?" his father asked. "You just started dating her!"

"From YouTubing. From posting videos," Tobin said when they still looked confused. "Just for a month, maybe a few. I'm burned out. I can't come up with any new ideas, and it's been like pulling teeth to stay on even a semiconsistent posting schedule. The video series with Lily was a godsend, but even as much as I enjoyed those, I'm hitting a wall."

"But what about your big plans?" his mother pressed. "I thought you said your agents had ideas for you. Maybe a TV series or something?"

"I'm keeping my options open," Tobin hedged, "but I don't think I'm going to be pursuing that. Not right now. There will be other opportunities."

"There will be other opportunities?" his father repeated, eyes wide. "This . . . this is your idea of a business strategy? Taking an extended vacation and then trusting that something's going to come up? That's not a plan! That's . . . that's . . ."

"Blind faith?" Tobin filled in.

"That's *crazy*!" his father thundered. "I may not have agreed with this . . . I can't even call it a job. This thing you do for income . . ."

"Technically, that's a job," Tobin said under his breath, causing his father to glower even more.

"But if you're going to do something, you damned well need to *do* it! Why in the world would you half-ass it? Why walk away when you're successful?" His father looked at him like he had indeed lost his mind. "Are you trying to sabotage yourself?"

Tobin sighed. He'd known they'd have a difficult time understanding it, but he had hoped it wouldn't be quite this problematic. "I am doing what's best for my business," Tobin said firmly. "I need a sabbatical."

"Oh? Is someone paying you during this little sabbatical of yours?" his father snapped.

"Actually, I will continue getting ad revenue from views of my previous content," he said as calmly as he could. "It'll be enough to pay the bills for a while."

His father's eyebrows knit together, and he could see that the man was trying hard not to yell or possibly even shake some sense into his recalcitrant son. "But aren't there new YouTubers all the time? I can't imagine people are going to sit around waiting for you to . . . to find yourself or decompress or whatever! You're throwing away everything you've built!"

The pressure on Tobin's chest was heavy and familiar. How many times had he had similar conversations—about high school or college? Or extracurriculars? They'd never been happy that he was a solid B student throughout high school, and dropping out in his second year of college had certainly solidified their disappointment.

"I just . . . I just keep waiting for you to grow up, Tobin," his father said, and he actually wore a look of disappointment, despair, disgust. Take your pick.

Tobin swallowed hard, the sandwich sitting like lead in his stomach.

"Hon, this doesn't have to be a bad thing," his mother interrupted, and Tobin stared at her. Not that she wasn't supportive, per se. But she normally presented a united front with his father. His father looked just as surprised. "In fact, it presents an opportunity."

"It does?" Tobin asked. Now he was the confused one.

"Of course." She smiled, a small satisfied smile. "Now you'll be able to go back to school and finally finish that degree."

Tobin felt aghast, even as his father tilted his head and nodded. "That's not a bad thought," his father agreed. "If you're taking a break anyway."

Tobin stared first at his mother, then his father. "Fuck. No."

"Tobin!" his father shouted. "Language!"

"I don't know how else to tell you. I am not going back to college. I don't need the degree. I am not spending that kind of money for something that ultimately is not going to help me."

"Tobin, education is important!"

"I value my education," he said. "I think it's great—for some people. But not me. Not with my ADHD."

"Oh, God, this again," his father muttered.

Something in Tobin shifted. Maybe it was finally admitting he was burned out. Maybe it was the fact that relief and freedom were so close. Maybe it was because being with Lily had somehow loosened things up in him. He liked the support. Now, he could almost imagine her next to him. Like when she'd first kissed him, and encouraged him, even let him do her makeup for a shoot when he knew she hated relinquishing control . . . all because he'd been so spun out.

He didn't have to be unhappy, trying to prove himself to people who weren't going to get it. Even if the people who didn't get it were his parents.

"I told you my decision because I love you," Tobin said, "and because there's a good chance I won't be here for the next lunch. I'm going to travel, recharge my creative batteries."

"Traveling?" His mother looked shocked. "Where?"

"I was thinking Australia and New Zealand, maybe," he said. "Or Japan. Hell, I might go to Iceland. Haven't decided yet. I just didn't want to leave the country without letting you know first."

"And this is your grand plan?" his father said. "How can you—"

Tobin held up a hand, then cut over his father's voice. "I know you're unhappy with my choice here. But the fact is, it's my choice. I love you, but I don't need to get your permission. And I don't want to disappoint you, but I am going to do this whether you're disappointed or not."

"Then what's the point?" his father yelled, getting to his feet. "What's the point in even talking to us? Why come once a month, your little grudging time? Why pretend that you respect our opinion!" He pointed at the door. "You might as well leave. And consider whether or not you want to even bother coming back!"

Tobin stared at him.

"Jacob," his mother breathed to his father, her eyes wide and glassy. "Now, come on. Tempers are a bit high, and . . ."

"I love you both," Tobin said quietly. He got up and headed for the door, his mother on his heels.

"He doesn't mean it," she said, sounding nervous. "He's just upset. This is a shock."

"I'm going to be traveling," Tobin said, giving her a hug. "I'll call, let you know how I am. And we'll talk when I get back."

He left the house and got into his truck, feeling low. This was hard, but important. He headed back to his house to get changed for the reunion.

CHAPTER 38

Lily walked into the high school gymnasium like she was walking through a time portal. There were bunches of Mylar balloons and streamers in their school colors of blue and gold, and tables set up here and there with candles. There was a podium on the stage, and even space for a dance floor, although the music was muted enough that you could hear conversations. She figured as drinking progressed, they'd probably crank up the music, and then there would be more of a party atmosphere. As it was, it felt a lot like a high school dance—or maybe even a middle school dance. People collected in little knots and crowds. She could recognize some of the cliques: the drama squad were enthusing over each other, the football team was cheering raucously about something, even the dance team had reconnected. She looked for her crew, the Nerd Herd. That's where Tobin would be—and that was who she wanted to see the most. She was wearing a flirty dress, sort of like Baby in *Dirty Dancing*, a pair of wedge heels, and her most devastating seductive makeup.

The man would not know what hit him, she thought with a mischievous grin. Then, it'd just be a matter of dragging him back to his house, making love to him until his eyes rolled back in his head, then asking . . .

Asking what? "Will you be my boyfriend?"

She winced. Well, they'd get to his house and then figure things out from there.

Someone bumped her on the shoulder, drink sloshing from his cup. Fortunately, thanks to years of influencer parties, she was good at dodging, so the offending liquid simply fell to the floor.

"Ah, shit," the man said, frowning at it, then at her. Then his eyes widened. "Lily? Lily Wang? Is that you?"

She studied him. He did look kind of familiar. He had brown hair and blue eyes that were a little bloodshot. His face was puffy, and he was wearing what looked like a respectable suit, except for the fact that the buttons strained around his midsection. He had broad shoulders, a decent if somewhat smarmy smile, and a hairline that receded at the temples. She blinked. "Um . . ."

"You really saying you don't recognize me?" he teased, but his eyes were sharp. "It's Travis."

She goggled. "Travis? Football guy Travis? Kylee's Travis?"

"Hell, I haven't been Kylee's Travis since the summer after we graduated," he said with a guffaw. She tried to smile, but really, how was she supposed to know that? "You are looking good."

"Thanks," she said, her eyes scanning the crowd. She thought she could see Asad in the corner, but there was a different crowd of people in the way, and she was short.

"No, I mean it," Travis said, stepping into her line of vision. "You look *hot*."

She couldn't help but feel amused. "Dude. You used to call me Big Wang."

He didn't even look embarrassed. "Hey, I was just teasing, you know that. You didn't need to be sensitive about it."

She shook her head. Apparently some things didn't change.

"But if you want, I can apologize properly," he said, and she realized that he was pitching his voice lower, leaning toward her. "I could buy you a drink."

"I didn't think they had a bar set up here, just, like, a punch bowl or something," she said, thinking there was no way in hell she was drinking anything this guy handed her. That might be unkind but . . . tough shit. She knew better.

He let out that donkey laugh again. "Not here, obviously," he said. "I was thinking somewhere a little more . . . private?"

Before she could say, "No chance in hell," a woman's voice cut in. "Travis? Where is my punch?"

He straightened reflexively, startled, and managed to slosh even more of what was in the cup out of it. He glared at it like it was at fault. "Uh, Betty. I just ran into Lily Wang here. Literally." Cue braying laughter.

The woman he was referring to was blonde, though apparently dyed, judging by her too-obvious symmetrical highlights. Her face looked tight, and her eyes looked pissed. "Lily?"

"Lily Wang," a new female voice chimed in. "Don't worry—we know her, Betty. I mean, obviously, she graduated with us."

Lily froze for a second. She hadn't heard that voice in a decade, but funny how the sound was like an ice pick in her ear.

Kylee Somers walked up. She was still blonde, too— still natural, and it looked better on her than Betty's dye job. She still had those high cheekbones, and her makeup was . . . all right. Lily might've suggested a slightly different foundation since her skin looked a little sallow, but that might be the lights, Lily thought charitably. Betty still looked upset.

"Why don't you go get me that drink, Trav," Betty said, then stopped him with a hand on his arm before he could head back to the refreshment table. "No more for you, though. Dad expects you in early for inventory."

Lily saw the bitterness in his expression, just the flash of it, before he nodded, brushing a kiss against the woman's cheek. Then he walked away with one last look at Lily—something that Betty apparently did not miss.

"I'm Travis's wife," Betty said sharply. "In case you were wondering."

Lily nodded, suppressing her gag reflex. Of course married Travis hit on her. *Ewwww.*

"Betty's one of my best friends," Kylee said. "I actually introduced her to Travis in college, if you can believe that."

Lily couldn't, actually, but she couldn't bring herself to ask Betty how she felt about getting Kylee's leftovers. She figured Betty had her hands full with Travis as it was. "Well, it's great to see you." She tried to extricate herself.

"Vanessa couldn't make it, because her husband's got a big case this week in New York," Kylee continued, as if Lily had asked something. "She's staying at the Waldorf Astoria. Her husband's a great lawyer, and really a great guy."

Great guy like Travis? Lily thought.

"So what are you doing these days?" Kylee asked, smiling. Betty looked curious, too, if still a bit wary.

This was Lily's moment, the one she'd waited for. She wanted to prove to Kylee and all the other popular kids that she was worth it . . . that they'd be sorry they didn't want to hang out with her.

"I'm a beauty YouTuber," she said. "I suppose an influencer is the better term, though—I mean, I post content on Instagram and TikTok too."

Kylee raised an eyebrow. "And that's . . . a job?"

Lily flinched. "Yes, it's a job."

"Wow. You make money doing, like, makeup tutorials and things?" She sounded almost admiring.

Almost.

"I had no idea you could make a living doing that!" Kylee continued with a cheerful smile. "You always did like makeup, so I guess that's kind of perfect. I just . . . I don't know, I thought you'd be doing more. You always got great grades. And didn't you graduate from UCLA?"

"I got my degree in business economics," Lily said, hating that her teeth were starting to clench. She forced herself to relax. She was too used to living in the YouTuber bubble—where people knew what she did and gave her respect for it. They knew the work, the struggle. The rewards.

"Well, I'd love to do something like that, you know, in my free time," Kylee said. "But with Kevin turning three, and then having baby Caroline a few months ago, I have not had a *moment*, you know?" She laughed, a trilling sound. "I mean, Chad does try to help out where he can, but he has his own construction company, and he works a lot. I can't expect him to be changing dirty diapers when he's spent the day fighting with contractors and architects, can I?"

Lily blinked. Her whole career, dismissed in a second.

"Are you married?" Kylee added the final blow, glancing at Lily's left hand.

Lily shook her head. "No."

"Seeing anyone?" Betty asked, no doubt thinking of Travis.

"It's complicated," Lily said.

"Isn't it always," Kylee replied.

"I'm seeing Tobin Bui, actually," Lily said. She didn't want to pretend that she wasn't. She was proud to be with him, if he was interested. She wanted to make that clear. Sure, it might be embarrassing if he rejected her, but she had to stick her neck out.

Kylee's eyes widened. "Are you kidding me? You're really seeing Tobin?" She shook her head. "I thought that whole thing was just a *joke*. You can't seriously be dating that guy. He just yells and plays video games all the time, for God's sake!"

Lily was about to rush to his defense when she realized . . .

How the hell would Kylee know about the "whole thing" being a joke? And how would she know that Tobin was a YouTuber?

Unless . . .

Kylee had lied. She *did* know about Lily, the videos . . . everything. And she was deliberately trying to put Lily in her place.

Lily shook her head. All this time, she'd wanted to stride into the reunion, walk up to Kylee and Vanessa and Travis and whoever thought she wasn't good enough, and point to her accomplishments. Her fame, her money, her popularity.

The thing was, it wouldn't have mattered. It *never* would have mattered.

"Gotta go," Lily said. "Sorry. My friends are waiting for me." With that, she walked away from Kylee and Betty. They were whispering, and they laughed. Only this time, Lily didn't give a good goddamn if they were laughing at her. It was like Tobin had told her: they didn't matter. She never should have given them that much power.

She walked over to where Asad stood. The whole Herd was there. Keith was telling Melanie a story about parasailing. Asad was taunting Freddie with what looked like a very sad crudité. Russell was laughing with Josh, who sent her a chin-up nod. Emily rushed to her, giving her a hug.

This was what home felt like, Lily thought absently, and for the first time since she'd hit the reunion, she felt relieved. She felt happy.

"You are going gangbusters!" Emily said. "I saw that last video, and I swear, I laughed my ass off. Although you two were *hot*, oh my God! That's not fair . . . you can't do that to a single woman!"

Lily burst out laughing. "Thank you, thank you. We worked hard for that."

"*Yeah*, you did," Hayden said, wiggling his eyebrows. Josh smacked him on the shoulder, but he was smiling too.

"You did a great job," Josh said, quietly. He was always quiet, thoughtful. He'd been joined at the hip with her good friend Tam, back in the day—not like a couple, but just best friends, so Lily had gotten to know him a bit better. She knew how hard he worked now, though, so she knew he didn't get to hang out with the Herd very often.

"You're going to have to make it down here more," Emily said. "If you and Tobin are really together, I mean. Do you think you'll be back in Ponto more often?"

"I . . . um." Lily felt her cheeks heat with a blush. "It's complicated," she repeated.

"Aw, boo," Emily said. "I miss you, sweetie. It'd be great to have you back. No pressure, though!"

"I do have a special spot in my heart for Ponto," Lily said with a wry smile.

"So do I," a new voice chimed in.

She glanced over to see Vinh. He was wearing a thousand-dollar bespoke suit in black, way more dressed up than anyone else there. It went with his black hair and nearly ebony eyes. He was looking at Emily when he said that, and now he was still looking at her like she was the only person in the room.

"Vinh," Emily breathed, going pale as a sheet. "I didn't think . . . what are you doing here?"

He smiled, something Lily doubted happened often. Vinh was always the serious one, unless he was with Emily. "I came to the reunion, same as you," he said with a tone of wry amusement. Then, again as if no one else was there, he added, "I wanted to see how you were. You look good, Emily."

"I would've thought you were too busy to come to something like this," Emily said. "Big job, big money, and all."

He sighed. "I took some time off," he said. "There are some things more important than money, Em."

Emily stared at him for a long moment. Lily saw the other Nerd Herd members squirming a little in the uncomfortable silence.

"Some things are more important than money?" Emily echoed weakly.

Vinh was staring at her with more intensity than Lily had ever seen. He nodded and took a step closer to her.

"Really, Vinh? Now? *Really?*" Emily snarled. "You can fuck *all the way off.*"

Then she turned on her heel and left.

Vinh was a step behind her, his face anguished. "Emily . . ."

Lily watched as Vinh quickly followed Emily out of the building.

"Well. That happened," Josh said, shaking his head. "I figure they'll work it out, or she'll kill him. Kind of like your dynamic with Tobin. Only less fun."

"Where *is* Tobin, anyway?" she asked.

She felt an arm snake around her waist, and she squeaked, before she recognized his scent and smiled.

"Miss me?" Tobin whispered in her ear.

She turned to face him . . . and he was close, like, face-to-face close.

She took a deep breath. Then she smiled. Then she closed her eyes, and pursed her lips. If they were going to be something, then she might as well give it a shot.

She was rewarded with a kiss that started out gentle and then rather quickly escalated to absolutely blistering. She only pulled away, panting, when she finally heard the cheering and applause of the Herd around her.

"Wanna go get some air?" Tobin said, stroking her cheek.

Unable to speak, she just smiled, nodded, and then followed him, her arm in his.

CHAPTER 39

Tobin just wanted to be alone with Lily for a few minutes before going back in and having fun with their friends. He had every intention of bringing her back to his house, if all went well, and then they'd enjoy each other . . . hopefully with the understanding that it was the beginning of their relationship. He wanted that more than he wanted anything, he realized. He was also more nervous than he could remember being in a long time.

He tugged her over to the abandoned Bowl, where the group of them had lunch so long ago. The moon was full, leeching color out of everything, making it all seem like a strange bluish-black-and-white movie. He smiled at her, nudging her. "I'm glad to see you," he said. "Missed you."

"I wasn't gone that long." She looked at him coyly from under her eyelashes, which were beautiful and long, as usual. She looked stunning, which he thought would always be true—even if she were a hundred, wearing a holey tracksuit and Godzilla slippers, he figured she'd look stunning, at least to him. But she was also smiling, and she just looked *happy*.

He loved to see her happy.

He loved *her*.

And telling her scared the crap out of him, because it seemed so damned soon.

"I don't think I've been down here in years," she noted, wrinkling her nose. "I can still see us all here, you know? Like nothing's changed, and we had everything in front of us."

"Well, I'd like to think we still have plenty of time," Tobin joked. He wrapped his arms around her, kissing her temple, then her cheek, then her lips. "We're only twenty-eight."

She smiled. "Yes, but we've just come so far in ten years, you know?" She grimaced slightly. "Not that everyone wants to acknowledge that, apparently," she muttered.

He thought about his parents, and how they downplayed what he'd done in the past ten years. "Yeah," he agreed on a sigh. "But hey, what they think ultimately doesn't matter, right?"

She shrugged, then pressed a kiss against his lips . . . one that lingered sweetly, one that went on long enough for his body to go tense and taut against her, his heart rate bumping up. "Please tell me you're going home with me tonight," he breathed when they pulled apart.

She laughed. "I was counting on it."

He nuzzled her nose. "Speaking of the past, and the future," he said awkwardly, wondering how to word it, "I was thinking about us. I've been thinking about it a lot, actually."

"Me too," she said in a low voice, rubbing her cheek against his chest. He wondered if she could hear his heart racing like a freaking castanet beneath her ear, showing how damned nervous he was.

"Hopefully we're on the same page," he said, laughing nervously. "Listen, I know we haven't been in each other's lives again for a while, and I know we've changed. I also know that in the past month or so that we've spent together, I have enjoyed spending time with you."

That sounded so tepid, he berated himself. Was he completely screwing this up?

"I know that I wanted to strangle you a lot when we were younger," she said, shaking her head, "but I figured out that a lot of that was just tension—and honestly, a lot of it was posturing. We were enemies, but we had fun with it. Then I got to know you, and I can't remember ever having as much fun as I have with you."

It felt like he'd swallowed the sun. Heat just expanded through him, warming him to his fingertips and toes. "I guess I'm saying I want to date you," he burst out, his voice breathless. Then he closed his eyes.

Awkward!

When he cautiously opened an eye, he saw her smiling at him, her lips curving in a bright, happy grin. "I guess I'd like to date you too," she teased, squeezing him.

He felt the tension that had plagued him for months—maybe longer—slowly unravel. It was like he didn't realize how unhappy he'd been, what a rut he'd driven himself into, until he found someone and something that made him happy. And a relationship with Lily made him almost giddy, which was admittedly a weird thing for a guy in his twenties, but fuck it. He was taking it.

He kissed her again—because he could, which in and of itself was amazing—and then smiled at her. "How do you feel about Australia?" he asked, cuddling her.

"It's . . . big? There are a lot of things that could kill you there? I hear it's beautiful?" She chuckled. "And you say I break out non sequiturs."

"It's not a non sequitur," he protested, "although I could've transitioned better. It's just . . . I'm going to be making a few changes, and I'd love it if you could be on board," he said carefully.

She tilted her head, her eyes widening slightly. "Changes?"

He released her with one arm and rubbed the back of his neck. He probably should've thought this through better, but here he was—and as with most good things in his life, he was just leaping in. "I'm going to go travel, maybe a month or two. I was thinking of hitting Australia, maybe New Zealand. And I thought, there is no one I'd love to visit them with more than you."

She was quiet, staring at him.

"It's a lot, I know," he quickly said, trying to fill the void of silence with his nervous chatter. "And I know we're just starting to date, and stuff. But it could be great. I know you like traveling—you used to go to Taiwan all the time, and you went to Europe, I think?—and I thought it'd be fun if we did it together, you know?"

She looked pensive. "So . . . you're planning on filming content there, I guess?" She bit her lip. "I mean, I'm sure I could come up with some things for content, and if we have enough time to plan, maybe get some cross collabs . . . actually, that could expand our international viewers."

He pulled away for a second. "I wasn't actually planning on filming anything. This would be a vacation."

Her mouth dropped open. "A vacation?" she echoed. "For a month?"

"Maybe longer," he said, and seeing her look of shock was like taking all the relief he'd felt and suddenly cramming it back into a tiny box as his whole body got squeezed in a vise. "Lils, I desperately need a break. I've been getting more and more burned out. I can't come up with new content. I'm kind of hating what I do. And I don't think it means I need to abandon it entirely, and I'm not looking for a new career. I just need a breather. Sabbatical. Just . . . a break."

"But you're at the top of your game!" she said, and he laughed mirthlessly.

"No pun intended, I suppose."

"You have nearly ten million subscribers now. Your social stats are huge," she pointed out. "I heard your agents. They have stuff—voice-over stuff, that live tour. There are so many opportunities for you right now!" She looked scandalized. "You realize that if you decide to just bum around Australia or whatever for a few months, all that would go away, right? When were you even planning on going?"

He felt his shoulder blades pinch together. He couldn't help but notice that she kept saying "you"—no mention of herself in this plan at all. "I was planning on leaving as soon as I could, honestly," he said.

"But I could wait, if you're willing to go with me. But I'm still not going to film anything, and I'm not collabing or doing any live events or anything. That's not what this is about. I need a mental health break."

She looked at him like he'd grown a second head. "But . . . you know how this business is."

"Yeah, I know," he said, and he couldn't help the note of bitterness that crept into it. "My agent Jeffrey's pointed out that it's like being a shark: if you don't keep swimming forward, you die."

"He's not wrong," she protested. "You'll lose viewers when you don't have consistent content. You're going to get replaced. You can't want that."

"What if I do? What if I don't give a damn?" he found himself spitting out, then winced. "I don't mean to sound ungrateful. I value each and every one of my viewers. But if it means my sanity—if they don't give a shit about my well-being, what the hell am I killing myself for, doing something I hate for people who will just push me for more?"

"It takes hard work!" she argued. "It takes effort, and time, and dedication. Sometimes it just takes pure brute force."

"Apparently I don't have that endless well of brute force, then," Tobin shot back. It felt like a tiny ball of ice had formed in his stomach. "I don't have to ask if you'd go with me, because it's obvious that you wouldn't. And it seems like you're judging me pretty hard for not doing what you'd do."

"I just . . ." She sighed. "I think we should think this through, talk about it."

"I've already thought it through," he said. "And I've made my decision. I already told my agents that I turned down the show and the live tour. I'm taking the break, ill advised or not."

She looked wild eyed. "Jesus, Tobin, this is crazy."

It was the final straw. "No. You know what's crazy?" he asked and let out that bitter, humorless laugh again. "Thinking that we were going to work."

"That's not fair," she snapped. "Just because I think that you're not living up to your potential, that you're going to turn your back on people who have made your career, that you're basically self-sabotaging, doesn't mean—"

"It means you don't believe in me," he said, and it felt like his heart was being shredded. "It means you don't give a shit about my mental health either. And it means this conversation is over."

He pulled away, stuffing his hands in his pockets.

"See you around, Lily," he said, then abruptly turned and headed toward the parking lot.

CHAPTER 40

The next morning, Lily found herself at Juanita's coffee shop with Emily. It was a Sunday morning, and there were families breakfasting, kids hanging out in the play area, a steady thrum of voices. Emily seemed subdued, but willing to listen.

"I can't believe he just walked away," Lily said, sipping at her chai and slowly demolishing her orange-cranberry muffin into a pile on her napkin. She'd planned on spending the night at Tobin's, but obviously that hadn't happened . . . and frankly, she was too upset to drive all the way back to LA. She'd been crying at the Bowl, sitting on the concrete circle and completely wrecking her makeup, when an equally upset Emily had found her. Emily was more angry than tearful, though, and she'd repeatedly said, "I don't want to talk about it," so Lily had respected that. She'd crashed at Emily's one-bedroom, tossing fitfully on an air mattress, getting nearly no sleep. She was sandy eyed and heart sore, and she felt torn. She got the feeling she'd screwed up, but at the same time, she felt like Tobin had a part in that too.

"I mean, I worked too hard to get where I am," she told Emily. "I don't think it's unreasonable to tell him that!"

"No, of course it isn't," Emily said, her voice soothing. She tossed back some of her drink, some four-shot monstrosity that apparently she lived on, since Juanita had claimed it was her usual. "But what I don't understand is what exactly happened to break you two up?"

"He wanted me to go to *Australia* with him!" Lily said. Well, wailed, really. She shook her head at herself. "With no notice! I mean, I have a job to do. And I'm just getting where I want to be. I have contorted myself and put out content relentlessly, and now I'm getting noticed. I finally got that palette deal I wanted. Things are *happening*, and I worked so hard."

"You don't have what it takes to succeed," she imagined in Daisy's mocking voice. *"Your numbers are going to tank."*

"So obviously you couldn't go with him," Emily agreed, studying Lily shrewdly. "What I don't get is, why does that mean you have to break up? I mean, it's not like he's never coming back, right? He wasn't asking you to *relocate* to Australia, right?" She paused. "Actually, was he? With Tobin, you never know."

"No, he wasn't," Lily admitted. "But . . . I mean, he had offers for work. I heard him talking with his agents. Do you have any idea what kind of opportunities he's gotten, especially since our collab? He's in the perfect position, and he's just . . . just squandering it!"

Emily's eyes narrowed. "I don't suppose you told him that."

"I was just asking what he was thinking, that's all," Lily said, knowing that her tone was stubborn. She squeezed the muffin crumbs into a cube. There was no way she was eating the pulverized baked good now, so she wrapped the napkin up around it.

"So you told him that," Emily corrected, and her voice was tart. "Lily, I love you, but let's face it: you've always had your eyes on the prize."

"You say that like it's a bad thing," Lily grumbled.

"It is," Emily said softly, "when you're willing to leave all your friends behind to do it."

Lily blanched. "That . . . I don't . . ."

"Remember? That day in high school, when you said that you weren't going to eat lunch with us anymore—then came back, horribly embarrassed?" Emily's voice was sharp. "I never said anything, because

Tam begged me not to and because I saw how upset you were. But what you did was hurtful. You basically said that we weren't good enough for you, and you needed to be with people who were better."

"Oh, God," Lily said, feeling sick to her stomach. "That's . . . it's not what I meant. It had nothing to do with you or the Herd."

"Felt like it," Emily said. "I got over it, though, because I knew that what you wanted wasn't something you were going to get and that it was going to hurt you more than it hurt us. Besides, you know we didn't hold grudges."

"No," Lily said. "You never did."

"Hell, we didn't hold grudges when you basically disappeared for years and never got in touch with any of us," Emily said, rubbing salt in the wound. "But we could have, believe me. And we could've shut you out, even back then. You were always kind of a handful."

Lily felt tears pricking at the corners of her eyes and dabbed them with her fingertips. "I took you for granted," she said. "All of you. Tobin showed me that. And I'm sorry. I guess . . . I thought because the Herd seemed to take in anybody who didn't feel welcome, we were just the outcasts. The dregs. And I thought everyone else saw us that way."

"Maybe they did," Emily said. "Who gives a shit? We were accepting. That's not a bad thing. We knew what it was like to be treated like shit, to be judged for our qualities—good qualities, I might add—which were seen as somehow undesirable. For fuck's sake, we were the top of our honors classes, we kicked ass at instruments and chess and academic team and art, and people thought we were just a bunch of socially awkward dipshits. And it was *their loss*."

Lily stared at her friend like she'd never seen her before.

"I have never, *ever* been ashamed of what we were," Emily said.

"I'm not ashamed either," Lily said. "And I am so, so sorry if it seemed like I was, or that I was trying to shame any of the Herd."

Emily seemed mollified, nodding. "Tobin felt it, too, you know," she said. "He was never angry at you, not really. Just baffled."

Lily sighed. "I'm baffled by him," she said. "Hard work is one of my good qualities. Hell, almost all of us had that drive. We wouldn't have known each other if we didn't. Why does he act like I'm persecuting him just by pointing out that he's going to derail all his hard work if he makes this choice?"

"Was he asking you what he should do?" Emily said. "Or was he telling you what he needed, and you told him that he'd made the wrong choice?"

"I didn't . . . ," Lily started, then stopped.

Had she?

She swallowed hard.

She *had*.

"If that's the case," Emily said sagely, "then yes, sweetie. You fucked up."

"Oh my God, I so did," Lily moaned, resting her head in her hands and covering her face for a moment. "I can't believe I did that."

"What, exactly, did he tell you?"

Lily quickly ran the conversation back in her head. "He said that he needed a break. He needed to take a sabbatical, because he was starting to hate what he did." She bit her lip. "And . . . I told him that was a bad idea. And then gave him a bunch of reasons why it was a bad idea."

Emily shook her head.

"But he could've just told me he wasn't looking for my opinion," Lily protested, still feeling wretched. "I screwed up, but if we're going to have a relationship, he needs to *talk* to me."

"I get the feeling our good buddy Tobin has been depressed for a while," Emily said. "Maybe not clinically or anything—I'm not a doctor—but I would say that he's been desperately unhappy. Tobin and I have hung out a lot since we all graduated. There's the Herd, sure, but then there's the townies, and we tend to stick together. I know that wasn't something that you necessarily wanted—you left Ponto Beach with a vapor trail, I swear—but for the ones that stayed, we never lost that sense of family, you know?"

Lily didn't know, not quite. But suddenly, desperately, she wanted to know.

"The more unhappy Tobin is," Emily said, toying with the collar on her coffee cup, "the harder he pretends to be happy. He gets . . . hyper. Super jovial. But it's a front."

Lily felt her heart pinch painfully. She knew that. She remembered when he'd come to her apartment, so upset. The first time she'd kissed him. How the mask of "weaponized silliness" had slipped, and she'd seen the raw, real, deep emotions Tobin was harboring.

That was the moment she started falling in love with him, whether she realized it or not.

"I screwed up so badly," Lily said again. "And I don't know how to make this right."

"He should have stayed and talked it out, true," Emily said. "I just get the feeling he doesn't have the emotional energy to do that now. He's got to take a break, and I think you have to let him."

Lily blinked. She'd been ready to jump in her car and rush over to his house, throw herself at his mercy, and force him to talk it out. "But . . ."

"He didn't ask you for your opinion on what he was doing as far as a break—he was telling you what he needed," Emily reminded her. "So you don't get to decide that he has to talk to you now. He walked away. When he's ready, then he can always come back and talk to you."

"But I'm in love with him," Lily whispered.

Emily sighed, her eyes clouding. "Sometimes love isn't enough, trust me," she said, her voice edged in personal pain. "But it'll be okay. Trust me. It'll work out if it's supposed to, right?"

Unfortunately, Emily didn't sound like she believed it herself.

"Besides, you've got this gangbuster career going on," Emily continued. "You two would've needed to discuss how that was going to work. You live in LA, for instance."

"Two hours isn't too far apart," Lily said, but she nibbled at the corner of her mouth in thought.

"And you film all the time, and you go to all those parties. You wouldn't stop that, I imagine," Emily continued. "Doesn't leave much room for him. You expect him to do what's best for his career. Would that have meant insisting, or at least suggesting, that he move to LA?"

She blinked. Lily could suddenly see, in startling detail, that she'd probably do exactly that. That it may have already been an idea that was forming in the back of her mind: thinking of a place big enough for the two of them, even though they hadn't even discussed dating yet.

And he would've hated it, she realized. But it wouldn't have stopped her.

Lily swallowed against tears again. She sucked. She *so* sucked.

"The question is, What is it you really want?" Emily said. "Because if what you want is the big career, then you need to stick with that—and stop torturing the person who can't or won't follow. I speak from some experience on that."

Lily was struck with a thought. "Vinh was there last night," she said. "You seemed really upset. Are you all right?"

"I'm fine," Emily said tightly. "Vinh went back to New York last night—private plane. And I still don't want to talk about it."

Lily nodded. She'd respected Tobin little enough—she needed to respect Emily's boundary.

Emily's phone buzzed, and she glanced at it, grimacing. "Sorry. My mom needs me . . . something to do with my brother," she said, shaking her head. "I imagine you're going back to LA, but drive careful, okay?"

Lily stood up and hugged her friend. "I'll be back soon, Tobin or not," she said and felt Emily hug her tighter.

"That'd be good," she said. "I've missed you." Then she waved and walked off.

Lily sipped at her now cool chai, forcing herself not to track Tobin down. She scrolled through her phone. Ordinarily, she'd be rushing back. She was missing out on posting content, and she really, really needed to. She didn't want to miss her schedule. But for the first time, she asked herself, *Why? Why is this so important to me?*

"Kevin, TAKE THAT OUT OF YOUR MOUTH," a woman said, her tone frazzled. A baby was squalling, and a toddler was shrieking and hitting a coffee table with a toy truck after sucking on it. Lily winced and started to get up to escape until she saw the mom in question.

"Kylee?" she said, shocked.

Kylee did not look like she had at the reunion. Her hair was in a haphazard ponytail. She was wearing makeup, but her concealer game was off: the bags under her eyes were rampant and dark. Her lipstick was mostly on her go-cup of coffee. She was wearing high-end yoga clothes, but there was baby spit on the leg of her ice-blue pants, and her T-shirt was smeared with chocolate, apparently from her toddler's iced doughnut.

"Hi, Lily," Kylee said, obviously trying to rally and present a dignified front. That would've worked a lot better if the baby didn't choose that moment to yank the end of her ponytail, hard enough to make the woman's eyes water. "I didn't expect to see you here."

"Same," Lily said, still feeling stunned. They stared at each other in silence for a moment.

Lily was about to ask about her kids or something, but she was interrupted by a giggling group of teenage girls, who walked up to her. Several wore Ponto High School Cheer T-shirts. "Excuse me," one of them said with a toss of some perfectly round curls. "Are you . . . EverLily?"

Lily smiled, then nodded.

They squeed in unison, and Lily couldn't help it. She grinned.

"OMG, I told you!" another chimed in. "Can we get a picture with you? Please?"

Lily nodded, letting them take several selfies. She couldn't help but notice Kylee watching her, the baby continuing to fuss.

This was her moment. Kylee was the original Daisy—the one who told her she wasn't good enough, that she'd never be good enough. The one who wouldn't *let* her be good enough by moving the goal posts of acceptance and exclusivity. It seemed like Lily had spent her life proving herself, working hard, in order to be a success—which she'd always thought meant being popular, one way or another.

"So they actually know you?" Kylee tried.

"You *don't* know who she is?" one of the girls shot back derisively as the others rolled their eyes.

"Oh my *God*," one muttered under her breath, and the others snickered.

"Hey, don't be mean," one said. "Old people don't know YouTube."

Kylee started, then winced.

The girls wandered away, laughing, oblivious to the destruction left in their wake. Kylee looked defeated, completely at a loss.

This was Lily's moment of triumph. The picture-perfect Kylee, finally being the one to know what it was like to be judged, belittled, excluded.

In an instant, and as a result of her talk with Emily, she suddenly *saw* Kylee. Here was a woman who had curated her external life as carefully as any Instagram influencer. She hadn't had friends who would stand by her unconditionally, like Lily had with the Nerd Herd. Kylee's "success" and "popularity" were based on keeping up an unachievable perfect facade and fending off all perceived threats to staying on top.

Just like Daisy.

Just like me, Lily thought, aghast. She'd become so fixated on succeeding she'd lost track of *why* she wanted it.

Lily found herself sitting next to Kylee on the low couch. "Why don't you let me hold her," she said, holding her hands out to the baby, "and you can grab yourself a scone or some more coffee. Sound good?"

Kylee's eyes widened. Then it was like her expression broke, and she looked . . . exhausted. And sad. And surprised.

And a little grateful.

CHAPTER 41

Tobin had spent the day after the reunion holed up in his room, eating a variety of cheeses and a serving bowl of mashed potatoes—the ultimate in comfort foods—and binge-watching the worst action movies he could find, just as a way to distract himself. He felt bruised, body and soul. Still, once he'd slept, he realized that he needed this trip more than he would have otherwise acknowledged. And there was nothing really holding him back.

He spent Monday posting his "taking a break" video, then comparing airline prices and looking up things to see in Australia and New Zealand. He wasn't about to take an organized tour like the Lord of the Rings Tour that was offered. As much of a fan as he was, he didn't feel like waiting until the next tour was offered some months later, and he hated feeling constrained by schedules. He remembered one particularly sucky trip he'd taken with his parents as a kid, a European bus tour of the continent after they'd visited his mother's parents in England. The bug-eyed tour director had run them like a Swiss train, yelling when there were stragglers, keeping them herded like sheep being penned. When someone had gently suggested that she lighten up, she'd blinked at him in harsh judgment. "This isn't a *holiday*," she'd said sternly. "This is a *tour*."

So yeah . . . no tours for him. The fact that he usually had jet lag the first couple of days made that a no-go, anyway. He liked taking things at his own pace, exploring things as he felt like it. He'd just keep it open. He could still handle hostels and little Airbnb places, and if push came to absolute shove, he could reach out to his network online and see if there were some YouTubers who might have a couch he could crash on. He had faith that it'd be a decent experience.

Now it was Tuesday. He was ready to go the next day, for however long it took.

"I can't believe you're just up and going to another continent," Asad said, accepting Tobin's spare key. "Who does that?"

"I actually know a guy who decided to up and go to a Morrissey concert when he was in high school," Tobin noted absently. "His parents were out of town, and he took all his savings, flew to London, watched the show, and then flew home to San Diego. That is baller, my friend."

Asad let out a low whistle. "That is actually pretty cool. But . . ." Asad let his sentence peter off, looking uncomfortable.

Tobin sighed. "What?"

"Is this because things didn't work out with you and Lily?"

"That obvious, huh?" Tobin shook his head. "Other way around, actually. Things didn't work out with Lily and me because I'm just jumping into this trip. Guess it didn't line up with her expectations of what a successful YouTuber is supposed to do, you know?"

Yeah, he still felt bitter. It was forty-eight hours ago. *Sue me.*

Asad nodded, looking sympathetic. "You know how driven she is. Always has been," he pointed out. "And you haven't been dating that long."

Tobin grimaced. "Had just started, actually, or just agreed to it. Then I sort of dropped this travel bomb on her." He felt an unwelcome ping of sympathy. "I suppose it's a lot to take in. And it is kind of impulsive."

"Kinda," Asad agreed, his voice neutral.

"But I know that I need a break," Tobin said. "That's nonnegotiable."

"And you absolutely should take one," Asad said. "There's too much emphasis on hustle culture as it is, and people being proud that they don't take breaks and work themselves to death. Freddie was like that before he left LA, and every now and then, I see him turning into the Gordon Ramsay asshole I know he hates being."

"Really?"

Asad shot him a lopsided smile. "It's a hard habit to break. Thankfully, I take care of it, and then he relaxes and knocks that shit off."

"How do you take care of it?"

Asad's grin was wicked. "Really want to know?"

"Since I'm not going to have sex in the foreseeable future, no," Tobin said, trying not to sound bitter and failing miserably. "I really love her, you know. Even when she drives me crazy. Even though she can be pushy. She is just . . . funny, and sexy, and smart. And determined. And just good at what she does."

"You do have that competence-porn thing," Asad agreed.

"But I don't know what I was smoking to make me think that we would work out," Tobin said. "I am the opposite of all of those things. We didn't get along for years. I should have just understood and embraced that the first time."

"Don't be so hard on yourself," Asad said. "Love's not easy. It takes work, and time, and a shit ton of effort."

"Yeah, well, ask anybody—that's not my MO."

"If you're going to be self-pity boy, I am leaving," Asad said, half joking. "And then your lawn is going to die while you're off stalking platypuses in the Outback."

"Thanks for keeping an eye on the place while I'm gone," Tobin said. "I appreciate it."

"Anytime."

There was a knock at the door, which startled Tobin. He looked at Asad, who shrugged.

He went to the door, and his jaw dropped. "Mom? Dad?" He stared at them. They were dressed in work clothes, which made sense . . . it was a workday, probably around lunch. "Is everything all right? What's going on?"

"We wanted to talk to you," his father said, and his mother nodded.

"You look like you've got stuff," Asad said quickly, grabbing the spare key and fleeing, adding a pantomimed "text me" behind Tobin's parents' backs. "See you later!"

Which left Tobin alone with his parents, in his living room. They settled on his couch, and Tobin stayed on his feet, nervous.

"Um . . . can I get you something?" he asked, feeling like an idiot. His parents rarely visited—he always went home to their house for their lunches. "Or, um . . ."

"I only have a little time," his mother said, "so maybe it's better if we just hash this out."

Tobin sighed. "There really isn't anything to talk about," he said. "We've said enough."

"Then you can listen," his mother said, looking at his father. He brooded, then nodded.

"We came to say we're sorry," his father growled.

Tobin wouldn't have been more surprised if someone had clubbed him with a crescent wrench. He gaped at them.

"You have to understand," his father said slowly, "I—we—just want you to be safe. We want you to make sure that you survive. You know your grandmother's story, of how she came from Vietnam with your grandfather, and how hard it was. We didn't have a lot of money when I was growing up. I got good grades, I got my degree, and I worked very, very hard to make sure that you and your mother never lived the way I did."

Tobin nodded, feeling guilty. "I am not trying to—"

"Just listen this time," his father said, but he didn't yell, didn't grumble. It looked like his eyes were a little teary, and he was just trying to keep it together. "I don't even know how to talk to you sometimes. You are so different than I ever was. I take after your bà nội, you know."

Given what he knew about Bà Nội, his father's mother, he could see that. She was a strict woman, despite having a soft spot for her grandchild. She'd died when he was young, so his memories were hazy, but he remembered her speaking in rapid-fire Vietnamese, usually telling his father to do something or not do something.

"Your bà nội was not an easy woman to grow up with," his father added. "That doesn't mean I didn't love her or respect her any less. And I never would've dreamed of talking to her the way you spoke with us."

"Dad . . ."

"That said, she never wanted me to be an architect."

Tobin blinked. "What? Why? It's not like you wanted to be a punk rocker or something. Architects are a completely respectable profession!"

"I lied and said that I was taking a double major with premed," his father said with a small, surprising smile. "I thought she would murder me when she found out I was just going for architecture. We had a very, very bad fight."

"How am I just finding out about this now?"

"My point is," his father continued, ignoring his outburst, "I was angry with your grandmother, I was frustrated with her. But now I see she was just doing what she thought was best. She thought being a doctor would be something that would make me a lot of money, and I'd be respected, and I'd always have work. 'People always get sick, don't they?' she'd always say." He laughed after mimicking perfectly what he remembered of the older woman.

Tobin sat down in a nearby chair. He'd never talked with his father like this. It felt intimate, and . . . like they'd turned a corner.

"She meant well," his father said. "But I love being an architect, and it's been the best choice for me. I didn't realize that I was doing to you what she did to me."

Now Tobin felt his own eyes go glassy with unshed tears. He took a deep breath, getting himself together.

"And I know I'm driven," his mother said. "I can be a bit fixated on certain solutions. But I believe in your potential, Tobin. I won't pretend to understand you—I swear, sometimes I thought you were a changeling . . ."

"Um, thanks?" Tobin said dryly.

"But that was just my expectations," she said. "I was frustrated because I just couldn't seem to get through to you. You were always funny, even as a child. You didn't approach things the way I would; you never made the choices I would. But you are making a success of yourself, and you're living your life your way. My family wasn't thrilled when I decided to stay in the United States rather than going back to England. But I made the right choice."

"So you're both rebels, and you're just now getting that I am too?"

His parents looked surprised, then looked at each other.

"I don't know that I have ever considered myself a rebel," his father admitted.

"I have been called many things, but 'rebel' has not been one of them," his mother added, then smiled. "But . . . yes? I suppose you are. We are."

Tobin grinned.

"Still planning on traveling, then?" his father said.

Tobin nodded. "As soon as possible. Probably be on a plane to Australia tomorrow. After that, who knows? Europe, maybe. Or Iceland. Hell, maybe even Asia." It didn't really matter, as long as he was *gone*. "I might just play a game of plane roulette and get on the first plane that has an available seat, I don't know."

His parents looked aghast, which made him smile. His father tugged nervously at his earlobe.

"Are you sure that's the . . ."

His mother laughed. "Oh, go on. I took a gap year and wandered around Europe when I was younger than him. I'm sure he'll be fine."

Tobin gawked at her. "Who are you, and what have you done with my mother?"

"Well, you are twenty-eight. You're not a child anymore, I suppose," she said wistfully. "You're a fully grown man."

"A full-grown man who appears to have a life-sized cutout of the Mandalorian and that Yoda thing, as well as some sort of castle made of LEGO, right in his front room," his father muttered, almost under his breath.

"Those are collectibles," Tobin said loftily. Then he hugged them. "I'll keep touching base—don't worry, okay?"

"We love you, Tobin," his mother said, squeezing tighter. His father clapped him on the shoulder.

"Just be safe," he said gruffly. "That's all I ask."

Tobin swallowed against the lump in his throat and nodded. "I'll do my best," Tobin said, then closed the door behind them. He closed his eyes, resting his forehead against the door.

It felt like things had changed. It might not be full-throated support, but it felt like they understood, and right now, that's all he could ask for. He had people who loved what he did. He just needed his parents to believe in him—and it seemed like, maybe, they were working their way toward it. But most importantly, they loved him enough to worry about him. He didn't want to be too optimistic, but he desperately hoped that things would only get better from here.

CHAPTER 42

The next day, Tobin sat in the back of the town car he'd ordered. He was going to LAX, which sucked, but he didn't want to deal with a shuttle, and he didn't want to bother any of his friends. Driving to LA almost always sucked already—dealing with LAX was one of the lower rings of hell, and he wouldn't wish it on anybody he liked.

He'd slept like shit, but that wasn't a surprise. He'd gotten a ticket to Melbourne, and from there he was going to see where adventures took him. He figured he'd probably spend the first few days just getting acclimated—that was what usually happened. He'd fight insomnia at night and pseudonarcolepsy during the day, and then, once he'd settled in and gotten his bearings, he'd start exploring. Everything he'd read and all the YouTubers he knew from Down Under suggested that Australia was pretty cool, and he was looking forward to doing something, anything, new.

He just needed the break. His chest still hurt, and thoughts of Lily were like a toothache, dull and sore and pervasive.

"There's some traffic," the driver said, nodding at the parking lot of cars on the 5. Tobin sighed.

"I figured. It's no problem . . . I left extra early just to be safe."

Still, that meant he'd probably be in the car for more than three hours. He'd kept his phone off since the night before, mostly so he wouldn't be tempted to text Lily like he'd almost done about twenty times the day before. He would've stuck it in the freezer if he wasn't certain it would screw the device up completely. He turned it on now, thinking he'd fire up *Among Us* or *League of Legends* or even *Clash of Clans*. Hell, solitaire or *Candy Crush* would give him something mindless to do.

His phone started buzzing immediately, and he groaned. He had an unusual number of text messages, he noted, scrolling through.

HAYDEN: Dude, have you seen Lily's video?

ASAD: Please tell me you saw Lily's video.

SHAWN: Hey Goof—this you?

Attached was a link to an EverLily post. She'd put it up sometime that night—late, from the time stamp. He frowned.

He didn't want to watch. It hurt just seeing her face in the tiny thumbnail. But he had, legitimately, twenty texts from friends telling him he "had" to see it. But, interestingly, nothing from Lily.

He was being a masochist. He didn't care. He fired it up, opening the video and expanding the screen.

"Hi, it's EverLily," she said, in that soft, calming voice that he loved. But she sounded a little off, rough-husky with emotion. Even stranger, her face was free of makeup—which she'd done before, obviously, since it was the blank canvas from which she started all her makeup tutorials. This showed that her eyes were red and puffy from crying, though. She looked vulnerable. He'd never seen her exposed like this, and it shook him.

"This is going to be a little weird, but I wanted to let you know that I'm going to be making some adjustments to the channel," she said, her voice faltering ever so slightly. "I've been doing a lot of thinking about what I want, and why I want it. I've been working so hard on this channel, building a following and 'developing my brand'"—she held up her fingers in air quotes—"that I sort of lost sight of what I was really doing."

305

Tobin felt blindsided. She was thinking about all of this? Since when?

Finally, a little part of him thought, but he shook his head. She was hurting, and that killed him. He wanted to rush over there and gather her up, tell all the haters to fuck off, and tease her or cuddle her until she felt better. He wanted that so badly.

She took a deep breath. He noticed that her hair was in a loose ponytail, and she was wearing her old, faded Ponto Beach High School shirt. Her smile was lopsided. "I figured out I still love beauty and fashion. That's a given. I also want to promise you: I am not going to be about the drama. I am never going to negatively review a product on this channel. There are plenty of other beauty influencers that do that, and I'm not judging their choices. I just know it's not the right decision for me."

Tobin straightened, feeling proud of her. Not that he'd done anything. Just that he got to see her make this decision and state it so straightforwardly.

"Today isn't going to be a tutorial, or a fashion post," Lily said. "Today, I'd like to make an apology."

Tobin stiffened.

"I need to apologize to a lot of people," she said, "but . . . well, let me put this into some context first."

She went off camera for a moment, then came back holding up a photo. It was a matte eight-by-ten, and he recognized it immediately. It was her senior high school photo, one of those professional studio shots.

"In my defense, this was ten years ago, and those eyebrows and bangs were popular," she said with a rueful smile. "Anyway, I was always interested in YouTube beauty videos. My family owned this clothing boutique, and . . . well. Long story short, I wanted to be popular. And I wasn't."

She pulled out another photo. She was scowling at the camera as she ate an ice cream cone. Next to her was Emily, who was laughing at something someone off camera said. Asad was shoving Hayden, and Josh was grinning. Tam was smiling at all of them.

"These were my best friends," she said with a small smile. "We called ourselves the Nerd Herd, because we were all geeks and nerds and honors students. We got straight As. Weren't invited to parties. Not many of us dated. Lot of social awkwardness. And I thought that I could prove I was good enough to get into the popular crowd. Needless to say, I got shot down."

Tobin couldn't help but stare. He didn't know why she was peeling back the mask on her brand, but he felt his heart expand as he watched her take a sledgehammer to her carefully cultivated facade.

"The thing is, those friends? They had my back no matter what I did. I thought it was because we were all losers and we didn't have anywhere else to turn. But I was stupid, and wrong. *So* wrong. I didn't realize what I'd lost until recently. And a lot of that has to do with Tobin Bui."

Tobin's mouth dropped open.

"I mentioned that we've known each other for over twenty years," she said, a small smile on those rosebud lips of hers. "For most of that time, I thought he drove me crazy. I thought he was ridiculous. But despite all that, he helped me when he didn't have to, even when he knew we'd fight like cats and dogs—almost literally—when we started. Through him, I got to reconnect with the Nerd Herd. I'd forgotten what it was like to have friends who just wanted to be with me for me. I still have friends in the beauty community, like Mikki MUA and Valkyrie, but these friends have known me since before I had subscribers. One of them *is* my original subscriber." She shook her head. "I have been such an idiot."

Tobin stared raptly at the screen as Lily wiped at her eyes with the back of her hands.

"Tobin helped me with my career when he didn't have to. But he also showed me there's more to life than my brand and my channel," she said. "He has been more wonderful than I can say. He's one of the best people I know. And I love him more than I've ever loved anyone."

He choked.

She said it. Right there. In front of millions of people.

"What started as a gag turned into something very real," she said. "He's taking a break, which he not only deserves but has every right to. And I wasn't supportive. I was so fixated on pushing and stats and being a big success that I missed what mattered. He matters."

This matters. You matter.

She suppressed a hiccup, then sent the camera a watery smile. "I just wanted to let you all know that my channel's going to change a little. I'm still going to do beauty and fashion stuff, because I truly love it, and I love sharing my finds and tips with you. But I'm not going to be as crazy about my schedule. And I'm going to share more real stuff with you too." She bit her lip. "I'm also going to keep some things private. I'm giving Tobin all the space he needs, and I know things might not work out, no matter how much I want it, or how hard I would push for it. He deserves all the time and love and support he can get. And for not seeing that sooner . . . I am unbelievably sorry."

She signed off. He stared at the paused screen in blank shock for a long moment.

Was it real?

If it was . . . did he want to risk it?

She'd brought up the Herd. She'd posted an undeniably embarrassing picture of herself. She'd seen that she'd pushed him, and she'd apologized. She hadn't called him herself, because she was respecting his boundary.

It was everything he'd wanted to hear.

God help him, he still loved her. And if there was a chance . . .

He needed to clear this up.

"Excuse me," he said to the driver. "How hard is it to change the destination?"

CHANNEL: *Everlily*

Subscribers: 6.1M
Video views: 303M
Most recent video: "An Apology"

RECENT COMMENTS:

Breathless Belle: This is so real. I am so sorry. Hugs, and hope you two fix things

Hai Mai: Oh no, did you two break up??? Noooooooooo

Gina Pagano: You didn't do anything wrong, queen. There are plenty of other men out there.

Decemberist Girl: Why did you do that? He's been awesome, and you shit on him?

Annabel Lee: I am low-key impressed that you were so authentic. Thank you for being so open with us. (And Decemberist Girl—STFU.)

CHAPTER 43

Lily felt hungover, even though she'd barely drunk the night before. She had posted the video around eight o'clock, and for hours she'd come close to taking it down. After seeing it, Mikki had called her, praising her bravery, which helped. He also came over with a pizza, which they split, and a bottle of prosecco "to celebrate her recent epiphanies." She sobbed on his shoulder at one point, and then they spent the rest of the night watching various adaptations of *Pride and Prejudice*, which Mikki did under duress. "I must love you," he muttered, shaking his head.

He'd left around one o'clock in the morning, telling her he'd text and check in on her the next day and admonishing her to "leave the video up." She'd shut down her computer and her phone, trying to avoid temptation. She'd tossed and turned, barely sleeping. She finally gave up and got up at seven and had spent the day torturing herself by watching old Tobin videos. Not theirs, though. That would hurt too much.

She didn't have anything in her apartment to eat—or, if she was honest, nothing she *wanted* to eat—so she put in a big sushi order for delivery. It was one of her favorite comfort foods, one she didn't indulge in often. Probably because she knew they were going to send four sets of chopsticks with her order. She'd just do what she always did: turn up her TV and pretend that there were other people in the apartment, rather than admit that one woman was eating all those rolls and sashimi.

Although if ever there was a time to say "screw you" to convention, it'd be now, she thought obstinately. She was heartbroken. Hell, she should've ordered a sheet cake to go, as well.

The door knocked, and she looked down at herself. She was wearing a pair of fuzzy flannel pajama pants and a tank top, no makeup, her hair probably sticking out at all angles. Well, screw it. They'd probably seen worse, right? And what did she care if they thought she looked awful?

She opened the door, steeling herself . . . then paused, blinking in disbelief when she realized who was at the door.

Tobin was wearing a T-shirt and shorts and his red sneakers. His laptop bag was slung across his broad chest, and he was tugging a roller bag behind him. "Hey there," he said, looking surprisingly uncertain and serious. "Can I come in?"

She nodded, mute, and stepped aside so he could walk in. She shut the door as he toed his shoes off.

"I know this is kind of without warning," he said slowly. "Honestly, I didn't expect to find myself here."

She nodded again. She certainly didn't expect to see him here at all, much less this soon. She took a deep breath. "I . . . did you see my video?"

He took off his laptop bag, putting his stuff off to one side. He looked at her, his whiskey-brown eyes alight. "Yeah. Everybody I know linked me to that thing." He paused. "Except you."

"You told me you needed time, and space," Lily said, biting her lip. "I wasn't sure if what I did was okay. I wasn't trying to manipulate you or anything . . ."

"Lily, it's okay," he said, reaching out and rubbing her arms gently. She almost fainted with sheer relief.

"I know it could've looked fake," she said. "I'm trying to be more . . . real. I want to be the Lily I was when I was with you," she said. "Not this curated, crafted, plastic Lily. Even if it means sometimes I'm a mess, or

I curse, or I do stuff that's silly. I don't want to keep trying to be perfect. I want to be me."

He smiled, one of his hands coming up to cup the side of her face. She sighed, curving her cheek into his palm and enjoying the warmth. "You absolutely should be you," he said.

"I'm so sorry," she breathed. "I never should've pushed you like that. You were telling me you were burned out, and all I could think of was your career and how successful you should be."

"You were looking out for me," he said. "I get that."

"I was being pushy, and I wasn't looking at how you were feeling," she protested. "I was hurting you."

"Not deliberately."

She shook her head. "Doesn't matter. I don't ever want to hurt you, Tobin. And I especially don't want you to feel like I don't believe in you." She sniffled a little.

He wrapped her in his arms, and she rubbed her face against his shirt, inhaling the scent of him. God, she'd missed this. How could she have gotten addicted to the way somebody smelled so damned quickly? "I'm sorry too," he said. "It just . . . between my agents and my parents, I just felt like I really needed somebody in my corner. And I thought we were going somewhere . . ."

"I am! We are!" she said, the sound a little muffled against his chest. She pulled back to look at him, seeing him smiling at her, that lopsided smile she loved. "I believe in you, Tobin. That is part of why I was pushing, but . . . I was just so fixated on what being a success was, and what being a failure was, that I missed entirely whose opinions on both success and failure *mattered*. And . . . I want us to, um, be going somewhere. With you." She paused. "Like . . . a relationship. That's what we were talking about that night, right?"

He smiled. "You said you loved me, in your video," he said softly. "I mean, I assume that was me."

She smacked his arm. "Of course it was you," she said, rolling her eyes. Then she softened. "And . . . yes. I love you."

"I love you too," he said, pressing a kiss against her lips. "It's kind of sudden, but I've never been as sure of anything in my life."

"It's over twenty years coming. It's not that sudden," she pointed out with a grin. He smiled back, holding her tight.

"What does that mean for us from here?" More kisses. He kissed her temple, the space behind her ear. She felt herself squirming as heat rushed through her veins.

Her breathing went uneven, and she struggled to focus. "Yes. Talking. Important," she said, causing him to laugh against the skin at her throat. "Um . . . when is your flight?"

"I changed it to tomorrow," he said. "I thought, one way or another, we'd need to talk. I wanted to see where we were, and what we were going to do moving forward."

She nudged him back. "If you want to talk, you need to stop kissing me like that," she scolded him playfully. "Because I can't think when you do that."

He nodded, his eyes low lidded and heated. "Good point."

"Do you still want me to come with you?"

He startled. "Would you?"

She bit her lip. She hadn't thought this opportunity would come up, so she hadn't decided, hadn't planned. Still . . .

"I don't want to abandon my channel altogether," she said slowly. "I love you, but it is still important to me. I don't think that's unfair."

"It's not," he reassured her, stroking her hair. He seemed eager to touch her, almost unable to help himself, and she found she felt the same. She kept stepping closer to him, feeling his body heat. "I'm not asking you to do what I do or feel the same way about your career that I do about mine. I'd love it if you could come with me, but that's because I love being with you, and I do hate the idea of being away from you for a few months."

"I don't like the idea of that either," she admitted, her mind whirring. "If I decided to go, it might not be for the whole trip."

His eyes shone. "A few weeks, maybe?"

"And I would want to film at least a bit," she said. "Not as much as I have been posting. But at least one or two."

He nodded. "As long as I have . . . let's say a week, where we can just hang out? Just us?"

"That sounds good, actually," she said with a smile. "I can't remember the last time I took a real vacation."

"Then this might be exactly what you need," Tobin said, framing her face in his hands. "You can go back to LA whenever you like. And then I'll come back, and we can be together whenever we want."

She nodded, then frowned. "There is the little fact that we live in different cities," she pointed out.

"Just a few hours away," he said. "I hate the commute, but you are more than worth it. I'd put up with eight hours of traffic if you were at the end of it."

"That," she said with a grin, "is possibly the biggest declaration of love I have ever heard. I know how much you hate traffic."

"Hell, maybe I'll move up here," he mused.

Her eyes widened. "But you said LA was a cesspool!"

"I love you," he said. "And I'm going to spend as much time as possible to show you just what that means."

She smiled. She wasn't sure that would be necessary—but then, she didn't want to show all her cards just yet. They'd have plenty of time to discuss it, and make plans . . . and spend time *not* making plans, and seeing where things went.

She stood on tiptoes, kissing him thoroughly, thrilling in the feel of his arms wrapping tight and holding her flush against his rapidly hardening body. "God, I missed you," she said against his lips and felt him smile.

The door knocked, and she jolted. Tobin's eyebrow rose.

"That's my lunch," she said, quickly getting the door and grabbing the delivery. "Um . . . hope you like sushi?"

"Sushi in a minute," he said, putting the order in the fridge. Then he tugged her to the bedroom, where he proceeded to show her just how much he missed her, and she returned the favor. And then some.

CHANNEL: *GOOFYBUI*

Subscribers: 11M
Video views: 397M
Most recent video: "Taking a Break"

RECENT COMMENTS:

T3Ch Warrior: Seriously, bro? You're just up and leaving? What the hell?

Hai Mai: Shut UP T3Ch. BRO. If he wants to take a break, he can take a fucking break!

Han Solo Cup: Hah! Get rekt, T3CH! She told you!

Skeptic_Sketcher: Self care is important. Subscribers don't want you to die so they can watch a playthrough. Take care of yourself.

Hayden the Greaten: Enjoy the Great Down Undah. Then come back and make epic videos (when you're rested and healthy and all that!)

CHAPTER 44

A few days and some rescheduled flights later, Tobin found himself standing in a hotel room, thousands of miles from Ponto. "So this is Australia." He looked out the window. "It's dark."

Lily hit him with a pillow. "It's two in the morning," she said. "We should at least try to sleep, or you're never going to get used to the time change."

"I slept on the plane," he said. "Sort of. And now I'm wired. I don't even know what day it is."

It was always like this—he always took a few days to get leveled out. He couldn't remember the last time he'd done it with someone else, though. Certainly not with a girlfriend.

He smiled. *Girlfriend.* He liked the sound of that.

He went over to the bed, stripping off his clothes in the process, gratified when Lily's smirk slipped and her gaze went hot. "What?" he said coyly, smiling as innocently as possible. "I'm just trying to get some sleep, like you said."

"If you really think you're going to get naked and then just go to sleep," Lily said with a purring growl that shot right to his groin, "then you have got another thing coming."

"Is it *thing*?" he said. "Or is it *another think coming*? That's how I've always—*mmrph*!"

He was quickly silenced by Lily tackling him, and he burst out laughing. "Shhhh!" she said, covering his mouth with her soft palm. "We've got neighbors."

"You started it," he hissed back and promptly tugged at her little nightie. She wriggled out of both that and her panties until she was just as naked as he was. The sensation of her, pressed and hot against him, was just what he thought heaven would feel like. "Did I mention how much I missed you? Not just for this, but . . . well, this is awesome."

She kissed him ravenously, to the point where he felt light headed. She pulled away, panting for breath. "I missed you too," she rasped, stroking his chest. He cupped her breasts, and she arched her back, rubbing against the most sensitive part of him.

"Whoa, whoa." He held her hips as they rocked against him. "I need to get a condom." Then he felt his muscles tense, and not in the good way. "Shit. *Condoms.* I never packed any."

"You didn't?"

"Well, I wasn't planning on having sex with anyone," he pointed out, and he saw her amused expression soften. She kissed him again, tenderly.

"Lucky for you," she whispered in his ear, "I happened to pack some. Quite a few, actually."

He groaned. "See? You are wickedly organized. That is so hot."

"Stick with me," she said, then rolled over, scrambling off the bed delightfully naked, perfectly pert ass swaying like she knew he was watching her. She went to her (perfectly matched) luggage, opening a (perfectly packed) set of toiletries and whatnot. She pulled out a box of condoms before grabbing a handful of the foil packets and dropping them on the nightstand.

Little did she know, he had every intention of sticking with her for as long as she'd let him. He hadn't felt this way about anyone. In a million years, he never would have expected it to be Lily—but now that they were together, it seemed like his entire life had led him to this moment, this woman.

"I love you," he said as she handed him a condom.

"I know." She smiled as he got himself sheathed. "I love you too."

"No more death threats, then?" he asked.

"Hey, no promises," she said, straddling him and kissing him again. He could feel her nipples, pebbled with excitement, brushing down his chest. He groaned against her lips, loving the little mewling sounds she was making as she wriggled against him, smooth hot skin sliding against his. He forced himself not to grip her hips too hard, to let her direct the action. This was her show, and he was just glad she was letting him be a part of it.

She reached down, positioning him, a move that made him gasp. Then he felt her lower herself onto him. She felt impossibly, unbelievably tight.

"Missed you," she said, her breathing harsh.

"Take your time," he said, gritting his teeth himself. It felt incredible, but he didn't want her to hurt herself. Still, it also felt like torture, since she was sinking down slowly, centimeter by centimeter.

When she was finally fully seated, resting on his hips, she shivered, and he felt it like a live wire. She tilted her head back, stretching out like a cat. Then, like a dancer, she twisted slowly. Her hips moved like goddamned Shakira, sinuous and deliberate, and he felt his eyes roll back in his head.

"Oh my God," he muttered, unable to stop his hips from punching up slightly.

When he pried his eyes open, he saw her smiling down at him, her eyes half-mast. When she stroked her own breasts, his mouth went dry. Then she grabbed his hands from her hips, smoothing them up to replace hers. He kneaded gently, and she gasped, gyrating slowly.

"God, Lils," he said, his hips rising. She started riding him more deliberately, pulling up almost completely off him, then rocking back down. Her hips began to snap, and her breathing was completely composed of sharp, moan-laced gasps.

"Tobin," she breathed, grabbing his shoulders, giving herself more leverage as she thrust herself down on his cock. "Oh, God, oh, please . . ."

"*Ngh*," he groaned, meeting every one of her motions with his own. What had started out graceful was quickly turning into almost clumsy, frantic grasping—like they couldn't help themselves, could barely control the movements of their bodies. They were doing everything they could to fuse themselves closer together, to become one person.

He felt it, the tightness settling just behind his balls, and he breathed as deeply as he could, taking in her scent. "Baby, I'm gonna come soon," he pleaded. "But I'm waiting for you."

She nodded, showing she had heard him. She moved with determination, her breathing speeding and going sharp and staccato. He could feel it, and the excitement made his body respond. He shifted, making sure his cock dragged just where she needed it.

Her eyes flew wide open. *"Tobin!"*

She shuddered convulsively, and he could feel her gripping around him. It shoved him over the edge, and he came, gasping, his body shaking and jolting into her as she clenched her thighs against his waist.

After what seemed like forever, she collapsed on top of him. He waited to catch his breath, then withdrew, already missing her heat. Missing *her* . . . even though she was right there with him.

"I am so glad," she said, out of breath, "that I came with you."

He looked at her, making sure that he heard her right. Then he burst out laughing, which he had to hide with a pillow when Lily shushed him.

"I don't mean *that*," she said, shaking her head but grinning. "I mean . . . came with you here. To Australia. On vacation."

He smiled, pushing a sweaty lock of hair away from her face. "I am too," he said.

"And it's okay that I'm only staying two weeks?"

He nodded. "I don't know how much longer I'll be," he said. "But we can keep in touch over Skype or whatever. And I promise I will see you as soon as I get home."

She sighed, nuzzling his shoulder. "We'll figure this out," she said. "Even if we don't plan it."

He smiled. "Hell, yeah, we will," he agreed, then kissed her on top of her head.

EPILOGUE

One year later . . .

"Lily, have you seen my dice box?"

Lily smiled at Tobin, who was looking around, disgruntled. She took his hand, tugging him into the now spotless and organized spare bedroom. It had an actual bed in it, so guests could stay over, and the thousand rubber ducks had been distributed to kids at a local festival. It had been a lot of fun. Lily had made letting her help get the house a little more organized one of the conditions of her moving into Tobin's house. They'd been together for a year, but she'd just moved in a few months ago. Tobin was still getting used to the changes, and he grumbled about them, but he appreciated a lot, too, which made Lily feel nice. It still felt like Tobin's house, though . . . something they were going to rectify by looking for another house, one that better suited both of them, by the end of the year.

She went straight to the new bookshelves, where she grabbed the dice box and then handed it to him.

"Thanks, babe," he said, kissing her cheek. "D and D night is not the same without my special dice, you know that."

"I know," she said. Her phone started buzzing in her pocket, and she grabbed it as Tobin disappeared back to the living room. She saw it was Mikki texting. She grinned.

MIKKI: So how is living with the Goofy guy?

LILY: We are making it work, and he's wonderful.

MIKKI: I still can't believe you live back in your old hometown. Who does that?

Lily laughed. She did miss Mikki, but he was so busy with his classes it wasn't like they would've been able to hang out much anyway. Besides, she was doing work with the makeup brand, and she still had the occasional meeting with Maria, so she could catch up with him for dinner when she was in town. She also was still collabing with YouTubers—even Chrysalis, which was amazing. It was one of Lily's new "just living" videos, where she hung out and did normal or silly or fun things. She and Chrysalis had tried cooking a soufflé, with unintentionally funny results that viewers had loved. Even better, Lily and Chrysalis had become friends.

After a full month in Australia and a week in New Zealand, Tobin had come back refreshed and raring to go on his channel. He'd asked, politely but firmly, for Jeffrey to be removed as his coagent, and the agency had complied, which was a big win. Bastian had gotten him a voice-acting gig on top of his videos, but it was usually short assignments for a sketch-comedy thing, and he could record on an ISDN line out of his house.

Tobin had spent a lot of time in Lily's apartment in LA, but she had missed not only him but also the Nerd Herd. With all the time she was spending in Ponto Beach, she'd been able to catch up with Emily, as well as get closer to their other friends. Their renewed friendship had meant the world to her.

So it was a no-brainer that she moved back to Ponto Beach.

Now it was a Friday night, and most of the crew were going to come over to play Dungeons and Dragons. She wasn't completely on board with the game, but she loved spending time with all of them. Most of all, she loved, loved, *loved* being so happy with Tobin.

LILY: You're just jelly. Come visit, I'll show you.

MIKKI: Ugh. Winter break, probably, if I keep my grades up. And of course, I'm going to the launch party.

MIKKI: Although are you sure about doing the launch party for your palette in Ponto Beach? No big influencer-packed party? It would make Daisy *nuts*.
Lily bit her lip, then kept typing.

LILY: I thought about it, but I'm happier doing a launch with actual fans, as well as my crew here. I don't want this to be some unapproachable, envy-inducing, exclusivity thing. I want it to be for the people who get me.

MIKKI: Well, you must know what you're doing, since your channels are kicking unholy ass.

Lily smiled. He wasn't kidding—EverLily on TikTok was outperforming her YouTube channel, and between all that, a few new sponsorships, and her upcoming makeup launch, she was doing very, very well. But more importantly, she couldn't remember feeling this relaxed *ever* . . . not even when she was in grade school. It was freeing, and almost an adrenaline buzz, to take the risks and then to do "aggressive self-care" as Tobin said. He'd helped her learn to enjoy exercising, something she'd *never* thought would happen. Most importantly, she had fun with him. She helped him stay on track when he wanted it; he helped her shake loose when she was taking herself too seriously.

They were a good match. They still had disagreements, but they were getting better about talking things out. They'd even taken to playing video games to help settle things down. She was getting pretty good at killing him in *Call of Duty*, it turned out.

LILY: Gotta run, guests going to be here soon.

MIKKI: If you told anyone I was playing DnD, I would shoot myself.

She could almost hear Mikki laughing. He didn't mean it, obviously, but she knew that was an outcropping of who they hung out with in LA. She'd thought like that—cared about that. It was great *not* to.

LILY: Hey. Joe Manganiello plays DnD. With like Vince Vaughn or someone.

MIKKI: Okay. I would play DnD with a hot guy. That's acceptable.

LILY: LMAO. As long as you have standards.

MIKKI: Have fun with your Nerd Herd, sweetie.

LILY: Talk soon!

She shut off her phone and saw Tobin standing in the doorframe, his eyes twinkling.

"What?" she asked, suspicious.

"I was just thinking . . ." He sat next to her on the guest room bed, sidling closer. "We've got about twenty minutes . . ."

She burst out laughing, half shoving him away. "Are you kidding?" She got up, heading for the hallway, Tobin hot on her heels, reaching for her hips and gently tugging her to what was an obvious hardness. "Oh my God, Tobin! People are going to be here any minute! We can't just . . ."

He kissed her. Hard, and slow, and serious. Until she was out of breath when he pulled away.

"I mean, we can't just . . ." She lost her train of thought when he nipped his way down her throat. "They're going to be . . ."

He kissed that spot right on the back of her neck, the one that made her shiver every damned time.

"Twenty minutes, you say?" she heard herself rasp.

He laughed against her skin, his breath hot. "I can do a lot in twenty minutes," he said.

She shook her head. This was life with Tobin. And it was awesome.

"Race you," she said, and they grinned at each other as they both sprinted for the bed.

Acknowledgments

I want to thank the fantastic team at Montlake for helping me get this book into the world. And big thanks to my amazing agent, Tricia Skinner at Fuse Literary. This is the way, my friend. All gas, no brakes.

About the Author

Cathy Yardley is an award-winning author of romance, chick lit, and urban fantasy. She has sold over 1.2 million books with publishers like St. Martin's Press, Avon, and Harlequin Books. She writes fun, geeky, and diverse characters who believe that underdogs can make good and that sometimes being a little wrong is just right. She likes writing about quirky, crazy adventures because she's had plenty of her own: she had her own army in the Society for Creative Anachronism; she's spent New Year's on a three-day solitary vision quest in the Mojave Desert; and she had VIP access to the Viper Room in Los Angeles. Now, she spends her time writing in the wilds of East Seattle, trying to prevent her son from learning the truth about any of said adventures and riding herd on her two dogs (and one husband).